"DON'T YOU DARE BACK OUT ON ME NOW, JOHNSTON!"

She scrambled up, yanked her nightgown over her head, and hurled it across the room. It settled like a discarded white flag. "Well, what are you waiting for?"

Grinning like a fool, J.J. scooped her into his arms.

"What are you doing?"

"I'm taking you to bed." His smile disappeared, and his eyes grew tender. "Please, Angel. Let me."

Even now, he was giving her one last chance to be sure. And that alone determined her decision. She laid her palm against his jaw, and he turned his head to place a kiss in it. "Oh, yes. Just hurry!"

By Susan Kay Law

Journey Home
Traitorous Hearts
Reckless Angel

Available from HarperPaperbacks

Harper
Monogram

Reckless
Angel

⊰ SUSAN KAY LAW ⊱

HarperPaperbacks
A Division of HarperCollinsPublishers

This is a work of fiction. The characters, incidents, and dialogues are products of the author's imagination and are not to be construed as real. Any resemblance to actual events or persons, living or dead, is entirely coincidental.

HarperPaperbacks *A Division of* HarperCollins*Publishers*
10 East 53rd Street, New York, N.Y. 10022

Cover illustration by John Ennis

First printing: February 1995

Printed in the United States of America

HarperPaperbacks, HarperMonogram, and colophon are trademarks of HarperCollins*Publishers*

❖ 10 9 8 7 6 5 4 3 2 1

For the Reverend David and Kay Martens

*To Daddy (the preacher) and Mom (the librarian)
for letting me spend most of my youth with my
nose in a book.*

I guess it's paying off.

Love you both.

Reckless Angel

1

San Francisco, 1858

"Damn it, Angel, I'm gonna kill you!"

Jeremiah Johnston grabbed for the reins of the huge chestnut stallion that danced and snorted in front of him.

"Ah-hah. Gotcha this time, you overgrown monster." He took a cautious step forward and, for the third time, tried to shove his foot in the stirrup bouncing against the horse's muscular side. Once again, the horse skittered away, and J.J. swore loudly.

"Uh, Mr. Johnston?"

J.J. turned to glare at the young stableboy, Tommy. Where had he come from? He'd deliberately chosen a time when there'd be no one around to see him. This early in the morning, there shouldn't have been anyone up and about at the Naked Rose Saloon. And the thick, dense fog that shifted and slipped around him should have made doubly sure no one witnessed his failure.

"What do you want, Tommy?"

"Um." Tommy scuffed his toe in the dirt of the

courtyard. "Well, I was wondering if'n you'd like a little help."

"No," J.J. said sharply. His shoulder ached from hanging on to the reins; the stupid horse kept trying to jerk away from him. It was all he could do to keep from wincing in pain. But there was no way he was going to let this half-grown kid, who couldn't weigh 110 pounds, know that the leather straps were just about to cut his hand in two. Not when Tommy had absolutely no trouble handling this misnamed monster himself.

Tommy hesitated, his gaze sliding from J.J. to Angel and back again.

"Go back to bed."

Finally Tommy nodded. Giving one last dubious look over his scrawny shoulder, he scooped up the mangy gray cat that had been slinking around his feet and slouched back into the stables.

"Now." J.J. turned to the animal again. Angel leaned away from him, his brown eyes wild in the beautifully molded head.

It was his brother-in-law's fault, and J.J. knew it. Everyone thought the handsome horse was an incredibly generous gift, but he was certain that, somehow, his sister's husband had managed to train the horse to behave properly for everyone but him.

"Come on, boy," J.J. crooned. "I'm not gonna hurt you." Even though the idea was taking on more appeal all the time.

The animal stilled, ears flattened against his head and nostrils quivering.

"That's a good horse." Lord, he hated this animal. All animals, for that matter. They were completely unreliable and unmanageable. But it galled him that there was one thing in his carefully ordered life that he was unable to control.

Somehow, he was going to handle this, too.

He sidled a little closer to the horse's side. Damn,

the thing was big. J.J. eyed one of the huge hooves. He knew from experience that it hurt like hell when one of them landed on someone's foot.

Despite the clinging chill of the damp morning, a trickle of sweat ran down J.J.'s temple. He dashed it away with his perfectly white sleeve.

He could do this. It was further than he'd ever managed to get before. This time he'd gotten the saddle on the blasted thing, after all.

"Come on, baby," he said, pitching his voice low, the tone he used in bed when he wasn't interested in sleeping. Well, it worked then. That, at least, he could control.

Almost there. He jammed his foot into the stirrup, then dragged himself across the saddle.

The horse bolted. J.J. nearly tumbled off over the horse's rump but managed to grab the saddle horn.

"Whoa!"

The horse paid no attention to his frantic call. J.J. threw himself down across Angel's back and clutched the horse around his neck just as they ran through the gates of the yard.

The street in front of the saloon sheared down at a sharp angle, ten blocks directly into the waterfront from where the Rose drew some of her less elite clientele. J.J. shut his eyes against the sickening tilt of the earth and felt their speed increase as the horse thundered straight down, heading for the bay.

Well, at least he knew how to swim.

"Damn it, Angel, I'm gonna kill yooouu!"

Only the faintest pearling of the air told Angelina Winchester that dawn was approaching. The heavy fog absorbed sound and light and emotion, leaving only dense, lush gray and a faint, distant prickle of fear.

When the stagecoach driver had dropped her off

late the night before, he'd made it clear that the Barbary Coast, San Francisco's waterfront, was no place for a woman. Then, she'd been too tired to care. She'd simply sneaked her horse into the stable behind a busy tavern—one too busy for anyone to notice an additional horse—and found herself a quiet corner around the back. The niche was well hidden by an overgrown bush that had leaves like nothing she'd ever seen, so she'd wrapped her arms tightly around her bag and gone gratefully to sleep.

Now she pushed herself reluctantly to her feet, every bone and muscle protesting with painful clarity. Shivering, Angie pulled her shawl more snugly around her shoulders. Lord, it was cold. It was June, for heaven's sake. Back home, the air would be warm and sweet by now, fragrant with flowers and new grass, settling around her like an old, favored blanket.

And, for the first time, she wondered if she'd done the right thing. Throughout the entire trip, even as it had taken her three extra weeks and a good deal more money than she'd thought, she hadn't wondered. Not even when she'd been left behind at several coaching inns and had to wait for the next stage, when it became clear her horse wouldn't be able to keep the pace set by the coach's teams, which were fresh from frequent changes.

No, she'd never questioned it once, because she knew the only way she would ever have the home she always wanted was to leave it first.

But she was no longer so sure. Her family always claimed she was too impulsive—reckless—and couldn't take proper care of herself. She *knew* they were wrong.

If only she had a bit more of the money she'd started out with. If only the air didn't reek with the stench of rotting fish, salt water, and the sour smell of the dingy saloon.

And if only it weren't so dark, if she could depend on the welcoming glow of the street lights. But it was relentlessly dark; the driver had told her the lights had been shut off the year before, when the city refused to pay the gas company. The depression that had set in when the gold fields played out had darkened the bright, beckoning light of San Francisco. She felt an equal, suffocating dimming of her hopes.

Ruthlessly, she shoved her loose braid down the back of her blouse, hoping that, for once, it would stay tucked safely out of her way. She jammed her shabby hat back on her head, ignoring the grumbling protests of her stomach.

After all, she was here. There was little use in second thoughts now. First, she needed a job. It wasn't as if she didn't have the skills to get one.

Grabbing her satchel, she peeked around the corner of the stable. The yard leading to the back of the saloon was empty. Satisfied that any remaining inhabitants of the saloon were resting up after last night's revels, she headed for the stable door.

Yes, she had her talent, and she had Lance. What more could a woman need?

Though breakfast would be nice.

There was no help for it. He'd fought the horse, Angel's hooves thundering wildly on the planked street, all the way down to the waterfront. The increasingly dilapidated buildings were a blur, flashing across the edge of his vision as he clung to the horse's back.

He had just enough impression of his surroundings to recognize a large, brick warehouse. Just two more blocks to the wharf, and then there was only a long, deceptively sturdy-looking dock that he had a sneaking suspicion just might collapse under the weight of the overgrown, ill-mannered moose beneath him.

Maybe, if a little of his usual luck returned, the thing was too stupid to know how to swim. Good riddance.

He blinked, trying to clear his eyes, and saw the

other horse. It pounded along beside him, keeping pace with his own horse. This one was every bit as big and as fast as Angel, but a woman huddled on its back. He caught a quick glimpse of dark hair, streaming along behind her like an unfurling black silk flag whipped by gale winds.

Lord, she must be scared to death, swept along on that runaway horse.

Hell. It was going to be up to him to save her. And it was going to beat the dickens out of his new suit.

He took a great gulp of air and gathered his strength. It wasn't easy to loosen his fingers, twisted tightly in Angel's mane, but he forced himself to do it.

And then, without giving himself any time to think more about it, he jumped.

2

She screamed when he grabbed her and took them both down toward the ground. The sound echoed in his ears, piercing and ear-shattering. J.J. twisted in the air, just barely able to get his body under the woman's before they hit the ground.

The impact was stunning, slamming the air from his lungs and sending sharp shards of pain slicing through his body like a thousand huge knives.

The damn horses were too close. He heard the impact of a heavy hoof, perilously near his head. The horses hadn't kept running. Swearing, he rolled the woman beneath him and covered her small body with his own.

She was struggling violently beneath him, her arms and legs thrashing about.

"Quit it, now. I've got you."

Evidently she hadn't heard him, for her struggles only increased. Poor thing. She probably was so frightened that it hadn't registered that she was better off beneath him, with the protection of his body.

She felt small and fragile. Her head was tucked against the crook of his neck, and her feet flailed wildly about his shins. It was as if he had captured a humming-bird, all vibrant energy, thrumming with heat and vivid life.

He sucked in a breath when a pointy elbow connected with his side.

"Would you cut it out? I'm trying to be noble here. It doesn't happen all that often."

He winced as he heard one of the restless horses stamp beside him. Why didn't they just get away? Because they were idiot horses, that's why. Couldn't be counted on to do a simple thing like move away from humans lying on the ground.

"Would you"—the woman shoved hard at his chest—"get off me!"

"It's not safe! The horse was running away with you." He gritted his teeth when she worked one of her legs free, whipped it around his, and slammed him in the back of the leg with her heel. "They're wild. They might stomp on you, or kick you—could you cut it out!—or do God only knows what kind of damage. Stop it, you little—!"

"He wasn't running away with me!"

"What?" She'd gone still beneath him, though her body still vibrated with energy. "What did you say?" J.J. asked.

"Lance wasn't running away with me, you fool! I was trying to catch up with you and head you off before you ended up in the ocean!"

Hell. *She'd* been trying to save *him*.

"But—"

"Get *off* me," she repeated, giving him one last push.

"Sorry." He glanced around. To his immense relief, both horses had backed away and were standing quietly against the grubby brick wall of the warehouse. *Now* they move away. Took them long enough. He rolled to his feet and stepped back.

She sprang up and flashed over to her horse. His first impression had been correct, he saw. She was very small. The huge red horse, almost the color of the mellow brick behind them, towered over her tiny frame.

"There, there, baby, I'm all right. The silly man didn't hurt me." Her voice was unexpectedly slow, low and rich and smoky with just a suggestion of southern drawl. Just like the best whiskey he served at the Rose. It was a voice that should have belonged to a high-class courtesan, not a small woman wearing a plain, faded, dirty dress, her tangled, dusty black hair tumbling down her back.

She stroked the horse's muzzle gently, calming him. J.J. dusted off his clothes as best he could, grimacing in disgust at the begrimed state of his new white frock coat and pants. He sidestepped over to Angel, who flicked back his ears and snorted, sending the reins that hung loosely to the ground swaying back and forth.

J.J. lunged, grabbing Angel's reins, then jumped away again, out of reach of the horse's kick. There, he had him. Now what?

He supposed he had to ride the thing back home. He sighed, thinking of having to go through that torture again. Far better to suffer the ignominy of hiking back, dragging the fool horse behind him.

Of course, *her* horse was well behaved. She was still murmuring and cooing, whispering sweet nothings to the blame animal and rubbing her cheek against its nose. Disgusting.

She stepped back from the horse and whirled on J.J. Her small, sharp features were almost quivering, and the light of battle blazed from her large, dark eyes. Oh, boy, he thought. That was one angry lady.

Once, he'd seen a small, fierce sparrow attack an alley cat, the tiny bird determined to chase the predator away from one of her fledglings that had fallen from the nest. She reminded him an awful lot of that bird.

She'd made sure her horse was all right. Evidently now it was his turn.

"What in the holy horse apples did you think you were doing!" Her loud shout was still tinged with a faint, appealing whisper of the south. "You could have killed us both!"

"I thought I was saving you," he said calmly, thankful he was still able to retain that much control. "I thought the horse was running away from you."

She snorted. "That'll be the day."

"Well, I had no way of knowing that."

"Humph. The day I start riding like a city-born rube who doesn't know the rear end of a horse from his own—"

She broke off abruptly just when J.J. was beginning to feel a bit insulted. He watched in fascination as her eyes, rich as the color of fine chocolate, went all unfocused and misty. She smiled softly, and he had to admit the termagant did have a sweet smile, her cheeks curving into deep, flirtatious dimples.

"Oh, Lord," she drawled slowly, seductively. "You are . . . magnificent."

Well, well. Magnificent. J.J. straightened his shoulders and tugged at his cuffs. Now, he'd been called a number of extremely flattering things by women in his day, but magnificent? He felt a smile pull at the corners of his mouth when she began to walk toward him.

He had every intention of turning her down, of course. But that didn't mean that after the fiasco of his attempted morning ride, his pride couldn't use the bolstering of her admiration.

She walked with unusual grace, her feet skimming silently but surely over the ground. Her eyes were dreamy, her face rapt with absolute absorption. She wasn't more than a few steps away now, and he couldn't stop himself from tensing with ridiculous anticipation.

She lifted her arms, her hands reaching out . . . and went straight past him, to his blame-fool horse.

"Oh, yes," she whispered again. "You are magnificent."

At that, Angel pricked up his ears and stopped straining to pull away. The relief in J.J.'s shoulder was acute, even though he wasn't particularly happy about the cause of it. The horse neighed softly and nuzzled the woman's shoulder.

Not even bothering to look away from the horse— what kind of woman was she that she didn't at least *pretend* to be interested in him?—she asked, "What's his name?"

J.J. made an inarticulate sound of distaste. "Angel."

"Angel," she repeated, rolling the name off her tongue. "That's perfect for you, isn't it, my fine young man."

"How'd you know it was a he?"

She glanced at him then, a quick flick that clearly registered her disbelief. Darn it, it was rough on a man's ego when a woman was more interested in a horse's sex than his.

"Well, mates, whadda we got here?"

Hell. J.J. stiffened at the sound of the voice behind him, then slowly turned.

The man wasn't young, but he wasn't old. He was merely alive. His clothes were ripped, loose, carelessly dirty, looking no worse than J.J. knew his own did, but the stench of sweat and sour wine emanating from the man clearly said that, in his case at least, it was his usual condition.

His chin was stubbled with gray, and his flat eyes appeared sunken over sharp cheekbones. But what held J.J.'s attention was the large, silver knife that, even in the foggy gloom, seemed to gleam with a life of its own.

He heard the woman gasp, but he didn't dare turn around to reassure her. He couldn't take that risk.

"Don' know what the likes of you are doin' down

here at this time o' the day, but I guess it's a lucky mornin' for me." The man's empty grin showed the gap where his front teeth should be.

"Damn," J.J. muttered, his worst fear confirmed. A Sydney duck. Of all the immigrants that had poured into San Francisco in the last decade, the least welcome—and most dangerous—were the convicts from Australia who managed to find their way to California. Unscrupulous, unprincipled, and thoroughly dangerous, they often took the easiest route to their own bit of the riches to be found here: by stealing, swindling, or murdering for it. Worse, they didn't seem to harbor a conscience about any of it, killing as much for sport as profit.

"Look," J.J. said quietly, his gaze fastened on the glittering tip of the knife as it wavered back and forth. Although the man was unkempt, that blade was in prime condition. "I don't have much with me, but let me give it to you and we'll get this over with as quickly as possible."

"Don't bother with trifles." The man's eyes wouldn't stay still, twitching back and forth. "I want the horses."

"The horses?"

"Yeah. They's worth a pretty penny, ain't they? 'Specially with the purses that been showing up at the racin'. Look like they'd be pretty fast."

The horses? J.J. felt a faint glimmer of hope. Maybe his luck was returning after all.

"No!" the woman shouted. "You can't have the horses!"

"Don't move." The knife swung around to follow her as she sidled to her horse.

"Lady," J.J. said out of the side of his mouth, "let him have the blasted horses." He knew he couldn't sell— or give—the creature away. His idiot brother-in-law would never let him hear the end of it. But if it was stolen, how could that be his fault?

"He cannot have Lancelot!" She broke into a run and headed for her horse.

For all his apparent carelessness, the thief was quick. He jumped to his left and took off after the woman.

J.J. swore viciously. This was getting out of hand. Twice in one day was really asking too much.

He took a few running steps and leaped, aiming for the thief's legs.

It had all happened so quickly. She'd been running to her horse and had heard the shout and thud behind her. She'd turned to see what was happening, and by the time she spun around, the thief was on the ground, moaning, and the man in white was standing over him with a knife.

"Well, now," he said calmly, turning the knife in his hand. He appeared to study it as the blade winked in the hazy light. "This is really quite a fine weapon. I think I might keep it." He lowered his gaze to the thief, and his eyes narrowed. "You wouldn't mind, would you." Despite the deceptive friendliness of his tone, his command was clear.

The thief bobbed his head in agreement and scooted a little farther away.

"Get out of here."

The thief looked incredulous at his good fortune. "You're letting me go?"

"I certainly have no use for you."

Tentatively, the man pushed himself to his feet and scuttled away. He gave one last look back, as if still unable to understand his release, then raced around the corner.

"Well, now." He ran his hand quickly through his hair, restoring it to order, and turned his attention back to her. "Rather an eventful morning we've had, isn't it?"

"Why did you let him go?"

"This is San Francisco, lady. The only justice you get is your own. He wasn't worth the trouble."

Angelina nodded absently as she considered what to do next. Say a quick good-bye to her erstwhile savior, use up a bit of her precious coin for breakfast, and look for work, she decided. Yes, this little adventure needn't delay her any more than it already had.

"I can tell you're rather fond of the animal, sweetheart, but next time a man with a knife asks, you'd do well to let him have the creature. He may well have caught you before you got on the horse and away."

"I wasn't going for the horse."

"No?" he asked, a hint of amusement seeping into his smooth, controlled voice.

"No." She walked quickly over to Lancelot. Her satchel was still tied onto the saddle, and she dug into it, unearthing the Navy Colt that had stood her in such good stead on the trip west.

She held the weapon out to show him, knowing the large gun looked almost absurdly oversized in her small hand. The contrast made it all the more effective. Even though she only stopped at the most reputable coach houses, occasionally she'd been the recipient of more attention than she wanted. The Colt had been a potent deterrent.

He stared at the gun for a moment.

"You know how to use that?"

She spun the chamber with practiced ease. "Of course."

He slowly lifted his gaze to her face, his expression faintly bemused. And then he grinned.

Holy horse apples. She'd scarcely noticed him before, only vaguely noting that he was a handsome man. Then she'd dismissed the thought and turned her attention to what had truly interested her—the horse— because, to her, *handsome* had never made up for the appellation of *man*.

But the man could sure smile. His hair was thick, wavy, gold; his face, almost too cleanly sculpted; but it was the grin that caught her.

It seemed like every drop of warmth in the world was contained in that smile; it beamed on her, melting into her soul, like pure sunshine pouring on her and warming her from the inside out.

Maybe there was something to this handsome business after all.

When he'd held her down on the ground, she'd paid no attention to his body on top of hers. She'd been too busy trying to get him off. Why then, could she now remember it with such startling clarity? He'd been hard and large, the comfort of his weight a complete surprise. And there'd been heat, that same spreading warmth that his smile brought. She couldn't help but smile back.

Almost of its own volition, her hand flew up to smooth her hair. It was hopelessly snarled. "My braid came undone. I lost my hat."

"So you did." His grin broadened, his white teeth gleaming even as the dark mists swirled around him. "What's your name?"

"Ang—" She broke off just in time. Without thinking she'd almost blurted out her full name. But, if she knew her father, it was more than likely there were a good half-dozen Pinkerton men on her tail right now. Better not to have her real name bandied about San Francisco.

Her gaze flicked to his horse, stamping impatiently over by the brick wall, and back to him. She felt a quick, irrepressible bubble of amusement.

"Angel."

3

Jesus, not another one.

This obviously was not meant to be his morning.

"Angel? Angel what?"

She gave a quick laugh that sizzled and sparked through the gray fog, a bit of light in the lifeless street. "Just Angel."

He shook his head slowly. It made an annoying kind of sense. "Okay, Angel, where do we go from here?"

She'd already tucked the gun back into her bag and hitched up her skirts, preparing to mount her horse and be gone. One foot already planted in a stirrup, she stopped to look at him. "We?"

"Yes, we. It's perfectly obvious it's not safe for you to wander around here alone."

She dismissed him with a wave of her hand, gave a quick hop, and mounted the huge horse with fluid ease. "You said you aren't too fond of being noble. You're released from duty."

"Maybe I'm developing a taste for it. I'll escort you wherever you're going."

It had been so easy for her to get up there. Obviously, it wasn't that difficult to mount a horse. He had the advantage of much longer legs, after all.

He managed to snatch Angel's reins, then moved around to the left side of the horse, who promptly danced away.

"Don't know where I'm going yet," she said briskly. "I guess I'll just have to stay with you until you make up your mind."

"Don't be ridiculous." She gave an unrepentant smile. "You'd have to get on your horse then."

He glared at her. "I'd manage."

And he would. There was a hardness in his expression, a determination in his stance, and the ease and confidence in the way he'd handled the thief, that let her know he was a man who would always do what he set out to do, who would control life, rather than the other way around. "I guess you would." She sighed in resignation. "Why does it matter?"

He frowned slightly and followed his horse. "I have a sister."

She understood that. She had a protective brother herself. Not to mention that nearly every man she'd ever met had immediately cast her in the role of little sister, something she was immensely grateful for. It made things easier.

"Really, I haven't decided where to go yet. I'll be all right, though."

"You probably would, but we're not going to find out." He was almost to the horse now, his hand slowly creeping up to grasp the saddle horn. "You'll just have to come home with me."

"I don't even know your name!" She saw the horse flick his ears and knew what he was going to do, although there was no time to warn the man. He jumped aside just as the horse lashed out, the hoof barely missing the man's kneecap.

"It's J.J." He stepped back and studied the horse carefully, as if planning his next attack.

"But what about your family? What'll they think about you bringing home a stranger?"

He smiled again then, and she felt a faint, warm flutter in her midsection. It shouldn't be allowed, a man to have a smile like that. It was far too dangerous to unleash on the female population.

"My 'family' won't blink an eye."

"Well, then." It was no use sitting around here arguing about it. She knew a man who'd made up his mind when she saw him. If he turned out to be more than a friendly stranger, she'd get out quick. It certainly couldn't be more dangerous than wandering around down here.

The big stallion twitched another ear, and she rushed to forestall impending disaster. "Maybe you'd let me ride your horse?"

He gave her a dubious look. "You can't be serious."

She laughed and leaned over to pat her horse on his neck. "Lance will behave, won't you? He understands chivalry."

"Uh—"

"Oh, come on." Angie swung her leg over her horse's back and slid off. "Please?"

"All right." J.J. bowed slightly. "He's all yours."

Angel was smaller than Lancelot, his body less massively muscled. The fine, elegant bones of his head hinted at rare Thoroughbred ancestry. His body was sleek and deceptively strong. This one, she thought in admiration, was built for speed.

J.J. went to stand in front of her horse. He planted his hands on his hips and stared at the huge animal. "You're sure he'll behave?"

"Of course," she said, laughter glinting through her voice.

He raised one brow in question.

"If I ask him to," she qualified.

"Great." J.J. sighed and prepared to mount the horse. "What's his name again?"

"Lancelot."

He dragged himself up on the horse, somewhat surprised to find success on the first try. It might not have looked elegant, but at least it worked. "Romance and chivalry and knights in shining armor. Why is it, all women believe in such nonsense?"

"Who said we do?" She was on Angel's back in a flash, looking for all the world as natural as if it were the only place she'd ever been.

"You named your horse after it."

"Maybe to remind myself what not to expect from a man." She was wearing some odd, loose kind of skirt that was split in the middle, and she efficiently tucked the extra material under her legs and out of the way. "Which way?"

"There." He pointed up a steep slope that arched rapidly away from the waterfront. "Up the hill."

"Let's go."

She shifted her weight almost imperceptibly, and Angel took off, the clopping of his hooves echoing through the grayness, which was just now beginning to lighten to something approaching daylight. To J.J.'s little surprise but extreme frustration, the horse responded beautifully to the woman's commands.

He banged his heels against Lancelot's sides. As the horse clattered after his mistress, J.J.'s backside thumped against the hard leather saddle, and he gritted his teeth against the pain in his lower back. Why would anyone want to do this to himself, when nice, springy coaches were so much more comfortable?

To his immense relief, the horse appeared to need little guidance, and J.J. finally relaxed enough to watch the small figure riding ahead.

She rode like a dream, easily, naturally, as if it were

the one thing she'd been born to do. Grace, motion, and crackling energy all combined into a surprising allure.

He had a sudden, disturbingly clear image of what it would be like to have her naked, moving over him, steadily rising and falling, her small, trim body vibrating with heat and intensity.

He quickly shut the unwelcome thought away. Though Jeremiah Johnston couldn't control horses, he could control everything else in his life. He could certainly control a wayward thought or two.

Her entire life, Angelina had loved three things wholly, completely, and without question: her family, her horses, and Winchester Meadows. If there had been little else in her life, it had never mattered to her. She had exactly what she wanted.

Nothing in that life had prepared her for the Naked Rose.

The wooden building was certainly one of the largest and finest they'd passed, but Angelina had barely had time to glance at it before J.J. led her around back to the low-slung stables. He'd quickly turned the horses over to the stableboy and headed for the back door to the saloon, gesturing for her to follow.

She would have refused just on principle. As if he thought he could order her around with a casual wave of his hand! But it had taken only a brief argument—well, an argument on her part, a discussion on his—before she convinced him that she'd stay and see to Lancelot herself. She trusted no one else to make sure he was properly settled.

So she'd barely seen the outside of the building, and the decrepit courtyard and garden that framed the back door hadn't warned her about what she'd discover inside.

It was like crawling inside a topaz, shiny and glittery

and rich. The two-story central room was massive, gleaming with crystal, bounded in warm, burnished oak, accented with polished brass. Saffron-colored cloths spilled across shiny tables, and plump round settees sprouted golden velvet cushions.

Fascinated by the place, Angelina wandered through the room. Her fingers glided over waxed wood. No dust, no smudges, just shine. She weighed a huge hunk of glittering fool's gold that sat on a side table and shuffled through the stiff pack of playing cards that must have been left out from the evening before.

The fog had finally lifted outside, and sunlight poured through the two tall front windows, warming the room with mellow bronze light. A long bar, simply but elegantly carved, stretched across the back of the room. To the left, before the staircases that curved sensually up to the balcony, an arched doorway led into another, cozier room.

Curious, she peeked inside. This room was still and quiet, also luxurious but slightly more businesslike than the sumptuous main room. It held mostly tables, spread with maize-colored cloths, tables for keno and poker and any other game of chance a well-heeled customer might try.

Angelina whistled through her teeth. She'd bet her last dollar that there were no dollar bets placed in this room.

"Like it?"

She jumped and turned to find J.J. coming down the stairs. He was tightening a black string tie that, along with his black boots, was the only dark note in the unrelieved white of his suit.

"You changed clothes," she said, then cursed herself for the obviousness of her comment.

"Yes." He stopped before her, a little too close, and she took an involuntary step back. Distance. It was always a good thing to maintain, from a dangerous horse or a dangerous man.

"Better, don't you think?" He lifted his arms and

turned, unselfconsciously giving her a good look at the perfectly tailored suit and the equally perfectly constructed body in it. Broad shoulders, lean strength, elegant muscles. Everything a man should have, and nothing she'd ever bothered to notice before.

He belonged here. Here, in this place of elegance and temptation and sin. As right in his saloon as the moon was in the sky, as the water was in the sea. As right as she was in Kentucky.

"Would you like something to drink?" he asked, his voice smooth and polished.

"Yes. Thank you."

She was still here, he thought, and wondered at the distinct relief he'd felt when he'd come down the stairs and found her in his place. He'd half expected her to get on her horse and take off.

It was simply his protective instincts kicking in, he told himself. Can't rescue a woman once and not have the urge to keep her safe. Besides, he was a bit out of practice. Hadn't had his sister to practice on for a long time. It felt surprisingly good.

He pulled a low-backed stool up in front of the bar and rounded the back. "What would you like?"

"Hmm?" She perched herself on the stool and tried not to look at the painting that unfurled almost the full length of the wall behind the bar. She hadn't seen it from the other side of the room, had only noticed that there was some artwork hanging there. Now, it seemed impossible to look at anything else.

"A drink? Would you like one?"

"Oh, yes. Certainly."

"What kind?" he asked patiently.

The woman in the painting was naked, Angelina thought in amazement. Stark, bare-assed, both-bosoms-to-the-wind naked. She didn't think the large red rose that dangled over one hip counted as coverage. "Um . . . water," she mumbled.

"You're sure? Just water?"

She dragged her gaze away from the painting and wondered if her cheeks looked as red as they felt. "I'm sure."

From beneath the bar he pulled out two chunky crystal glasses and a simple metal pitcher. He worked quickly, competently, his hands elegantly graceful as he poured one glass full of clear water and handed it to her. His skin was darkly tanned against the flawless white of his cuff and she had the oddest notion that perhaps the painting was a safer sight than watching his long, lean fingers.

He wore a ring on his right hand, a big nugget of gold that retained its original shape and had only been worked enough to be made into a ring. It was set with a large turquoise so intensely blue it looked as if it would be hot to the touch.

He turned and frowned at the long triple rows of bottles and decanters that marched down the shelf. They glowed in shades of amber and brown, some almost invisibly clear. He carefully readjusted the two that were slightly out of line until the bottles aligned so evenly Angelina was sure that even a measurement would show them to be exactly spaced.

He selected a round bottle of colorless liquid, poured himself a splash, then set it down on the bar in between them.

"You're drinking already? It's not even lunchtime."

"Around here, it's not even time for breakfast yet." He braced his elbows on the bar and leaned forward.

"So, Angel, what part of the South are you from?"

Thick, golden lashes lifted up and he looked intently at her. Lord, his eyes—they exactly matched the hunk of turquoise in his ring, profoundly blue and overwhelmingly pure. Unable to hold his gaze or to ignore the strangeness of his close regard, she dropped her own gaze to her glass of water.

"Whoever said I was from the South?"

"You did—every time you opened your mouth."

"Excuse me?"

"Your accent. But don't worry. It's as alluring as hell."

Alluring? She took a quick gulp; as she lifted the glass, it caught the light, bent and reflected it, sending tiny rainbows chasing down the length of the polished bar.

"Virginia maybe?" he guessed.

When she didn't answer, he sighed and tried again. "What are you doing in California?"

This one she was willing to answer—up to a point, at least. "Looking for work."

"Well, in that case."

She sneaked a peek at him; the impact of those eyes hadn't lessened, but she supposed a person would grow used to them after a time. Maybe.

He smiled slowly. "Perhaps I have something for you."

She started and looked around the glittering saloon. Oh, no, she thought wildly. What work could there be in a place like this? "I don't think—"

"I want you to teach me to ride."

4

Well, she was certainly a long way from home, Angelina thought as she looked around the room—*her* room, she corrected. This was where she lived now, at least for a while.

After she stammered her agreement to his job offer—her choices, at the moment, were limited—he'd waved off her tentative questions about salary. They would settle that later, he'd said. He was certain they could come to an agreement.

Telling her it was the cook's afternoon off, he'd fed her—a quick, precisely stacked sandwich in the sparsely furnished kitchen near the back of the building. Although he certainly wasn't proficient in the kitchen, he didn't seem at all disturbed by the fact that he'd made lunch for a woman. Then he'd whisked her upstairs to her new room and left her to unpack before she had a second to catch her breath.

When she'd left Kentucky, this wasn't precisely what she had in mind.

She dropped her satchel on the floor on the deep spring-green rug and turned in a circle. The room was sumptuous, brass and glass, green and peach and ivory.

Yes, a very long way from home, indeed.

She wandered over to the huge brass bed. She stroked the peach cover; it was satin and soft, stuffed with down and scattered with fat green pillows. Laughing, she turned around, threw up her arms, and let herself fall back on the bed. It squeaked under her weight, and she nearly groaned in pleasure.

After two months on the road, of grabbing snatches of sleep in jostling stagecoaches and hard, strange beds, this seemed as close to heaven as she'd ever found.

She tugged a pillow close and wrapped her arms around it, smiling as she drifted off to sleep.

"What do you mean, you hired a stablegirl?"

J.J. winced inwardly and took a fortifying gulp of whiskey before answering Rose. "You should see her with the horses. Amazing."

"So? Since when do you care?" Rose tugged at the neckline of her rose satin gown; her breasts threatened to pop out of the heart-shaped neckline.

"I don't. You know that."

"Why did you hire her, then?" she demanded. "We already have Tommy."

J.J. had never quite figured out the proper label for Rose. She was his partner, yes. His lover; though, now that he thought about it, he couldn't remember the last time they'd . . . Mostly, he just called her friend.

He knew her candy box pink-and-white beauty hid a mind far sharper than anyone would expect. And he knew, too, that her objections to his hiring the woman had absolutely nothing to do with jealousy.

He chucked her under her softly rounded chin. "You just don't want to add another salary."

She folded her arms across her impressive chest and made a luscious pout. "True."

"It won't be expensive, I promise. Mostly a room and board, I expect." His smile faded. "Rose, she didn't have anywhere else to go."

Rose sighed and gave in, as he'd known she would. "All right."

"Thanks. Now, have you seen David this afternoon?"

"Nope." Rose frowned. "There was a letter delivered just after lunch, when you were down counting stock. He tore right outta here, and I haven't seen him since." Without missing a beat, she smiled and waved at a customer who'd just arrived. "Think there's somethin' wrong?"

"I'm sure there's not." He gave her a light swat on her rump. "Better get back to work."

She shrieked but sashayed over to take orders from the new arrivals.

J.J. went around to the back of the bar. Snatching up a soft cloth, he stroked it down the wooden surface, erasing any smudges. He didn't see any, but that didn't mean they weren't there.

It was late afternoon, and the Naked Rose was beginning to fill up, humming with the murmur of low voices and the clink of glassware. Four men, ex-miners who had the sense to get out while the getting was good, were playing a halfhearted game of poker while two of the "upstairs girls" kept them company. Around the room, perhaps a half-dozen more men drank and talked. The place was clean and shiny and relaxed.

Later, the Rose would take on a different air. As dusk rolled in, the soft, hissing glow of the gas lamps would make the room seem smaller, cozier. It would also be louder, ringing with shouts from the gambling room, lively tunes from the piano shoved in the far corner, and laughter. The air would be filled with smells of good tobacco and brandy and perfume.

J.J. tossed the cloth over his shoulder. Nodding in response to a gesture from a customer at the end of the bar, he poured a long glass of whiskey. He slid the glass expertly down the length of polished oak.

Bracing one hip against the bar, he surveyed the Rose, and couldn't suppress a swell of pride.

He was a man who had it all.

He had two partners he called friends, better friends than he probably had a right to. He had a family, a sister and his nieces, close enough to see frequently.

And he had the Rose. He'd come close to losing it only once, when the gold played out and depression hit San Francisco in '53. But when the other saloons were retrenching, they'd scraped together enough money to expand. Whatever business there was to be had, they'd gotten it. Now, most of their competitors were long gone, and the Naked Rose was without question the fanciest, best-known saloon in town. Soon, it would turn a decent profit again.

Most of all, it was his place, exactly the way he wanted it.

Yes, he thought as he poured a drink for yet another new customer, he'd finally arranged his life precisely to his satisfaction.

There was something odd tonight.

Rose sashayed through the saloon, nodding at regular customers, stopping to tap a favored one lightly on his shoulder, her laughter tinkling above the raucous tunes pounded out on the piano. Her smile was bright, her dangling earbobs danced when she tossed her head, and no one noticed that she was rapidly assessing everyone and everything in the room.

The customers seemed unsettled, prone to drinking just a touch more than usual and gambling recklessly. It was good for business, and it should have made her happy, but she couldn't shake a faint waft of apprehension. The air was unusually heavy and thick, weighing down on her shoulders.

And that stranger was still here.

Planting her hands on her hips, Rose studied the man who'd settled at the end of the bar since midafternoon. A long time to sit in one place, especially since he clearly wasn't here for company. He hadn't spoken to anyone, merely sat there and sipped at a glass of whiskey.

She'd noticed him the moment he came in; but then, she noticed every new customer. He'd barely acknowledged her friendly welcome, just plopped himself down at the far end of the bar, his back to the wall, and waved for a drink.

It wasn't as if he'd done anything to make her worry. He'd been the soul of circumspection, sitting there in his ordinary, dark, made-to-blend-in clothes.

But there was no way that man would ever, ever blend in. Extremely tall, thin almost to a fault, he moved with an oddly disjointed grace. A long swath of silver hair fell to his shoulders, and Rose pegged him on the far side of forty.

She hadn't survived this long in the West without knowing trouble when she saw it. And this man was serious trouble; everything from the set of his shoulders to the arrogant tilt of his head told her that. He was a man used to command and equally unused to compromise.

And having a man like that in her bar was going to cause trouble, sooner or later.

Unless, of course, she could get him quietly out of the way.

Rose tugged at the bodice of her dress, showing off her bosom to best advantage. She knew her assets and was an old practitioner of the "catch more flies with honey" school. If a little display of flesh made things easier, well, she wasn't above making use of the few advantages women had.

He barely glanced up when she neared him, just flicked a quick look her way and returned to staring into his small glass of smoky whiskey.

Slightly piqued at the unusual experience of being completely dismissed by a man, she leaned against the bar and rested her elbow on top of it.

"Hello, stranger. You've been here a long time."

He didn't answer. Giving the barest of nods in acknowledgment, he took a slow sip of his drink.

"Is there something we can do for you?"

He looked at her then, his gaze slowly sliding from her head to her feet and back again. His eyes were the palest blue she'd ever seen, so light they were almost silver. Yet, she could read little in them, not appreciation or speculation or any one of the dozens of things she usually saw in a man's eyes when he looked at her. She got the impression he was simply absorbing information—no judgments, no assumptions—but when his gaze finally returned to her face, she was absolutely sure he's missed not the slightest detail.

"Maybe."

A woman wouldn't call him handsome, she thought, all lean, sharp features that met at striking angles. But it wasn't a face that a woman could look away from, either.

"You got a name?" she asked.

"Yes."

It was a full minute before she realized he wasn't going to offer it up. She gave an exasperated sigh. "You gonna tell me?"

He smiled then, a slow grin that she would have sworn he was incapable of. "Eventually."

"Mine's Rose," she offered.

"So I gathered." The smile stayed as he nodded to the painting of her that reigned over the back of the bar.

He turned sideways, looking out over the chaos that bubbled in the rest of the saloon. He sure didn't talk much. She'd only meant to find out what he wanted, to see if she could hurry him on his way before trouble started, but she found herself intrigued. Sure, they'd had men of few words in here before, but usually they were cold and angry. His silence was . . . comfortable. Almost easy.

"Nice place." He straightened and looked down at her. Lord, she'd known he was tall, but she found herself level with his ribcage and had to crane her neck back to look at him. "Who owns it?"

"I do." She caught a quick flash of surprise, and she was pleased she'd managed to provoke that much reaction in him. "Well, me and my partners," she corrected.

"Partners?"

"Yep." She grinned. "Best ones in the world. David and J.J."

He stared at her for a moment. "And which one do you think you're in love with?"

Rose felt her smile freeze in place. "I don't know what you mean, stranger."

"No?" He lifted his hand and laid one lean finger along the curve of her cheek, just rested it there like a butterfly lighting on a flower. "You sure are one pretty lady, ma'am. Shame there's so much hurtin' in your eyes."

She jerked away from his touch as if it burned her. She wasn't hurting. And, even if she was, it sure wouldn't show in her eyes. A bright smile, a gay laugh; everybody always commented on her cheerfulness. She'd made damn sure she was good at it.

"There's no pain," she said sharply.

"Shit." He said it so mildly that at first it didn't register. "There's always pain. Some of us just hide it better'n others."

She forced her smile wider. "There's no pain."

The corners of his strange, light eyes crinkled, and he reached for the dark brown hat that rested on the bar at his elbow. He clapped it on his head, then tipped the brim to her. "Whatever you say, ma'am."

She watched him saunter out of the place, all long limbs and bones and assurance. How could he know? she wondered. No one knew.

One of the girls laughed, the sound sharp and piercing above the hubbub of conversation. Glassware clinked, and, down the bar, a customer shouted for more gin. Rose shook herself slightly, tucked the curly pink ostrich plume more securely into her hair, and went back to work.

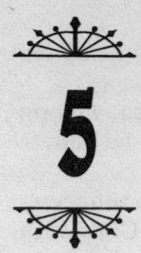

5

Angelina peeked carefully over the edge of the balcony, then jumped back and plastered herself against the wall before anyone could see her.

Lordy, the place looked different at night.

She hadn't planned on coming down. Her new job revolved around the stables and the morning, and had no part in the goings on in the saloon the rest of the night. Indeed, she was half-convinced that if she set one foot downstairs after sundown, somehow either her mother, father, or brother would find out and come bursting in and drag her out by her ear.

Better she stay safely tucked away in her room and plan what she was going to do next. For while this was a fortunate and interesting stopover, it was hardly a giant step on the way to her own breeding farm.

But, from her room, she could hear the merrymaking downstairs. Cheerful barks of laughter mingled with the pounding, rhythmic notes of the piano, and had drifted through her tightly shut door to her shamefully receptive ears. It had proved irresistible, calling her with gaiety and the bright, seductive lure of the unknown.

She knew it was probably sinful, the curiosity that led her from her room to this perch that would allow her to see the frivolity downstairs. But she knew she was weak when it came to temptation. She'd been weak when, at ten, she'd tried to ride her father's new stallion, the black devil she'd been forbidden to get near. That had been a near disaster, also. She'd broken her arm and her mother had tried to keep her from ever riding again. In the end, though, she'd been able to ride the horse as no one else could.

And, at twelve, she'd sneaked out to watch a mating. That would have shocked her family if they'd caught her nearly as much as the size and raw power of the stallion had shocked her. At least, it had at first; but there'd been elemental beauty as well and life at its most basic. By the time she was sixteen, she'd talked her father into letting her help. By eighteen, she was managing breeding herself, although none of their customers had any inkling of it. That would have been too much of a scandal.

Now her curiosity was, more than likely, going to lead her into trouble again. But the music and the sounds beat in her blood, gaiety and temptation and the draw of the unknown and unsuspected.

She sidled closer to the edge of the balcony, grasping tightly the polished oak handrail. Hers was the last room, far from the steps, and the place where she stood was cloaked in shadows. Surely no one would see her here.

Beneath her, the large, open room was much darker now. The pale, flickering light from the hissing gas lamps high on the walls left large swaths of darkness in the corners and between the tables. The room no longer glittered and glowed; it seemed smaller, more mysterious, and infinitely more sinful.

The room was filled with milling people. Men, mostly, in tailored suits and grubby denims. It didn't seem to make much difference how they were dressed; they mixed easily, settling at the bar or around one of the tables. She caught the low, rich rumble of masculine laughter. Off to her left, the piano rang with "Camptown Races."

The saloon was hazy with smoke, filled with the mellow scent of tobacco and the yeasty warmth of beer. There were a few women there, their shiny dresses of ruby and emerald and pink standing out brightly among the dull colors the men wore.

If the room itself glittered less at night, the women made up for it, light winking off beads encrusting their bodices and dangly jewels at their ears. Their clothes sparkled as their laughter tinkled above the men's.

Among the colors, dull and vivid, she caught a flash of white, cool and pristine. Gripping the railing tighter, she leaned over for a better look.

J.J. was behind the bar, smoothly filling two glasses while he chatted with three more customers. The pure gold of his hair gleamed as he threw back his head in laughter, exposing the strong brown column of his throat.

He stopped and turned, looking up. Quickly, she jumped back into the shadows, but it was too late. He'd already seen her.

He grinned and waved, beckoning her down.

She shook her head. No, she couldn't go down there. She'd never intended to. It was wrong, wicked. All she'd wanted was a bit of a peek. She ignored the niggling suspicion that perhaps this was what she'd wanted all along.

He frowned at her refusal, then gestured again.

"Come down." His words couldn't be heard above the hubbub of conversation, but she could read his mouth as they formed.

No! she mouthed back, underscoring it with a slash of her hand.

He regarded her for a moment, his brows drawing together. Then he shrugged and headed for the stairs.

Oh, Lord! Angelina considered bolting for the safety of her room but couldn't seem to make her feet move. What good would it do, anyway? He could certainly drag her out of there, too, if he wanted to; it was his place, and he must have keys to every room.

She frowned over the impropriety of that thought. It hadn't occurred to her before, but it was certainly something she was going to have to rectify as quickly as possible.

He'd rounded the top of the stairs and was advancing on her, his white suit almost glowing in the shadowy darkness of the hallway.

He stopped mere steps from her. "Come on down."

She shook her head vehemently.

He leaned down, his mouth close to her ear, insuring that she could hear him over the din from downstairs. She felt a whisper of his breath curl around her ear, stirring the hair that looped loosely against her neck. "Couldn't you hear me? You're welcome to come on downstairs. One of the side benefits of the job."

"I can't!" Her fingers curled in the fabric of her plain brown skirt. She'd never paid much attention to her clothes but she knew, among those brightly dressed women, she'd look as plain and drab as a dull brown wren somehow stuck in a flock of gay, colorful finches.

"Don't be silly. Of course you can." He would have been hard-pressed to say why he was so insistent on her coming downstairs. Perhaps it was simply his instincts as a host, as if he needed to make sure everyone was entertained. It certainly couldn't be that he merely liked the idea of having her there.

Ignoring her protests, he grabbed her wrist and tugged her along behind him down the hallway and the stairs, down into the midst of the gaiety. She tried once to pull away, but she knew, deep down, she was glad he hadn't listened to her. It was too hard to be shut away while the rest of the world was enjoying themselves. Was it so bad, then, to just have a bit of fun?

He settled her on a stool at the far end of the bar, safely away from most of the customers. He wheeled around the open end, planted his hands on the glossy surface, and turned his attention to her.

"Something to drink? It's past suppertime now."

"Oh, well." She'd already broken with propriety by being down here; what was a bit more? She looked out over the crowd, who all seemed to be having more fun than anybody should, and then back at J.J., comfortably ensconced behind the bar. He was smooth, sophisticated, and completely relaxed. What would he think of a woman who'd hardly ever been in a big city, who'd been tucked away in the country her whole life? Who'd never even tried a forbidden sip of alcohol? "Whiskey."

He raised a brow. "You're sure."

She swallowed. "Of course I'm sure."

"All right." He splashed a modest amount of dark amber liquid into a glass and set it in front of her. He nodded in acknowledgment to two customers down at the other end of the bar and turned to draw two tall, foamy beers.

Angelina lifted her glass and gave it an experimental swirl. It was really sort of pretty, all gold and smooth, sparkling in the flickering light. She tried a tiny sip.

Heat trickled down her throat and spread in her belly. She pinched her mouth together to prevent a cough.

There, that wasn't so bad after all. She'd managed to drink the stuff without embarrassing herself. She peeked at J.J. to see if he'd admired her sophistication, only to find he was too involved with customers to notice.

"Ready?" he called down the bar. He put one large mug on the shiny surface and gave it a small shove. The glass slid easily down the slippery wood and Angelina took a quick breath, sure it would go crashing off the other side.

It slowed to a stop precisely in front of the customer.

She gaped at the drink, then stared at J.J. He grinned at her. "It's a gift."

"How did you do that?"

He shrugged. "I'll teach you if you'd like."

"I would."

"If you can manage to teach me to ride that mangy beast, I'm sure I can teach you to tend bar."

She was going to learn to tend bar. Oh, her family was just going to love that.

But if only they had given her a chance, one single opportunity to do what she really wanted, what she knew she could do, what she was *meant* to do, she wouldn't be here. She silently vowed to worry no longer about their disapproval. She must make her own way now.

"Who's the new girl, J.J.?" the customer shouted. "Gonna have to dress her up a bit if'n ya wanna make any money off her!" He slapped his knee and guffawed loudly.

She stared blankly at the man. It wasn't until J.J. yelled "Shut up" that she realized what he'd been suggesting.

"Why, you—you . . . " She rose off her chair. "I'm not—not *that,* you idiot. I'm just here to—"

J.J. coughed sharply. She turned and was surprised to see a dark red flush creeping up his neck.

He was embarrassed, she realized. Embarrassed to have his customers know that he'd hired a woman to teach him to ride, a skill most westerners took for granted. And she was warmed by this show of vulnerability, a tiny weakness in his armor of smooth sophistication. A weakness that *she* could help him with.

"I'm just the new kitchen help."

"Oh. Sorry, ma'am. Din't mean no harm."

She nodded stiffly and returned to take a quick gulp of her drink. Really, she could get to like this stuff. It wasn't all that bad.

"Angel." J.J. touched her hand, and she raised her gaze to find him watching her intently, an odd half smile lifting the corners of his finely sculpted mouth. "Thank you."

A slow glow warmed her from the inside out. She felt slightly lightheaded, almost giddy. The whiskey must work more quickly than she realized; she'd better slow down.

"No problem."

"Thank you anyway." She had to return that smile. It was too appealing to ignore, and, caught by the approval in his turquoise eyes, she felt the glow spread to her chest.

"Well, this must be the new employee." A woman strolled casually up to J.J. and draped herself against his side. She was beautiful, spun-sugar blond hair piled high, skin the color of rich cream, and plump lips the exact shade of pink peppermint candy. She was covered—barely—in lustrous rose satin, the generous curves of her breasts swelling over the low neckline.

Angelina couldn't prevent one quick glance at her own chest. She had no reason to believe that her own weren't fully functional, but still, in the face of such lavishness . . . She shook off the unwelcome rush of insecurity. Why would she want to look like that? They were completely impractical things. Would probably get in the way when she rode.

"Yep." In a gesture so easy and natural it had to be utterly familiar, J.J. slung an arm around the woman's shoulders and tugged her close. "Rose, love, this is Angel. Angel, meet Rose, my partner, the brains of the place."

Rose laughed and snuggled into J.J.'s embrace, turning her head to drop a quick kiss on his shoulder. "Nice to meet you, Angel."

Of course. She should have known. Of course a man like J.J. would have a woman like Rose in his life. Had she really thought he would be alone? She took a breath and squared her shoulders. "Angie."

"Huh?"

"Angie. You can call me Angie." She darted a quick glance at J.J. He frowned at her, but his eyes were twinkling.

"Angie it is, then." Rose straightened and, for all her soft, fluffy prettiness, became all business. "How's the till tonight, J.J?"

"Not bad." He gave her a quick buss on the top of her head. "Probably not good enough to satisfy you, though. How about you. Heard anything good?"

She swatted at J.J.'s arm and patted her hair, checking to make sure he hadn't mussed the careful arrangement. "Everything seems pretty calm. Lotta talk about a horse race a coupla high muckamucks are settin' up. Not much else."

Angie sipped carefully at her drink and watched them as they talked easily about their evening's work. They were so comfortable together, relaxed and casual. Both earthy, sensual, worldly. As the unfamiliar bite of whiskey slid down her throat, she felt an equally unfamiliar envy for the ease and friendliness of their relationship. What would it be like to have a partner, a friend, so evenly matched?

"Ah, there he is, finally." His arm looped around her waist, J.J. steered Rose around the end of the bar and headed for the door. "Come on, Angel, I want you to meet our other partner, David."

"I told you. It's Angie."

"Nope. Too late." He grinned. "We're both stuck with 'Angel.'"

At first glance, the man who'd just entered looked

ordinary. Pleasant features, jumbled sandy curls, medium height. But then he looked at her and nodded a vague greeting. He had extraordinarily beautiful eyes, filled with flecks of green and gold and glazed with a soft, aching sadness that made her want to comfort him.

"Angel, David's been my friend—well, forever. We came out here together. Don't believe a word he says about me."

David swallowed visibly and lifted one hand. Clenched in his fist was a crumpled scrap of paper.

"I'm going home."

6

J.J. stared blankly at David. "What did you say?"

David shoved the ball of paper into his hand. "I'm leaving. Read it." Blinking, he shook his head slightly. "I have to go."

J.J. carefully smoothed the small scrap against his thigh before starting to read. His jaw twitched, and when he finally looked up, his shoulders were lower, as if someone had just placed a heavy burden on them.

He handed the letter back to David. "We can't talk about this here. Come on."

Uncertain, Angie watched the three of them head for the stairs. This was obviously private business, no concern of hers, and it was probably best she just stay out of the way. Yet, she felt an undeniable curiosity.

She took in the customers milling around the room. With J.J. and Rose gone, someone had to keep things rolling down here. Though it was hardly part of her duties, it was just as well she begin earning her keep now. She darted over to the bar and slipped behind it, snatching up a limp rag to wrap around her waist as a makeshift apron.

Her brow furrowed as she contemplated the bewildering array of glittering bottles. She didn't know scotch from dishwater. If she was lucky, all the customers would order beer. Surely she could figure out how that spigot worked. And if they ordered something else, she suspected that as long as she was generous enough with the liquor, no one would care much if she gave them the proper kind.

She whirled around and smiled brightly at a skinny old man in a battered brown hat. "What'll you have, sir?"

J.J. hadn't gotten halfway up the steps before he remembered Angie. He couldn't leave her downstairs without being there to watch over her. The vultures would take one look at that little bit of a country girl and smell fresh meat. She was bound to be frightened.

"You go on ahead. I'll be up in a second," he told Rose and David before heading back down the stairs. There was Angie, dancing back and forth behind the bar like she owned the place, frowning as she contemplated two brown bottles before she dumped a splash of the contents of each in one glass and set it before a customer.

So maybe she wasn't frightened. But that was only because she didn't know enough to *be* frightened. He did, and until he was sure she could handle herself, he was keeping a very close eye on her. Things could get far too complicated otherwise, and the last thing he needed in his life was more complications. Keep It Simple was his motto.

It was equally clear that he couldn't just order her to her room as if she were a disobedient child. He knew her just enough to suspect just how well that would go over.

She was trying to draw a beer now, and ended up

with a mug that was at least three-quarters foam and spilling over the sides and onto her hands. But she laughed when she handed it to a young cowpoke, and the fellow was charmed enough by her display of dimples to accept it without protest, mooning at her as he dunked his nose in the foam. She licked her sticky forefinger, puckering her lips at the taste. Then she shrugged and popped another finger in her mouth.

The goggle-eyed cowboy was clearly entranced, grinning at her with a mouth rimmed in white suds.

"We need you upstairs," J.J. said.

She started. "I was just trying to help out. To fill in while the rest of you were busy."

"Yes, I appreciate that. But you're part of the staff now, and any decisions we make will affect you, too."

She scrubbed her palms on the towel tied to her waist. "I didn't want to intrude."

"You won't." She would, though. J.J. knew David wouldn't mind, but Rose would wonder why he'd brought Angie along. He couldn't think of any other way of getting her conveniently out of the way, though, and he was downright certain she'd get into more trouble than he wanted to deal with if he left her down here by herself.

"But who's going to tend the bar?"

"Josiah can handle it for a while. He's not much for talking, but he'll take orders well enough."

He headed for the stairs, not bothering to check to see if she followed him. He'd done his duty; his conscience was clear. He'd tried to get her out of here.

"Won't Josiah—whoever he is—"

"I'll introduce you later. He works for us, too."

"Then won't he feel left out?"

"Nope." His rapid steps were quiet on the sanded wooden steps. "I told you, he's not much for talking. He wouldn't be interested in a meeting of all the employees."

Except it wasn't a meeting of all the employees. Just

the three owners, and a woman who was already causing him more bother than he'd intended.

He'd worried about her. He'd actually had to stop and *think* about her, damn it.

He hated that.

"Here." He ushered her through a door that opened off the long balcony, several rooms before her own. His own sitting room, she supposed, filled with dark wood, spare lines, and once-rich fabric of wine and forest green.

"David, first I'd like to introduce you to our newest employee," he said formally. "This is Angel, our"—he paused, the corner of his mouth lifting slightly, "horse mistress?"

"I'm sorry," she muttered. David couldn't want her here. Surely he needed to be alone with his partners, to deal with whatever was causing the darkness on his pleasant face. "I know I'm intruding, but J.J.—"

"Doesn't take no for an answer. We know." David came smoothly to his feet, bowing briefly over her hand. His green-gold gaze washed over her, and a small smile of approval broke through the darkness. "'Angel.' How appropriate."

"I'd really prefer 'Angie.'"

"'Angie', then. Would you like to sit?" He settled her into a dark green wing chair almost before she knew it, then sat back down on the couch. He was outwardly calm, but she saw the tight curl of his fist against the expensive gray fabric that covered his thigh.

"Now that we're all here," Rose said coolly, lounging elegantly next to J.J., "what is it, David?"

He swallowed, the slow slide of his Adam's apple betraying the thickness in his throat. "It's my father." His booted feet shuffled against the cream-and-burgundy carpet. "He's dead. Nearly a month ago."

Rose gave a soft, inarticulate cry of comfort, then rushed over to sit next to David, wrapping her arm around his shoulder.

J.J. was absolutely still. "I'm sorry."

The utter lack of emotion and the cold inflection of J.J.'s voice shocked Angie; he seemed to be completely unmoved by his friend's pronouncement. Yet, David seemed comforted by that short phrase; his taut shoulders relaxed a bit. "I know, J.J.," he said softly.

Angie felt completely out of place. She was an outsider, unable to offer anything of worth. And it brought a quick, irrational fear. What if something happened to her own father while she was gone? How would she even know? She wanted to rush back to Kentucky and watch over him nearly as much as she wanted to be able to do something, anything, for this man she hardly knew.

"There's more." David crinkled the paper he still held clenched in his fist. "He'd been ill, more so than any of them had guessed. The store . . . he hadn't been taking care of things. Mother had no idea until he died."

"Oh, no." Rose's bell-like voice was soft with sympathy.

"Yes. There are debts, many of them. Taxes, suppliers." His hazel eyes glistened with moisture. "They'll lose it all."

"When are you leaving?" J.J. still hadn't moved, a sculpture in white and bronze.

"Friday. There's a stage that morning. I have to be on it." He closed his eyes. "I only hope it's not too late."

"It won't be." J.J. nodded briskly. "How much do you need?"

David stared at him for a moment, then gave a deep sigh. "Two thousand dollars."

There was an almost imperceptible tightening of J.J.'s jaw, a sudden stiffening of his body in the elegant white suit. "Your share of the Rose is worth more than that."

"Only a little."

"Can you take a thousand now, and I'll send you a thousand later?"

"No." David's voice was heavy with worry and regret. "The bank is threatening foreclosure."

"Well, then, you'll have it."

"I'm sorry, J.J." David shook his head. "I didn't mean to do this, without warning—"

J.J.'s hand jerked in a negative gesture, cutting him off. "It's your money. I couldn't have done this without you."

"I know it's impossible."

"We'll get it somehow."

David looked at J.J., a long, slow moment broken only by the steady ticking of the mahogany clock on the carved mantel. Why did it seem they were saying so much to each other without any words at all?

"Friday, then?" J.J. asked suddenly.

"Friday." David rose to his feet with restrained, unnatural movements, like a man under a heavy burden. "I think I'll go to my room now."

Rose swept up in a rustle of heavy satin. "Let me get you settled."

David gave her a wan smile. "There's no need to mother me."

"Hush." She smoothed a sandy curl off his forehead. "Who else will let me?"

Angie was left alone with J.J. He sat, unmoving, staring at an exceptional oil of a sun-drenched mountain meadow that was hung over the fireplace. She wanted to help, to show some appreciation to the man who—however unnecessary it had been—had dragged her in off the streets. But if she had had enough money to help, she wouldn't be here.

"Does he have a large family?" she tried.

"Five younger sisters." His tones were clipped. "A mother. A social, kind, and totally helpless mother."

"Oh." How easy it had always been for her, she realized, responsible only for herself and her horse. What freedom it had given her. "You don't need to pay me until you're able," she offered.

His bark of laughter was without a trace of mirth. "I'd planned on paying you ten dollars a month. That won't even make a dent."

"Oh." Ten dollars a month. She would have given it up, easily. It wasn't enough for what she needed, not nearly enough. And she would stay for nothing. There was no place to go . . . not yet, anyway; she wasn't desperate enough to fall back on her brother. Besides, she'd seen the clientele the Rose attracted. If there was any possibility of finding someone to back her in this venture, she was as likely to find him here as anywhere. "I really don't need it," she said, knowing it was futile, unable to think of anything else to offer.

"No." His pride wouldn't allow him to take the wages of his workers. He gave a small smile. "Ten dollars a month. I guess that makes you a sawbuck angel."

"I guess so." She was unaccountably pleased she'd been able to lighten his mood, just a bit. "Perhaps we can cut back on Angel's oats instead. It will be cheaper, and maybe he won't be so ready to run away with his rider," she teased lightly.

"If that works, I'm never letting him near food again." He looked at her, his even features glowing bronze above the stark whiteness of his collar. "I'll wait until he's too weak to carry me. It'll serve him right."

She smiled, happy to hear a hint of animation return to his voice. "We must start lessons in the morning, before he's unable to throw you properly. How would I have any fun otherwise?"

"No," he said flatly, any trace of amusement gone. "Tomorrow morning I must come up with two thousand dollars."

7

The morning was nearly as depressing as his mood when J.J. stepped out of the shelter of the Rose's back doorway and into the yard. Thick, wet mist surrounded him with cold wind and damp moisture. Nearly eight o'clock, and there was no hint of the warmth or light that should have come with the rising of the sun hours ago.

He sighed in relief when, off to his left, he saw his buggy pulled up in the yard, just as he'd requested. No need to go roust Tommy out of bed, then.

The buggy was one he'd bought in better times, its glossy sides a rich, deep, wine red, the button-tufted cushions a matching shade of plush velvet. He'd been unable to pay for a new paint job for several years, plowing any extra money back into the Rose, so the enamel showed a few chips here and there, and the upholstery was getting a bit worn. But it was spotlessly clean, and the half-canvas top, raised, as usual, against the weather was neatly mended. The vehicle did him no shame. Too bad it wasn't newer. He could sell it for a bit of the money.

Clapping his white hat on his head, he walked forward, climbed into the buggy, and settled himself on the seat, about to order Tommy to head for the bank.

Except it wasn't Tommy on the driver's seat. There was Angie, wrapped in a red poncho as bright as St. Nicholas's robes, her toes tapping as she hummed underneath her breath, her arms waving the short whip as if she were conducting a grand orchestra.

Her name came out in a long groan. "Angel."

"Hmm?" She twisted in her seat to look at him, peering through the condensation dripping off the brim of the sorriest black felt hat J.J. had ever seen. Her arms stopped flailing in the air, but her feet kept moving, as if she was incapable of keeping her small body completely still. "Good morning," she said brightly.

"Where's Tommy?"

"I sent him back to bed."

"And just who gave you authority to do that?"

"Well." A drop of water clung to her nose and she huffed it away. "He was tired. So I said I'd take over for him."

"It is not your job," he said sternly. He did not want this, not one little bit. He had enough on his mind without dealing with a lost little rabbit who couldn't sit still. Tommy, he could simply order to drive and ignore him the rest of the way.

Angie was another sort entirely. He doubted he could sit back here without feeling as if he should be the one up front, giving her the grand tour of the city as she sat back and took in the sights with those shining brown eyes. She'd probably want to carry on a conversation, too. He didn't have the time or the energy for dealing with her this morning. His own thoughts were quite challenging enough.

"Oh, come on," she said, the vivid red of her cape

bringing out the honey tones in her skin. "You hired me to help with the horses. I'm helping with the horses."

"I hired you to teach me to ride. Nothing more."

"But you won't let me! You didn't want to start the lessons!" she protested. Then a quicksilver change of mood, and her dimples flashed. "Oh, let me. I'm really quite competent, you know. I drive nearly as well as I ride."

Of course she did, he thought. He'd expect nothing less. He could drive, too, when he had to, though *competent* probably wasn't the right word for it. "You've had a long trip. You should get some rest before I put you to work," he said, hoping his generosity would get her off that seat and him on his way.

"I'm fine," she chirped, bright and fresh on her perch, a slice of warmth on the gray day. "Besides, there's nothing else to do. I've been up for hours. I've already mucked the stables, and I'm not one to sit around and twiddle my thumbs."

He should have known. A morning person, up with the birds, bright and annoyingly cheerful. A saloon was filled with creatures of the night, and the morning was the only time around the Rose that he'd ever managed to have to himself. Without someone wanting his help, his ear, or his presence. Now, it seemed, he'd given that up, too.

"Drive, then, if you're so insistent on it."

"Good." She spun on the seat and braced her feet against the high front board, then twisted to look back at him again.

"What is it?" he asked, frustration breaking through his smooth voice.

She wrinkled her nose. "Well, um . . . "

He sighed heavily. "Two blocks down, then a right on Sacramento."

"Right, boss." She tipped her hat at him, the black whip clutched in her hand trailing a shower of drops, then clicked to the horses.

He sagged back against the seat, safely under the canvas top.

It was not proving to be a promising morning.

She'd told him the truth. Sort of.

She *had* been up for hours, and she'd finished all of the work she'd managed to find. The Rose's stables were small, with only a couple of horses, and she was used to the Meadows' huge barns. Feeding, watering, and cleaning had taken no time at all. She'd been looking for something to do, and Tommy *had* seemed inordinately sleepy.

Until J.J. climbed into the carriage, she'd honestly not realized that the reason she offered to drive was that she wanted so badly to see him again. There he was, all golden and citified and completely out of her realm of experience.

She tried to tell herself it was simply her blasted curiosity again, an interest in a type of person she'd never met before, the lure of trying to figure him out, the way she would a puzzle.

But that didn't explain the way her breath wedged in her throat. And it didn't account for the undeniable pang in her chest when she wondered if he looked that perfect when he just rolled out of bed, and she realized that Rose knew the answer.

She clicked the reins over the horses' backs and they started forward with a rough jerk, snapping her neck. Soon they were out of the protected courtyard and into the sharply sloping narrow streets that were hedged with an odd, unmatching array of buildings.

Thick mist swirled around her, dampening her lashes and blurring her vision. It made the buildings appear almost unreal, unconnected to the ground, undefined from the sky. There was no reason or pattern; great granite monoliths sat next to neat wooden boardinghouses;

tumbledown stores crowded imposing brick manors. Few lights pierced the thick fog, only an occasional yellow glow from a paned window that sent warm light spilling across the cobbled street. Mostly, the buildings were dark and silent. San Francisco, it seemed, was not a morning town.

Dark and silent, too, was the man behind her. Pulling her team to a stop at a crossroads, she sneaked a quick look over her shoulder in the guise of checking for traffic.

He was utterly without expression. Gone was his "host" face, the jovial and welcoming man who greeted customers at his saloon. But neither was there any sadness nor worry that she could detect, no drawing together of his brows or a pulling frown on his beautifully shaped lips. He was still, utterly controlled, fog and light playing across the planes of his face.

"Is something wrong?" he asked suddenly.

"No."

"Then why are we stopped?"

"Oh. Sorry. Which way?" she asked quickly, though she remembered his directions well enough to know it wasn't time to turn yet.

"Straight on."

"Of course." She chirruped to the horses again, as sorry a mismatched team as she'd ever seen. The right horse was a gray gelding. When she'd brushed him that morning, there were many, long-faded scars under his mangy coat. The animal had obviously suffered horrendous abuse at some point. If only she could—just for a few minutes—have her hands on the person who'd so mistreated the animal.

The other horse was an ancient mare, long past her best years, her coat a dirty dun color. Sway-backed, bow-legged, she perked up her ears and turned surprisingly eager when hitched to the buggy.

Her father wouldn't have even termed the animals

horses; he'd have considered it an insult to put them in the same species as the fine steeds he raised, and would have been embarrassed to have had them hitched to his wagon.

Angie rather liked them. They had personality and the wear of their years, but they also showed just how precarious J.J.'s financial situation was, if these were the best he could afford.

"How long have you had these horses?" she asked, keeping her voice as even as possible, not wanting to give a hint of just how hungry she was for any information about him. It was her inconvenient curiosity again, latching on to a new interest. A completely inappropriate interest, and one most unlikely to be flattered by her attention, but she couldn't resist indulging herself, just a bit.

His gaze remained on the passing buildings. "Six years. Maybe seven. I don't pay much attention."

That long? He'd bought them back in the boom years of San Francisco, when the town was still heady with gold and success. Her brother had written her about it, about the money pouring into the saloons and dance halls and gambling parlors. Certainly he would have been able to afford better then. Perhaps he simply didn't care?

"The gray . . . he was abused, you know. He bears scars."

"Yes. When I saw—" He stopped abruptly. His voice was flat when he continued. "I don't know his background. I bought him from a customer, that's all."

Puzzled, she twisted around to look at him. His gaze, deep blue and unreadable, flicked over her once and returned to his apparent absorption in the passing city.

Subject closed. She sighed and tried another tactic. "How long have you been here? In California, I mean?"

"Forty-nine."

"You were a forty-niner? Somehow I can't picture you as a miner."

"I was."

"Did you strike it rich?" She smiled at him, expecting an answering jibe.

"No."

"Why'd you quit?"

His answer was slow in coming. "Hitting it rich mining depends on luck. I'd much rather depend on myself."

"What was it like? I've heard stories, you know. That it was very wild, big nuggets there for the taking by the man who was big and bold enough to get there first."

"It was cold."

"And then? What did you do next?"

He didn't answer her, merely stared into the gray mists, his golden hair the only note of sunshine in the dismal morning.

She'd been dismissed; that much was perfectly clear. "Giddyap, now." She snapped her whip over the heads of the horses, urging them to pick up their pace to a speed that might possibly be approaching slow.

She felt sorry for badgering him when he clearly didn't want to talk. Probably, he was worried about his friend. But, darn it, she wanted to know about him.

Obviously, it wasn't going to be that simple, just ask him questions and he would answer. She'd have other chances. If she was to teach him to ride, they'd be spending a good deal of time together.

She cursed herself roundly for her slight quiver of anticipation at the thought. If she could investigate him as an example of a species—Sophisticated Western Man—she'd be fine. But she must never, never be drawn into the trap of thinking of him simply as a man.

Thankfully, there were other interesting things to hold her attention. She began to study the passing city. It had been nearly dark when she arrived, and she'd been much too concerned about finding a place to sleep to pay much attention to her first glimpse of this city of dreams.

Yesterday, she hadn't set foot beyond the saloon. There'd been enough to explore and absorb there.

It certainly wasn't a place where she could ever feel at home. The streets were too narrow, the buildings too dark and near. She felt as if they were closing in, trapping her in the cold damp. She needed sunshine and warmth, and the open spaces filled with green and freedom.

Yet she could see the appeal. This was a place where anything could happen, where anyone could reinvent herself anyway she chose, for who would tell her not? A person was all of her own making.

When she began to ask questions about the city, J.J. proved a bit more forthcoming. He translated signs in Spanish and pointed out Delmonico's, a leading restaurant. They passed a large theater, the gaudy sign above the door advertising the current production of *Uncle Tom's Cabin.*

"What's that?" She pointed to a small white building, its sign bearing black, oddly shaped characters.

"It's in Chinese. That's Man-Fai's, the laundry."

"Chinese?" She craned her neck to watch the disappearing sign as they turned the corner. "I've never met any Chinese."

"When the miners first came out, they were unwilling to take time away from the diggings even to wash their shirts. So they sent them to China to be cleaned. When they came back a year later, the ships were filled with people, too, ready to take their chances in the gold fields."

He chuckled, the first bit of lightness she'd heard from him this morning. "It didn't take them long, like me, to learn it was much easier to get your share of the gold by opening a business catering to the miners, instead of mining yourself."

"Oh." She noticed a small group of men in ragged

coats and dirty denims, squatting in a circle next to the plain brick wall of an unidentifiable building. "What are they doing?"

"Gambling."

"Right out on the streets like that?"

"San Francisco is a gambler's town, Angel. We all came to take our shot at the riches. Isn't that what you did, too?"

"Maybe."

"It's really calmed down quite a bit. In Fifty-one, there would have been games everywhere you looked, betting on everything you could think of—when the next ship would come into the harbor, how many sunny days there would be in June, who would get first shot at the new dancer at the saloon. Thousands of dollars at a time."

"Thousands!" How wasteful. If she could have gotten her hands on just a bit of it, what she could have built with it.

"Thousands. It's not as frequent now, but most are still gamblers at heart. And there are a handful of men who had the foresight—or the luck—to get their money out before the crash came. They haven't stopped trying to beat each other, one way or the other."

Thousands. People were willing to gamble away thousands on the turn of a card or the role of the dice. Surely there was someone who was willing to risk a bit on a much surer thing—a hard-working woman who could turn a spot of land and a small stake into the most profitable horse farm on the west coast. She was certain of it.

"Stop, Angel. We're here."

She quickly halted the team. The large, gray, granite front of the bank loomed over her. Three stories high, it was utterly square, its front devoid of any ornamentation, its hard lines unsoftened by the sickly light of the two gas lanterns fixed over the double doors.

The buggy quivered lightly as J.J. stepped out of it. He turned, lifting one hand to help her down. "Come on, then."

She shook her head. "Nope." She didn't want to go in that gloomy place, and she could be of absolutely no help to him whatsoever. She had no hint of how to deal with the humorless men who ran places like this. She'd probably say something that got her tossed out on her ear. "I'll stay here, with the horses."

"As if anyone is going to steal those horses."

"They might."

The corner of his mouth lifted, just a bit. "Little girl, haven't you learned the streets of this town aren't safe for you alone?"

Little girl. It was just enough to get her back up. "Oh, for heaven's sake," she snapped. "It's the middle of the morning, and we're in front of a bank. What could happen?"

The hot blue of his eyes went cold, and she shivered in the damp air.

"If you don't know that, Angel, you're even younger than I thought you were," he said quietly.

It was such a simple thing. She wasn't sure herself why she was so determined not to follow his instructions. She only knew that if she gave in to him so easily now, it would be terribly tempting to do everything he asked, as long as he asked it in that low, intent voice.

She lifted her chin. "I'm staying here."

He stared at her a moment, long enough for her to fiddle with the plain lace trimming the edge of her sleeve.

"Do you have that gun with you?"

"Right here." She patted the bulging bag next to her on the bench. "Not to worry."

"I never worry." He turned and, without a backward glance, went up the broad steps and into the bank.

8

It didn't take Angie long to discover that waiting outside like a proper driver, though certainly the appropriate thing to do in light of her new career, was decidedly boring.

She looked up and down the empty street until she was sure she knew every brick of every building. She clambered down to further her acquaintance with the horses, checking them over carefully. If they'd been mistreated before, they were the picture of health now.

She paced up and down in front of the bank and made a complete inspection of the buggy.

Sighing, she clambered back up into her perch and stared at the entrance to the bank. It certainly didn't seem to be doing a booming business. No more than half a dozen men had gone in and out of the place during the eternity she'd been waiting.

The mist of the morning had turned into out-and-out rain. She shivered and tugged her cape closer around her neck, grimacing as a trickle of cold water ran down her spine.

What could possibly be taking so long? She hoped they were giving him lots and lots of money. Maybe even enough to stake a bright, ambitious young person in a promising new business.

Someone like her, for instance.

Her foot beat a staccato rhythm on the bottom of the buggy. In front of the bank, in the yellow glow of the gaslights, stones gleamed wetly. Lots of dark round stones, and if she had to sit here much longer, she'd be reduced to counting the blasted things.

The door opened.

Finally.

J.J. strolled down the stairs. He moved with the controlled, casual grace she was learning to associate with him, lean elegance that drew her eye and held it in the most disconcerting way.

There was no hint of how his business had gone. No triumph in his expression, but no defeat. No frustration or satisfaction. She was beginning to learn just how closely he guarded his emotions, how little he gave away to the world. And it only made her all the more curious about what went on beneath that controlled surface.

He stopped in a puddle of light near the side of the buggy and looked up at her. He seemed not to notice the rain. Tiny droplets sparkled in the gold of his hair and sheened the prominent angle of his cheekbones.

"Well? Did you get it?"

She was waiting for him.

It had given him the oddest sort of pleasure to know that, all the time he was talking himself hoarse with that pompous fool of a banker, his new employee was just outside, awaiting his return.

He'd even managed not to check on her safety more than twice, taking a quick peek out one of the narrow front windows. He knew this compulsion to feel responsible for her was simply a reflex. He hadn't had anyone to watch out for since his sister had up and done the fool thing and gotten married. For some strange reason, that protective instinct of his, satisfyingly dormant for the past five years, had reared its inconvenient head and settled on this woman.

He had every confidence he would conquer it, however. He'd almost managed to conquer his curiosity. On the entire drive this morning, as she'd shot questions at him and bubbled over with her own curiosity, he hadn't asked one single question back.

It wasn't as if they hadn't occurred to him, which was strange enough in itself. California was a place where people came to leave their pasts behind, and that suited him well enough. He was comfortable taking things at face value. Life was much simpler that way.

When he picked her up on the waterfront, though, he'd felt that unfamiliar—and completely unwelcome—prickle of interest. Where had she come from? What was she doing here? It had soon become obvious that she, like so many here, wanted the past left alone.

That was fine with him. Soon, he wouldn't even wonder anymore.

And he wouldn't feel this idiotic pleasure at seeing her waiting for him.

The bright red fabric draped around her in rich loops. She looked warm and vibrant, utterly out of place in the cold gray street, and he almost felt as if he could warm his hands on her.

He ignored her question. It was none of her business. He wasn't ready to talk about it—to even think about it—yet, and she'd get her pay either way.

He smiled at her instead. It was a smile he often used consciously, aware of the effect that it had on women, satisfied that he could bring that sparkle into their eyes. It cost him so little, and pleased them so much.

Their reactions had ceased to move him long ago. But he was strangely gratified with the flare of warmth that lit her eyes in response.

"So, Little Red Riding Hood," he said slowly. "Are you going to show me the way to your house?"

He knew she was unused to flirting, but he did it anyway, expecting her to fluster and stammer. Instead she stared at him a moment, then leaned forward, closing a bit of the distance between them.

"That depends. Are you the big bad wolf?" Her voice was low, husky, the smoky hint of the South more pronounced than usual.

He felt his smile widen with genuine amusement. "Of course."

She paused to consider.

"Well, in that case," her dimples flashed, "hop in."

Rose leaned over the balcony railing that stretched along the upper floor of the Naked Rose.

It was just past noon, and the place was still mighty quiet. They had a few daytime drinkers, men who worked nights and came in for lunch, not wanting to eat alone.

The girls were still in their rooms, sleeping off the night before, resting up for the evening to come. No one had ever said being a working girl wasn't work.

Both David and J.J. had hied themselves off first thing in the morning, long before she'd rolled out of bed.

She sighed and trailed her fingers over the smooth finish of the bannister. The satiny texture felt almost warm beneath her fingertips, as rich and lush as the rest of the place.

Even after all these years—nearly eight—she still didn't feel as if she belonged here. There was a part of her that still felt she deserved to be back in the seedy bar on the waterfront where J.J. had found her.

It didn't even make any difference that he'd made her a full partner, as he had David. This was J.J.'s place, and they both knew it. He simply let them come along for the ride.

She was grateful, still completely stunned that he'd welcomed her into his place and his life, clean and warm and shiny. Maybe, if she stayed here long enough, it would even fill up that cold, dead place that still yawned inside her.

Old one-armed Josiah was tending bar. He didn't need her help. There weren't that many customers. She didn't have anything else to do right now, however. The books were balanced—she never let them fall behind, so it never took much time to keep them up to scratch— and J.J. was gone. And there didn't seem much point in making plans when she didn't know what, exactly, was going to happen when David left.

There was one thing she was pretty darn sure of, though.

This nice, comfortable, shiny life she'd made for herself was never going to be the same again.

Most of her was scared to death, afraid she was going to fall back into that icy, dark place where she'd been so long.

But there was a small, shivery part of her that thought that, maybe, just maybe, it was long past time for a little shaking up.

Not the kind of shaking up, though, that had just walked into her saloon.

It was that stranger again. Dark arrogance in the golden warmth of the bar, he paused just inside, taking in the place from beneath the shadowed brim of his battered hat. It was an instinctive gesture, the habit of a man who was used to watching his back.

She gave one quick reasonable thought to bolting to her room, back to the safety of that pink-and-white refuge where she often hid. Then she found herself walking slowly down the steps, as drawn to him as she'd been to California, terrified of the danger, but hopelessly intrigued by the unknown.

His gaze landed on her before she reached the bottom of the steps, and she resisted the urge to fidget with her skirt and hair. She knew she looked good. She always looked good. She was Rose.

The polished oak breadth of the floor had never, ever seemed so wide.

"Hello again."

His face was unsmiling, the strange, unsettling eyes steady. "Hello, ma'am."

She waved her hand in a careless gesture. "Call me Rose, please. Everyone does," she said with the practiced smile of a professional hostess.

"Rose, then." They walked to the bar together, side by side, his long steps slow and easy. He put his hat down on the top of the bar.

He nodded at Josiah, who slid a tumbler of whiskey in front of him. Good, Rose thought in satisfaction. The bartender had remembered what he drank without asking. It was one of the things drilled into everyone who worked at the Naked Rose: Always remember what the customer likes. Always.

"Back so soon?" Her crinolines rustled when she leaned against the bar. "You must like it here."

His gaze didn't waver from her face for an instant. "Perhaps I do."

She looked down at the glossy surface of the bar. She couldn't remember the last time someone had made her feel so jittery, so young and unsure. She hadn't been young in so very long.

She signaled to Josiah to bring her a drink, ignoring the man at her right while she studied the far more familiar—and more comfortable—face of her cook and sometimes bartender. Josiah's dark, deeply lined skin was in stark contrast to his white hair. She didn't know where he came from. She didn't know how he'd lost his arm. No one had ever asked him.

"So," the man said suddenly, his voice low, "are you goin' to tell me about it?"

Her gaze snapped back to his face. He'd taken off his hat, and the soft afternoon light did nothing to blur the hard edges of his angular features.

"About what?"

"About whatever put those little wrinkles into your forehead."

Her hand flew to check. He was right, damn it. She forced herself to relax the strained muscles of her face, and the furrows smoothed out. There. That was better. Wouldn't do to look like she was worried. People came to the Rose to escape their worries.

"It's none of your business," she said crisply.

"Which is probably why ya should tell me."

"Excuse me?"

"Easier to talk to a stranger. Sometimes."

He was certainly a stranger, the like of which she'd never seen before and was in no hurry ever to see again.

"Though I ain't much of a talker, I'm a pretty good listener," he promised.

He might have something there. In her line of work, she'd seen how much easier it was to talk to strangers. People did it to her all the time. Easier than telling your troubles to someone whose opinion you cared deeply about, someone who looked to you to be strong or perfect or whatever. She'd been on the receiving end many a time. Maybe she could try it out herself.

She took a quick swallow of the whiskey, ignoring the burn as it slid down her throat. She rarely did more than sip her drinks now, for she remembered far too well times when she used to gulp them down. But it seemed an appropriate image for the proprietress of the Naked Rose to drink good whiskey, so she'd learned to sip it in moderation. Right now, however, she welcomed the warming glow in her belly.

"One of my partners must leave," she blurted out. It felt odd. She wasn't in the habit of talking about herself at all. She was good at her job because she was so good at talking about others.

He slid closer to her, hitching one foot up on the rail. Any other customer and she would have leaned closer to him, flattering him, flirting, making him feel like this saloon was one of the few places where he was appreciated, where his special qualities were noticed and understood. It was a situation she could control.

He was another sort entirely, leaving her unsettled and wondering if she had any control at all. She fussed with her skirts and shifted a bit away, hoping she'd done it smoothly enough so he wouldn't notice.

No such luck. He gave a low chuckle and moved to follow her, making no pretense that he was doing anything else.

She stayed. It wasn't as if he were even that close. His lean body just seemed to take up more space than it should.

"Which partner?" he asked.

"David. He has to go back to his family in Chicago," she said in a rush.

He frowned and hooked a thumb in the waistband of his narrow black pants. "You wanta go with?"

"Go with?" She contemplated the shimmering liquid in her glass. "Why would I want to do that?"

"Ah." His face cleared. "What's the problem, then?"

"He needs the money for his share of the Rose."

He glanced around the luxurious room quickly. "And?"

"And I don't know how we're going to come up with the cash."

He had such clear eyes, she noticed. Eyes that seemed as if they could see right through her. And this talking-about-it stuff wasn't so bad, once you got the hang if it. Maybe it *would* help. "I know it looks rich," she continued. "But we've got everything invested in the place. There's not a whole lot sitting around to buy out a partner."

"So get a loan."

"J.J.'s trying. But you know what the banks are like now. Not exactly free with a buck since the crash."

"Yeah." His eyes narrowed. "I know."

"Yeah." She blew out a breath.

"What about taking on a new partner?"

"We couldn't do that!" she said, plunking her glass back on the bar so abruptly that whiskey sloshed over the side. "This is *our* place."

"I see."

She reached over the bar and grabbed a towel. "That would change everything."

"Probably." He picked up his hat, turning it around and around in his large, bony hands before placing it on his head. "Would that be so bad?"

Would it? Depends what it changed *to,* she supposed. And that was always the trick, wasn't it? She took her time blotting up the whiskey, making sure no dampness would spoil the golden wood.

When she looked up, he was gone.

"Well," she muttered to herself. "He could have said good-bye."

9

Angie wasn't quite sure how she could be living and working in the center of the most popular saloon in San Francisco and still be lonely.

She grabbed a pitchfork and started spreading out a fresh layer of straw in Lancelot's stall. Though it was a cool morning, her light blouse clung to her. The pervasive dampness of the air made sure that none of the sweat she worked up mucking out the stables would evaporate.

She'd been here three days. She was well fed by the Rose's cook, who made meals for all the employees as well as the customers. She was well rested; her bed was almost sinfully comfortable. Her duties were ridiculously light.

And she was restless as hell.

She was used to being busy, darn it. Though he would never let her deal with the customers or the books, her father had let her manage most other aspects of Winchester Meadows. She'd been surrounded by family, enough so she often wished for more solitude.

She hadn't seen J.J. since she brought him back from the bank that morning. He'd announced he was going to drive himself, and took off again, clumsily maneuvering the team out of the yard and into the street. He'd been gone every morning and afternoon since. She took that to mean he hadn't gotten his loan and was off trying to drum up money.

In the evenings, she supposed he, and the rest of the people who lived at the Rose, were downstairs, tending to business. She'd managed to keep to herself, in her room. It was one thing to indulge her curiosity—once. However, spending her free time in the middle of a saloon wasn't in her plans. People got caught up in the light and the entertainment and never got around to getting on with their lives, or so she'd heard. That wasn't happening to her.

About the only person she saw regularly was Tommy, the stableboy. An oddly quiet and self-possessed adolescent, he wasn't likely to provide much companionship. He had his nose stuck in a book every time she saw him, and seemed more than happy to turn over most of the stable work to her and go back to his reading.

The only company she had were the cats who lived in the stables. One gray, one tan, one a spotty blend of both, they were a motley crew, with raggedy fur but plump bellies.

She shoveled one last forkful of straw into the stall and headed for the next one. This was how she spent her time, cleaning stables and riding the horses, who had no one else to give them much exercise. Heck, she might as well have stayed home if this was all she was going to be doing. She had to find a way to start working on her future.

As her frustration built, she started shoveling the straw faster and faster, not quitting until the stall held far more than it needed. Angel would have a soft bed tonight.

Propping herself against the wooden side of the stall, she tugged off her leather work gloves. Most of her hair had escaped its braid and was straggling down around her face, and she considered starting over and binding it up again, though she knew it was in vain. It simply was too fine and straight to stay tucked away.

"Hello."

David entered the stables, leading his own bay gelding. The horse had been worked hard, and he grabbed a cloth and began to rub it down.

"Would you like me to do that?" Angie offered.

He smiled at her and ran the cloth over the horse's back. "You don't need to do that."

She shrugged. "It's my job."

"Not really."

"I wouldn't mind." Surely he had enough to do, to get ready for his return home. Yet she felt it wasn't her place to mention that.

"If you'd really like to help, you could finish putting my saddle away."

She scurried to do the job, finding the saddle already cleaned and ready for storage, the saddle blanket neatly folded. She was finished long before he was done rubbing down his horse.

"Well," she said awkwardly, "I guess I'll leave you alone."

"Please don't." He glanced at her before he bent and lifted his horse's hoof, checking for stones. "I wouldn't mind the company."

"Of course." She fiddled with the tack hanging on hooks along the walls, trying to think of something to talk about. She'd spent much of her life with men, her brother and her father and the men who worked for her family, but this was entirely different. She wished she could think of an appropriate conversation, but all that popped into her head were questions. Questions about how long he'd known J.J., how they'd ended up in California, and how long Rose had been a part of their lives. Questions that had answers that were absolutely no business of hers.

"I'm leaving tomorrow. You know that, don't you?" he said lightly, concentrating on his horse's neck.

"Yes."

"I was wondering if you'd be willing to watch my horse for me. I'm going by stagecoach, as fast as I can, and I won't be able to take him with me."

"Of course." Surely he knew she would do that. She doubted that that was all he wanted to speak with her about, but it was obvious he didn't want her here just for the company.

"I'm sorry about your father," she tried tentatively.

"Thank you." His movements careful and unhurried, he returned the cloth to the storage room and settled his horse in his stall. He leaned casually against the side of the box and studied her. Self-conscious, she rubbed her hands on the plain wool of her skirt.

"What is it?" she asked finally.

His smile was completely unaffected, and he crossed his arms across his chest. "What do you think of J.J.?"

"What?" she sputtered, completely unprepared for the question.

"What is your impression of J.J.?" he repeated calmly.

"Well." Her hands were really sweating now, and she resisted the urge to pluck the damp fabric of her blouse away from her skin. "He's very . . . elegant."

David's green-gold eyes lit with amusement. "He is that."

"He seems nice enough."

"Nice." He chuckled. "I would bet my last dollar that you're the only woman who's ever described him as *nice*."

"Isn't he?" Perhaps she'd jumped into this whole thing rather quickly, she thought, wondering if this was David's subtle way of warning her about something.

"Of course he is." He stopped, studying her carefully. Apparently satisfied, he nodded briskly. "As I said, I am leaving tomorrow."

"Yes."

"J.J. may need someone. I'd like to know you're going to be around for a while, if he needs you."

"Me?" she asked in shock.

"You."

"But why me? Certainly there are plenty of people around here who would help him in every way they could."

"Have you ever noticed the way most of them treat him?"

"Very well, I should think. I haven't been around that much."

"They treat him like the second coming."

"So?"

"Perfection can be very wearing."

"I wouldn't know," she said.

Wisps of fog like curls of smoke crept through the open doors, blotting out the lantern light and blurring David's features. "Oh, yes." He crossed to her, stopping a few feet away. A man that close to her usually served to make her uncomfortable, pointing out her lack of size. Somehow, there was no sense of that from this man.

"Sometimes J.J. needs someone to remember he's only human, after all."

"All they'd have to do was see him sit a horse to know that," she blurted out.

With the tip of one forefinger, he lifted her face to the light.

"Yes," he said, satisfaction lacing his voice. "You'll do."

The saloon was quiet, the last of the customers having left some time ago, and all of his employees long retired to their homes or their beds. The room was spot-less, the cleaning ladies never overlooked a corner, or they wouldn't still be working for J.J.

He was always the last one to leave. This last check was necessary to him, making certain everything was just as it should be for the next day, the next customer.

Aimlessly, he wandered the room, pushing in a chair unpended over a table, wiping a smudge off the smoked glass of a lantern, adjusting the position of one of the deeply tufted circular sofas.

Bracing one arm on a table, he looked around one last time. It was perfect. It was his. He waited for the surge of satisfaction and pride that always accompanied that realization.

He could not lose this place, by God. He could *not*. It had taken too long and too much of him to get it to be like this. It was the only place he belonged, the only place on earth he could make sure things were done right.

"Sugar? Aren't you going up to bed?"

He smiled down at Rose as she leaned softly against his side. She was all feminine curves and sweet smells, as familiar as every inch of the saloon was to him.

"Soon," he promised, his attention returning to the room.

"Everything's going to be all right," she said softly.

"Of course it is."

"It *will*. You'll make sure of it."

"Mmm-hmm," he replied.

She sighed, knowing that was as much as she would get out of him, as close as he'd ever come to confiding in her.

Years ago, he gave her a reason for living. It was still hard for her to believe that she had the right to touch this perfect man, to take him by the hand and lead him up to his room, to sleep beside him all night long. She would do anything for him, would have given up all she had to make his life easier, but she knew he didn't want it, wouldn't take it. She'd tried it, and always been turned down.

She leaned her head against his shoulder.

"Come on," she suggested. "Let's go upstairs."

"All right."

J.J. allowed her to take him by the hand and lead him up the stairs. Staying down here wasn't doing him any good, anyway. He'd been over it in his head again and again, and he couldn't think of any way to get the money as quickly as David needed it.

A hollow coldness settled in his belly. His oldest and best friend hadn't been able to depend on him when he needed him.

It had been a very long time since he failed to take care of his own, to arrange their lives for the best. He still couldn't understand why the bank had refused to give him the loan, even though he'd offered to put the Naked Rose up as collateral.

Rose walked ahead of him, her soft hand in his. He watched her shapely rump as she swayed up the stairs, the soft swish of her shiny pink skirts, and the curly tumble of her white-blond hair down her back. He wondered if he would fail her, too.

That was why he'd kept people at a distance as much as possible. The deeper the emotion, the deeper the sense of failure and loss. With the exception of his sister, there was no one in his life that he could say he loved. Friends were about the best he could manage, and he even kept them to a minimum.

He had hundreds of acquaintances. He had almost none who ever bothered to look even the slightest bit below the surface.

That was how he liked it.

Rose paused in the long, shadowed hallway at the top of the stairs. "Your room or mine?"

"Mine, of course." He never slept in her room. He liked being in his own space.

He ushered her into the room, closing the door softly behind him.

Angie leaned back against her door, cuddling her old robe tightly around her. She'd woken up thirsty and headed downstairs for a glass of water, but when she saw J.J. and Rose making their way up the stairs, she'd shrunk back into the shadows and waited, unwilling to interrupt them.

They'd done nothing but walk down the hall hand in hand, smile at each other, and hold a murmured conversation. She hadn't heard anything, hadn't seen anything untoward, but she felt like she'd intruded. As if she'd been spying.

She pulled on the belt of her robe, tugging it tighter.

David was wrong. There was no way J.J. needed her.

He didn't need her at all.

10

The sun had finally broken through the clouds. Warm, mellow light flooded the room from the high front windows. The Naked Rose was uncharacteristically empty of customers, and most of the staff was taking advantage of the opportunity to grab an undisturbed dinner.

At the long bar, Angie was digging into fried ham, crispy browned potatoes, and biscuits. Her mother made excellent southern-style beaten biscuits, but Josiah went her one better. Slathered with sweet butter and honey, these were good enough to live on.

Angie kept her gaze carefully on her plate. There was no other safe place for it. If she looked to her left, she saw J.J. and Rose. They were only a few feet away, hunched over the books and talking in hushed tones while they picked at their own food.

To her right was no better. The three "upstairs girls" were laughing loudly as they tucked away an amazing amount of food. Angie had met them the second day she was here; Rose had introduced them as casually as if Angie were meeting a new neighbor. Angie had stammered a polite greeting, unable to forget what the women did for a living, but as curious as she was shocked.

Angie darted a quick glance at them out of the corner of her eye. Maria was dusky-skinned, tall and elegantly slender; tiny Mei Ling was quiet and still. Crystal was obviously older than the other two, a fleshy dyed blond.

Crystal threw back her head in raucous laughter. Quickly, Angie returned her attention to her plate. It was no use getting curious about the "girls"; they were not part of her life and weren't going to be if she was smart. There were some things her family wasn't likely to forgive.

She sawed off a bite of ham and tucked it in her mouth, concentrating on chewing. But her ears weren't as easy to close off as her eyes.

"So where we going to come up with money?" Rose asked.

"We're not. We'll just have to send him what I've scraped together so far and the rest as soon as we can."

"You didn't let him down, J.J.," Rose reassured him.

"Yes, I did," J.J. said, his voice flat.

"What time's the stage?"

"I don't know. Soon, I expect. He should be down to say good-bye any minute."

"Uh, J.J.?"

Angie looked up to see Tommy standing awkwardly in front of J.J., shifting back and forth from foot to foot. His faded jeans and cotton shirt hung around his thin frame, and he clutched a folded sheet of paper in one bony fist.

"What is it?" J.J. glanced up from the books.

"Well, sir. It's Mr. Marin, sir."

"David?" J.J.'s attention quickly went to Jimmy. "What about him?"

"He gave me this." Jimmy shoved the paper at J.J. "Told me ta give it ta you after noon."

J.J. slowly reached out and took the paper. "Thank you, Jimmy." He stared at the paper, making no move to open it. "Have you had lunch, son?"

"Uh, yes, sir. Josiah fed me in the kitchen, same as always."

"Good." The paper trembled in J.J.'s hand, the movement so slight Angie wondered if she'd imagined it.

"Can I go now, sir?"

"Huh? Oh, of course. Go right ahead."

Jimmy tumbled out of the room, clearly anxious to be gone.

"J.J.?" Rose's gently curved brows drew together in concern. "Do you want me to open it?"

"No." He unfolded the paper in precise, unhurried motions, then scanned it quickly.

"What does it say?"

"He left this morning."

"Oh, J.J."

"Didn't want to say good-bye. Says he's no good at that kind of stuff." The paper made a crinkly sound and his fingers tightened on it. "And he says we have a new partner."

"A new partner!" Rose burst out.

"Yes." J.J. tossed the paper on the bar. He was quiet for a moment, then gave a brisk nod. "A new partner."

"How could he do that to us?" she wailed.

"He had no choice, Rose. You know that."

How did J.J. manage that? Angie wondered. No hint of anger or worry or sadness. His voice was conversational and friendly. It couldn't matter to him as little as it appeared to. She'd seen the slight tremble to the paper, seen the small narrowing of his eyes.

It was something she'd never learned to do, to hide her feelings for even the briefest period of time. Her emotions rolled out of her, for all the world to see, and the truth was, she rather liked it that way. It made life interesting.

But she had to admit there was something intriguing about a man who kept himself under such tight control. She figured most women would want to test that control, to see if they could shake it up just a bit, to discover what was going on underneath. Because there had to be more than that easygoing charm and lighthearted smile.

Thank heavens she had no intention of testing his control. The role men played in her life would, of necessity, be a very small one. He was her employer. To look for anything more, even a simple friendship, would be more than foolish. It was the kind of thing that got women in trouble all the time, that kept women all over the world from realizing their dreams and fully utilizing their talent.

It was fortunate she was far too determined to allow that to happen.

"A new partner." Rose shook her head in disbelief. "Does he say who it is?

"Nope."

Angie caught a whisper of black out of the corner of her eye. The man was tall and lean and moved so soundlessly she hadn't heard him come up. Neither, apparently, had anyone else, for J.J. and Rose were still huddled over the note.

"I'm your new partner," the man said evenly.

"You!" Rose's eyes widened. "Not you!"

"Yes." The man planted himself in front of J.J. and Rose, his legs spread wide on the polished floor, and his gaze locked with Rose's.

J.J. got to his feet and put himself between the man and Rose, standing comfortable and elegant in his white suit. He looked relaxed, almost at ease, but no one with any sense would believe it, for there was strength in the breadth of his shoulders and danger in the set of his jaw. "I'm J.J."

"Stitch."

J.J. crossed his arms before him. The two faced each other, a lean, graceful figure in white and a thinner, taller one in black: the old warrior and the young lord.

Except this time, it was the young one whose territory was being staked out.

"Do you have anything to prove your claim?" J.J. asked.

"Papers. Signed by David and me this mornin'."

"How did he find a buyer so quickly?"

"I found him."

"You low-down, snaky, sonovabitch!" Rose screeched, looking as if she were ready to launch herself at Stitch's head. "You used me!"

"No." Stitch hooked his thumb in the waistband of his pants. "I saw an opportunity. I made an offer. It was accepted. That's all."

Hot, red color flushed Rose's cheeks. "You rotten—"

"That was business." Stitch looked intently at Rose. "It had nothing to do with anything else."

"Why, you—"

"Hush." J.J. pulled Rose against his side, placing a calming hand on her shoulder. "Stitch . . . Stitch what?"

"Just Stitch."

"Stitch, then. I'd like to buy you out."

"Sure," Stitch said. "I'd be willin' to sell for four thousand dollars."

"Four thousand dollars," J.J. said flatly. "That's absurd. Your share is barely half that."

"That's my price."

J.J. smoothed the satin over Rose's shoulder, his fingers long and bronze against the shiny cloth. "It appears we're partners, then. What are your plans?" he asked in an almost casual tone. "I would suggest you leave the running of the place to us. We know how to do it. I'll send your share of the profits to wherever you request."

"You'll know my plans when I'm ready to tell you."

Stitch squinted at the sparkling chandelier high over-head. "But you can count on my bein' around. I kinda like it here."

"Fine." J.J.'s voice remained even, but a cold glitter crept into the warm blue of his eyes.

The color drained out of Rose's face, leaving her skin white against the deep rose-pink of her bodice. "He can't stay," she protested. "I can't have him here."

"It appears we must," J.J. said.

"He can't," she whispered.

"We'll have to put up with him. At least until I can buy him out." J.J.'s brows lowered. "There's one thing you should remember, Stitch. I will tolerate your pres-ence, but the Naked Rose is mine."

Stitch shrugged casually, but his gaze focused sharply on Rose. "We'll have to wait and see, won't we?"

God, he hated mornings.

Too bad he didn't seem to be able to sleep through them like everyone else.

The main room was empty. He glanced out the large front windows; it was a typically gray morning. No cheery sunshine warmed the large room. Its usual warmth and sparkle seemed dimmed, vaguely depressed, and he felt the heavy weight of failure.

J.J. wandered through the room, his boot heels echoing against the shiny wood floor. He wedged a chair more tightly against the side of a table, then rubbed a smudge off its surface with his shirtsleeve.

He was rarely up quite this early in the morning; he liked the night, dark and secret and seductive. But after spending far too many hours staring up into the shadows of the ceiling, he—as he had every morning this week—had given up and slipped away.

The place wasn't meant for emptiness. He liked it when the Rose was stuffed to the gills with customers.

Among the hubbub of people and music, there was little room for empty space, little allowance for loneliness. No time for a man to dwell on his failures.

Leaning one hip against the bar, he fiddled with the nugget ring that was his only souvenir of his stint in the gold fields. He'd failed David, been unable to get him the money he'd promised. And, somehow, he'd failed Rose, too. The thin, hollow thread of her voice last night when she'd said that Stitch couldn't stay had told him that much. He'd never heard that tone before.

Failure was rare in his life. It wasn't something he dealt with well. But, Jesus, when he did fail, it always seemed to be on a grand scale.

The twisted smoothness of the gold ring was warm under his thumb. He'd nearly failed in the gold fields; the cold, draining, miserable year was one he never wanted to repeat. But, in the end, he and David had taken out enough gold to set them up in here, and they'd never looked back.

He no longer accepted that there were things he couldn't win, situations that he couldn't turn to his own advantage. He may have believed it as a child, but he was grown far beyond that now. He'd find a way to make this right, too.

But not this morning. He was no longer an impetuous young man. He'd learned to control his impulses nearly as well as he had his emotions. So he would wait, to observe and plan, and when he made his move it would have a reasonable chance of success.

Still, there was one failure he could begin working on this morning, one he'd neglected far too long. Perhaps working with his body was just what he needed to give his mind a rest.

He tapped a staccato beat on the bar and headed for the stables.

Long before he reached them, he could hear her singing a bright, sprightly version of "Jim Crack Corn" in that husky voice that was so at odds with Angie's ordinary appearance. She must be the only person at the Naked Rose who really liked mornings.

She had on a plain white blouse with the sleeves rolled to her elbows and one of the split skirts that seemed to be the only things she wore; this one a faded blue.

She was sweeping out the center aisle of the stables. Only she was dancing with the broom, spinning around with the heavy silk of her dark hair flying behind her. Her voice lowered a few notes, and she changed to "Buffalo Gals." The broom made one big sweep, chaff and dust flying in the air as she did a quick two-step.

She wasn't conventionally graceful. Her movements were quick, glimmering with energy, and he wondered if there was a man alive who could watch her dance and not dream of capturing just a bit of that life for his very own.

"I'm glad to see you're enjoying the morning so much," he said.

The broom clattered to the floor as she whirled to face him, her mouth popping open in a startled O. Then she grinned, and he realized that he'd been entirely wrong about her looks being ordinary.

"Yes," she said. "The morning has such possibilities."

She didn't need beauty. She had radiance, and that was far better.

Which meant he was going to have to keep a very, very close eye on his customers. Freshness like hers was too rare, and he knew only too well how quickly it could dim.

"How old are you?" he asked abruptly.

Faint puzzlement crinkled her brow. "Twenty-three."

Older than he'd thought. She'd managed to retain so much exuberance. When he was her age, he'd been old, well on his way to submerging all those dangerous emotions. He knew her spontaneity was just asking for trouble; only those who learned to depend on things much more stable than feelings made it through life without being battered. But he couldn't bring himself to chip away at her intensity, to teach her that it was better to be controlled and logical.

He would simply have to watch over her for a while, he thought. Until he could make her understand that she needed to protect herself better.

"And you?" she asked, brushing the length of her dark hair back over her shoulder.

"Nearly thirty."

"As old as all that!" she said, a teasing lilt in her voice.

"Yes." Unwillingly, he felt himself drawn into a smile. "Too old to teach to ride, perhaps?"

"Of course not," she scoffed. "I can teach anyone to ride." She snapped her fingers. "Like that."

He mimicked her gesture. "Just like that, huh?"

She laughed and looked him up and down. "Well, maybe not just like that."

11

"*Well, we'd better get started* then, hadn't we?"

"Now?" she said, and J.J. wondered why she looked so delighted by the idea.

"Might as well," he said casually, slipping his hands into his pants pockets.

She eyed him critically. "You're going to get those clothes dirty, you know."

He looked down at his crisp white cotton shirt, white pants, and narrow black string tie. Hell, he'd taken off his coat. This was about as casual as he got. "This will have to do."

"Okay, but you should think about getting some plainer clothes. Ones you won't mind dirtying up."

"I'll see what I can come up with next time."

"Good." She picked up the broom, leaned it against the roughly finished wooden wall, and indicated a spot next to it. "You just stay here out of the way until I'm ready for you."

He choked back a laugh and nobly refrained from making a reply that had absolutely nothing to do with horses. He obligingly took up his post.

So far, so good.

He watched as she tugged open the door to the tack room. Soon she emerged with a bunch of leather straps looped around her neck, lugging a large saddle that looked as if it must weigh near as much as she did.

"Can I help you with that?"

"This is my job, remember?" she said sternly. "You just stay right there."

"Draped in leather and giving orders," he muttered. "What more could a man want?"

"Did you say something?"

"Not a thing."

She paused in the center aisle, looking suspiciously back at him over her shoulder. He innocently raised his eyebrows.

Apparently giving up, she toted the saddle over to a long timber propped between two stands. "You should get all your tack ready before you go for your horse. That way he doesn't have to stand around waiting."

"Wouldn't do to keep him waiting."

"No, of course not."

He was beginning to enjoy himself. Really, this wasn't so bad. Apparently, he'd just never had the proper instructor before.

She hefted the saddle over the board in one big heave. For such a small thing, she was amazingly strong. She handled the big saddle matter-of-factly. He felt a bit ungentlemanly propped up against the wall like an unwanted tool, but she managed it all so well.

"Now," she said once she had all the tack arranged to her satisfaction, "you can go get your horse."

She headed for the box stall that held the old gelding.

"Oh, no," J.J. protested. "I'm not riding that old thing."

She planted both fists on her hips. "Yes, you are."

"You were hired to teach me to ride Angel."

"I've seen you ride, J.J." She waggled one finger like

a disapproving schoolmarm. "We're going to have to start from scratch."

"You said Angel was well trained." He tried to glower down at her, but he doubted he pulled it off. She certainly didn't back off one inch. He wondered if she had any idea how cute she was, her dark eyes snapping while she tried to draw herself up to a height that might possibly approach his breastbone.

"He is, but—"

"So prove it."

She shook her head at him. There was a dark smudge on the soft curve of her left cheek and straggly strands of hair settled around her neck.

Yep. Cute.

"It really would be better to start slowly," she said severely.

"Aw, come on." He waved a hand in the direction of the ancient gray, who blinked and went back to chomping on his hay. "Leave me a little pride. If I'm going to fall off something, at least let it be a horse that can walk faster than I can."

"Oh, all right," she relented. "But we'd better make one thing clear right now. I'm the expert here, and I'm in charge. I expect you to follow my instructions without arguing about it."

"Yes, ma'am." He gave her a crisp salute.

"Now, then." She dragged out an old three-legged stool, plopped her rear down in it, and looked at him expectantly. "Saddle your horse."

"What?"

"Saddle your horse."

"I don't saddle my own horse. I pay people to do things like that."

"No arguments, remember?" she said archly.

"And I used to think a demanding woman would be fun," he muttered under his breath.

"What did you say?"

He scowled at her. "You don't want to know."

"Ah." She didn't appear the slightest bit concerned. "Go fetch your horse, then."

Conscious of her gaze upon him, J.J. cautiously approached his horse. The animal hadn't shrunk any since the last time he tried this, but this time, at least he knew that she was there to step in if he needed her. She wouldn't let him get trampled. He did pay her salary.

Angel was surprisingly docile as J.J. led him out of the stall. The horse shook his head only once before J.J. was able to place the bit in his mouth and slip the bridle over his head.

"Hey! It worked."

"Of course it did."

He glanced over at her, still perched on her chair, her knees tucked primly together and her back straight.

"What did you do to him?" J.J. asked accusingly.

"Not a thing."

"Yes, you did," he insisted. "It's never been that easy before."

"I thought you always paid someone to do it."

"Well . . ."

"It was your confidence, J.J. Horses can sense when you're uncertain."

"I'm never uncertain."

"Of course not."

He snorted, but her expression was calm, without a hint of sarcasm. Either she hadn't meant it that way, or she was more adept at verbal bantering than he had expected.

"Okay. The saddle now, right?"

"Oh, no. You should curry him first."

"Curry him? Why?"

"He likes it."

He stared at her. "You're kidding, right?"

"Nope." She smoothed the worn fabric of her skirt over her knees. In cheap, old clothes, her rump planted on a rickety, three-legged stool, she still managed to have the airs of a princess.

"Angel, I don't particularly care what he likes."

The horse nickered softly at the sound of his name. J.J. glared at him. "No, not you. *Her.*"

"You'd better start caring what he likes."

"All I want to do is make him do what I tell him."

"You can't *make* him do anything."

"I sure as hell hope I can."

She pursed her lips and gave him a small, negative shake of her head. "Not a chance. He weighs at least seven times what you do."

"He does what you tell him," J.J. said, exasperated.

"Only because he wants to."

"He's just a *horse.*"

"Shh." She jumped up and dashed over to the horse. She crooned softly to it, gently rubbing his nose, and Angel nudged his muzzle against her shoulder.

Her laugh was low, quiet, and intimate in the warm stable. She rubbed the horse's neck, her small hands gliding in slow sweeps over the dark red coat.

"You have to seduce him into it," she said in a seductive whisper. "Make him want to please you, make him want the same things you do."

She nuzzled the horse, moving closer to the beast without any trace of fear, the slow whiskey murmur of her voice and the even strokes of her hands almost mesmerizing.

"Begin a relationship with him." The shining swath of her loose hair slid over her shoulder, a gleaming length of near-black silk. "If you force him into it, it's no good. He'll always be fighting it. The rhythm will always be off."

She smoothed the length of the horse's mane. "It's much, much better if you move the same, think the same, *feel* the same. It's the difference between a duty and a pleasure."

His throat was dry. When had it gotten so warm in here? He could have sworn it was chilly outside. Must be all these big animals breathing out hot air.

"Fine," he said, his tone clipped. "I'll curry the damn thing." He snatched up the curry brush and used it to point at the stool. "You go back and sit over there."

She looked at him curiously, then darted back over and sat down. Jesus, the woman moved fast. Except when her hands were stroking that damn horse.

He gave the horse a cursory brush. At least Angel wasn't dancing away from him but standing docile and still. "Showing off for her, aren't you, fellow?"

"It's good you only have geldings and old mares here, you know."

"Why?"

"Otherwise Angel and Lancelot would be after each other. Showing off for the breeding mares."

"Oh."

"Like all men."

He resisted the urge to ask what would impress her. "There." He tossed the brush away and turned to face her.

Her hands were up, elbows pointing up in the air as she plaited her hair. She had a length of twine clenched between her teeth, and the washed fabric of her blouse pulled tight against her breasts. Small, upturned, aggressive little breasts, clearly outlined by the faded cotton.

He swore softly.

"Hmm?" She lowered her arms, grabbed the twine, and tied the ends of her braid. She looked up at his frowning face and shook her head.

"You're supposed to enjoy it, you know."

"I was?" Did she realize he'd been looking at her? Had she *wanted* him to look at her?

"Yes," she said briskly. "That's the problem men often have. They're too impatient. They don't want to enjoy the process. They just want to get to the riding."

"Really?" he asked in a strangled voice.

"Yes."

"Can I put on the saddle now?"

"No. You need the pick first."

"The pick?"

"You really don't know anything, do you?" She went to a shelf against the far wall, stretching up to fetch something and bring it over to him.

"Here." She slapped it into his hand.

He grimaced. "Forget the leather. This one's too much, even for me." The instrument had a wooden handle topped by a gleaming, sharp hook. "What am I supposed to do with this?"

"Clean out his hooves."

"Un-uh," he protested. "Hard telling what might be in there."

"My point exactly, J.J. You have to clean it out before you can ride. There might be stones or something else that could hurt him in there."

"There's probably shit in there."

"Very likely," she agreed.

He tried to stare her down. There had to be *some* advantages to being the boss. She merely lifted her chin and looked at him expectantly.

"Oh, all right." He gripped the pick like a dagger. "How do I do this again?"

"Lift his hoof and brace it against your leg, then use the pick to dig out any debris in his hooves."

J.J. gave a deep sigh. He was beginning to doubt whether this was worth it. But giving up had never been part of his nature. Every other man west of the Mississippi was a competent horseman. His pride demanded that he become not only competent but exceptional. He *would* do it.

Somehow.

"Run your hands down his leg," Angel instructed. "He should lift his hoof for you almost automatically."

"I can do that." Then he looked down at the huge hoofs and wondered. He set his jaw and bent.

Somewhat to his surprise, it worked exactly as she'd said. He began to dig out the dirt, straw, and other stuff wedged in there, grimacing at the ripe aroma. Though his brother-in-law insisted that horse shit smelled better than any other kind, J.J. didn't figure that was much of a recommendation.

Three hooves later, he gratefully dropped the animal's leg and stepped away. This horse stuff was hard work. Fragrant black smears decorated his white pants, and his light shirt clung uncomfortably to his back.

He looked up to find Angie standing still, swaying, her hands clenched at her sides. Her delicious brown eyes had that glazed, unfocused look he'd seen once before. Probably admiring the damn horse again.

"Angel?"

"Hmm?"

"Can I do it now?"

"What?" She shook her head. Strands of hair, already coming loose from her braid, flew into her eyes and she shoved them away. "No, of course not. You have to put the saddle on."

His shoulders sagged. "Oh, come on. Can't I pay someone to do that? Please? I'm good at that."

"Not anymore you're not, remember? You don't have enough money."

"Yeah." He frowned, wondering why it didn't bother him as much as it had a half hour ago. "I have enough to pay you, though," he said hopefully. "And I'd be eternally grateful. I have some really interesting ways of showing my gratitude."

"No." Her mouth pinched in a good imitation of a maiden schoolteacher. One that every boy in school old enough to sweat would have fantasies about. "How are you going to know the saddle's on properly if you don't do it yourself?"

"I hire competent people?" he said hopefully.

"It's important to have the saddle on correctly. You know what happens if it's too loose?"

"I slide around too much?"

"You slide *off.*"

"Shoot, that happens all the time anyway."

Resigned, he went to fetch the saddle. It was heavier than he remembered, and he was surprised she'd been able to lift it.

"J.J.?"

"What now?"

"You have to put the saddle blanket on first."

12

"*Do you think it's getting kind* of stuffy in here?" Angie asked. She tugged at the scratchy neck of her blouse, wishing she'd put on something a bit looser this morning.

J.J.'s rear was pointed directly at her. His upper half had disappeared somewhere underneath Angel's belly. He was supposed to be tightening the cinch that held on the saddle, but she was absolutely certain he'd maneuvered it so she had an unobstructed view of his nicely rounded backside.

She was quite positive he didn't mean anything by it, the rat. It was probably just a reflex. There was a female there, so, like any good male of the species, he started showing off his assets to best advantage.

It had started when he half knelt to clean out Angel's hooves. The motion had tightened the legs of his pants over his thighs.

He always looked so lithe and elegant in his loosely draped suits. Never had she suspected what was underneath.

Her father had praised her for her unerring eye in selecting stallions for breeding. She had a keen eye for muscle definition.

And, Lord, did J.J. have it.

Her breath had begun to catch in her chest.

He'd rolled up his sleeves, exposing strong brown forearms and sinewy wrists, and her heart thudded. He'd hefted the saddle, his shirt strained across his back, and the air grew thin.

"There. Done." He straightened and beamed at her. His clothes were rumpled and stained, disarranged golden waves tumbled over his forehead, and she had never, ever suspected the effect that seeing him sweaty and mussed would have on her.

"Holy horse apples," she muttered. It would do her well to find herself an investor and get out of here as quickly as possible. She suddenly knew why women gave up lifelong dreams to follow men down the path of stupid distruction.

When one was in the grip of lust, the brain did not function properly.

"What's wrong? I did it right, I'm sure. You can check it." He tugged on the strap that ran along Angel's muscular side.

"That won't be necessary. I'm sure you did just fine."

"What's next?"

"Getting out of here." Yes, it was becoming absolutely necessary to get out of here.

"Good."

Turning her back on him, she headed out of the stable. He could follow. It would be better if she didn't have to see him.

"Maybe we'll even get you up to a walk today," she suggested.

"A walk!" He'd caught up with her just before she made it to the door. At her suggestion, he stopped cold and planted his feet. His arm was sticking straight out from his side, his fist gripped around the very end of the leading reins, so the horse was trailing along behind him at as large a distance as possible. "We have to do better than that."

She chanced a glance at him. "Slow has its advantages."

Looking at him had been a bad idea. Mussed-up perfection had a decided appeal. It made him look far too approachable.

He grinned. "I'm very good at slow."

She didn't answer, just stepped out into the yard.

Gray descended. Fog blurred the outlines of the Rose, not more than thirty yards away. The packed earth between the buildings was dark, wet, and muddy. The few trees and bushes drooped, their limp leaves a sickly gray-green. The air hung heavy with the scents of the sea and damp vegetation.

Angie looked up. The sun was a faint and utterly useless yellow ball.

At least she would cool off quickly.

"How can you stand it?" she asked.

"What?"

"The weather. It's so gloomy all the time. Don't you miss the sun?"

"Oh." He glanced around with a faintly surprised expression on his face. "Never thought about it much, I guess."

"And it doesn't bother you at all? Don't you ever want to go someplace where it's warm and fresh?"

"Nope." Angel stamped impatiently, jingling his bridle, and J.J. took a few cautious steps farther away. "This is where my place is, and that's the only thing that really matters to me. The rest is just trimming, anyway."

"Hmm." She wondered if the rest of California was like this. She hadn't paid all that much attention when she came through on the way here—she'd been too busy worrying about running out of money—but now that she thought about it, she was certain the land had been much more to her liking. When she found someone to back her venture, she would have to make sure to find a place where she could ride and breathe, where the air was light and the sun was strong enough to make you feel like dancing just because it was shining that day.

"Time to get you up on the horse."

"Well, ah . . . " J.J. cleared his throat. "Angel, you don't suppose you could lend me your wings so I could just fly right up there? I'm really not so good at mounting. At least, not on a horse."

"Come now. Have to do things more than once to find out if you like them."

"Speaking of which, I haven't seen you downstairs since the first night."

"Trying to change the subject?"

His smile was unrepentant. "Maybe. But I'm curious, anyway. You know you're welcome. I won't even put you to work."

"How generous." It had been more than a little boring, hiding out in her room every night. She wasn't used to spending that much time boxed up. She liked to keep moving. But she knew she no more belonged in that place than she did on the bottom of the ocean.

"Afraid we'll corrupt you?"

"Well, I . . . " He wouldn't understand. Certainly he could handle himself in any situation, with any person, and be at ease.

"Only if you want to be. I promise."

"I'm really not all that good with people," she blurted out. "Things just seem to pop out of my mouth. I communicate much better with animals."

"You do fine with me."

"As I said . . . " He understood her intimation, and his quick amusement warmed her. "With you, I didn't really have any time to think about it."

"True. Still, it looks like you're going to be here at least a little while. Might as well get to know us a bit."

Precisely what she was afraid of. "Perhaps."

"Good." He seemed to assume that her "perhaps" meant "yes." To her chagrin, he was very likely right.

"Enough stalling," she said sternly. "Let's get you up on that horse."

Rose frowned at the books. Something just wasn't right.

She quickly added up the long column of figures, flipped a page, and compared it to another.

There it was. Somehow the thirty-eight cents extra that they'd paid to the gas company had gotten entered under receipts.

She dipped her pen in ink, drew a steady line through the entry, and corrected the figures. Perfect. Every last cent accounted for.

Her back was stiff from the hours hunched over the ledgers, and she arched in an attempt to stretch it out. She blinked at the burn in her eyes from staring at the tiny black numbers that marched in precise rows up and down the page.

At least she had good light. The afternoon sun streamed through the front windows, cutting a wide slash of gold across the floor.

J.J. had often offered to find an office for her where she could sit when she did the accounts. But she liked being out here where she could keep an eye on things and be readily available when needed. It wasn't as if she'd be distracted. When all those lovely dollars were tallying in her brain, she didn't notice what went on around her in any case.

And the proof of that was trudging up the stairs right now.

She was vaguely surprised to see Stitch in the daylight. He seemed so much a creature of the night, cloaked in black and mystery.

She was even more surprised to see a bulging black bag slung over his shoulder.

Rose tossed the pen on the table, swearing when it splattered dark black dots of ink across the surface. "Damn!" No time to clean it up now. She had to keep Stitch from getting up those stairs and into her private domain.

She rushed over to stop him, holding up her skirts in both hands as she raced up the stairs.

"Just where do you think you're going?" she demanded.

He flicked her a glance but kept on, his boots barely whispering on the steps. "Upstairs."

"What for?"

"Movin' in."

"Don't be ridiculous." She edged past him, planted herself two steps above and threw her arms out to the sides.

He paused with his foot on the step below her. His gaze rested, just for a minute, on the impressive display of cleavage highlighted by her stance. "I'm not."

"You can't move in."

"David lived here. Bought his share of the place."

"Yes, but he was a friend."

"So who said I won't be a friend?"

Her mouth fell open. "You?"

He brushed by her easily. "Yep. Besides, you live here. Johnston lives here. Seems to me the owners always live here. That includes me."

He'd reached the landing now, and she trotted along beside him. "You really wouldn't want to. It's noisy. A man your age needs his sleep."

The corner of his mouth twitched. "Gotta keep an eye on my investment."

"I'll make sure you get your share. Honest I will."

"How about this one?" He shoved open the second door to the left. Rose caught a quick glimpse of naked, writhing flesh. Maria was entertaining her regular Saturday-afternoon client.

"Guess not." He tugged the door shut. "Business seems good."

Undeterred, he tried the next one. Mei Ling was curled up on the bed, sleeping peacefully, her dark hair spilling over the pillow. Stitch closed the door quietly.

"Would you just stop?" She grabbed his arm and pulled him to a stop. "The girls need their rest. It's the busiest night of the week."

"Okay. You pick one."

"What do you want?" she asked, knowing her agitation was creeping into her voice but unable to stop it. Though she couldn't explain, she just knew that she couldn't have him here. All the time. Every day.

He didn't even pretend to misunderstand her question. "I'm retired. Missed workin'. Thought this would be a good place to spend the rest of my days."

"That's it?" There didn't seem to be a trace of duplicity in his clear eyes. It couldn't be that simple. Nothing about this man was simple; every instinct she'd honed in all those years down on the waterfront told her that.

"That's it," he said flatly.

"I won't let you take this away from me," she said fiercely.

For the longest time she thought he wasn't going to answer. He just stood there, the bag still slung over his shoulder, one bony hip thrust out. Then he lifted his hand, gently fingering the tendril of hair she'd carefully curled against her cheek that morning. She meant to snatch away, she really did. But the soft whisper of his knuckle against her cheek seemed more like an apology than a threat.

"I don't want to take anything from you," he said quietly.

But he could. She knew he could.

He turned away from her, facing back down the long hallway. "Which room?"

She gave in to the inevitable. It was going to have to be up to J.J. to handle Stitch, she decided. Clearly, she couldn't budge the man. She must be losing her touch.

"David's old room, I suppose," she said, resigned. It was empty. And the sitting room and J.J.'s room were between it and her own.

"Which one?"

She pointed two doors down.

He was there in three easy steps. The door creaked a bit when he opened it. She'd have to see that it was oiled. They took good care of the place. Perhaps Stitch would realize that and go on about his business, bothering them only to pick up his profits.

He dropped the bag next to the bed and inspected the room. It wasn't nearly as luxurious as the rest of the Rose. David had never bothered with things like that. But it was clean and comfortable. It would have to do for him.

He checked the place quickly, testing the bed, peering into the washbasin, tugging at the clothes hooks that marched the length of one wall.

"I'll have water brought up, and I'll get the sheets on the bed as soon as pos—"

"What's that?" His finger jerked toward the door on the far wall.

"It leads to the sitting room."

He strode across the room and yanked the door open. She followed him, peering around him. What was he looking at? Surely there was nothing to object to in there. It was the nicest private room in the entire place, for J.J. and David had used it as a combination office and study as well.

"What's that door over yonder?"

The twin of the doorway they were standing in was on the far side of the sitting room. "That's the other door into J.J.'s room. David and he shared the sitting room."

"Shit." He strode back through the rooms, scooped his bag off the bed, and went back into the hall. Rose had to hustle to keep up with him. "Won't do."

"Why not?"

"I like being alone." He took off down the hall, past the door to the sitting room.

"Then lock the door, you idiot!"

"Nope." They were already past the outside door to J.J.'s room. There were only three more doors until the walkway dead-ended. "What about the one down on the end?"

"No, the new stablegirl has that room."

"How about this one?" He entered the second-to-last room, Rose trailing along behind.

The room was little used, and so was almost bare. The single small window was draped in faded checked cotton, the finish on the iron bed was chipped, and the nightstand was battered.

"This'll do." He began dumping the contents of his bag out on the bed.

She stared at the flurry of denims and long cotton underwear. "It most certainly will not!"

"How come? Ain't nobody living here far as I can tell."

"Because my room's right next door!"

"So?" He shrugged, angular shoulders lifting and falling under the black cotton shirt. "I don't snore all that loud."

Two faded blue work shirts were already hanging limply from hooks along the green-painted wall.

"But—" She gave up, turned on her heel, and sailed out of the room.

She couldn't possibly explain that he took up too much space, that his mere presence in the next room would make her own feel crowded.

She couldn't even explain it to herself.

13

It was a real dress, not one of the split ones she used for riding. Plain blue, buttoned up to her chin, but it still felt odd.

Angie leaned forward and inspected herself in the small silvered mirror that hung over the low dresser. She'd ruthlessly scraped her hair back in a low knot, but strands were already falling loose around her face. She licked her fingers and smoothed the hair back.

She was going downstairs. She was tired of being stuck up in her room, and Lord knew she couldn't go down to the stables and get any work done. Too much commotion, what with all the customers coming and going, and no telling who she'd run into in the dark. Better she stay inside.

Except the fluttering low in her belly told her just how dangerous it was for her to go down there, where he was. It reminded her just how necessary it was to find a way out of this place as quickly as possible.

She was a determined woman. She'd spent her

whole life dreaming one dream, and she wasn't about to let it slip away just because some man smiled at her. She'd seen it happen to other people and hadn't suspected she was susceptible herself.

Obviously she was. So she'd put on this dress and made herself look as businesslike as possible for two reasons. First, to remind herself that her relationship with J.J. was strictly business. She knew that it was so on his side, and it was no use letting herself be tempted into dreaming about anything else on hers.

And second, tonight, Angelina Winchester was going to commence to find herself an investor.

Because the only thing that was going to get her started on the future she wanted was money.

She marched through the door and into her future, managing to make it almost all the way down before her confidence began to waver. Color. Angie stood uncertainly at the bottom of the steps as color swirled around her. Nobody seemed even to notice her. Why would they? Raucous music and loud laughter bounced off the high ceiling; the upstairs girls spun just fast enough for their brightly hued skirts to twirl and give a quick glimpse of their legs; black-and-red playing cards spilled across the gold cloth that covered the tables.

Well. She took a sharp intake of breath, narrowed her eyes in determination, and started looking around for the richest man in the place.

"Would you like to dance?"

Shoot. She was just getting started.

J.J. stood in front of her, impeccably attired as usual in white, lamplight gilding his neatly trimmed hair. And she'd thought she was only susceptible to him all messed up.

He held out his hand for her, an odd half smile on his face. The gold in his ring glittered, and the steady beat of the piano thrummed through her head.

He bent down so she could hear him over the noise

that swirled through the place. There was the faintest wash of his warm breath over her ear.

"Come on. How are you supposed to find out if you're immune to corruption if you won't even try?"

It was a long night yet; she could find an investor later. One dance couldn't possibly hurt.

She slipped her palm into his.

He led her out onto the tiny dance floor that was wedged in between the tables and banquettes next to the piano. Three other couples were out dancing already, enough to nearly fill the small floor, but she suddenly wished it was more crowded. She felt conspicuous, conscious of just how out of place she was.

"I really don't dance all that well," she warned him.

"Not to worry," he said, smoothly tugging her into his embrace. "No one who moves as you do could possibly dance poorly."

The warmth that heated her cheeks was nothing compared to the warmth of his hand at the back of her waist, the thin cotton no barrier to the slight pressure of his fingers as he guided her through the motions.

He might be awkward on a horse, but he was complete elegance on the dance floor, his movements a smooth, even glide, flowing seamlessly into one another.

The bright music slowed, and his steps slowed, too. She couldn't bring herself to look up into his face, and his chest didn't seem a much safer sight, so she looked around at the other dancers.

It wasn't much like a dance back home. The couples pressed together, and the women's hips swayed back and forth rhythmically. Maria's partner was shorter than she, and his cheek was resting very comfortably on the satin clad shelf of her bosom.

J.J. leaned down to her. "You dance very well."

"Thank you. So do you." She nodded at the crowd filling the room. "Are you always so busy?"

"Usually."

"They all seem very . . . friendly."

He gave a short bark of laughter. "People don't like being alone. Always looking for the illusion of love."

"You don't sound very impressed by it."

"Keeps me in business." She felt the subtle shift of muscle under his coat as he spun her with the music. "At least here they know it's an illusion. Probably better that way."

Surprised, she looked up at him. His jaw was smooth, clean-shaven, and she felt the most irrational wish to lay her palm against it and see if she could feel the remnant of the stubble he'd scraped off. "What do you mean?"

"Love's an illusion, either way. At least here, they know it, even if they choose to forget it for an hour or two."

"You don't believe in love."

"Nope." His teeth flashed even and perfect when he smiled. "Are you going to give me a lecture on the power of love now?"

She shook her head. "No."

"I knew you were a sensible woman." He deftly guided her around Crystal and her partner, who had planted themselves in one corner of the floor and were swaying back and forth, apparently without any intention of moving an inch.

"I wouldn't mind if you told me a bit more about your theory, though."

"Love's just the excuse people use to let their emotions take control of them. They do utterly stupid and unbelievably foolish things."

"Such as?"

"Well, my sister went and got married to an idiot, for one thing, and he took her off to this dreary little farm up in the middle of nowhere."

"Maybe she likes it there."

"You've got to be kidding." He was shocked enough to almost miss a step.

"I probably would."

"Yeah," he said thoughtfully. "You probably would."

"But not you?" she asked. "You'd never let your emotions run away with you?"

"No." His eyes went soft and blue, his voice pitched low and husky. "Of course, maybe I haven't met the right woman yet."

She scowled at him. "Is this where the corrupting part comes in?"

He threw back his head and laughed. "Not going to work on you, huh?"

"Not a chance," she said, but even as she knew he was playing, a small corner of her acknowledged the seductive pull of his suggestion. "How do you do that, anyway?"

"What?"

"That." She pulled her hand from his grasp and waved at his face. "That thing you did. Looking at a woman like she's the only thing you see."

"Practice, darlin'." He grinned as he spun her through another sweeping turn. "Practice."

Everybody in California was too tall, Angie decided. She stood on her tiptoes and craned her neck, trying to see over the press of bodies that filled the small gambling parlor that opened off the main saloon.

After their dance, J.J. had deposited her next to the bar and gone off without a backward glance. Not that it bothered her. She knew he had duties to attend to.

She'd turned her attention to her search for a backer. She'd had to climb three steps in order to get a good view of the crowd, then selected three likely-looking prospects. Clean-cut, well-dressed, elderly men who looked as if they might have a ready source of funds.

After she'd approached the first one, though, she

decided to add sober to her list of requirements. Her first candidate slipped under the table before she got the second line of her proposition out.

The second man had outright laughed in her face. The nerve of the man. He'd very kindly suggested that if she needed a job, she could go find herself a nice young farmer and commence to breeding. He obviously had no idea that was precisely what she was trying to avoid.

The third man had been the worst of all. He'd been interested in a business relationship all right, though not exactly the one she had in mind.

She was rather proud of herself. She'd actually managed to walk away without dumping something over his shiny bald head.

She must be improving. Back home, when a customer had made some less than flattering remarks about doing business with a woman, she hadn't always been so restrained.

Which probably had something to do with her father's refusal to allow her to take over the Meadows, now that she thought about it.

Then she realized the place to find an investor wasn't in the main room. It was here, in the gambling parlor. Surely the men who came here had deep pockets. Even better, they clearly had no reservations about risking their gold on a long shot that might pay off big.

She thought she could probably give them better odds than the keno table.

No one paid much attention to her as she circled the room, and she didn't think it was because of her plain dress or lack of cleavage. Here, the focus was clearly on money. It was much quieter, only the steady chink of coins being counted interrupted the low murmur of conversation. A haze of smoke and greed hung low over the closely spaced tables.

She elbowed her way through the crowd, disregarding

someone's grunt of pain. If he didn't have the manners to get out of the way of a lady, he deserved it.

The men in front of her gave way, and she bumped against a table. The poker players hunched around it scowled at her, then returned to brooding over their cards.

She gasped. There were immense heaps of coins on the tables, gleaming gold and silver and seductive.

Money hadn't ever been anything she'd thought much about before she left for California. Her family was really all that mattered to her, her family and the land and the horse farm they'd built together.

Even now, money, in and of itself, meant little to her. It was only a means to an end, the tool by which she could prove herself to her father, the way she could take the place in her family she *knew* she was meant to have.

But she couldn't deny that all those piles of metal were more than a little tantalizing. She translated all that money into land, grass, and horses, and wondered if she had a latent, unsuspected talent for gambling.

"It's quite a pile, isn't it?"

She spared a brief glance at the man standing next to her left elbow. She registered pleasant, middle-aged features and bushy, graying mutton chop whiskers before her eyes were drawn back to the piles of metal. "Yes. Yes, it is," she agreed, then sighed. No use fantasizing about it. Whatever she got, she no doubt would earn, not win.

"Of course, there are so many better ways to spend money, if you so chose," he said conversationally.

"True." She wrenched her gaze away from the coins on the table and focused on the man. A round face, ruddy cheeks, and an expensive gray suit. And, stuck in the cloth tied around his neck, the biggest diamond stick pin she'd ever seen.

The glitter was blinding. "Is that real?" she blurted out.

"This?" Chuckling, he flicked his neck cloth. "Yes, yes it is. Quite a sparkler, eh? Though I save the really nice ones for special occasions."

"The . . . the really nice ones?" He'd seemed like a nice, unexceptional man at first glance. She was rapidly readjusting her opinion. "Mr. . . ?"

He rocked back on his heels. "Ezekiel Hermanson." He looked at her expectantly, as if his name should bring some reaction from her.

She grabbed his hand and pumped it enthusiastically. "I'm Angelina, Mr. Hermanson. Pleased to meet you."

"That's good to know." He smiled broadly. "You must be new around here."

"Yes, I am. I've been here under a week." Here was her opportunity, she thought. The man was obviously just looking for a wonderful investment. Now if only she could put it to him the right way.

She tugged at her hand but he seemed unwilling to relinquish it. She gave him a smile and pulled a bit harder.

"I thought so." He patted her hand just before she managed to wrench it from his grasp. For such soft palms, he had a surprisingly strong clasp. "Not exactly the usual type they get in here. Which is good, in my opinion. Fresh. From the country, are you?"

"Well, as a matter of fact—" He clearly had the cash and wasn't prone to rash gambling. If only she could put it to him the right way. "Mr. Hermanson, you seem to be a rather, uh, successful man."

"I have been described that way, yes." His friendly eyes twinkled.

"Sir, I just might have a proposition that you would be interested in."

"Oh, my dear." The crowd closed around them, and he moved closer to her. "I thought you just might."

14

It was a night like any other. J.J. moved among his customers, expertly seeing to all their needs. Liquor, female companionship, a friendly ear or a less-than-friendly game of poker. The Naked Rose had everything a man could desire.

But it wasn't a night quite like any other, after all. For every few minutes, his gaze would fall on her.

He wasn't even entirely sure why he'd been so insistent she come down. He told himself it was merely a way of keeping an employee happy. If she was bored, she'd take herself off, and then he'd never learn how to ride. With everything else in his life teetering on the brink, he was damn well going to get at least that one thing right.

But even as he told himself that, the words were hollow. Because his gaze fell on her more often than necessary for her protection. Even now, as she zigzagged into the side room, he got the same little spark of interest he had every time he'd seen her all evening.

She didn't mingle much. Just wandered around,

taking it all in, her feet tapping with the music, her eyes alight with curiosity and her body fairly buzzing with life.

Damn. He looked in surprise down at his feet, which had taken two steps to follow her into the other room.

He wheeled around and headed for the bar, draping his arm around Mei-Ling and introducing her to a new customer.

He wasn't going to do this.

The last thing he needed in his life was someone else to look after. So why did he have the overwhelming feeling that he had to arrange her life properly? To make sure she was fine and healthy and happy?

Mei-Ling and the customer quickly became absorbed in each other, rendering his presence not only unnecessary but unwelcome. One more thing suitably organized.

He headed for the bar. Surely there was some cleaning up to do. He liked things spotless.

The smudges and rings on the bar soon disappeared beneath his steady scrubbing. He bent over and put a little more elbow grease than necessary into the job.

If only he hadn't danced with her.

It had merely been a gentlemanly gesture. He'd probably danced with every woman who'd ever set foot in the place. They liked it, he liked it. Though there were certainly few women of her sort that ever came here.

When his arms went around her, he'd realized it was the first time he'd touched her since pinning her to the ground on the waterfront. The way she felt was something he remembered far better than he'd realized.

The rag bunched in his fist as he straightened, staring off into the gambling parlor. He couldn't see her there. She was too short.

She hadn't been too short when they danced. He would have thought they wouldn't fit right, but somehow they did.

She wasn't willowy and lissome and all those other things that were supposed to be so desirable in a woman when she danced.

Angie didn't float; she sizzled. Beneath his hands, she wasn't soft and curvy. She was athletic and firm and very, very warm.

For some reason, he found he liked that very much.

Maybe some other man would, too. It was damn sure she didn't know how to handle cowboys like the ones who came in here.

The rag fell to the floor as J.J. took off for the back room.

Behind him, Josiah stared in puzzlement, then bent down and scooped up the cloth. He folded it in a precise rectangle and hung it carefully on the hook where it belonged, just like Mr. Johnston liked it.

Her business proposition wasn't going as well as she would have liked.

Mr. Hermanson had certainly been agreeable enough. Maybe a tad too agreeable.

He'd listened to everything she had to say, nodding all the while. But he hadn't asked many questions, as she'd assumed a prospective investor would. Once or twice, he'd leaned closer than she thought necessary to hear her words.

She couldn't quite believe he meant anything by it. He reminded her of a friendly uncle, the kind who never quite understood what children wanted but tried hard all the same. And if he'd wanted feminine companionship, there were certainly plenty of women of that sort who worked here.

"Now, then," she went on, fingering the pleats of blue cotton at her waist. "I thought I'd start small. I'm sure I could get by with perhaps thirty acres. The land here is rich, I'm told."

"Hmm-hmm." He smoothed the whiskers that

swooped along the length of his round jaw. "It certainly is."

"Good. I've got one stallion, and he's the best there is. I think with perhaps four or five mares—"

An arm thudded around her shoulders with enough force to make her bend a bit. Under any other circumstances, she would have been spinning around and taking aim with her knee.

Despite the fact that she'd felt it around her only twice before, however, this arm was familiar.

This was more than simply a friendly gesture. For one thing, J.J. had never made friendly gestures like this toward her. For another, she could feel how heavy his arm was around her shoulders, and the stiffness of his body as he stood next to her.

His voice was calm as he spoke to her potential investor. "You may leave now."

"J.J.," she whispered to him, "he and I have business together."

"Yes." Hermanson drew himself up to his full height, which was only half a head taller than hers, and smiled. "We do, at that."

"She has no business with you." J.J.'s grip tightened, drawing her closer against his side.

"Perhaps you don't realize who I am, Mr. Johnston. I am—"

"I know who you are, Hermanson. And I don't want you here."

It took Angie a moment to figure out what was different. The room had gone quiet, without the steady shuffling of cards, clink of metal, and hum of voices. Everybody had turned to them, forming a tight circle, their faces turned expectantly toward J.J.

Rose and Stitch had appeared somewhere along the way, and Rose was frowning pointedly at J.J.'s arm wrapped around Angie's shoulders.

She didn't want Rose to get the wrong impression.

Angie tried to slip away, but J.J. merely curled his fingers, pressing gently into the muscle of her upper arm, and held her there.

"Angel," J.J. said without taking his gaze from Hermanson, "you will not talk to this man again. You do not know who—or what—he is."

What he was? She found it hard to believe that this twinkling, soft-spoken man could be anything but what he appeared to be. "But, J.J.—" she protested.

"No." He looked down, giving her a slight shake. "I'll explain later."

Her mouth opened, ready to protest his arrogant assumption that she couldn't decide for herself, until she saw the look in his eyes. Pure blue, not a hint of softening gray, they were almost startlingly intent. The man was serious.

"All right," she agreed.

"Good."

"Well, well." Hermanson looked them both up and down. "If that's the way it is, then. Though I should think the lady would have the right to make up her own mind."

"She already has."

What in the world was going on? She could feel Rose's cold glare, and the hushed expectations of the gathered crowd. Explanations were definitely in order.

Hermanson shrugged. "In that case, I have a business proposition for you as well."

"No."

"You haven't even heard it yet."

"Doesn't matter. I've heard enough about you to make up my mind for me."

"I want to buy the Naked Rose."

J.J.'s laugh was harsh. "You can't be serious."

"Oh, I assure you, I am." The huge diamond on his round chest glittered coldly.

"Why? This place is hardly worth your time."

"Not normally, of course." He smiled genially. "But when I own every other piece of property on the block— well, we have something worth my interest."

Angie winced as J.J.'s fingers dug into her shoulder. She looked up into his still, expressionless face and knew he had forgotten she was there, that he had no clue that he was holding on too tight.

She kept quiet. If he needed to hold on to her, just for this moment, she would let him. She knew what it was like to lose something that was yours, although in her case she'd never had it—not really.

"I don't care if you own the entire goddamn city, Hermanson. The Naked Rose is not for sale."

"Hmm." Ezekiel Hermanson rocked back on his heels and again ran his thumb down the length of the sideburns that hugged his jaw. "We shall see, won't we?"

"No, we won't." J.J. gave a slight bow. "I think perhaps you are ready to leave now."

Hermanson's broad, friendly smile remained unchanged, but a cold glint hardened his eyes. "As you wish."

"Just a minute." Stitch lounged easily against the nearest table. "He ain't the only owner here. I wouldn't mind hearin' what ya got to say."

"Ah." Ezekiel turned to Stitch. "And you are—"

"A businessman, ya might say."

"Well." Hermanson extended a hand. Stitch stared at it pointedly but didn't take it. Hermanson finally shrugged and dropped his hand. "I wouldn't deal with anyone who doesn't have clear ownership."

"I do. A third of the place."

"I hadn't heard that," Hermanson said. "When did this happen?"

"Just yesterday."

Hermanson looked at J.J. "Is this true?"

J.J. nodded curtly. "Yes."

"Interesting." Ezekiel nodded thoughtfully. "This is

my offer. I'm willing to pay four thousand dollars a share to each of you. Or I'll buy the place outright for fifteen thousand. Take your pick."

There was a collective gasp. In the midst of the madness of the gold rush, the saloon might have been worth ten times that. No more. It was a price that no one could hope to match from another buyer.

"It's not for sale," J.J. said again.

"It will be." Ezekiel turned to leave, and people moved aside to let him pass, leaving a wide, empty swath behind him as if no one wanted to get too close.

J.J. grabbed Angie's other shoulder and turned her to face him.

"You won't talk to that man again, do you hear me?" he said softly.

"What do you mean? He seemed so—"

"I know he looks harmless." She'd never seen him so intense. "You don't know what he's capable of. I do. He'd chew you up and spit you out before you realized he took the first bite. Please, Angel, you've got to trust me."

Trust him she did. Without reason or sense, she supposed, for she was accustomed to making up her own mind, not taking a man's word for it. But this was J.J.'s place and J.J.'s town, and she'd done enough foolish things already.

He must have sensed her assent, for his grip on her shoulders loosened, and he rubbed gently, as if in apology for his roughness.

"Who is he?" she asked.

"A land speculator. He made millions in the early fifties, most of it in ways that were less than honest, but that's hardly news around here. The only thing different was he was one of the few who managed to hang on to it." His hands still stroked her upper arms, softly, automatically. "That, and that people who oppose him have a tendency to disappear."

"Disappear?" The word clogged in her throat. Surely he couldn't mean that the way it sounded.

"Sometimes their bodies are found. More often, no one ever knows what happens to them. Except that Ezekiel always seems to get what he wants."

This was such a different world than the one she came from. For the first time, she felt the sharp, cold clench of fear. Perhaps she had been utterly foolish to believe she could do this, that she could prove herself in a place like this and convince her father to give her her rightful place.

She raised her hand and brushed her fingers down the clean line of his jaw. "You will be careful, won't you?" Then, realizing what she was doing, she jerked her hand away and let it drop helplessly to her side.

"Me?" His smile was unexpected and utterly captivating. "I'm always careful."

"Well . . . " Her voice trailed off. There was nothing she could do, nothing she could say. "I think I'll just go up to bed."

"Good idea."

"You have to let go of me."

Surprised, he looked at his hands, then pulled them away and shoved them awkwardly into his pockets. "Sorry."

"It's okay," she whispered, backing away slowly before turning and dashing for the stairs.

The familiar sounds of his saloon were muted and distant; the lights, far too bright. He closed his eyes against them.

He could lose it all.

Ezekiel Hermanson never lost. Never. Once he set his sights on something, he always got it. No matter what stood in his way.

J.J. tried to imagine his life without the Naked Rose. He had no place of his own to go, nothing else he wanted to do. Nothing that wouldn't require him depending on another for a time, and he wouldn't—couldn't—do that.

Pride had sent him to California in the first place. Pride, and a demanding father who had never let him find his own way.

He'd found his place here, where he could make sure everything and everyone were safe, where the beer flowed as freely as the laughter, and no one poked around into dark, soulless corners best left alone.

Tension speared down his back, a sharp pain that stiffened him abruptly.

He would not lose this place.

They'd survived the fires. They'd survived the end of the gold and the swindlers and the vigilance committees.

Somehow, they'd survive Ezekiel Hermanson, damn his jovial face.

"J.J.?"

Rose had come to his side without him realizing it, "Hmm?"

"Have I something to worry about?"

His nails bit painfully into his palms. "Of course not. I'll find a way around this."

"Not that." The curly plume in her elaborate hairstyle bobbed as she shook her head. "I know you will."

Such faith. He hoped to God he was worthy of it.

"I meant her."

"Her?"

"That girl." She nodded in the direction of the stairs. "Have I too much competition?"

"Don't be ridiculous."

"Am I?"

"How long have we been friends, Rose?"

"You know that as well as I do." Light danced off her dangling earbobs as she turned her head.

"And have I ever give you reason to worry? Even once?"

"No."

"Why now, then?"

"You don't usually rush in to defend quite so quickly, either."

He wasn't entirely sure why he had. He'd simply acted, before he thought or felt or considered. For some reason, Angie had that effect on him. "Most of the women around here can take care of themselves." The constant chatter of too many voices was beginning to grate on his nerves. "She doesn't belong here, Rose."

"True. That lil' country gal will never belong here."

"I know that. But I don't want her chewed up by this city, either."

He leaned down and gave her a perfunctory kiss. "I'm going for a walk."

She watched him saunter away, a lean, elegant figure in white among a sea of dingy gray and blue.

"No, you've never given me reason to worry," she said softly. "But you've never once given me a reason to stop, either."

15

Rose found Stitch in the old, neglected garden. Silver moonlight poured over a drooping orange tree and edged the stone walls, lushly covered with tangled, overgrown vines.

She picked her way carefully along the path, stepping over fallen plants. The darkness was close, misty with moisture, and unexpectedly warm. Stitch, tall and thin and dark as a slice of the night, stood in the center of the garden. The moonlight lit his silver hair but left the rest of him cloaked in blackness.

The center clearing was circular, paved with stone, and she stopped beside his still figure. His legs were widespread, hands clasped behind his back, and his face uplifted to the sky.

She stopped beside him. A snarled growth of poppies still bloomed along the edge, and she stooped to pick one of them, jerking the tough stem off. The dark red petals looked almost black in the night.

"Hello, Rose."

He hadn't even glanced at her, merely turned away and spit out his chaw of tobacco. She twirled the bloom between her fingers.

"You didn't have to do that."

"Yep. My ma said I shouldn't never chew around a lady."

"Nice night," she said, knowing it was trite, but unsure how to approach him.

"Yeah." Shadows fell under the stark bones of his face, silhouetting his hollow features.

"How did you know?" she asked softly.

"Huh?"

"Just stop it," she said, anger seeping into her voice. "You knew about Hermanson. You knew he was going to offer for this place. Why else would you want it?"

"Maybe I told you the truth before. Maybe I just wanted a place to retire."

"Stop it!" The stem of the flower bent double between her fingers. "Stop it and look at me!"

He swallowed, then turned to her, his pale eyes now dark and shadowed.

"You knew," she repeated.

"Yeah, I did."

"How?"

"My old partner." He shoved a hand through the length of his hair, pushing it back from his high forehead. "Pudge's wife is a cook at Hermanson's mansion. She heard him talkin' 'bout the hotel he was gonna build here. Be even better than the Ward House or the St. Francis."

"And?" she demanded.

"An' the only piece of property he had left to get was this 'un."

"And you just figured you'd get here first."

"No." His bony shoulders lifted and fell. "I din't know, at first, if there was somethin' here for me. Just came to look around."

"You used me!" The poppy fell from her hands, disappearing against the flat, dark ground when it fell there. "You got me talking and found out about David's leaving, then snuck around and bought the place behind our backs!"

"Shit, Rose." He bent and scooped up the flower. It looked absurdly small in his long-fingered hands. "It was just business. You can understand that, I reckon."

She went still. She'd been used before, but not in a very long time. At least, not without her knowledge, consent, and her doing more than a little using back. "I thought we were friends. Of a sort," she said softly, then cursed herself for saying it. It was the kind of thing weak women said, and she'd stopped being weak right about the time she'd stopped being used.

"I don't see that one has much to do with the other."

But it did. Oh, but it did. "Sell it back to us for what you paid for it."

"Didn't think you had the money for even that, or you woulda bought it from David."

"We just didn't have any time. We'll come up with it eventually."

He shook his head slowly, moonlight glancing off the sharp angles of his cheeks. "You heard my offer."

"Damn it! Why do you need the money so badly?" She knew it was a stupid question. Who didn't need easy money?

He waited so long she was surprised he even answered, knowing he rarely gave away this much of himself. "Got my eye on a piece of land. Good piece of land, raise a few horses, maybe a coupla cows. Need just a few thousand more and I'll be ready."

"Can't you get it someplace else?"

A muscle in his jaw ticked. "I'm tired, Rose." Moonlight glimmered between them, softening her anger, leaving a slow sadness. "I want to retire. I'm done. I just want a place of my own."

She didn't want to know what he was retiring from. It was all too easy to guess that it was something dangerous, illegal, and more than a little lonely. The loneliness she recognized, even as she denied that it was part of her life.

"I can understand that. But this is my place. You'll be taking it away from me."

"Aw, shit, Rose." He held the forgotten poppy loosely in his hands, and the petals quivered. "I don' wanna take nothin' away from you. But maybe it's time for you to leave here, anyway."

"No." Her stomach clenched in fear even at the mention of leaving the Naked Rose. "This is where I belong. It's all I have, Stitch."

"It wouldn't have to be," he murmured.

She nearly asked what he meant, but the words wouldn't form. She didn't want to know this, either. It wasn't something she was ready to deal with.

"We need some time." She felt moisture filling her eyes and willed it away. Crying was a weakness she couldn't afford. "Please. Just the summer. Time to come up with the money to buy you out."

"Let it go, Rose."

"I can't," she said hoarsely.

He lifted his hand and trailed the poppy down her cheek. The petals were as soft as the mist, a whisper of the night. "All right, Rose. I'll give you the summer."

J.J. strode across the muddy yard between the saloon and the stables the next morning, wondering why, even with all else that was going on, he was going to a riding lesson. Certainly he had better ways to spend his day, yet here he was, bright and early, heading for that blasted horse.

He should be thinking of a way out. Yet he'd spent the entire night thinking, turning in his rumpled bed, and it had done little good. His head hurt from lack of sleep, and his thoughts seemed muddled and slow, murky as the morning fog. He figured he might as well get his brain pounded out, for all the good it was doing him.

Of course she was already there. He'd had every expectation she would be, and a tiny, dangerous suspicion that she was the reason he'd headed out here this morning niggled at him. She wasn't important to him, not one little bit. But she was amusing, and her energy seemed to make him a bit more optimistic, more aware of the possibilities. Perhaps she'd jar something loose— if the horse didn't do it first.

Her head was bent over a tangle of straps, her fingers working nimbly and quickly at them. She looked up at his footsteps and smiled, and he knew the reason he'd sought her out, after all, was so she could smile at him just like that. Not with an expectation that he would save the world, but with simple, uncomplicated pleasure.

"Good morning," he said. "Ready to try it again."

"Of course." Holy horse apples, she thought. When she'd told him to get less expensive clothes, she hadn't thought he'd look like this. His billowy shirt was white, open at the throat, draping elegantly on his lean torso. Close to what he always wore, though usually he covered it with a frock coat. Today he tucked it into a pair of denims, so old the blue was faded to nearly white in the creases, and so snug his leg muscles were clearly outlined.

"I see you found some older clothes."

"You approve?" He lifted his hands wide. "The britches were David's. He left them behind. It was all I could find."

"I'm sure it'll do nicely." As long as she didn't look at him too closely.

"So," he said, rocking back on the heels of his scuffed brown boots and shoving his hands in his pockets,

"I suppose you want me to start grooming that horse again, huh?"

"Not right away." Angie jumped up and dug in her pocket. "I think it's probably best if you just get to know him a bit first. You two didn't seem to have much of a rapport yesterday."

"Noticed that, did you?" He strolled over to Angel's stall. "So, fella, how do you suppose I reintroduce myself to a horse?"

"Like this." She followed him, then plopped a lump of brown sugar into his palm. "He's susceptible to bribery."

"Guess he belongs in San Francisco, after all." J.J. stuck out his arm stiffly, cupping the sugar in his hand.

"No. Flat."

"Excuse me?"

"You have to flatten your palm. So he can get to it." She grabbed for his hand. His skin was warm, the pads of his palm firm, as she showed him how to hold the sugar.

"Oh, yes. Now I remember."

She jerked her hand away. "You knew how to do that," she accused him.

"Who, me?" he said innocently. "You think I'd pretend to be so stupid I didn't even know how to feed a horse a lump of sugar just so that you'd hold my hand?"

She knew her cheeks were turning pink, but she couldn't hold back her quick bubble of laughter. "You're hopeless."

"Yes," he said, his voice low and even. "Sometimes I am."

He turned his attention to the horse so quickly she could only wonder what he'd meant. There was no point in asking; the rigid set of his jaw told her that much.

"Come here, Angel. Got something sweet for you."

"I assume you're talking to the horse."

She was rewarded by his low chuckle. "Oh, I don't

know. I imagine I could think up something for you, too."

The soft silk of his shirt captured the light as he bent and it shimmered softly, silver like stolen moonlight, a bit of the night on a man of sunshine. She turned her attention to the horse; safer that way.

A light cluck of her tongue brought the horse over to them. Her practiced gaze swept over the animal, and she felt a quick surge of pride. He'd always been magnificent, but with the extra work she'd been giving the animal since her arrival, he was taking on a depth and tone of muscle that very few animals would ever match.

"Oh, my fine Angel, you are looking very good," she said, noting the even copper sheen of his coat. Beautiful, strong, and sleek. She knew she was just the person to help this horse be what he was meant to be, though she supposed that sounded arrogant. There were few people who had the touch with horses she did; it was as much a part of her as having dark hair.

"Healthy as a horse?"

"Without a doubt."

J.J. hesitated a minute, then stuck his hand out farther, edging his palm toward Angel's mouth. He leaned his upper body away, his movements tentative, and gave an almost undetectable start when the horse lipped the lump of sugar off his hand.

He still had some fear. There was a very long way to go if she was to teach him to be a competent rider—never mind good. She would have to take it very slow, for they couldn't afford to have any disasters or they'd be in worse shape than when they started out.

He pulled back his arm and rested it on the top board that bounded the stall. "Angel. Is this really an exceptional horse?"

"Oh, yes."

"You're a good judge of horseflesh?"

"Very good."

He eyed the horse speculatively. "How much would you say he's worth?"

"I don't know the local market that well, but . . ." She frowned. "Not enough, I don't think. Maybe two thousand at best."

His quick exhalation was the only indication he'd been holding his breath. "That's it, then."

"If there were an established racing community here, maybe—"

"No." His fist tightened around the rough board. "It's very disorganized. A race is put on only when someone takes the notion. Or a couple of fellows fall into a bet, and let others join in."

"I'm sorry," she said, though the words seemed so useless.

Bits of dust floated in the soft morning air, settling down around his shoulders. Even in the dim light, his hair glimmered with gold, and his eyes were like a slice of Kentucky summer sky, warm and richly blue.

"Why is it," he said finally, "that you've never suggested I simply go ahead and sell out to Hermanson? Take the money and run?"

"Others have?"

"Who hasn't?" He snorted. "Only Rose. And you." His touch was so light it was almost a whisper when he brushed a lock of hair back over her shoulder. "It's a lot of money."

"So?"

She looked as if she was ready to do battle, he thought, with her fists jammed on her hips, her dark eyes snapping, and the energy fairly crackling from her small body.

"What's that got to do with it?" she continued.

"A lot, I should think."

The dark silk of her hair flew as she shook her head adamantly. "No." A sweet-sad gentleness seeped into her voice. "I know what it's like."

"Know what what's like?"

"Having a place. A place where you are *you,* in a way you are no place else. A place where you feel right, where you can make sure everything is good. A place that you belong to as much as it belongs to you." She gestured as she talked, the movements crisp and quick and round.

"That's it. A place where you can make sure everything is right." He was startled by the words, surprised he'd actually said them out loud. He rarely gave up anything of himself, rarely even looked inside himself. It had slipped out so easily. And it hadn't even hurt.

"A place where you fit."

"Yes. Fit," he repeated. Apparently becoming impatient with being ignored, the stallion stuck his head over the stall side and nudged her shoulder. She smiled brightly, rubbing his nose. "So, then, what are you doing here if you have a place like that?"

"Just trying to find a way back there."

"Why'd you ever leave?"

"It wasn't really mine." She stood on her toes to reach properly, and her hands rippled over the horse's neck. "When I go back, I'll be able to prove that it should be."

She stepped back and dusted her palms on the dull brown linsey-woolsey of her split skirt. Her gaze met his squarely. "What are you going to do?"

"Do?" He grinned. "The only thing I can. We're going to have a party."

16

THE PARTY OF THE CENTURY
at the fabulous
NAKED ROSE SALOON AND GAMING PARLOR
Return to San Francisco's Golden Days
and Celebrate the Return to the Stage of the
LEGENDARY, BEAUTIFUL, EXCEPTIONAL
ROSE
Tomorrow Night!

It took them two weeks to get ready.

Josiah spent every moment in his kitchens, preparing the most delectable assortment of temptations a glutton had ever salivated over.

The upstairs girls bought themselves new dresses in honor of the occasion, flimsy, glimmering bits of fabric that left just enough to the imagination. They spent the remainder of their time in bed, sleeping, resting up for what surely would be a glut of new customers.

Rose dusted off all her old costumes, finding they

fit her every bit as well as they had five years ago. They were due for a bit of alteration, though, so she lowered the necklines another inch and raised the hems a good two. Once she was satisfied, she turned her attention to her old act, limbering up her voice and her legs. She'd only lost a shade of the height off her kicks, and she figured nobody would mind—as long as there was enough skin exposed.

Stitch did little. He slipped into the main room from time to time, drank a tumblerful of whiskey, watched the proceedings through hooded eyes, and disappeared again. He paused only long enough to take in one of Rose's rehearsals. When she twitched a hip and kicked his hat right off of his head, he said nothing, merely scooped it up, jammed it back on, and headed out the front door.

The handbills were Angie's responsibility. Printed in screaming big letters on blue paper, a whole series of announcements counted down to the big event. At J.J.'s insistence a sleepy but unprotesting Tommy accompanied her all over town—for her "protection," though Angie was sure her Colt would do a much more adequate job—and the two of them plastered the brightly hued papers on every bare surface they could find.

J.J. did everything else. He supervised the cleaning staff, making sure each lampshade was polished to a fine sparkle and each floor was scrubbed free of dirt. He ordered supplies and washed glasses, counted bottles of whiskey, and calculated profits, scratching out the numbers again and again on numerous scraps of paper. He watched the rehearsals, tasted new stock, approved costumes, and climbed a teetering ladder to wash the chandelier crystals with vinegar-laced water.

He did everything but sleep. At night, he paced the floor and re-added his figures, knowing as he did so that this was a long shot. Even in his best estimates, there was almost no way he could boost business enough to meet Stitch's price. But since this was the only shot he had, he'd make it work.

There was one more thing he didn't do. He didn't stop taking his morning riding lessons.

It was a ridiculous thing to waste time on, when he had so much more pressing business. He told himself he needed the exercise. He convinced himself he'd made a commitment, and he could no more give up on this goal he'd set for himself than on any other.

What he didn't admit was that his lessons were the one bright spot in a life that was becoming increasingly edged with desperation.

Not that the lessons were going well. Angie barely let him up on the horse. Instead, she had him grooming the darn thing until Angel's mane was the cleanest, shiniest, smoothest hank of hair in the entire place. He saddled and unsaddled the mangy beast until it was second nature, until he could reach under and fasten the cinch without bracing himself for the blow of a hoof.

She spent a fair amount of time trying to convince him to start on another horse, one that, she claimed, was more "suited to your size." He was having none of it.

But she made him laugh. It was that simple. Where Angie was, there was joy. Life and energy charged the air whenever she hummed by. At a time when his own life was crowded with work and uncertainty, it was something he found irresistible.

Even today.

Though it was barely past eight when he slipped out the back door, he had to squint against the glaring sun. The weather had taken an unusual turn, warming to a point where the normal humidity became extremely uncomfortable.

The air was heavy, weighing down on his shoulders as he crossed the packed earth of the yard. He wished he could think of the sun as a good omen, but the heat felt oppressive. This wasn't the town he knew, always shrouded and mysterious and cool. San Francisco in the grip of a heat wave was no more familiar than his life had become.

The grand party was tomorrow; by midnight, he would know if there was any possibility of salvaging his saloon. There was nothing he could do now to change things. If only he could get rid of the acid that ate away at his insides.

He *would* save his saloon. And he *would* learn how to ride that damn horse.

The door to the stables slid easily with his too-hard shove. His eyes adjusted slowly to the darkness within, and he blinked.

Angie was shoveling fresh straw into an empty stall. The air swirled with chaff and dust that her energetic work had stirred up. Her cheeks bloomed with the exertion, and a damp tendril of hair clung to her throat, just above the collar of her plain blouse.

It would be so easy to brush it away, then allow his finger to slip underneath the limp cotton. To forget the future and his responsibilities, to lose himself in trying to make her body hum with pleasure.

All three cats were there, sitting in a line, watching her work, their tails twitching back and forth.

"We should get rid of those damn cats."

She propped the pitchfork in a corner and whirled to him, her eyes bright with anticipation. "Well? Are you ready?"

He flushed and looked away. It was probably the wrong morning to be doing this. He was edgy, tense, and far too susceptible to thoughts he had no business entertaining. Try as he might, he couldn't quite seem to keep himself under his usual calm control. The best thing he could do was duck out while he had the chance.

"I'm ready," he said anyway.

*　　*　　*

"Let me try it myself," he demanded.

The lesson hadn't gone well from the start. Angel had been skittish during saddling, and J.J. just managed to avoid being nipped on the shoulder. It had taken him three attempts to mount, a skill he thought he'd conquered a week ago.

And now he was on the horse's back while Angie led them—once again—around the yard on a long rein.

"Give me the reins."

She shaded her eyes from the sun and looked up at him. "I don't think you're ready."

"I'm not a child. You've been circling me around this yard for a week. I feel like a toy top."

"You need to get a feel for it, J.J. A good seat is the most important thing for a rider."

"I always thought my seat was just fine."

Angie was proud of herself. She'd actually learned not to react when he made comments like that; her gaze hadn't dropped to his body. She couldn't help the image that popped into her mind: J.J. bending over to pick up a fallen bridle, faded denims stretched taut across tight, muscular buttocks. Oh, yes, his seat was better than fine.

But she learned to ignore it, to go on with the lesson as if nothing had happened. He didn't mean anything by it. She didn't think he was even conscious of the provocative comments he made. It was second nature to him, to flirt and to tease.

She'd be a fool to think anything else. It was perfectly obvious his affections were firmly fixed.

"I just don't think you're ready yet," she insisted.

"And I think I am. Just let me try."

"You agreed that you would allow me to make decisions like that."

"That was before I knew you were going to keep me going around in circles until I got dizzy."

"No, I don't want you to try anything too soon. It would set you back too far if it didn't work out."

"I can't get set back because I haven't gotten anywhere." Lord, couldn't he even do *this*? A thing that so many people did as a matter of course? How was he supposed to believe he could stand up to Ezekiel Hermanson if he couldn't even learn to ride the damn horse? "Just give me the damn reins!"

"No." One small fist still curled tightly around the leather strips; she planted the other on her hip. "You'll get them when I think you're ready. And you're not, no matter what your inexpert opinion is."

"Look, brat, I've allowed you to think you're in charge here—"

"Brat!"

"But that was before I knew you were going to use it to keep me under your thumb. I didn't expect you to get so much enjoyment out of leading me around like a trained bear that you'd keep me doing it forever. Let me ride him myself!"

Angie set her jaw. "You think I'm doing this because I like the power?"

"Aren't you?"

"Look, barkeep, I'm doing this for your own good. If you can't get past the fear—"

Warm sunlight gleamed off the fine gold of his hair, but his voice went cold. "What did you say?"

Oh, no. Tactful as always, she scolded herself. No man ever liked to hear that a woman saw him as less than the bravest of the brave. "I only meant—"

"Here." J.J. swung his leg over and slid off the horse. "He's yours."

"What?"

She saw only the wide expanse of his back as he strode toward the saloon.

"The horse. He's yours."

"You can't mean that," she shouted after him.

"Oh, I do!" He paused and turned back to her. "I have more important things to do!" he hollered. "The last thing I need is to waste my time following orders from an undersized brat who hasn't got the slightest clue what she's talking about!"

He turned again, giving her one more brief flash of his back before he disappeared through the door.

Too bad, she thought wistfully. He really did have an exceptionally nice seat.

"Where is he?" Angie burst into the main room of the Naked Rose.

As soon as J.J. had left, she turned to put Angel away. It had taken only a few seconds before she worked herself back into a good, righteous anger.

He should have been putting his own horse away, instead of leaving it to her as if she was cheap labor— even if she *was* cheap labor. He had promised her that he would listen to her, that the lessons would proceed according to her instructions.

And the first time he got a little impatient, he lost his temper and stormed off, leaving her to clean up. Not to mention leaving her to wonder if she was out of a job, a job she wasn't ready to leave until she got a backer lined up. Starving in the streets lost its charm rather quickly.

She'd quickly tethered Angel to a nearby post, promising she'd come back soon and rescue him from the sun, and charged after J.J.

How dare he disappear on her. Where she came from, people stood and fought. They *would* have this out, she decided, gaining the central room of the Rose.

It was nearly empty. The place was closed for the afternoon in preparation for tomorrow's party. The air was warm and still. Bright light streamed through the open front door and windows, spilling across the oak floor, polished shiny as glass, and fell on the only occupant of the room.

Rose, clad in the lace-iced pink cotton that was her

version of an everyday dress, was perched by the bar, mumbling as she bent over the account books.

"All right, where is he?" Angie demanded.

"Shh." Rose held up one finger as she scribbled on the page with her pen. "Just a minute."

Angie impatiently tapped her fingers on the gleaming surface of a nearby table. She knew he was just hiding from her, the rat.

"There." Rose laid down her quill and looked up. "What did you want?"

"I want to know where he slunk off to!"

Rose's brows came together in a delicate frown. "J.J.?"

"Of course J.J."

Rose rubbed her fingertips along the surface of the bar. "He's quite busy these days. Why do you want to see him?"

"I don't *want* to see him." Angie gave an exasperated huff. "We need to get a few things straight. He hollered at me, darn it! If he thinks he can—"

"He what?" Rose pursed her lips for a moment, then indicated a nearby chair. "Why don't you just sit down for a moment and see if you can tell me what happened."

Too restless to sit in the chair, Angie began to pace back and forth. "I told you." She made wide, agitated circles with her hands. "He yelled at me, just because I wouldn't let him try something he wasn't ready for."

"J.J. never yells," Rose said calmly.

"He certainly did!" The heels of her boots clicked rapidly on the plank floor. "All I was doing was trying to protect him. He didn't have to get so mad at me."

"J.J. never gets mad."

"What?" Angie stopped walking long enough to gape at Rose. "Of course he does. He turned red, and he yelled at me, and he stomped off. And he called me a brat!"

"A brat?" Rose's hand went very still, pale white

against the golden wood. "He calls his sister 'brat,' " she finished softly, as if to herself.

"He does? What happened to his legendary charm—"

"Angie," Rose broke in, her voice soft but laced with an odd, low thread of steel. "I think perhaps you should go back to the stables now."

"But I want to settle this, if I'm ever going to teach him to ride."

"I don't know where he is."

And if you do, you're not telling me, Angie thought. "Fine." Angie marched back out of the room.

Rose was still, a study in white and pale pink in the center of the golden room, her gaze fixed on an empty point in space.

Finally, she picked up her pen and bent over the books once more.

17

Faint strains of gay music drifted out of the Naked Rose, wafting through the hot, calm night air and into the stables.

Even tonight, J.J. couldn't afford for the saloon to be closed. Last-minute preparations were going on right around the regular customers, who were more than willing to put up with the inconvenience in order to get a good glimpse of Rose practicing her act.

The peach-and-green softness of Angie's room had begun to wear on her; it simply didn't feel like *her,* would never feel like home. Tonight, the room had been hot, stuffy, and noisy, making her long for the green hills and simple lines of her home.

She'd had no desire to join the crowd downstairs, either.

J.J. was the only lure that drew her, and that would be folly. She'd been unable to find him that afternoon, and her anger had soon dwindled away. He was under a great deal of strain; she knew what she would feel like if she were close to losing the Meadows for good.

Despite the fact that she understood his anger, she still felt awkward. The easy, lighthearted companionship that had marked their time together had been damaged in that moment of intense emotion, and she wasn't entirely sure how to repair it.

Finally, unable to stand her frilly room any longer, she slipped down the stairs unnoticed and out to the stables.

The doors were wide open, to catch a stray hint of night breeze. Though it must have been past midnight, the sounds of merriment spilled out the open windows of the Rose and showed no sign of abating.

The tack Angie was oiling really didn't need it. She simply needed something to do with her hands, out here in the one place in San Francisco that she was certain she belonged.

She glanced over at Tommy, who lay slouched in his customary pose, his lanky body sprawled on a ragged blanket thrown over a mound of hay.

He had a lamp of his own, and the wavering light played over the limp strands of his light brown hair and his sharp features. His nose was where it always was the instant he finished a chore—in a book—and he was yawning hugely.

"You really can go on to bed, you know. I'd be happy to take care of any customers for you," she offered.

"No," he mumbled, never taking his eyes off the fat, leather-bound volume he'd propped up on his knees, the gray cat curled up against his side. "Couldn't ask ya to do that."

"It would do you good to get some sleep."

"No." There was a soft rustle as he flipped a page over. "Want to finish this first, anyway."

"Ah, I see. It's not that you work too hard, you just stay up too late reading."

"Yeah." He looked up long enough to flash her a quick grin. "I din't have any books for such a long time."

"Making up for lost time?"

"Uh-huh." He bobbed his head in agreement.

His gaze kept sliding back to the page. She should let him get back to it, but curiosity got the better of her. He was very young, a boy just edging into manhood, obviously quick and studious. He was comfortable with the horses, but there was no natural affinity there; it wasn't something he was choosing to do, as she was. Why wasn't he in school? Home with his family?

"What are you reading?"

He gave a good-natured sigh, marked his page with his finger, and held the book up for her inspection. "*Moby-Dick.*"

"Ah. My father read that to me. Where did you get it?"

"J.J."

"Really?" she asked, as casually as she could manage. "I never pictured him as having much of a library."

"Oh, yes. Ain't got enough money to buy my own, so he lets me use his." He settled back into the hay, cradling the book in his arms. "'Course, I know he doesn't buy 'em for himself, but I let him think that."

She'd been rubbing the same section of strap, over and over, way past the time the leather had become pliant under her thumb. She laid it aside and picked up a new piece. "Why is that?"

"'Cause he doesn't like thanks, ma'am. All of us know that."

"All of you?"

"Yep. Everybody who comes to the Naked Rose."

Maturity far beyond his years gleamed in his light eyes. "J.J. don't do too well with people being beholdin' to him."

"And why is that?" It wasn't any of her business. No reason she needed to know, except an irrepressible urge to understand him, to know the way his thoughts ran.

"Guess, if'n nobody thanks him, he ken pretend he

din't do nuthin'. That he don't care what happens to anybody."

The flame in her lamp wavered, and she bent to turn up the wick. "And does he?"

"Oh, yes'm," Tommy said eagerly. "But I reckon you knows that."

"Yes, I reckon I do," she murmured. The brighter glow of the flame filled her corner of the stables, casting odd-figured shadows on the rough wood wall. "Tommy, how did you come here?"

"The Rose?"

"Yes."

"Din't have no place to go." His bony shoulders lifted and fell under the thin cotton of his blue work shirt. "My ma and pop died on the trail out here."

"Oh, Jimmy, I'm so sorry." He was too young to have lost so much.

"It was a long time ago." The light threw dark shadows under his cheekbones. Someday, he would be an exceptional-looking man. "They let me stay with the train, but when we got here, I din't have anyone to live with. So I just stayed down at the waterfront." He darted her a furtive glance. "I . . . " He cleared his throat. "Sometimes I took stuff that din't belong to me."

"You were just doing what you had to. I understand."

"You do?" he asked hopefully. "That's what J.J. said, too. He caught me once, when I was trying to snitch his wallet."

He took the cover of the book between his fingers, lifting it up and letting it drop. "I wasn't that good at it, I guess. I got caught a fair amount. But J.J. din't hit me, like most o' them did."

"Of course he didn't."

"Naw. He gave me a job, even though I didn't know how to do nuthin'. Let me stay here, gave me food as part o' my pay. And when he found out I could read, he let me use his books anytime I wanted."

"Yes," she said, her voice a stark whisper. "He would do that."

Her hands slowed in their task, lightly caressing the oiled leather. Yes, that was J.J., who took in strays to keep them safe, even as he tried to keep himself away from them. To keep himself from caring.

She saw it all so clearly now. She, who was only another one of his strays, whom he picked up on the waterfront out of his basic kindness, a kindness he'd hidden beneath roguish charm. And perhaps he did feel some vague, brotherly fondness for her.

But that was all there would ever be from him. She'd never deluded herself in her life, and she wasn't about to begin now. Not when the delusions could lead her into something so painful.

As painful as falling head over heels in love with him. Ah, she could do that so easily, if she were stupid enough to allow it.

But she wouldn't, even if—for a moment—she regretted that she couldn't. The lure of possibilities was strong, of the kind of emotion she hadn't truly thought existed.

She still wasn't sure that it did. It was a dream people wanted to believe in, to justify their actions, to relieve themselves of the responsibility of controlling their own lives.

It would not do to give up her dreams for something so ephemeral and so illusive. Especially since she was absolutely certain that it would be one-sided.

No, she couldn't let anything stand in the way of her future. Not when she'd planned so long and come so far.

The flame in her lantern gave one last flicker and went out, cloaking her corner of the stable in shadow. The air was filled with the comforting, familiar scents of hay and horses and lamp oil. She set aside the bridle and picked up another harness. All the tack would be in perfect condition before the night was over, for that was all she could leave behind.

Because there was only one way to make sure she wouldn't fall into the trap her heart was setting for her. And that was to make sure she left here, before these gentle, tentative feelings had a chance to grow.

She'd stay until after the party tomorrow. She needed to make certain J.J. would be able to rescue his saloon. When she was back in Kentucky, when she and her horses were famous throughout the state, perhaps she'd remember him there, laughing behind his bar.

18

They just might make it.

The place was packed, more people jamming every table than he'd seen here since the first heady days they'd opened, right in the thick of the gold rush. Shouts rang out in appreciation as Rose flipped up her skirt one last time and headed off the makeshift stage over the dance floor after her second performance of the evening. He'd have to make sure he thanked her for this.

The gay notes of the piano could scarcely be heard among the hubbub of conversation. A paunchy, middle-aged man chased Mei-Ling up the stairs, and her squeal echoed behind.

J.J. flipped the tap and poured yet another beer for a new customer. They weren't out of the woods yet. He needed more than new customers, more than one good night. He'd upped their percentage of the take at the gambling tables. Last he saw, satisfyingly high stacks of chips had threatened to topple over onto the heavy green tablecloths.

He slid the mug down the bar and it coasted to a stop in front of the customer, who nodded his thanks before upending it, foam leaking out around his mouth and spilling over his chin.

"Hey, J.J.! 'Nother round here!" shouted a boisterous group of ex-miners that crowded around the nearest table.

"Whiskey?"

"What else?"

J.J. automatically reached for the bottle, then his fingers tightened around the cool round neck. God, what if it wasn't enough?

If only they could begin to turn a real profit. Perhaps enough so that Stitch would see that the Naked Rose was worth more to him, in the long run, than Hermanson's quick money would be in his pocket now.

If only.

"J.J.!"

"Sorry." He plunked the bottle down right in the middle of the table. "Might as well have the whole thing, boys."

"Hoo-hee, don't you know it!"

Stitch had been here since they opened, selecting a table with a clear view of Rose's makeshift stage. No one had joined him; no one had even spoken to the man all evening, as far as J.J. could see. Clearly a friendly sort.

Stitch had his chair tipped back, just touching the wall, and the brim of his dark hat shadowed his face. He gave nothing away.

After a moment's thought, J.J. grabbed a fresh bottle of whiskey and two glasses.

"Hey, Josiah, can you handle things by yourself for a bit?"

Josiah was bartending tonight. Food wasn't high on anyone's priority list, and he'd done enough in advance to keep the bellies filled of the few customers who wanted it.

Josiah stuck a mug beneath the tap and hitched it open with his hip, so smoothly and quickly it sometimes took customers a bit before they noticed he had only one hand.

Josiah looked at the bottle in J.J.'s hand, then glanced over at Stitch's table. "Sure."

If Stitch noted his approach, it didn't show.

J.J. set the bottle on the table and kicked out a chair. He sat down, splashed a good shot of whiskey into each of the glasses, and set one down in front of Stitch.

"Enjoying the show?"

The golden liquid caught and bent the light as he swirled his glass. "Anythin' wrong with that?"

"Just a comment."

Stitch pushed back his hat with his thumb and glared at J.J. "Are you warnin' me off?"

J.J. laughed. God, it felt good to be able to do that. "Rose is a big girl. She can do her own warning. Always has, always will."

Stitch was clearly not inclined to conversation. He said nothing, just turned his gaze back to the empty stage.

J.J. tossed back half his glass of whiskey, welcoming the raw burn as it slid to his belly. "Are you going to stick to the agreement?"

There, he'd asked. He waited for an answer, gripping his drink so tightly the glass was sure to shatter if he squeezed any harder.

"Yeah."

Air rushed out of J.J.'s lungs in a fast, sweet breath of relief. "You'll keep your word?"

Stitch's eyes narrowed. "I promised Rose. You'll have the summer."

The summer. He had time. He listened to the crowds of customers swirling around him. He was getting money.

And, as he picked up the bottle and headed back

to the bar to relieve Josiah, he had the best thing of all.

He had hope.

He found himself watching for her.

Even in the midst of his relief, of knowing that his life wasn't going to fall completely apart, J.J. wanted to see her.

The surface of the bar was stained with damp rings, and J.J. picked up a towel to polish it clean. He glanced once more at the stairway to the upper floor, waiting for Angie to appear.

He knew she wasn't fond of the bar. It seemed to cage her in, to be too small to hold all her humming energy. And she clearly wasn't adept at small talk, wasn't comfortable making lighthearted, meaningless chat with strangers.

The few nights she'd come down, she'd poked her nose into every corner, inspecting the place from top to bottom. Then she'd started looking for something to do. The truth was, there really wasn't much work that he could assign her. She worked hard enough during the day, and he wanted her to relax in the evening. And something easy, like chatting up the customers, making sure they were comfortable—it just didn't seem to be the kind of thing she liked to do.

She was obviously much happier out with the horses. But surely tonight . . . surely tonight she would join in the celebration. Hell, at least now he was certain to have enough to pay her.

He folded the wet rag into neat squares and stowed it away. The two large mugs he pulled out were still warm from a recent washing. The kitchen help were being kept busy tonight; he was going through glasses as fast as they could clean them.

If only he hadn't yelled at her.

Maybe she was still upset with him. Lord knew *he* was.

When he was young and very stupid, he'd had one helluva temper. A temper that had often put him at odds with his equally strong-willed father.

The blowup when he was nineteen had been the final straw. His father had demanded that J.J. prepare himself to join the law practice. He'd thought it was long past time J.J. settle down and make something of himself. If J.J. didn't agree, he was no longer welcome to live in the house.

He knew his father hadn't meant it. But J.J. had been mad enough at the ultimatum to leave for good. He'd always planned to go back someday, when he could prove he'd made something of himself on his own terms.

It had never occurred to him that his father wouldn't be there when he was ready. That he'd have to spend the rest of his life knowing that the last words they'd spoken had been in anger. And that he'd failed his sister, too, who'd had to spend too many years alone, watching their father die.

Golden beer flowed easily into the glasses, a deep head of foam billowing up and threatening to overflow. J.J. snapped the tap shut.

He'd struggled to master his temper, to make sure that useless emotion never caused him to waste so much time again. He thought he had.

Until yesterday.

There were plenty of ready excuses. He'd been under a strain.

But the truth was, *she* affected him. Her small body was packed with so much life. She wore her emotions so close to the surface that it pulled a bit of his own out, made him wonder what he was missing by holding on to control so tightly.

Look what happened when he let go. That's why he was always so careful, so calm. People said foolish, stupid things in the grip of emotion. They hurt each other—and themselves.

He put the mugs down on the bar, and a bit of foam sloshed over the rim. He automatically measured the distance down to the customer; after seven years, sliding the glass to a perfect stop was no longer a challenge.

He didn't know why he bothered to sneak another quick peek at the stairs. Obviously, she wasn't coming down tonight.

Except she was already down, standing just to the other side of the bar, her hair straight and long, rippling down over her shoulders. The lace edge of her cotton blouse feathered against her honey-toned skin. Her smile was tentative; her color, high.

There was a loud thud, the splatter of spilled liquid, and the crack of broken glass.

The mug had sailed clean off the other end of the bar.

"Hey!" A cowboy in a double-buttoned shirt and faded denims jumped up, displayed the dark stain seeping down the front of his trousers.

J.J. winced. "Sorry."

He grabbed a handful of clean rags and headed for the end of the bar. Josiah waved him off. "I'll take care of this one, boss."

The cowboy grabbed the towel Josiah proffered and dabbed at his stained front, glowering at J.J. all the while.

"Josiah, all this man's drinks are on the house tonight, all right?"

The cowboy's scowl quickly turned into a grin. What was a little dampness compared to all the free whiskey he could drink?

J.J. planted his hands on the bar. "You came down."

"Uh . . . yes." A loose, silky strand of hair fell across her cheek. Angie impatiently brushed it away and tucked it behind her ear. "Wouldn't miss it for anything."

"Can I get you something?" He jerked his thumb toward the long, even rows of bottles.

"No."

"You're sure?" he asked, needing to offer something.

"Yes."

"You don't want a drink?" He moved to pick up a glass.

"No!" She gave a small, negative shake. "I meant, yes, I'm sure. No, I don't want anything."

"Okay." He rubbed the inside band of his ring. The gold was warm from his body. It felt almost soft to his touch. "Angel, about yesterday morning—"

The motion of her hand was quick and jerky, cutting him off. "Forget it."

"But I'm sorry. I shouldn't have called you a brat."

She smiled slightly. "I should be used to it. My brother used to call me much worse."

"Yeah, I'm the same way with my sister."

Her gaze skittered away: up, down, side. Anywhere but directly at him.

"Look." He turned his ring all the way around and stroked the smooth curve of the turquoise. "Would you like to sit down? Rose will be back on in a bit, and—" He stopped. He could just about guess what her reaction to Rose's show would be. Perhaps that wasn't the best idea. "Are you hungry? You could go back to the kitchen. Josiah's left some cold beef sandwiches."

"No." She squared her shoulders. "J.J., could I have a bit of your time later? I need to talk to you about something."

"You don't want to do it now?"

"No. It's . . . private."

"Sure," he agreed, puzzled. What could she possibly need to tell him that required privacy?

"Good." Her hands fluttered for a second before she jammed them deep into the pockets of her dark blue skirt. "You seem to be very busy tonight."

"Yes, it's going well." Out of habit, he pulled out a cloth and began to rub down the bar again.

She met his gaze squarely, her brown eyes shimmering with dark emotion. "I'm really glad it's all working out for you, J.J."

"Maybe." He removed two empty glasses from the bar and set them in a pan of cold, soapy water. "At least now I've got something to work with."

The jovial, flexible laughter was Ezekiel's trademark. It was one of his great advantages as a businessman; few believed that someone who seemed like a genial uncle could have the instincts of a shark. Yet when J.J. heard it, the friendly rumble warmly rising above the noise in the room, tiny hairs prickled at the back of his neck.

Hermanson bellied his substantial bulk up to the bar. Angie unobtrusively slid just a bit away. Good. At least she'd heeded his warning.

Ezekiel confiscated the glass of whiskey Josiah had been serving to the customer just to his left. He sipped it slowly as he perused the hubbub in the saloon.

"I must congratulate you, Johnston. Business is booming."

"Yes," J.J. said warily.

Ezekiel's smile was broad, gold flashing next to equally shiny teeth. "That's good. Might as well make a bit extra before you have to sell out to me."

"I have no intention of selling out, Hermanson. You may as well start looking for another site for your hotel."

"Oh, but you will." His smooth pink fingers wrapped loosely around his glass, cradling it gently as he lifted it to his lips once more. "Don't you know, boy? I always win."

J.J. pressed his hands down on the bar, feeling the hard surface beneath his palms. "Not this time."

He chuckled. "Of course I will."

The band of J.J.'s ring cut into his finger. "What are you planning?"

"I don't need to plan anything." He shrugged. "Things just go my way. Always." He held the glass of whiskey up so that light, liquid and amber, flowed through. "I'm the luckiest man in the world, don't you know that?"

"I have work to do." J.J. turned away, heading for the storeroom. They had plenty of supplies, but he needed to get out of there, away from Ezekiel's false charm before J.J. began to wonder whether it would be easier simply to give up and start over.

Start over where? How? This place was all he was, all he had to give. It was the only thing he'd ever done that he'd managed to make work out right.

"Gold!"

A hoarse shout from the front of the Rose froze him in his tracks. There was the slam of the door, a low, astonished murmur, and then silence.

The man who'd just tumbled in was young and underfed, his dirty, ragged clothes hanging on his narrow frame. Blond, stiff hair stuck out in ragged spikes around his head, and his eyes were bright with something J.J. recognized all too well.

Gold fever.

"Din't you hear me?" he shouted. "They found gold!"

The Naked Rose erupted with wild, exuberant cheers. Hats flew in the air, men scrambled to their feet, and entire bottles were upended over the stranger's head.

Gold was the one tie that bound all the residents of San Francisco together, the siren call irresistible to all. It was the thing that had brought them here, the foundation for thousands of bright, golden dreams.

"Wait!" The wrinkled, frail-looking old man was a veteran of the gold fields, a miner to the depths of his fragile bones. He climbed on top of a table and shouted with all the strength left in his aged body. "Wait!"

The cacophony slowly receded. The miner snatched the hat off his bald head, pointed it at the young man, and said only one word: "Where?"

"The Fraser River! Half the town's on their way out now!"

Any semblance of civilization disappeared as every man in the place headed for the exit. There was gold! And every man was certain that if he could just get there first, could get himself one small piece of earth, that all those precious yellow rocks would fill his hands and his pockets and his life.

They surged through the door, spilling out into the warm, crowded street, joining the men who'd already streamed from boardinghouses and restaurants and gin joints. What did it matter if they weren't entirely sure where the Fraser River was? Someplace to the north. They'd find it. They could *smell* the gold.

J.J. stood, motionless, in the center of the Rose and surveyed his deserted bar. Two tables were tipped on their sides; one of the saffron curtains that billowed around the front windows was torn half away, a ragged swath lying against the scuffed oak floor. The splintered remains of a broken chair scattered across the center of the room.

"Yes, a good business," Ezekiel commented, his voice as warm and smooth as always.

J.J. didn't glance his way. He bent, righting a side-tipped chair, setting it carefully square with the table. Its legs squeaked against the oak floor.

Then J.J. turned and walked down the long hallway, out the back door, away from the remnants of his life.

19

"*All right, where is he?*" Rose demanded of the near-empty room.

After J.J. left, Ezekiel had excused himself and, whistling happily, strolled from the saloon. Angie had waited for a moment, then disappeared without a word. Now there was only Stitch, leaning back in his chair with his dark, scuffed boots resting on a tabletop.

He pushed back his hat and looked up at her. "Who?"

She smacked his feet off the table. "Don't put your dirty boots on the furniture. And you know very well who I mean. I was changing for the next set when Crystal ran in and told me what happened. Where's J.J.?"

He nodded in the direction of the hallway. "Back there."

"He left?"

"Guess so."

She whirled in a pouf of short pink satin skirts, ready to follow.

"Wait."

She spun. "Don't tell me what to do."

"Stay."

She advanced on him slowly. "Did you have something to do with this?"

"No."

He looked far too comfortable, too unsurprised. His silver hair swept the shoulders of his black cotton shirt, and his mouth was unsmiling.

"You're lying." she accused him.

"No." There was a brief flicker in his pale eyes. "I don't lie to ladies."

"I haven't been a lady for a long, long time," she said, surprised at the harshness that crept into her voice.

He straightened and leaned forward, suddenly intent. "I don't lie to *you*."

She was shocked at how much she wanted to believe him. Shocked enough to take off down the hallway as fast as her spool-heeled boots allowed.

"Don't go after him."

"I have to," she said without turning back, wondering why she even bothered to answer. "I love him."

She hadn't heard him follow her, and gasped in surprise when his long hand closed gently around her upper arm.

"No, you don't."

Shadows filled the narrow hallway, enveloping them, cloaking his face, leaving only the pale gleam of his eyes.

"Yes, I do," she said. No one had ever doubted that before, not in all the comfortable, steady years she'd spent in the Rose.

"No." He moved closer, and she shuffled back until her shoulders came up against the solid bulk of the wall. "You worship him. That's somethin' very different."

"I do love him," she repeated, clinging to the one thing that had been a constant in her life since she first edged back from the darkness.

"Love is sharing it all. Not hidin' the bad stuff, makin' it all easy and nice for him."

I don't do that, she wanted to say, but she knew it was true. She'd always been afraid that if she was anything less than sparkling and cheerful and lively, J.J. wouldn't love her. Not that he had, anyway. He'd never pretended to.

"When were you ever greedy with him? When did you ever cry on his shoulder?" His voice was low, mesmerizing, slipping over her ears and past her defenses. "Ask him to share the burden?"

"No." she whispered again.

"You worship him." He stepped closer, crowding her, making the breath wedge in her chest. "It's easier that way. Easier than riskin' really lovin' someone. Someone you could lose."

She closed her eyes, looking for refuge, unable to escape the frightening touch of his words.

"I love him," she said helplessly.

"No, you don't." His hand came up to brush her cheek, a whisper of the soft night air against her skin. "Shall I show you?"

She meant to say no. She would always believe she had *meant* to say no. But then his lips settled gently over hers, and she lost all grasp of reason.

His mouth was exactly what she'd expected, though she'd failed to realize, right until that moment, that she'd expected anything. Firm, lean, overwhelmingly male.

She had heat in her life, had passion and aching and shivering want. She was familiar with that heat, knew how to deal with it, how to give in and how to turn it off at will.

What she'd never, ever had was warmth.

A flooding, spreading warmth that seeped into her veins and her weakening limbs. Into her soul. A warmth that lured rather than seduced, that persuaded instead of demanded. That made promises, instead of fulfilled them. She was unprepared for the absolute and total devastation of it.

She jerked away and raised one shaking hand to her mouth, a mouth that felt like a stranger's. She was certain he would pull her back, and wondered if she would even try to get away again.

He didn't, simply stepped away, fading into the darkness of the deserted hall, his dark clothes becoming one with the night. Only the silver fall of his hair and the compelling fog-gray gleam of his eyes echoed the absent moonlight.

She ran. Down the hall, through the main room, and up the stairs, her heels clattering loudly, echoing in the empty spaces. Only after she had gained the safety of her room, slamming and locking the door behind her, did she realize she hadn't gone to J.J. after all.

The room was designed to mirror its owner. Rich, warm, and welcoming, it impressed and disarmed equally effectively. One tended not to notice that it had only one well-guarded exit until one was thoroughly ensnared.

The young man wiped his damp palms on the baggy legs of his britches before he was admitted by the impeccably correct butler. Jack tried hard not to gape at the richness that surrounded him. Though he'd seen it before, its impact was little diminished. Especially since, tonight, he'd be getting more riches than he'd ever dreamed of owning at one time. And for so little work, too.

"Went good, huh?" His voice squeaked in the silent room, then was quickly absorbed by the heavy, forest green drapes.

"Yes. You performed exactly to specification." Ezekiel made no move to rise from his massive, simply carved armchair. Nor did he invite the young man to sit down. "All the others did their parts well, too. Though yours was clearly the most important," he said in his fluid voice, making Jack swell with pride at his accomplishment. He'd done well!

"It went 'zactly as ya said. Town's almost empty of all but old men and ghosts."

Jack's eyes bulged when Ezekiel hefted a plush, deep blue velvet pouch. He was riveted by the lumpy sack that clanked with each motion.

"Um." Jack licked his dry lips. "Not goin' ta be good for your business, with ever'body outta town."

"It's of no matter." Hermanson smiled negligently. "They'll be back soon enough for me. But too late for Johnston, poor soul."

He tossed the pouch at Jack, who grabbed it in his eager hands and clutched it safely to his chest. He impatiently ripped open the thong fastenings.

Round gold coins winked dully in the soft gaslight. Beautiful. Prettier than any girl he'd ever seen, even the one who served him the day he'd gone to check out the Naked Rose and plan his performance.

He closed the pouch quickly and shoved it deep into his pockets. "Thank you, sir." His words tumbled over each other. "Any time I can be o' any more service, sir, ya just call on Jack. Any time."

"I'll bear that in mind." He gestured toward the door. Jack backed out, still babbling his thanks, until the butler softly closed the door behind him, slicing off his final offer of more help.

Satisfied, Ezekiel sat back in his comfortable chair, enveloped by soft light, soft fabrics, and the perfume of the good brandy warming in the crystal balloon cradled in his hand.

Perhaps this was the atmosphere he should create in his new hotel, he mused.

Angie stood in the entrance to the old garden, gasping, struggling to draw the thick air into her lungs.

As soon as she watched J.J. head out of the saloon, his head bowed, a lonely, golden figure garbed in white disappearing into the dark hall, she'd gotten the idea. She'd had to go two blocks to find what she vaguely remembered seeing while papering the town with advertisements, and she'd sprinted all the way there and back.

She'd wondered how to find him, if she'd have to look through half the grounds. She knew he'd be here somewhere; no way would he have left the Naked Rose tonight. However, the place was fairly large, and she was reluctant to ask Rose for help in locating J.J.

She'd leaned for a minute against the old stone gateway to catch a breath, trying to guess where he would go, when she heard a soft whisper of sound, the brush of leaves.

J.J. stood in the far side of the garden, looking back at the bulk of the Rose. The moonlight was yellow, blurred by the heavily moisture-laden air, and the light misted over the golden sheen of his hair and the stark whiteness of his suit. His features were sharpened, skin drawn tautly over bone.

She walked slowly through the remains of the garden, her feet sinking into the damp earth, and the green, warm smell of crushed vegetation rose with her passing. He watched her approach in silence, his face half in shadow, half in moonlight.

He didn't seem to welcome her coming, but he didn't ask her to leave, either. When she reached him, she stopped, shoving her hand in her pocket. Her fist curled around the crumpled paper she'd ran so hard to find and then ripped off the hitching post it had been nailed to.

"Hello." she said, unsure of where to start. If only he would do more than look at her. If only she had a bit of the charm of the rest of her family, to whom simple conversations and comforting words came so easily.

"I was just saying good-bye."

"Good-bye?"

"To the Rose." He looked down at his hands, at the contrast of dark skin and white cuffs, the dull gleam of gold in his ring. "I can sell the ring, my paintings, the horse . . . " He frowned. "Oh, that's right. I gave you the horse, didn't I?"

"Don't be ridiculous."

"No, mustn't be ridiculous." The corner of his mouth lifted, just for an instant, before dropping back into an expressionless line. "I'm sorry, I didn't mean to be sharp. Thank you. But what would be ridiculous was believing it all would be enough."

"J.J.—" She stopped, searching for a way to put it so he would believe that it was possible, to give him hope when he'd so clearly given up.

"What is it?" he asked gently. "Oh, that's right. You asked to speak with me about something. I don't know that now is a good time, Angel. Your job's gone, along with the rest of it."

"It's not that." She pulled the paper from her pocket, its blue color turning a sickly green in the yellow light, the edges torn in her haste to pull it free. "I had an idea."

"An idea?" He sounded distantly amused, his face schooled into blank, controlled lines.

"Yes." She thrust the crumpled paper toward him.

He looked at her for a moment, then reached out and accepted the handbill. He squinted, trying to make out the words in the dim light. " 'The Horse Race of the Century'," he read aloud. " 'All Comers Welcome', Angel, I really am not interested in this right now."

"How much of a gambler are you?"

"That depends on what I'm gambling on. I came out here, didn't I?"

"Read on."

He continued, his voice empty of inflection. " 'All Comers Welcome. Winner Take All. Entrance Fee Is

One Thousand Dollars In Gold'." He paused, and the paper rustled as his fingers tightened. "'Minimum Prize Is Ten Thousand Dollars'."

An almost imperceptible hint of animation lit his features. "Do you really think he's good enough?"

"Oh, yes. Absolutely." She was certain of that much. "It says a flat mile and a half. There's no horse I've ever seen that could possibly match him over that distance."

"Can we have him ready?"

"I think so. It'll be a fair amount of work, but it's set for August fifteenth. We've got two months." She grinned. "Read the last line."

"The last line?" He stared at the paper. A slow, simmering laughter came from him, swelling, growing, the jubilant sound of regained hope. He threw his arms wide, then scooped her up and twirled her around, the sounds of her delight mingling with his, bubbling up to the hazy, moon-washed sky.

"Angel, you're an absolute genius!"

THE PRIZE IS GUARANTEED BY MR. L. J. HOOPER
AND EZEKIEL HERMANSON, ESQ.

20

She was flying, held up by the strong hands at her waist, the solid shoulders beneath her hands. She was spinning in a world of light and shadow, filled with the scents of ripe summer earth and warm male skin.

He set her down, bringing her back to earth with an abrupt jolt. He shoved his hands in his pockets, unable to figure out what to do with them.

"Do you really think they'll have the race? Even with everyone out of town?"

She looked so alive, her breath coming in short pants, her hair swinging loosely down her back, and her eyes alight with enthusiasm. For a moment, when he'd held her aloft, he'd actually thought of bringing her down slowly, of gliding her small body lightly along his. He'd wanted to feel her slight curves, to know the firm strength of her limbs.

The thought had shocked him so much he nearly dropped her when he put her down. The vague, brotherly affection he had for her was fine. Anything else was not.

"Of course they will. Hooper and Hermanson absolutely detest each other. Something about some old land deals, in the early days. They each claim the other one swindled him, and they've been trying to show each other up ever since. I'm sure they don't even care whether anyone else shows up."

"Can you come up with the money?"

"Yes." He stepped back to a safe distance, where there was no chance he would reach out and touch her. "We'll split the prize, right down the middle."

"I can't do that. It's your horse!"

"And it's no good at all without you to train him."

She'd given him a chance; he could give her back this much.

"I've heard you talk, once or twice, about starting a business," he continued. "Something you wanted to do, more than anything. This could get you started, Angel. Enough to put you on solid footing without having to take a partner. The place could be entirely your own."

She tried not to think of it. It was never a good idea to count on something that wasn't sure. It was too tempting. It would give her enough to start out right. She could prove to her father in no time that she was capable of taking over the Meadows. "Partners?" She stuck out her hand.

"Partners," he agreed, pumping her hand once, quickly, before he let go and she felt the touch of the first cool breeze that crept through the garden. "I suppose if you're going to teach me to ride well enough, we'll have to do nothing but practice."

"You! I assumed I would ride."

"Of course not. It would be too dangerous."

"I'm the best rider you'll find, and you know it."

"I know that." No way in hell was he going to entrust his future to anyone else's hands. Not even her small, capable ones. "But you have no idea what a race here is like. It's not a social occasion, Angel."

"I never thought it was."

"It'll be dangerous. With that kind of money at stake, men will do anything to win. Including hurt you."

"I weigh less than you. Angel will go faster with a lighter load to carry."

"Nearly all the men riding will be my size. It will be no handicap."

"It's just ridiculous!" She was not letting this opportunity slip through her fingers to satisfy some male notion of pride. No one could ride that horse the way she could.

He looked down at her, with her arms folded across her chest and her stubborn chin stuck way out. He knew a woman who'd made up her mind when he saw one. It was pointless arguing with them when they got like that. He wasn't fond of wasting his energy.

"Fine," he agreed. When the time came, he'd make certain he was the one riding.

Though it would probably be a good idea if he learned how first.

"I still want you to teach me to ride."

Her eyes narrowed. "Why?"

"Why?" He shifted. "Because it was our original agreement. Backing down, now that you've found the challenge is too much for you?"

"Of course not. I can teach you to ride. I can teach anyone to ride."

"Well, then, let's get to it."

"Just a moment." She jumped forward, her skirts swirling around her ankles. "I want to make an addition to our agreement."

"Oh, no, I'm not that cheap." He grinned. "It would take more than being taught to ride a horse. Though I might be open to negotiation."

"What?" The weak light was just enough to show the darkening of her cheeks. "That's not what I meant at all."

"Oh," he said, sounding entirely deflated.

"Oh, you." He would persist in making her laugh, she thought, just when she was doing such a good job of being businesslike and forgetting that they were alone in a dark, secluded garden with only the moon and a few faded roses. "You were right when you said I wanted to start a business. The thing is, I've been watching you lately, and—"

"You have?" He fluttered his eyelashes. "I'm flattered."

Business, she reminded herself. "I've realized that I'm not all that well versed in some areas. I need to be."

"You want me to teach you to run a business?"

"Yes. To keep books, deal with customers and suppliers, to—"

"Will you do exactly as I tell you?"

"Yes."

"You mean I'm in complete charge in these lessons?"

"Yes."

"You'll follow all my orders?"

"Yes." She barely managed to force the word out through the back teeth she had clamped together. He was using all her own rules against her.

"I think I'm going to like this." He grinned brilliantly, sweeping away the night and darkness. That was the reason she had planned to leave tomorrow. Because he had a smile that could make her forget every single plan and dream she'd guarded so carefully for so long.

"Probably."

They were partners. Friends. Entirely acceptable.

But what she must never do was believe there was a chance for anything more. She couldn't let herself even think that she *wanted* anything more, because it would mean giving up so much.

"I'm going to bed."

He nodded agreeably. "That's probably a good idea."

"Right now."

"I'll walk you in."

"No!" She backed away, bumping her knee against the side of an old stone bench. "Ouch!"

"Are you okay?"

"As much as I'm going to be," she muttered.

"Good. I'll help you back to your room."

"No, I can manage just fine," she said quickly. "You stay here. Enjoy the evening."

"You're sure? I really have better manners than this. I know a gentleman should see a lady to her room."

"Don't think of me as a lady. Think of me as your business partner."

She whirled and scurried away.

"First thing tomorrow?" he called after her.

"First thing tomorrow," she agreed.

She reached the safety of her room, slammed the door behind her, and leaned up against it weakly.

Business partner. She could do that. She was a strong woman.

"A business partner," she said out loud, liking the sound of that. A business partner had a business, right? And that was what she wanted above all else.

She'd take care of it, and it would take care of her, and she'd finally be able to prove she could take care of herself.

J.J. scrawled another set of figures on the scrap of paper and frowned at them.

He had to find a way to not only come up with the money to stake his horse in the race but keep the Rose going through August. It was going to take some tricky juggling.

He sat back against his pillows, propping the paper and the book he'd been using to scribble on against his knee, and watched the morning light begin to leak through the gauzy cotton covering his bedroom window.

It looked as if it was going to be another warm day. Even this early, the sun had a strong, steady intensity that was rare here.

He hadn't slept the whole night through. Not that he ever needed much sleep, but usually he managed to snatch at least a few hours. He should be exhausted.

Instead, he felt the kind of energy and anticipation he hadn't felt for a very long time. Maybe since the early days of the Rose, when he'd first battled to make it, to stay in business against heavy competition. He liked the challenge, enjoyed the heady feel of invincibility.

He idly twirled the pen through his fingers. An hour, perhaps. Then he could go down, grab some breakfast, and meet Angel. Angie. He really should get used to calling her by her real name. It probably wasn't all that flattering to a young woman to be referred to by the name of a stallion. But if this worked, she truly was an angel.

There was only one drawback. For, if he did manage to salvage the Rose, he was going to have to owe his brother-in-law a huge debt of gratitude for the gift of the horse. He wasn't sure how long he could sustain being polite, thankful, and admiring. Of course, Tony might simply expire from the shock.

A hesitant knock sounded at the door.

"Come on in."

The door creaked open a bit and Rose peeked around the edge. "Can I come in?"

"I just said you could. And when have you ever needed to ask?"

She slipped inside, a whisper of pink silk and loose, spun-candy hair. "J.J., I—" She stopped and stared at him. "What happened to you?"

"What do you mean, what happened to me?"

"I mean . . . " She waved her hand at him. "You're a mess."

"Huh?" He glanced down. His linen shirt was

unbuttoned, the crushed, limp fabric hanging straight down, exposing his chest. His white pants were hopelessly wrinkled, the bottoms smudged with earth from his late-night walk in the garden. He ran a hand through his hair, trying to push it back into some semblance of order. "Yeah, I guess I am. Listen, Rose, I—"

"Me first," she interrupted, then seemed to lose the train of what she planned to say. The plump pink curve of her bottom lip quivered slightly.

"Why don't you sit down?" He shoved aside a cascade of loose papers, sending them flying to the floor.

"You have stuff all over the place."

"Yeah. Never mind, I'll clean up later."

"Later?"

Surely it couldn't be so much of a shock. Yes, the staff sometimes teased him about his penchant for neatness, but seeing him—and his room—in a jumble shouldn't have this effect on her. Had he been that rigid about it?

He patted the thick burgundy-and-green quilt that covered his wide bed. "Come on, sit down. It was a long night. What are you doing up so early?"

"Early?" She sat down gingerly, just on the edge of the bed, as if she was afraid it would collapse beneath her.

"I don't know the last time I've seen you up much before noon."

"Yeah, well, a guilty conscience tends to do that to a person."

"Hmm?" Out of the corner of his eye, he caught sight of one of the papers he'd been working on. Yes, that was a good plan. He could delay the next shipment two months. They weren't low, and it wasn't as if there'd be a huge demand, what with half the men out of town chasing that fool rumor.

"J.J.," she said, an odd note to her voice.

"What is it?" he asked softly, pulling his attention

back from his plans. She was frowning, her brows drawing together, putting tiny lines in her forehead. She wouldn't like that, though he wasn't sure why she worried about it so much. They weren't unattractive.

"I'm sorry." She pleated and repleated the loose fabric of her robe, folding it against her knee, the buffed, perfect ovals of her nails nearly the same color as the pale silk. "I'm sorry I didn't come to find you last night. I know you needed me, with losing the Rose and all."

"That's what I wanted to tell you," he began eagerly. "We're not going to lose the Rose, I don't think. Maybe not, anyway. Angel had these idea, about racing Angel—the horse, I mean—in Hermanson's race. She really thinks he can win."

"Hermanson's race? Seems to me I heard something about that. Him and Hooper are at it again, huh?"

"Yes. Can't you just picture it? I'll buy out Stitch, right out from underneath Hermanson's nose, and with his own money. Isn't it perfect?"

"Stitch?" She went pale.

"Yeah. Rose, is there something wrong?"

"Yes. No. Maybe." Her blue eyes shimmered with moisture. "I don't want to lose you!"

"Rose." He took her hand, linked it with his, and gently smoothed the fabric over her knee. "Why ever would you think you would lose me?"

"I . . . " She looked down at their joined hands, at the contrast of her small pale one and his larger, bronzed, elegant hand. So familiar. Yet it was no longer enough. And he didn't even seem to notice that she hadn't been there to support him the night before. "I think maybe I'm not going to sleep in here anymore."

"What?" He sounded puzzled. "You mean ever?"

"I don't know. Maybe."

His free hand came up, and he lightly brushed the curve of her cheek. "If that's what you want."

"I don't know what I want! But I need to find out."
She wasn't making any sense. She only knew she could
no longer go on the way she had been, waiting, hoping,
living day to day, never thinking beyond the next
evening. It had kept her going for so long. When had she
started to need more?

"You still won't lose me, you know."

"I won't?" When had she ever really had him?

"Our friendship doesn't depend on sex. It never
did, Rose." He lifted her hand, pressing a quick kiss to
the back of it. "It never will."

She closed her eyes, trying to imprint the feel of
his hand. His touch was as much a part of her as her
own; she could hardly separate it from all the dozens—
hundreds—of times he'd touched her before. It seemed
as if it should be different this time. Somehow.

"When you've figured out whatever it is you've got
to figure out," he went on, "you just let me know, okay?"

"Okay." That was it. No questions, no probing
for what or why. When she first met him, that had
been such a relief, to be with someone who didn't
insist on poking around in corners of her memories
best left alone. Now it seemed a bit odd. As well as
she understood him, in some ways, they knew each
other so little.

"Well." She opened her eyes, finding him watching
her with concern. She disengaged her hand and grabbed
for the nearest sheaf of paper. "What's this that's got you
so involved you didn't even notice the mess you're making? Must really be something."

"Yes." He grinned, the smile she'd always thought
held all the power of the sun in one small slice of happiness. "I've just been making plans for the rest of the
summer, figuring the best way to get through this. I'm
assuming the majority of our clientele will be out of
town. If you look here, you'll see where I've shifted a
bunch of receivables into September."

"Yes." At least they still had this. "Now, just you wait. I need to re-add these figures. You know I'm better with the books than you are." She smiled, and bent with him over the numbers.

21

"*This isn't working.*" Angie frowned, crossing her arms over her chest. She was standing in the center of the yard, circling slowly, as she studied J.J. making a leisurely loop around the yard on his mount.

"What do you mean? I thought it was going fine. I'm still on."

He'd finally talked her into letting him try the reins. They'd been working on the long rein the whole time, and she kept insisting his seat wasn't right. Well, his seat was about as right as it was going to get, he figured. He might as well start learning to control the horse.

They'd made three circles around her, and he hadn't fallen off yet. He hadn't even had to grab for the mane and hang on, hadn't bobbled too much. He figured this was just about a record. He was getting the hang of it.

"Nope." Angie shook her head. J.J. was as stiff as a city preacher, his legs clamped around the horse's middle, and he was leaning too far back, as if trying to get away from something. Angel had smooth gaits, but J.J. was jostling from side to side in a rhythm that was absolutely unrelated to his horse's own.

"Oh, come now. You just don't want to give me any credit." She looked so small down there, J.J. thought. Not to mention darn cute, her brow furrowed in concentration, her mouth pursed in determination. She had on a plain white cotton blouse that billowed around her small frame and one of her brown riding skirts. Her hair was pulled away from her face, pointing out her sharp, alert features, and her braid was stuffed out of the way beneath her collar.

She wasn't a fussy woman. Not at all the kind of woman who'd worry about you mussing her hair if you got a little carried away in bed. Hell, *she'd* probably be the one to get carried away, if all that energy and intensity were ever completely cut loose. In fact—

Whoa, there, fella. He shouldn't be thinking like that. She was his partner. His friend, even. Rose had severed their relationship not more than what—two, three hours ago? He might be a bit of a jerk, but he wasn't that much of a bastard.

Of course, Rose and he hadn't had a relationship in that sense in ages. He wasn't sure when it had faded simply to friendship and habit. Long enough ago that his body was feeling the drought.

"Why'd you stop?"

"Huh?" He shook himself free of his thoughts to find that he had, indeed, stopped. Angel was standing motionless beneath him. "I don't know."

She gave a small snort of disbelief. "You said 'whoa.'"

"I did?" There was no help for his lessons if he didn't start paying attention to them.

"Yes." She sighed, then waved him down. "Come on, come on. Get off."

"Why? We can't be done. We've barely begun." He stopped, aware of what he'd just said. "Hmm . . . I would have thought that might be your line."

"Just go ahead and dismount, all right. Obviously, we're going to have to try something different."

He barely managed to keep himself from making a few suggestions. He had to get control of the pictures that kept popping into his head. Angie was clearly not the type of woman who had casual affairs, so he could just stop thinking about it.

He swung his leg over the horse's back and slid off. There. He didn't even wobble when he hit the ground anymore.

Angel flicked his ears and gave a quick little side step. J.J. jumped back.

Angie brushed him aside and went to bend underneath Angel's belly, working the buckle of the girth free. She looked ridiculously small next to the horse, the animal's muscular side towering over her.

"Maybe you should let me do that," J.J. suggested.

"Why?"

"Well, he could kick you or something."

The straps fell loose, swaying underneath the rounded side of the horse. "I thought we settled this a long time ago."

"Yes, I know."

"Besides, I've been kicked before."

"You have?" He felt sick. He could hear the crunch of bone, the scream of pain. See the blood dulling her long, glossy hair.

"Sure." Rising on her tiptoes, she reached up and tugged the saddle off. "Anyone who spends as much time with horses as I do is bound to, eventually."

Her voice was so casual, as if she'd merely said, "Oh, yes, I've seen a cow." It was inevitable, she'd said. Why, then, would anybody ever *want* to come near one of these animals?

"Here." She shoved the saddle into his arms, and he grabbed it before it fell to the ground, then juggled it to get a better grip. "Might as well put that away."

The leather of the saddle was warm from the body heat of both horse and man, the leather smooth. "Why do you do it, then? If you know you might get hurt?"

She shrugged, then looked over his shoulder, refusing to meet his gaze. "Maybe it's all I'm good at."

"Don't be ridiculous," he said, more sharply than he'd intended, but he felt a quick jerk of anger at the realization that she thought so little of herself.

"All right then." She squared her shoulders and looked at him then, her dark eyes bright with mischief. "Maybe it's the only thing I'm the *best* at."

"Ah, now that I can believe." The saddle was getting heavy, but he didn't want to go off to the stables now, when she was finally telling him something about herself. "What about your family? Is that where you learned about horses?"

"Now, wait a minute," she said sternly, pointing a demanding finger at the stable door. "You go put that away like I told you. Maybe if you follow instructions really well, I'll answer your questions."

He hefted the saddle more comfortably and started to walk back to the stable, but stopped to glance back at her over his shoulder. "What are we going to do, anyway?"

"We're going to ride bareback," she said.

"Bareback?" A warm wind blew through the yard, sending stray strands of hair whipping around her face and plastering the loose fabric of her clothes against her body. She impatiently shoved the hair away. "You mean . . . together?"

"That's right."

He rushed to put the saddle away.

By the time he returned she was already on Angel's back, firmly bent low over the animal's shoulders. The dull brown cotton of her voluminous split skirt was spread over the side, looking dreary against the healthy sheen of the horse's coat.

"Hop on."

He strolled over, eyeing the small space between her rump and the horse's. They were going to be very, very close, if he were to fit in that space.

"I don't know," he said doubtfully. "I know I'm of fairly average size, but are you sure this will work? Perhaps we should take that overgrown animal of yours."

She laughed gaily, a light, clear sound in the heavy summer air. "*Now* you want to ride Lancelot? After all the times you've insisted it would be Angel or nothing?"

"Well . . . "

"Oh, come on. I wouldn't recommend riding two on him regularly, but he's strong enough to handle it for a time. Might even be good conditioning for him. And, after all, I'm not that heavy."

J.J. measured the distance from the ground to the place on the horse's rump where she evidently expected him to perch. He'd finally mastered mounting. It no longer took him three tries, nor did he have to drag himself across by clinging to Angel's mane. But there were no stirrups this time, no saddle horn to grab.

"Are you coming?" she asked. "I thought you'd figured out how to mount, at least."

He frowned, his pride pricked. Which was, he assumed, what she'd intended. "I've never done it this way before."

"And you're going to let that stop you? I thought you liked to try new things."

"Well, usually, but by and large I rarely risk breaking my neck in the process, either. It's rarely quite so far a fall."

"Would you just get on!"

"Yes, ma'am." If she was just a bit bigger, she'd have made one helluva sergeant. Even if she was a female.

He took a deep breath, two quick steps, reached in front of her, grabbed a hank of mane, and threw himself upward.

"It worked!"

"Uh, yes," she agreed. "But do you think you could, maybe, loosen your grip a bit? I'm rather fond of breathing."

"Oh, sorry." He really did have to let go, he supposed. His arm was wrapped tightly about her upper body, and the inside of his biceps was pressed rather neatly to the side of her breast. She fit there amazingly well, trim and small and warm.

He loosed his fist, releasing the coarse handful of mane. It was a bit awkward, trying to figure out the best place to put his hands. Well, not the best place, exactly, but the safest. Finally he rested them on his own thighs.

"I know it wasn't elegant," he said. "But it worked."

"Yes," Angie agreed. She knew she was grinning like a fool. But she was used to seeing him so much in control. Even the warmth, the friendly welcoming smile he used so often seemed more like a mask than reality; he put it on because it was expected, and perhaps because it made everyone else feel so good. She doubted it really reflected what went on behind that polished surface.

Today, however, there was more. An exuberance in his voice, a warmth in those deep turquoise eyes. She didn't think she was imagining it. The challenge of saving the Rose and the hope that he might be able to pull it off seemed to have loosened something inside him, shaken free some of the emotions he guarded so well.

"You're going to have to, er, hang on," she said. She hadn't really thought this through all that well. Hadn't fully considered that he was going to be wedged up behind her, his chest hard and hot against her back, the long, lean span of his thighs tucked right along hers.

He was quiet for a moment, before his voice spoke softly near her ear. "Where?"

"Um . . . just around my waist, I think, would be best."

His arm slipped slowly around her, lightly, barely brushing her, yet his warmth seeped through the fabric and heated her belly. She looked down, and his muscular forearm looked brown and very male against the polished white cotton of her blouse.

Lord, she was small, he thought, her waist barely big enough to feel through the layers of fabric. Yet there was nothing fragile about her diminutive size; she was all fierce energy and toughness, packed into an efficient package.

Unable to stop himself, he leaned forward, breathing in the smell of her hair. Oh, she smelled good, like horses and—

Hell! What was getting into him? All this bouncing around on Angel's back must be softening his brain.

"If I start to fall, do you really think I'm not going to drag you off with me?"

"You could just let go."

"You willing to take that chance?"

"I guess not." She grabbed his free hand and tucked in a thick length of the horse's mane. "Here. Hang on!"

He hadn't felt whatever signal she gave, but apparently the horse did. Angel immediately went into a steady trot that had J.J.'s back teeth clicking together painfully.

"See there?" Angie said. "That's the problem. You're just not going with it."

"What do you mean?" His spine was being compressed with each bounce. Surely he would be an inch shorter by the time he was done.

"You have to relax, first. Sink down on the back of the horse."

"Relax." When his butt was getting pounded into tenderized beef?

"Yes. Your back should be straight, but you can't lean back."

"Straight." He stiffened his spine. "Ouch!"

"Come on. Close your eyes."

"I would think that would make riding a bit difficult."

"You're not trying to see where we're going right now. You're only trying to get into the rhythm of this."

"Rhythm." The only rhythm he felt was that of his bones rattling.

"Are your eyes closed?"

He pressed them shut. "Yes."

"Good."

"Now, just relax. Slowly. Feel the motion. Let it take you."

He felt the motion. He felt her trim back sliding ever so slightly against his chest. Up, down. Up, down. Her rump was lifting and settling, just a bit, between his legs. A whisper of motion, not enough to be an outright enticement, just enough to give him a hint of pleasure. Away . . . back.

He curled his arm more tightly around her. Why did everyone think that soft women were so feminine? He could feel the muscles in her waist working as she guided the horse, feel the supple firmness of her flesh. No overblown curve of hip had ever been so intriguing.

"There. You've got it!"

"Huh?"

"The rhythm. You've got the feel of it now."

"I sure as hell do."

"I'm going to pop him up to a canter now. It'll be a little bumpier at first, but you'll get the hang of it. How about we get out of here and go for a real ride?"

"Sure, Angel. Whatever you say. Aren't I your star pupil?"

"Of course you are."

She signaled the horse and they clattered out of the gate and into the street. The sharp angle down to the waterfront was probably more than they could handle right now, she thought, so she went up half a block, Angel's muscles bunching with the effort, and turned onto a cross street.

They were riding through a business district, the narrow street hedged with shops, brick-fronted hotels, and small restaurants built of unpainted wood. There were surprisingly few people out for this time of the morning; just last week, when she'd been through here with Tommy, putting up flyers, there'd been a fair amount of traffic.

"Where is everybody?" she shouted back to J.J.

He bent to her ear, and she could feel the soft flow of his breath over the skin of her neck. "They left already. For the new gold fields."

"So quickly?"

"Most of them have been waiting for another strike since the fields down here played out. They just grabbed their stuff and went."

"Oh." The near-empty streets were well suited to riding. There was no place near here that Angel could really stretch his legs, but since they didn't have to stop at the crossings to wait for carriages and wagons, they were able to keep up a decent pace.

The air was warm and heavy, settling in a low haze over the city. It seemed almost as if it had a thickness and texture of its own. She caught the scents of frying bacon and fresh coffee from a nearby restaurant, and, always, the briny tang of the ocean.

It had been so long since she'd ridden double. It was how she'd learned, as a child, clinging to her brother on the back of his pony. But she'd ridden alone for years, except for the occasional lesson she gave to her sisters' children.

Riding with her nieces and nephews in no way prepared her for riding with a man. She was conscious of his size, of the way his body wrapped around her, touching her full length. Of the loose, gentle circle of his arm around her waist, of the slow rise and fall of his chest against her back. She felt the thin cloth that separated them grow damp, and imagined that she could feel the texture of his skin through it.

He was getting the feel of the rhythm now, rising and falling naturally with the horse's paces, letting the motion rock him. Her star pupil. Soon, he would be riding well enough to try it on his own. And then there would be no more excuse ever to have him do this again. Rather a shame he picked it up so easily, after all.

They couldn't ride for long. Two was really more than Angel could carry for any length of time, especially in this heat. So, when she reached the end of the next block, she regretfully turned the horse around and headed him back the way they'd come.

"Are we going back already?" J.J. asked.

Angie smiled. He must be enjoying himself, if he thought it was too soon to go home. And she was glad she'd been able to give him a bit of the joy that riding could be, for it had always been simply work to him. He'd done what she asked, doggedly, determinedly, but he'd never had fun. And it should be fun.

She nodded to tell him yes, and felt the binding on her hair give way. Her hair unfurled behind her, flowing over her shoulder, blown back by the wind.

J.J. had long ceased thinking about the animal beneath him. Lessons would have to come another time. A time when he could concentrate on something besides the woman snuggled against him, the heat of her small body nearly scorching. Her hair came loose, flowing back, a banner of dark silk flying in the wind. He dared to take his arm from around her waist—surely he was safe enough with the grasp he had on Angel's mane—and closed his palm around a handful of her hair.

"Sorry! It's probably in your way."

"It's fine." Surreptitiously, he rubbed the strands against his cheek. God, it was so soft, as smooth and fine as it looked. Surely no fabric, no matter how rich, had ever slid over his skin so silkily.

They'd stopped. Beneath his legs, he could feel Angel breathing hard, his ribs going in and out.

"We're home."

Damn. Already?

"You'd better get off first."

He had to lean forward to swing his leg around, encompassing her even more fully with his body. They wouldn't be any closer if they were in bed together, he thought.

He slid to the ground, hitting the earth with a thud. She sprang off and landed lightly beside him. Holding the reins in one hand, she lifted her face up. She was flushed from the ride, her skin pink and shining with a light film of moisture, her glossy dark hair pouring down around her shoulders.

"See? You liked it, didn't you?"

"Yes."

"It was warm, though." She wiped at her forehead with her forearm. "How come you look so cool? Don't you sweat?"

"I never sweat," he said, looking affronted. "I . . . glow."

"You are completely ridiculous."

"It's part of my charm."

Her laughter was quick and low, her husky tones blending with his low rumble perfectly.

"Well," she said finally, "I'd better go rub Angel down and put him away. He's earned his rest today, as have you."

"Yes." He watched her lead the horse to the stable, the sure, energetic pace of her steps drawing his eyes, and wondered how he'd ever manage to survive another riding lesson without forgetting himself.

Next time, he was likely to do more than *dream* about touching her.

22

"*Okay, ready to start the lesson?*"

"I think so." Angie eyed J.J. nervously. Though she'd asked him to teach her the elements of running a successful business, she wasn't entirely sure she was ready for this. He had entirely too anticipatory a look in his eye. "You aren't going to take advantage of this, are you?"

He grinned innocently. "Why, whatever do you mean?"

"Making me do silly things. Ordering me around. Making demands. Things like that."

He fluttered his eyelashes at her. "Would I do that?"

"Stop that. You look like a gnat flew into your eye, and I'm not buying it for a minute."

"You mean you think I'd try and teach you in a less-than-gentle-and-nurturing way? Sort of like, perhaps, the way you taught me?"

"All right, all right," she said grudgingly, knowing he was right. It had been rather fun, having the right to order him around, and maybe she'd enjoyed it a wee bit too much. "Let's just get to work, shall we?"

They were in J.J.'s sitting room, which doubled as an office. He'd dragged a second chair over to the massive, rubbed oak table he used as a desk and seated her there. In front of them, a daunting array of ledgers, books, and sheaves of paper were piled, threatening to spill over to the floor with the slightest jar.

She'd shown up on the dot of eight, assuming that the first lesson of business was "Be punctual." She figured she'd gotten that one right, if nothing else. The rest didn't look quite that simple.

She'd woken up groggy, for she'd spent the night dreaming. Awake or asleep, her dreams were the same—disturbing, sexy, hot, and filled with J.J.

Once she'd splashed water on her face, dressed, gobbled two pieces of dry toast, and rushed to J.J.'s room, she'd thought she was much too tired to be an attentive student to his lessons.

But then he'd opened his door. He was bright and shiny new, garbed in flawless, elegant white, looking fresh and rested. The skin on his jaw shone from his recent shave, the clean lines of his features caught her anew, and she was suddenly wide awake.

All it had taken was one look at him, and she'd felt that sharp spurt of energy. Alert, aware, edgy, and ready to take on the world.

"Now, first things first." He leaned back in his chair and studied her, his gaze sweeping her from head to toe.

She fidgeted under his regard, tapping her toe impatiently against the floor and walking her fingers along the edges of the stacked books.

"Hmm," he said consideringly.

Finally she could take it no more. "What?" she burst out. "What is it?"

He shook his head sadly. "We simply must do something about your appearance."

"My appearance?" She looked down at her clothes, which seemed unexceptionable to her. They were clean. Her shirt was neatly tucked in. Her boots were free of stable residue. What more could he want? "What's the matter with my appearance?"

"You're simply going to have to dress better than that. At least when you're not in the barn."

"Dress better?" she sputtered.

"Hmm, appears there's an echo in here." He grinned unrepentantly.

"I'm planning to work with my customers, not seduce them."

"Well, I had that impression. Though I probably know more about that line of work."

"J.J., really, I hate fussing with my clothes. And the horses don't care."

"Ah, but your customers will." He tugged on his sleeve, aligning the edge evenly with his wrist. "It's all about image."

"Image."

"Yes. You want to be a businesswoman. One who's taken seriously in a line of work that's dominated almost exclusively by men. Overcoming that isn't going to be easy, even for someone of your determination and skill."

He thought she had determination and skill? She tried to submerge the warm spurt of pleasure, tried to concentrate on the purely businesslike nature of the lesson he was trying to teach. "So you want me to take advantage of that? To be all fashionable and frilly and feminine? I'm not sure that I can manage that, J.J."

"Well, the feminine's not a problem." His smile held a definite edge of wickedness. Oh, he was a dangerous man, absolutely deadly to any woman with a vulnerable heart. "You're going to need to look serious, but smart. Successful. Clean lines, pure colors. Your wardrobe doesn't have to be drab, mind you. You're going to stand out anyway, so you might as well take advantage of it.

"Your aim is not only to be noticed, but to be remembered. Of course you'll have the best horses. You'll have to be an owner to match. You should be fashionable, but not trendy. Nice, trim jackets and skirts, your hair neatly tucked away. Always good quality, nothing fluffy, but still distinctly feminine."

"J.J., do I have to?" She wasn't quite able to hide the plaintive note in her voice. "I don't think I could do that. My sisters are the decorative ones. They're so good at it! I'm merely efficient."

"Angel," he said warmly, "you're going to be damn straight wonderful at it."

Maybe she would. If he could look at her like that, confidence radiating from him, approval gleaming in those beautiful blue eyes, maybe she could. Maybe.

"I'll try it."

"Wonderful!" He grabbed the largest book and dropped it in front of her, stirring up a current of air that blew the fine wisps of hair away from her forehead. "Now then, you're going to have to learn how to keep accurate books."

"So," she said brightly. "Do you think the weather is going to break soon?"

"Yes. Now then, first you need to—"

"Today?"

"—decide what system you want to use, and then—"

"Will it rain, do you think?"

"Angel."

"You know," she went on, "I told you you shouldn't call me that anymore."

"Are you trying to avoid this?"

She grimaced at the stack of ledgers. "Of course not."

"Good. Then shut up and listen. You'll have to decide what type of system is appropriate for your business." He flipped open the book he'd selected. Rows and rows of tiny, squiggly numbers marched across the page in terrifying profusion.

"Oh, God," she whispered. "All those numbers."

She spent the morning listening to him delineate every aspect of the Rose's accounting system. In overwhelming, precise, and utterly incomprehensible detail. Debits. Credits. Receivables. Creditors. And always numbers. Rows and columns and lines of numbers.

She soon gave up. It was so much more interesting simply to watch him talk. He was precise and confident, utterly businesslike in his demeanor. She thought she'd do well to adopt such a mien. Though she had an almost uncontrollable urge to shake his composure, to see if she could surprise a flicker of reaction out of his calm restraint.

"Now, then," he was saying as he indicated yet another ledger. "This is for accounts receivable. They must be kept absolutely correct."

Accounts receivable? Oh, but his intensity was appealing. "Why is that?"

"Because otherwise you won't know who owes you money."

"Can't I just remember?"

"You'll need records."

"Why? I have a good memory, if it comes to that."

"To prove it, in case they decide not to pay."

"But of course they'll pay. Why wouldn't they?"

Now there was a reaction. His jaw dropped open before he snapped it shut. "Nobody likes to pay, Angel. They'd much rather keep their money."

"You've never been to Kentucky, have you? The men are gentlemen. They always pay their debts."

"Better not take that chance. That's the kind of thinking that has put many a nice man in the poorhouse."

She waved her hand negligently. "I'd never sell one of my horses to someone like that, anyway."

"Someone like what?"

"Someone who wasn't a gentleman or lady. Who wouldn't give one of my animals a good home."

"They're not adopting a child, Angel. They're buying merchandise. It's not your place to be deciding their fitness as owners. You should simply be worrying about the best price you can negotiate."

She shook her head. "No. If they're not going to properly appreciate one of my horses, they can't have one."

"Angel . . ."

"No," she said stubbornly.

He scrubbed a palm through his thick golden hair, which fell naturally back into perfect array. "Fine." He shoved the book aside and pulled out another one, flipping through the pages until he found a half-empty page. "Now then, here's where you'll record the moneys you owe."

"Why?"

"Why?" he repeated. The smooth, rich timbre of his voice was becoming oddly strained.

"J.J., are you all right? Perhaps we should do this another time." Any other time. Surely scribbling numbers was the least part of running her farm. If her horses were beautiful enough, the rest would follow.

"I'm fine. Now, why you need to do that is so that you will make sure you have the money available when your bills come due."

"Why don't I just pay it when I purchase something?"

"Because this way you'll have use of the money as long as possible."

"So?"

"So that's how it works. Because you never pay out any money until you absolutely have to."

"J.J., do you know that your right eyebrow twitches a little bit sometimes?"

He glared at her, and she sighed. "All right, I'll trust you on this. Why can't I just hire someone to handle it for me?"

"Because you'll never know if you can really trust them. If you don't understand the books, you're just asking for someone to rob you blind."

"I'll make sure I hire someone good then."

"No one will ever do it as well as you do, because no one will ever care as much. It's *your* business, so this is your responsibility."

She looked over the table of papers. Deadly dull, boring papers. She'd so much rather be out in the stables, working with the horses. She always had, much to her mother's frustration. She'd never had much interest in anything that required her sitting in one place for very long.

"I suppose so," she said woefully.

What was he going to do with her? he thought. She looked so dejected, the delectable curve of her lower lip thrust out, her small, sturdy shoulders drooping. Half of him wanted to tell her to head back out to the stables and forget it; he clearly didn't have the patience to teach this to her. The other half wanted to grab her and kiss her until every single scrap of paper on that table went up in flames.

It was a toss-up as to which urge he was going to give in to first. And he damn well shouldn't be giving in to either.

"I have an idea," he said finally.

"Yes?" She perked up slightly, hope lightening her dark brown eyes.

"I'm going to have Rose teach you about the books."

"Rose," she repeated doubtfully.

"Yes. They're really her responsibility, anyway. She's an absolute genius with them."

Somehow it made perfect sense, that Rose, that

gorgeous, utterly feminine woman would also be a sharp businesswoman who could understand all those blasted numbers. Numbers that Angie had never quite mastered completely. She'd always preferred riding to listening to the teacher, and Miss Pratchit had eventually given up, claiming she didn't know what use mathematics would be to a girl, in any case.

Now Angie knew, and it appeared it was too late to do anything about it.

"I'm sure she'll be able to explain it much better than I will," J.J. continued, his gaze fixed on a spot on the wall behind her left shoulder. Clearly, he was running out of patience with her; he couldn't even trust himself to look at her. "She is the one who keeps them up, after all. Keeping the customers happy, and the management of the staff, are really my responsibilities."

"Oh, come now. Did I give up on you so easily the first time you tumbled off the horse?" There wasn't any way she could ask Rose to teach her this. She was uncomfortable enough in the woman's presence, and it would be completely impossible for her to concentrate on those dadblamed books at the same time.

"Only because you were having much too much of a good time watching me make a fool out of myself."

"I'm not going to let you out of our bargain so easily."

"You said you wanted to learn how to run a business. I don't recall that it had to be me teaching you."

"That's not the point, and you know it."

"You were the best person to teach me to ride. It's obvious I'm not the best one to teach you about bookkeeping." She'd trapped her bottom lip with her teeth, and her lip puffed out, pink and delectable. Her teeth were small and white, with crisp, clean edges that he longed to slide his tongue over and see if they were as even as they appeared.

"Can't we just forget it completely?"

"No, for then I would be totally remiss in my part of the bargain."

"How do you know she'd even be willing to teach me? She has no reason to help me out."

"I'll ask her." He tugged at the high, tight collar on his shirt, feeling the damp heat of the room close around him. He was going to suffocate in here if they didn't get out soon. "She's a good person. I'm sure she'd be happy to help."

How nice. Angie tried to surpress the sharp, nasty bite of jealousy. Obviously, the woman had no flaws. Was that something to hold against her? Except being in her company only served to have Angie remember that she was far, far from the female ideal herself.

"Fine." She wouldn't give in to this. For all her weaknesses, she'd never disliked someone just because that person was so absolutely perfect. If some other juvenile characteristics had been popping up lately—like a ridiculous schoolgirl crush—she could certainly make sure she wasn't giving in to them without a fight. "Where do you think I could find her?"

J.J. looked immensely relieved. "She's down in the main saloon, I think. It's still closed, but she was doing some inventory before we open. Would you like for me to come along and arrange it?"

"No." If he was so anxious to have her out of his way, the least she could do was oblige him. "I'll go ask her myself. Do you think I should take the books with me?"

"Just leave them here. I'm going to go on out the back. I've got a few errands to run, so you two can go ahead and work here."

"Wonderful," she said, forcing an approximation of anticipation into her voice.

"Great." He jumped to his feet. "How about we have the riding lesson later than usual today? The Rose will probably be quiet enough that they can handle it without me, and if we wait 'til sundown maybe it'll be a bit cooler."

"Cooler would be good."

She watched him saunter out the door. In the warm weather, he'd eschewed his usual frock coat, and the loose cotton of his shirt stretched across his shoulders. For a man so lean, almost sleek, he really did have an astonishing amount of muscle.

Picking up a pad, she waved it in front of her heated face. Yes, cooler would definitely be good.

23

"*Don't you have anything better* to do?" Rose slammed the pad of paper she'd been using to keep track of the liquor onto the bar and glared at Stitch.

He was in his usual spot, sitting at the table he'd appropriated. He had his chair tipped back, his battered black hat resting on the table next to a barely touched glass of whiskey.

He was still watching her.

It must have been at least a half hour since he'd moved. He seemed to have no need to fidget, to burn off restless energy. He appeared completely content to sit there and follow her every move.

She'd tried to ignore him, tried to go on with her duties as if he wasn't there. With the amount of time he'd spent watching her in the last three weeks, she would have thought she'd hardly notice his presence anymore.

Not so. Her hands didn't seem to want to be still, constantly fussing with her hairdo or checking the position of her bodice. She didn't dare glance his way, knowing that her gaze would collide with his. And she'd had to count one set of bottles three—three!—times.

Finally she had been unable to take it anymore and whirled on him, determined to force him to either tell her what he wanted or leave her alone.

He tipped his head back, the carelessly trimmed ends of his silver-gray hair brushing his shoulders. "No, I don't."

"I have work to do."

"So do it."

"I can't. You're interrupting me."

"How'm I doin' that? I haven't said a word."

"You're watching me."

He smiled faintly. "I am, at that."

"You're always watching me," she accused.

"So?"

"So stop it! I don't like it."

The two front legs of his chair clunked against the floor as he sat up. "Rose, it's for sure you're used to men watching you."

"Not all the time." She rounded the end of the bar, her skirts swishing with each step. "And not the way you do."

"And how do I watch you?"

"You don't give away what you're thinking." She slowed, realizing she was getting too close to him. He was dangerous, unpredictable, and it wouldn't do for her to get too near him. No telling what he might do. And no telling how she might react to it. "I can't tell what you want."

He picked up his hat, turning it around in his big, rawboned hands, the only wasted motion she'd ever seen him make.

"I think ya know very well what I want."

Needing something solid to hold on to, she wrapped her fingers around the back of a nearby chair. "Why don't you go somewhere, do something, until the summer is over? Your investment will be well cared for. You know that."

"I'm not talkin' about my investment." He set the hat carefully on the table and rose, his lanky height unfolding slowly. "And you know it, don't ya?"

"What are you doing here?" she asked softly, a rare note of desperation creeping into her voice, but she didn't seem able to force it away. Her nerves were stretched taut, ready to snap at any provocation. What was going to happen when they did, she didn't know. She only knew she couldn't go on like this much longer.

"Waitin'."

"You could wait anywhere."

"No." He took a step toward her. When she tightened her fingers, clutching desperately to the chair, he stopped. "Not when what I'm waitin' for is you."

"Me?" she croaked.

"Yes, you." He crossed to her then, holding her in place with the intensity in his pale eyes. "Waitin' for you to be ready."

"For what?"

"To realize that you don't need this place anymore."

Fear, cold and insidious, welled up in her chest. "I'll always need this place."

"No, you won't," he said calmly, his low, hoarse voice soothing her, warming the fear, shrinking it to something less powerful. "You would be better off without this place, Rose. You've held on to it too long, long past the time you needed it. You're a strong woman. You're ready to go on."

"I don't think so." Her fingers began to tingle from lack of blood, so tightly did she grip the chair.

"Yes." He closed the last step between them, close enough so she could feel the warmth from his body, but he didn't touch her. At least, not with his hands. He touched her with the vibrancy in his gaze, with the tender concern in his voice. "I've been alone damn near my whole life, Rose. I'm tired of it. I don't wanna be alone anymore."

"I'm not alone."

"No." He drew one finger down her cheek, softly, oh, so softly. If anyone had ever touched her like that, it was too long ago to remember. "But I think maybe you're lonely."

She tried to force a laugh, something light and gay, to show him how absurd his ideas were. But the sound that came from her throat was strained and heavy, bare and lonely. "What do you want?" she asked again.

"Not too much." He drew back his hand, letting it fall to his side. "Just a little place. A quiet place. Someone to share it with me." His shoulders lifted and fell. "A kid or two, maybe."

"A . . . kid?"

"Maybe. If I'm lucky."

A child. She let go of the chair and wrapped her arms tightly around her hollow middle. She tried to gulp a breath, tried to force the air around the lump in her throat.

"When are you going to tell me about it?" he asked gently.

"About what?" The words were painful, burning the raw tissue of her throat.

"Whatever it is that hurt you so much." He bent, brushing his lips across hers, a soft whisper of hope. "When you're ready to tell me, then I'll know I'll know you're ready to give up this place."

She opened her mouth to tell him she'd never be ready. Tell him what he wanted to hear. Tell him . . . what could she tell him?

"What in the holy horse apples is going on around here?"

Rose jumped back at the irate shout. Angie was advancing on both of them, her eyes snapping with fury. What the hell was she so upset about?

"How dare you kiss him?" Angie positioned herself squarely between the two of them and rounded on Stitch. "And you, Mr. Stitch." She jabbed her finger into his chest, emphasizing her words. It was like a hummingbird attacking a panther. "Don't you have any sense of fair play? Don't you have enough honor to find a woman of your own?"

Oh, my. The little bird was watching out for J.J. Rose suppressed a quick giggle, knowing it wouldn't be appreciated and shocked that she could even think of laughing. A year ago, maybe even a month ago, she would have been violently jealous of any woman thinking she had the right to protect J.J. Now, she was only amused, and a little touched.

Stitch stared down at the small finger prodding his chest. He didn't even attempt to brush her away, though he could have as easily as he would a fly. He lifted his gaze to meet Rose's, and his cool, silver eyes were rich with laughter.

"I think I'll be going right now. Seems to me this is a woman's thing."

"Yes." What a relief. She'd have time before he brought the subject up again, time to think. To be certain she wasn't making a mistake, to decide what it was she truly wanted.

He slipped away and up the stairs to his room.

Rose turned her attention back to Angie, who was glaring in the direction of Stitch's back. Her arms were folded firmly across her chest, and her small foot was tapping an impatient staccato beat.

"Now, then," Rose started.

"How could you do that?" Angie whirled on her, her color high. "How could you kiss him? How could you hurt J.J. that way?"

"Well—"

Angie went on as if Rose hadn't spoken, the impassioned words spilling out of her. "You know that Stitch only wants to take the saloon from J.J. How could you betray him?"

"That's not how it is."

"Oh? Even if it wasn't, you shouldn't be kissing any other man. How would J.J. feel?"

She was certainly an excitable little thing. Rose hadn't really paid that much attention to the young woman when J.J. had hired her; the stables really weren't one of Rose's interests. Though she'd felt a prick or two of annoyance when J.J. seemed inordinately friendly with Angie, Rose had been too preoccupied with her own concerns to worry about it much.

"I don't think it would matter to J.J. one way or the other," she said, wondering if she could poke a little here. Certainly, it would be no surprise if Angie had developed a crush on J.J. But could there be more to it? It took a special kind of caring for Angie to want J.J.'s happiness so badly that she was willing to make sure his relationship with Rose wasn't damaged.

"How can you think that? I know he looks so perfectly unaffected, that nothing ever really touches him. But he really has a very soft heart. You should know that!" Angie accused.

"Is that so?" Angie certainly wasn't what Rose would have thought was J.J.'s type. Too young, too volatile, and too . . . country. But she supposed Angie had a certain appeal. There was that beautiful dark silk hair—though Angie had no clue about arranging it—and dimples were always a plus. And she did have that liveliness, that zest for life. If someone were to take her in hand—perhaps.

"Yes. Don't you care? If he ever found out, he'd be so hurt."

"If he was, then I guess you'd just have to comfort him, wouldn't you?"

Ah, there it was, a quick flash of guilt in Angie's open eyes. She would never make a poker player.

"I wouldn't do that," Angie said softly, all the indignation drained from her voice.

"No, but you've thought about it, haven't you?" Rose grinned suddenly. "Don't worry about it, hon. J.J. and I are no longer . . . " How could she describe what they had been? She settled for the simplest. "Together."

It stopped Angie cold. "You're not?"

"No." Well, now, that was interesting. The girl had nearly quit breathing. Rose clucked her tongue. "You mean he didn't tell you?"

"No," she said, her eyes unfocused. "He didn't say a word."

"Well, isn't that just like him?" Rose patted her piled curls of hair. "He should've told you, hon. Men can be such fools."

"He had no reason to tell me," Angie said crisply. "We're just business partners, after all."

"Uh-huh." Rose mentally wagered how long that was going to last. From the flush on Angie's face, she'd guess no longer than a couple of weeks. Three at the outside.

"Speaking of which, J.J. said you'd be the one to teach me about the bookkeeping."

"Why would you want to learn about that?" She could handle Angie setting her cap for J.J. It even soothed her conscience a bit, knowing that she hadn't left him alone. But there was no way any other woman was touching her ledgers.

"J.J. told you about the race, right?"

"Yes."

"I've got plans for my share of the winnings. I'm starting my own breeding farm. But if I'm going to do it right, I'm going to need to know how to handle the books."

"Good for you! Most women are always countin' on the men to handle the money. Which is why women get taken advantage of so much. A smart women knows exactly what's comin' in and goin' out, so she can get her share. Women are better with money, anyway. They don't have their pride all tangled up with it."

"I'd appreciate it."

"Good." Rose narrowed her eyes. Wasn't like J.J. to let an opportunity like this pass. Snuggled together for hours, bent over a book was exactly what the situation called for. Was he that out of practice? "Why isn't J.J. teaching you?"

"He said you were better with numbers. A genius."

"Well, that is true. Still, he'd probably be the one to ask."

"No," Angie said, deflating like a ripped balloon. "He tried. I think he got a little frustrated with me."

Frustrated. Hmm.

"Are you sure you wouldn't rather have J.J. do this?"

"Yes, I'm sure. I . . . well, you might as well know it. I'm no good with numbers. I never studied enough."

And you can't manage to concentrate with J.J. sitting there next to you, can you? Rose thought. Serve them both right if she sent Angie scurrying back. Still, she firmly believed all women should know how to handle their finances.

"Hon, that's the first thing you gotta remember. It's not just numbers down there on them pages. It's money with a capital M. *Your* money. And that makes all the difference in the world."

24

The sun had just edged into the sea, and darkness was falling with amazing rapidity. The harsh heat wasn't lessened by the disappearing light, and the smell of the sea and summer clung to the city like a haze.

J.J. pulled Angel to a halt in front of the stables—it only took him two tries—and dismounted. The faint sound of music leaked out of the open back windows of the Rose. Not the raucous, good-time melodies that would have poured from those windows a month ago and been nearly obscured by the shouts and laughter of customers, but a simpler, cheerful tune that drifted along on the still air.

He found he rather liked the change.

Lancelot and Angie clopped into the yard just seconds after him. He stepped over to glare up at her. "You let me win," he accused.

"I did not." Her face was sober, but her eyes were dancing.

"You did."

"Oh, all right. Maybe I did. Students need a bit of encouragement now and again, you know."

"I'll keep that in mind." He raised his hand to assist her dismount.

Angie stared at his uplifted hand. "You don't have to help me get down."

"I know."

His hand was unwavering. He simply waited for her, a chivalrous move he'd never before made. In the rapidly falling dusk, his skin was dark against the stark white of his cuff. He didn't have unusually large hands, for a man. Instead, his were elegant, beautifully boned, with lean, controlled fingers that held a deft, sure touch.

Wordlessly, she slipped her hand into his, and the warmth of his palm enfolded hers. She slid easily off the horse and landed lightly on the ground.

He held on to her for a few seconds longer than necessary, his thumb making a slow sweep of the back of her hand.

When he finally let go, she felt bereft, and wanted nothing more than to snatch his hand back. She shoved her hand into her pocket to prevent temptation.

"It was a good ride, wasn't it?" J.J. said. He shouldn't be doing this. He was making her nervous, standing this close; he could tell by the way she fidgeted, by the way her gaze flitted around the yard, unable to settle on a safe spot.

"Yes," she said breathlessly, her slow, southern drawl pronounced. "You're doing very well."

"I'm a fast learner."

She grimaced. "I wish I could say the same."

"You'll catch on soon enough. You have a quick mind." He chuckled. "Besides, I probably had a better teacher than you do."

"True."

"Hey! That's where you're supposed to protest and

tell me what a good job I'm doing. Don't you know how to oblige when a fellow is fishing for compliments?"

"Apparently not." She gave an exaggerated sigh. "One more thing to learn, I suppose."

"I should think so. Can't go around insulting your customers."

Silence fell as quickly as the night. A light breeze suddenly kicked up, and fog sifted in, creeping across the ground, flowing around their feet.

"Well," he said. "I suppose we should put the horses away. Unless you have something else to teach me tonight."

"No. It's too dark for lessons."

Not necessarily, he thought, even as he tried to ignore it. Ignoring his thoughts was getting more and more difficult all the time.

He'd spent years being rigidly in control, convinced that giving in to volatile emotions brought nothing but trouble. It was certainly all it had ever brought him.

He liked things on an even keel. Easy, predictable, orderly. Yet it was her emotion that intrigued him the most. The play of expression across her face, the energy that hummed through her, the ability she had to experience things, instead of just think about them. Unsettling as it was, it was also undeniably exciting, igniting a warm spark inside that he'd thought long extinguished.

She led Lancelot into the stables, and he followed behind with Angel. The darkness was thick now, impenetrable, and he paused to light a small lantern and hang it on the hook just inside the stable door. The yellow glow filled only a part of the space, making it seem smaller, cozier.

"Where's Tommy?" he asked.

"I told him he could have the old gray and take the night off. There was a lecture that he wanted to hear." She whirled on him quickly, concern in her voice. "I'm sorry, that really wasn't my place."

"It's fine," he assured her.

"Do you think he'll be okay?" She fiddled with the reins. "I mean, he's still young. It's very dark out."

"He'll be fine. Tommy's been on his own for a very long time."

"Not quite. Not since you found him."

"He told you about that."

"Yes."

"Oh, well." J.J. shuffled his feet, and Angie smiled at his discomfiture. "I just gave him a job."

"It was more than that, and you know it."

"No." His voice hardened, enough so that the horse's ears flicked back. "Don't make it into something it's not, Angel. I don't take care of people. I don't rescue people. I do it far too badly. The only person I take care of is me. If it helps a few others along the way, fine. But it doesn't have anything to do with me."

"I understand." She did. He wanted to deny it, because it was easier that way. There was no responsibility, and no disappointment if circumstances went beyond his control. But pretending that it wasn't there didn't change it. He was still a man who took care of his corner of the world, and the people in it, in a way that few men ever did.

She turned to unsaddle Lancelot and ready him for the night. J.J. did the same with Angel, finding, to his surprise, that the ritual was becoming almost routine to him. He couldn't do it with Angie's speed and expertise, of course, but he no longer embarrassed himself. And though his heart still kicked into a wild rhythm whenever the horse went faster than a slow trot, he was able to suppress the urge to lunge forward, throw his arms around the horse's neck, and hang on for dear life.

"J.J.? You mind if I ask you a question?"

"Probably not."

"I was wondering about the girls."

"What about them?"

She bent, checking Lance's legs. "How they ended up working here."

"There are lots of women like Maria. One of the first exports shipped up to San Francisco from South America were women. She worked in a brothel down at the Coast. Didn't like it much, so she came here.

"Mei-Ling just showed up one day. She'd been beaten once too often in the crib, and finally ran away from her owner."

"Her owner?" Angie was appalled.

"That's the way brothel owners think of it. Doesn't matter. He came looking for her once. He won't again."

Because you made sure of it, didn't you? She didn't think she wanted to know more. It made her feel vaguely sick.

"And Crystal—she's from back East somewhere. She won't say. I think she just likes the life, if you know what I mean."

He went back to quietly unsaddling his horse, leaving Angie to ponder just how uncomplicated her life had been, and to wonder if she'd ever been grateful enough for that.

She had Lancelot bedded down long before J.J. was finished with his tasks. Bent over to check the hooves, he was silhouetted in the puddle of golden light. His hair gleamed, thick and gold, and she wondered if it would feel as soft as it looked. The faded denims stretched over the tight, muscular curves of his backside and thighs, yet even in such casual clothes, doing such a mundane task, there was that indefinable elegance and sophistication that was so much a part of him.

Nothing in the world sounded quite as appealing as simply standing there, all night, and watching him work. Which was exactly why she had to leave.

"I'm going back to the Rose. Thought I'd turn in early."

"Wait. I'll walk you back."

"I'm tired."

"Wait." He looked up at her, even as he reached to inspect another hoof. The flame from the lamp was reflected in his eyes. "Please," he said softly.

How could she go? Wordlessly, she nodded her assent.

Nothing she could think of seemed worth saying, no topic of conversation that wouldn't reveal more than she wanted him to know. So she simply stared, drinking in the way he moved, the gentle touch of his hands as he checked the horse. The dark stable seemed like a world all its own, distant from realities she was no longer sure she wanted to face. She liked it in here well enough, in the hot, still air and the fuzzy golden light.

Lost in the quiet, she started when he spoke.

"Do you miss your family?"

"Sometimes." Less than she'd expected lately. Her mind had been otherwise occupied.

"Why did you leave?" He led Angel to his stall and sent the horse in with a light slap.

"There was no reason to stay." She realized how little she'd told him about herself. Somehow, she'd never thought he would care to know. "My family has a farm. Horses."

"What a surprise!" His grin was engaging.

"My father is getting older. He'd ready to turn the reins over to someone else, so to speak. I always assumed that he'd give them to me. It's all I've ever really wanted."

He latched the door to Angel's stall, and the horse snuffled quietly. "And he's not?"

"No." Her laugh was brittle. "I'm a girl, you see. Not that it ever seemed to matter when I was doing my share of the work. But he's quite convinced that most customers won't want to deal with a woman breeder."

"Is he right?"

"I don't know. Maybe." Her hair tickled her neck,

and she flipped her braid back over her shoulder. "I have to try. I would think, if the horses are good enough, no one's going to care too much who they have to deal with to get them."

"You're probably right."

"I thought he'd come 'round, soon enough. But I think he thought I'd marry one of the neighbors' boys eventually, and he could turn it over to both of us."

"You didn't want to?"

"They'd all want to tell me how to do things."

"And you want to do it your way."

"Yes." Was that so selfish? To want to care for her horses, horses she'd bred, animals she'd been the one to train and feed and raise, and do it the way she was totally confident was the best for them?

"I understand."

"You do?" She wasn't accustomed to simple acceptance, to respect for her dreams and plans. It was heady, making her giddy with warmth. The air in the stables, sweet with the smell of fresh hay, was thick in her lungs.

"Of course. I lost a lot of workers, in the early days of the Rose, because I wanted things done my way."

"Was it worth it?"

"It made the Rose what she is, if that's what you mean." It wasn't the exact truth, though it was the only answer he was willing to give her. It had made his place successful, but it had also made him lose things he was only now beginning to recognize. "What finally made you leave?"

"I think my father gave up on me." And it had hurt her, more than she realized right until this moment. She hadn't allowed herself to feel the sharp disappointment before, had simply shoved it away and gone on with her plans. "He's been making plans with my two brothers-in-law, trying to figure out how to divide up the place. I heard him talking with my mother. He doesn't want to split it, and my brother has his own place and doesn't want it, so in three years he's going to decide which one to turn it over to."

"And you can't work with either one of them?"

"It's mine!" she said fiercely. "They already have their own places. They only want it because it would make them richer. I want it because it's home!"

"Home." His voice was soft, low, as warm as the night. He stood easily across from her, leaning against the wall of the stables, the soft fabric of his light shirt draping loosely against his body. "Do you realize, this is the first time you've told me anything about your home and why you're here?"

"I guess so." She laughed self-consciously. "My father's not likely to leave it be. At first, I thought maybe you'd let him know where I was. To get me off your hands. One less person to worry about."

"You know you can trust me." He was intently serious, golden light shadowing the refined planes of his face.

She did trust him. Oddly so, perhaps, for it had been a very long time since she'd trusted anyone but her brother. Though she loved her sisters, they were loyal first to their husbands. And her mother, to her father. She'd trusted all of them, until she'd found out he was ready to pass on the Meadows to one of her sisters' husbands rather than take a chance on her.

She wasn't willing to say out loud, though, how much she trusted him, to admit just how completely she'd fallen under J.J.'s spell. She went back to the original subject instead. "Besides, neither one of them is as good with the horses as I am. I couldn't stand to take orders from them, and it would be worse sitting around watching them mess things up."

He threw back his head and laughed, showing a flash of white even teeth, exposing the strong brown column of his throat. "You're so modest."

"When I got old enough to figure out there was only

one thing I was really good at, I decided to be very, very good at it. I have too much pride not to. I'm not going to pretend anything else. It's all I've got."

"I like it." He sauntered over to her, slowly closing the distance between them. "Confidence has a certain amount of appeal, you know. Though I do not, for one solitary second, believe you have no other talents."

She had to force herself not to step back, to show that his nearness bothered her. But it was far, far too tempting to stay close, where all she would have to do was take one small step and she'd be pressed against him. "You have a tendency to see the good in people."

"Me?" He looked so astonished. Obviously, he had absolutely no idea how rare he was, how few other people in the world simply accepted others at face value. How utterly unusual it was to meet a man who didn't judge, who had no expectations that others were always failing to fulfill.

"Yes, you."

"Well." A rueful smile lifted the corner of his mouth. "I'm certainly not going to try and disabuse you of so flattering a notion, even if you are wrong. It would be impolite of me, wouldn't it?"

"Yes, it would."

He gave a slight, formal bow and offered her his elbow. "May I escort you back?"

"Of course." Yet she didn't take it, merely stared at his proffered elbow, trying not to believe that there was something more to his playful courtesy than a passing amusement and natural charm.

He and Rose weren't "together" anymore. She'd tried not to think of it, all through the evening, as they'd ridden through the narrow, hot, empty streets. As she'd watched him, gilded from the small circle of lamplight, care for his horse and put it away. And now, as he patiently waited to escort her back to his saloon.

For it had absolutely nothing to do with her. She'd

be foolish to believe that it did. Even if it did, she didn't want it to. Believing in things like that was what kept so many woman from achieving what they were meant to in this life.

But it was too tempting. She slipped her hand in the crook of his elbow and they left the stables, pausing for J.J. to extinguish the lantern. With the flame gone, they were cloaked in sudden, encompassing blackness. There was an intimacy in that, in being linked only by touch, hidden by darkness from the rest of the world. They stepped out into the yard. Angie's foot landed in a small dip in the earth, and she nearly stumbled.

J.J. caught her. "All right?"

"Yes, of course," she mumbled, embarrassed. She was not a clumsy woman.

"Let's just stop for a moment, for our eyes to become adjusted to the dark."

The air, warm and sweet, settled around her shoulders like an old, soft blanket. The cotton of J.J.'s billowy shirt was thin, and beneath her fingers Angie could feel the hard, sinewy muscles of his forearm.

She had never before stood alone in the dark with a young, handsome man. Had she missed so much? Her heart beat low and hard, breathing slowed to a pace that seemed to match the flow of the honeyed air.

Perhaps she had missed something vital. She only knew that, now, it felt like all else was pale compared to the texture and smells of being lost in the black, hot night with this man.

A gust of hot wind bellowed through the small yard, blowing her loose clothes against her skin. High above, someone lit a lamp in one of the back windows, a flare of light that illuminated a rectangle of pale gold on the ground below.

"How accommodating of them. I suppose we can safely find our way back now." His voice was every bit as warm and sweet as the night.

"Yes."

Neither moved. Unwilling, tempted, overwhelmingly drawn, she finally turned to him, to find him watching her with eyes shadowed by the night.

What was it about this woman, he wondered, that made him content—more, happy—to stand in a deserted yard on a sizzling summer night and listen to the subtle ebb and flow of her breathing?

The faint glow from the window bathed half her face in light. There, right there, on the soft curve of her cheek, was where he could put his finger, and if she smiled, would be the appealing, flirtatious dent of her dimple. He hadn't even realized he'd memorized the spot so exactly. Had he spent so much time looking at her?

"Or we could just stay here," he said when they made no move to the Rose.

"Could we?"

It was the faint hope in her question that did him in, the sweet-sad wishfulness. He was lost; no power in the world could have prevented it, could have brought him back to sense and control in time to stop.

He bent his head, wanting to drink in the flow of her breath, certain she would taste like spice and sugar, like the slow, whiskey-tinged sound of her voice.

It was her warmth that caught him off guard, though he should have known. Should have realized that the flame that burned so brightly in her would have translated into heat. And never once, in all the time he'd spent dreaming of her trim, muscled body, had he thought that her lips would be so soft, as tender as the first bloom of spring.

He touched her nowhere else, just the whisper-soft pressure of her lips and the light resting of her hand on his arm, yet he felt as close as if they were naked, bare to her touch, her presence.

So this was what it was all about, she thought.

She'd vastly underestimated the lure, the utter devastation, the whirling, spinning feel of a man's mouth gently resting against hers. Right at the moment, for that instant, she would have given anything to have this moment never end.

He gave a harsh, ragged growl, his arms came around her waist, and he pulled her to him, pressing her tightly against the lean, hard length of his body. Her world grew hazy, lost to sensation. When had her mouth opened? she wondered vaguely. When had his tongue found that slow, easy rhythm that thrummed through her entire body?

God, she was sweet, he thought, her arms clutched around his neck as if she never planned to let go, her body almost vibrating in his arms. She was shivering now, and he was unbelievably pleased that he could draw that response from her.

He was shaking himself, shudders that coursed through his body and resounded in his soul. He was cold at his back, but his front, and she, was so warm.

Cold? It was raining, icy water that soaked his hair and ran down his back. He pulled away, holding her by her upper arms.

She stared up at him, water sluicing down her face, slicking her hair against her head. She looked dazed, her eyes huge and dark as the night.

Oh, God. He'd nearly done it, nearly pulled her down in the hard dirt and made love to her right there. He'd been that far gone, so lost to reality that he'd had no concept of where or when or why. Had only thought of the way she felt, the way he would twist and shudder when he touched her.

He'd totally lost control, had been completely abandoned to passion. How had he come to that? To the point where the world could have fallen around his ears and he would have been powerless to stop it—and he wouldn't even have cared?

"I—" He paused, unable to think what to say, to explain that he could not do that, could not allow himself ever to feel that. He wiped his eyes, dashing away the cold water that blurred his vision. "I'm sorry. I can't. I'm . . . sorry."

He turned and escaped to the Rose, running through the rain and the night and the cold to the familiar haven of the Rose, the place where he was never lost to passion and abandon.

And she was left alone, standing in the icy, hard shower, trying to wash away a feeling she had never wanted and would surely never feel again.

For if she could not rinse it away, she would spend the rest of her life remembering and longing for it to come once more.

25

"Rose!"

She jumped as her door crashed open and J.J. bellowed her name. The needle she'd been using to mend one of her gowns pierced her forefinger, and she frowned as a bright crimson drop of blood marred the shiny pink satin.

"What?" she asked crossly.

J.J. stood braced in the doorway, his hair darkened by water and plastered against his forehead, his sodden shirt clinging to his chest.

"I have to talk to you."

"You're dripping on my floor."

"I have to talk to you now!"

"Oh, all right," she agreed, amusement creeping into her voice. "You seem a bit excited." She'd never seen him quite so flustered.

"I'm not excited!"

He was actually shouting. She laughed and waved him into the room. "All right, come on in. What do you want?"

Stepping into the room, he slammed the door shut behind him. He opened his mouth, then shut it again, seemingly unable to decide what to do with his hands. He ran them through his hair, shoved them in his pockets, then pulled them out and crossed his arms in front of his chest.

Curiosity got the better of her. "What is it?" she asked again.

'Why don't you move into my room?" he asked in a rush.

"Move in?"

"Yes. You have to do it right away, Rose." He'd run straight to her room, heading for the only solution that occurred to him.

Rose would protect him. His conscience seemed to be developed enough so that he couldn't make advances to one woman while being involved with another. Thank God.

Lord knew he needed help. He was becoming obsessed. He was losing control.

He could not let it happen. It was the wrong thing for Angie, and God knows it was the wrong thing for him. No telling what horrible thing would happen if all these damn feelings got a good hold and took over.

"Oh, J.J." Rose sighed and set aside the gown she was working on, its fabric glowing a soft pink in the low light of the single lantern. Inexplicably, her eyes began to shimmer. "I don't think I *can* move."

"What?" How could she do this to him?

"No."

"Oh, my God." He dropped down on the bed next to her and it bounced with his weight.

"I'm sorry, J.J.," she said, her voice quivering slightly.

"No, that's okay." If that's what she wanted, he couldn't ask anything else of her. Only, what the hell was he going to do now?

"If you need me, you know that—"

"No." He smiled at her, noticing for the first time that her hair was loose, curling softly against her shoulders, so different than her usual elaborate hairstyles. It matched a new softness in her cool blue eyes. "I like your hair."

Like a self-conscious girl, she reached up to smooth her hair. "Thank you."

"Is this really what you want, Rose?"

"Yes. No. Maybe." She swallowed visibly. "I don't know. I just know I can't do anything else."

He took her hand, lifting it to his mouth, hoping she would know how grateful he was for all the years of friendship they'd shared. "If there's ever anything you need, anything you want, *anything,* all you have to do is ask."

"I know that." Her fingers tightened around his.

He looked around the room, taking in the swaths of rose-colored fabric, the billowy quilts, and the heavy rugs. "We never spent much time in here, did we?"

"No. We were always in your room."

"Mine." Yes, that said it all, didn't it? Yours. Mine. Never ours. "Rose, why do you think that we never . . . I mean, why were we not . . . " God, what was he thinking of? What was he trying to ask? He felt new, muddled, cut loose, as if all the precepts he'd clung to for so long were now gone.

"Why we never became more than we were, you mean?"

He nodded.

"Maybe we were simply too much alike," she said.

"What?" He slid his fingers over the slick surface of the silk comforter, brushing them back and forth.

"It was easier that way. Neither of us was willing to risk any more."

"Maybe."

"Or maybe we're both just shallow and completely unlovable."

"That's probably it." His quick smile was brilliant, and Rose caught her breath. Even now, his smile had the power to make her heart trip in double time. That had been the thing that had drawn her to him in the first place, that had rescued her from the darkness where she lived for so long. She would be forever grateful for that.

He gave a heavy sigh, then rose to leave. Her question stopped him.

"J.J., why did you never ask? When you found me in that bar, down on the waterfront, why did you never ask what had brought me there?"

"I guess I thought, if you wanted me to know, you would have told me."

He was nearly out the door when she spoke again.

"You should have asked."

Maybe he was going to make it after all.

J.J., firmly ensconced at a back table in the main room of the Rose, stared glumly into his half-empty glass of whiskey.

He'd made it through a whole week, and he hadn't touched her again. Of course, he'd managed it only at the expense of his mood, which had become downright churlish and had all of his employees looking at him strangely. It was perfectly clear that they were all perplexed as to what had gotten into their even-tempered employer.

Crystal had, purely out of the goodness of her heart, offered him a free hour or two of her services, to improve his temper, and now was insulted at the speed with which he'd refused. Josiah had kept the whiskey coming. The rest had simply stayed out of the way.

His riding lessons had been torture. He'd taken to getting out there before Angie, having his horse saddled and himself mounted up by the time she arrived. Safely perched several feet off the ground on Angel's back, at least he couldn't touch her. Throughout his entire lesson, he kept his hands and his lips as far as possible from where he longed for them to be.

He was guiltily aware that he wasn't holding up his end of the bargain. He'd let Rose take over all of the business instructions, for he was damn certain he'd never be able to spend hours on end closeted away with Angie in a room, huddled over books, receipts, and business plans.

He took a quick gulp of his whiskey, noting that the quality was not quite up to par. He'd have to speak to his supplier.

He blinked, trying to clear his eyes of the gritty sting, for the other thing he'd sacrificed was his sleep. He knew darn well he couldn't survive many more of the hot, erotic dreams that kept slipping in as soon as he closed his eyes. So he'd thrown himself into work, checking the saloon from top to bottom, poring over books, and spending a helluva lot of time on tasks that he knew were utterly useless. But it was better than thinking about her.

Frowning at his glass of whiskey, he pushed it away. Despite his career, he wasn't really that fond of the stuff. Drowning his urges in liquor wasn't making them go away. It only made him more susceptible to stray fantasies.

A low hum of conversation swirled around the room. It was probably the best crowd they'd had since most of San Francisco cleared out in search of golden dreams. Halfway through the evening, there were perhaps a dozen customers scattered through the place. There were the usuals, of course, people too old or too lazy or too smart to go chasing after rumors of yellow rocks. But several young cowboys had come down from the hills. Lean faces already weathered by days spent in wind and sun, they were devoting themselves with equal enthusiasm to depleting his store of whiskey and entertaining the girls.

Perhaps there'd be enough customers tonight to keep him occupied with real work. Scooping up his glass, he headed for the bar, ready to send Josiah back to the kitchen and take over tending himself.

Yes, all these people around would be good. It would keep him from dreaming too much. Keep him from becoming so lost in memories of warm, clean lips and fresh, cool rain that he'd forget that he had nothing to offer her, that the last thing in the world Angie would want was a simple, uncomplicated, and very temporary good time. Not that that was such a bad thing. Just a little fun in bed had a good deal to recommend it, but he was pretty sure Angie wouldn't see it that way.

Yes, with enough distraction, maybe he would make it through one more night without touching her.

Maybe.

"Rose, are you sure about this?"

"Don't be silly. Of course I'm sure. Never been more sure of anything in my life." Rose flipped once more through the dozens of pink-hued gowns stuffed into the wardrobe in her room.

Rose had corralled Angie just as she was heading downstairs for the evening. "You're not wearing that, are you?" Rose had said, aghast.

Angie had looked quickly down at her usual white cotton shirt and brown split skirt. It looked no different than it always had. "I believe I am."

"No, no, no." Rose had clamped on to her wrist, pulled her into the room, and sat Angie on the bed while she proceeded to plow through her wardrobe.

In the last week, Angie had found herself in an odd, surprising friendship with Rose. She'd never suspected that she'd have anything in common with this beautiful, worldly, sophisticated woman with her clearly eventful past and a head for numbers. Angie had expected the time with Rose to be awkward at the least.

It had been nothing of the sort. Rose had a generosity of soul Angie had rarely seen, was a surprisingly patient teacher, and didn't seem to have even a bit of residual possessiveness toward J.J.

But that still didn't mean that her new friend had the right to criticize her clothes.

"Really, Rose," she protested as she watched Rose tug out a frilly candy-pink confection, frown, shake her head, and toss the dress away. "I am perfectly happy with what I'm wearing. It's comfortable."

"Hon, what has comfort ever had to do with women's clothes?" She waggled her finger at Angie. "We're going to blow J.J.'s eyes right outta his head. Just you wait."

Angie felt her jaw fall open. She hadn't realized she was quite that obvious. "Why would I want to do that?" she asked carefully.

"Oh, Angie. Just who do you think you're foolin'? This is Rose. Nobody knows what goes on between a man and a woman better'n me."

Holy horse apples. Did the whole world know of her absurd crush? Did J.J.?

"Rose, I'm am not trying to catch his eye. I don't want to. There's no future in it."

Rose stuck her head right into the bleached pine wardrobe. Her voice was muffled. "So whoever said we had to be thinkin' about a future? What's wrong with just havin' a little bit of fun?"

So what was wrong with it? The thought was sinfully tempting, as seductively appealing as anything she'd ever known. What was wrong with it was she was unconvinced of her ability to leave it at that, to stop dreaming dreams she had no chance of making come true. Better to keep concentrating on the ones she had some control over.

"Why would you think J.J. would be interested in just a bit of fun, even if I were?"

Laughter tinkled as bright as a new bell. "Hon, you're kiddin' me, right? I know that man better than anyone in the world, and I ain't never seen him so rattled. If that ain't a fellow that's got a burr under his saddle, I don't know what is."

Rose straightened and stared at the lush billows of fabric, frowning. "Damn it, everything I have is pink. That's the wrong color for you entirely."

"I suppose so." A delicate, feminine color like that was reserved for women like Rose.

"Absolutely. You need much warmer colors, to show up the honey in your skin and echo all that fire in you."

What was Rose babbling about? The only reason Angie was still sitting here was that the one thing she had learned in the last week was there was no stopping Rose when she had her mind set on something. She hadn't let Angie give up on the books, either, going over and over the numbers until a few of them sank into Angie's head. Rose had that same look on her face right now. "Rose, nothing of yours is ever going to fit me, anyway."

Rose stopped pawing through her wardrobe and looked over Angie's chest, her forehead creasing. "That is a problem."

"So I can just go ahead and go down like this?" Angie asked hopefully.

"Nope." Rose snapped her fingers. "I have just the thing." Rising on her tiptoes and digging on the top shelf, she pulled down a long, flat box. "I bought this once cause it looked so pretty in the window, only to find out it washed me out so bad I looked like an old sheet that had been bleached within an inch of its life. It'll be perfect."

"Rose, really—" What had made her think that she even wanted to go downstairs tonight? She should have stayed safely tucked away in her room where she belonged. She'd given in to the desire to just sit in the corner and look at him, and now she was getting what she deserved for being so weak.

"Now, hush up, hon." Rose set the box down on the bed and studied Angie, who shifted uncomfortably under her regard. "First, we gotta do somethin' about your hair."

"My hair? It's hopeless, Rose. It's so straight, it never stays where I put it, no matter how my mother tried to curl it."

"Straight, you think?" Rose's deft fingers quickly undid the braid, smoothing Angie's hair over her shoulder. "See?"

The long fall of her hair was rippled from being tightly braided all day. "It's all crinkled up. It always does that. It doesn't help it stay curled."

"We're not going to curl it. We're going to leave it down."

"Leave it down?" Just like that?

"Sure. It has beautiful shine, and now with all this texture—it'll look just right."

"But, Rose, that's so plain. I can't leave it just like that. And, anyway, it'll get in my way."

"What are you going to do that your hair will get in the way, hmm?" Rose teased.

Angie gave up, and Rose set to work.

26

There was no way in hell he was going to be able to pull it off.

All it had taken was one look at Angie coming down the steps toward him, one glimpse of the precise, quick way she moved, and his heart had turned over. He'd begun having the most unbelievable fantasies of vaulting over the bar, ignoring the reactions of all of the people in the saloon, rushing up the steps and sweeping her into his arms, and carrying her off to his bedroom.

And then the fantasies really started.

He had to stop it. He grabbed the nearest rag and began scrubbing down the bar, putting enough elbow grease into it to rub the varnish right off the wood. Except he couldn't help watching her out of the corner of his eye.

Rose was with her, whispering something to her when they reached the bottom of the stairs. Angie shot her an annoyed look, then squared her shoulders and started marching.

Straight over to him.

He forced his gaze to the surface of the bar, searching for something—anything—better to look at. Something safe. Anything that would keep him from messing up both their lives by giving in to this outrageous passion he most definitely did not want to have.

"Hello."

Lord, she was right there, standing just on the other side of the bar. The husky, smoke-and-southern tinged note to her voice never failed to make him crazy, even when all she said was one word.

He backed away, until he bumped into the shelf that ran along the back of the bar. "Hello."

She was standing there waiting for something, her fingers twisting together. Behind her, Rose was frowning at him. What the hell did they want from him?

He was caught, lost to the rose color that bloomed across the delicate curve of her cheek, entranced by the way her lips parted as she breathed. Why was this happening to him? Why now? Why her? He'd liked his life the way it was. He didn't need his body to get fixated on one woman and the one thing he wanted so desperately to do with that woman.

All right, perhaps there was more than one thing. Maybe there were hundreds of things, but they fell into the same general category.

"Do you . . . notice anything different?" Angie stammered.

Different? She was as alluring as always, a breath of color and life into the steady, even roll of his existence. He took a deep breath to steel himself, to keep him from giving in to the need to say something to make her smile, to make her flash those dimples that made him feel as giddy as a young man. God, shouldn't he have gotten this out of his system years ago?

What was the matter with Rose? She was waving wildly behind Angie. "Different? No, I don't think so."

Hell. Wrong thing to say, obviously. Her shoulders drooped, and the sparkle in her eyes extinguished. He wanted nothing in the world so much as to make it come back.

"J.J., you idiot—" Rose began.

"Stop, Rose." Angie cut her off. "It doesn't matter."

"But—"

"No," Angie said briskly. "Promise me, all right?"

They were up to something. Women with their heads together, plotting. Now that was trouble if he ever saw it.

Finally Rose gave in with a deep sigh. "Oh, all right."

"I'm just going to sit over there in the corner for a moment, all right?" Angie slipped away to a table apart from the others. His gaze followed her; Lord, had any woman ever walked like she did, quick, short steps that made her hips swing in that subtly intriguing motion?

"J.J., how could you do that to that girl?" Rose shouted at him.

"Do what? I haven't done anything to her." Hell, he'd been trying as hard as he knew how not to do anything to her, for Christ's sake.

"Are you really so slow? Didn't you even notice what she looked like?"

Of course he noticed what she looked like. He always noticed what she looked like, the way her head tilted when she listened to him, the way her eyes flashed just before she threw one of those quick little sallies his way.

"It took us damn near an hour to get her ready," Rose was ranting on. "Her hair, her dress, everything. Don't you realize she did it for you, you stupid man!"

Now that Rose mentioned it, she was wearing something different, a long, easy slick of gleaming red silk that nipped in sharply at her waist. It had flowed around her as she walked to the table where she was now hidden in shadows.

"Dandy that you are, you would think you, of all men, would at least notice her clothes!"

The only interest he'd ever had in clothes was how they would aid in projecting the image he'd chosen. He'd always suspected women had never quite figured it out, and Rose's current ire was proof: they didn't know that the only interest men had in women's clothing was what parts of their bodies were revealed by it.

"Why would I notice her clothes?" he said crossly. "All I ever notice is *her*."

Rose stopped her yammering. "Oh, so you *are* interested."

"What difference would it make if I was? We want two different things out of life."

"You should go over to her. Tell her how nice she looks."

"No."

"What could it hurt?"

Too much. He was shocked at the knowledge of how much it could hurt. "Leave it alone, Rose. I have to. For her sake."

Reaching across the width of the bar, Rose hauled off and slugged him. "Go over there, you fool!"

"I can't." If only it were as simple as Rose kept trying to make it, if there were a way to make it neat and clean.

She glared at him, then gave up, making a strangled squawk of disgust before she flounced away.

J.J. went back to work, mumbling under his breath. "Women."

Damn it, Rose thought. If she'd had any clue what an idiot J.J. really was, she never would have started this. She'd stopped a few steps from Angie's table, debating what she could possibly say, watching as Angie studied the room through eyes that were unfocused, wounded, and probably not seeing anything at all.

She could tell her that J.J. was simply trying to protect them both. It was a good part of the truth. But

Angie wasn't going to believe it; she was too vulnerable, and too young in all the ways that counted.

There was no help for it. She'd started this, and now she had to fix it. Squaring her shoulders, Rose headed for Angie, and nearly tripped over the large feet that were right in her path.

Though she couldn't say she'd forgotten Stitch was there—he had too much presence and took up entirely too much space for that—she managed to overlook it most of the time, simply because she was becoming accustomed to it. Apparently, this time he wasn't going to let her ignore him.

He was in his usual position, slouched on a chair pushed up against the wall, a bottle of whiskey and a small glass on the table in front of him.

Except this time, there was something completely new.

"What are you grinning at?"

"You."

Men. Idiots, the bunch of them, never saying anything that made a lick of sense. "Well, you can just cut it out."

He didn't, the lopsided smile looking strangely young in his weather-beaten face.

"And just what is it you find so funny?"

He nodded at J.J. "You've given him up."

"So?" she said defensively, crossing her arms over her bosom.

"So that's good."

"Don't you go thinking that means I'm going to come to you."

"You will," he said with complete confidence.

Egos, every single one of them. How she'd love to shake that confidence, just for a minute.

"I'm finding I rather like my freedom. Perhaps I'll test it out a bit before I settle down. It's been a long time."

His grin faded, and she felt inexplicably sad. It was what she wanted, but she wanted to bring it back.

"If you must," he said. "I'll be waiting when you're ready."

It was the last thing she'd expected from him. Her mouth fell open and she snapped it shut.

"It's nice," he said. "What you're doing for the two of them."

"Lord knows how long it would take them if they were left to their own devices. I'd like to be around to see the fireworks."

"Are you so sure they belong together?"

"No." She glanced over at Angie, who was still sitting alone, so uncharacteristically quiet and still. "But I do know that playing it safe isn't going to get you the brass ring, either. It's better to have the regrets."

"Seems to me you could take a bit of your own advice."

He was so male, lounging in the spindly wooden chair like a satisfied mountain lion who had nothing left to prove. Faint light from the gas lamps flickered across the sharp bones of his features.

"Maybe I will," she said. "Maybe I will."

Amazing that he hadn't noticed the dress right away. Now that it had been brought to J.J.'s attention, he couldn't keep his eyes off of it. It flowed softly over her, shimmering with light every time she breathed, highlighting the slight, delectable curves of her breasts. It shone with a soft light and was no more lovely than her hair, which rippled loose down her back and begged a man to bury his hands in it, to see if it felt as silky as it looked.

He knew it would, damn it.

She'd looked so sad, all night long, sitting there alone at the side of the room. He'd tried not to watch her, tried to keep himself busy, to focus on his job and remember all the reasons it was best he stay away from her.

He'd failed utterly. He bunched up the towel he'd

been using to, once again, wipe down the bar and threw it away. He was going to go to her. He was going to tell her how beautiful she looked, how totally alluring she was, and the consequences be damned. It would bring the light back into her eyes, and right at this moment, it was the only thing he cared about. Somehow, he'd find a way to make sure it went no further than that.

One of those blasted cowboys beat him to it. A young, lanky fellow with a square chin and a shit-eatin' grin strutted over to her and bent to ask her a question.

Tell him to go away, J.J. mentally urged her. He's not the man for you, either. He's just a no-account cowboy looking to have a good time. He'll never treat you right.

Angie smiled tentatively and nodded, and the cowboy grinned wider, yanked out a nearby chair, and planted his bony butt on it.

J.J. scowled and reached for a bottle of whiskey.

He spent the next twenty minutes giving customers the wrong drinks as he tried not to watch Angie and that damn cowboy. He'd wanted her sparkle revived, but not like this. Every time the cowboy bent over her shining head, J.J.'s stomach clenched. Each time he heard the quick bubble of her laughter, his hands curled into fists. And whenever there was the small flash of her dimple, he had to grab the bar to keep himself from rushing over and announcing she was only supposed to smile like that for him, damn it.

The scraping sound grated on his nerves when the cowboy slid his chair so close to Angie's that his knee nudged hers. J.J. thunked a glass down on the bar so hard that beer geysered up and over the edge.

That cowboy was getting just a touch too friendly now, looming over her as he bent his head to listen to something she had to say. It wasn't that loud in here; no way he had to get that close. He said something, and Angie stopped smiling. She shook her head and leaned away.

The cowboy's features went hard. He grabbed

Angie's arm, yanked her close, and planted a sloppy kiss right on her open mouth.

J.J. was over the bar and across the room in an instant. He caught fistfuls of the man's shirt and pulled him to his feet, jerking him close until they were almost nose to nose. Well, maybe nose to chin. He was a mighty tall cowboy.

"Just what did you think you were doing, putting your hands on her like that?"

"What?" The cowboy sneered. "Jes' gettin' friendly like."

"Looked to me like she wasn't interested in being friends."

The cowboy tried to pry himself loose, but J.J. held firm. "Then she shouldn'ta had such a nice chat with me, should she? I ain't lettin' no tarted-up bar girl get above herself with me—"

J.J.'s fist smashed into the cowboy's jaw with a loud crunch, sending them both crashing backward, through a chair and onto the floor.

The bar erupted. The girls squealed and ran for cover, from where they could safely call encouragement and jeers. One of the other cowboys, jostling for a better view, elbowed a gambler out of the way. The gambler promptly brought a nearby chair down onto his head.

Soon the melee filled the bar with the sounds of crashing glass, hoarse shouts of triumph, and grunts of pain. Tables toppled and a young cowboy took an enthusiastic dive off the steps, right into the midst of the chaos.

J.J. grinned and threw another punch at that sonovabitch who'd had the nerve to touch his Angie.

He'd absolutely, completely lost his mind.

An hour later, J.J. stood in the center of the room and surveyed what had become of his bar, and himself.

Glittering shards of glass spilled across the scuffed

floor. The chandelier was askew. A disgusting, smelly puddle leaked from an upended brass spittoon.

Grimacing, he flexed his hand. His knuckles were split and stiff. He looked down; dark splotches decorated his white suit. One sleeve was nearly ripped off his jacket, hanging awkwardly on his shoulders.

Damn it all, he felt good.

After he tossed that ass of a cowboy right out into the street, he'd closed down the place. He'd shooed out all the rest of the customers, several of whom had chosen to continue the brawl outside. Then he'd sent Rose, Angie, and the rest of the girls scurrying up to their rooms right before he dismissed the rest of the workers.

Stitch had been the last one to go. He'd stood at the base of the stairs, taken a good look at the place, then nodded to J.J. "Nice right," he commented, then shuffled off to his own quarters.

So J.J. was alone now, alone with the mess he'd created. He was aghast at the damage done in so little a time, but he couldn't quite bring himself to regret it.

He'd never, ever lost control like that in his entire life, not even when he'd been young and stupid and angry. And, damn it, it had felt good. It had been exhilarating, punching that cowboy who so richly deserved it. He liked the way the excitement had pumped through his veins, the way outrage had made his heart pound. It had felt good not to think for a change, just to *do*.

Insanity was the only explanation for it. If he didn't find a way to get himself back under control, no telling what he might do, what kind of fix he might get himself into.

He knew the cause. He was obsessed.

With Angie. With every quick, energetic move she made, with every equally fast leap of her agile mind. With the memory of her body pressed against his in the rain.

There was only one solution.

He'd simply have to seduce the woman and get her out of his system.

27

J.J. woke bright and early the next morning, ready to tackle the shambles downstairs, and more than ready to put his plan into action.

He tugged on his faded denims, pulled a loose shirt over his head, ran his fingers through his hair, and headed downstairs. Even the sight that greeted him failed to dim his mood.

A large slice of bread served as breakfast. He brewed a big pot of coffee, figuring they all were going to need it today, grabbed himself a mug, and headed back into the main room.

The damage wasn't nearly as bad as it could have been. It was mostly on the surface. First, though, he had to get rid of some of the useless, broken furniture.

He hefted the nearest damaged chair over his shoulder, tucked another one under his arm, and dragged them both out into the street. He'd start a rummage pile out there. He figured most of the stuff would get taken by people who would find some use for free things, and then he'd get the rest hauled away.

He propped the front door open, letting in the cool, damp morning. Despite the temperature, he worked up a light sweat, lugging out the broken furniture and planning his mode of attack.

His conscience was only slightly tweaked by what he planned to do. It had ceased to make any difference whether or not some mythical future husband of Angie's would be annoyed to find out that someone had got there first. The man should just be grateful to get a wife like that at all, damn it, J.J. thought as he threw a split chair unnecessarily hard on top of the pile.

Angie insisted that all she wanted out of life was her own horse farm. Though it seemed to him to be a strange dream—who wanted to spend the rest of their lives mucking out stables?—he would accept her at her word. Nothing he planned to do would interfere with the future she had planned for herself. And, hell, he intended to make damn sure that she came out of this with some good memories. Some hot, erotic, and extremely sensual memories.

The pile of sticks, torn seats, and broken tables was nearly as high as his head by the time he finished lugging out all the furniture that wasn't salvageable. He stood in the doorway and dusted off his hands, surveying the room.

Hell, he rather liked it this way. The room looked more open and spacious, uncrowded by so much stuff. It wasn't as if he had so many customers packing the place that he needed all those chairs. Maybe he'd just leave it half empty for a while. Give them all room to move around. Even dance, if they took a mind to. Long as nobody danced with Angie but him.

He grabbed a broom and started to sweep up the crushed glass that crunched under his boots and sparkled in the soft morning light.

*   *   *

Angie was certain her feet made no noise on the steps, but J.J. looked up as soon as she reached the bottom of the stairway.

He straightened, leaned on the broom, and grinned at her, and everything she had planned to say evaporated.

"Ah, it's a nice morning, isn't it?" Idiot! Certainly there was something better to talk about than the weather.

"Yeah, the fog broke early today. What are you doing up? I thought you'd still be recovering from all the excitement."

"I wanted to help clean up."

"It's not necessary."

"Yes, it is." It was taking a chance, stepping closer, but she couldn't seem to help herself. "I'm sorry. It was my fault."

"Don't be ridiculous." He laughed. "Most excitement we've had around here in ages."

His lower lip had been split, and was puffy and discolored. She touched it lightly. "You were hurt."

"You could kiss it and make it better."

She snatched her hand back. "You're awfully calm about this." She indicated the remains of the room. "It's such a wreck."

"Aw, heck, it was time to redecorate anyway. It's only stuff."

"Only stuff?" What was he talking about? This couldn't be J.J., who was wont to lecture the employees if the whiskey and gin bottles weren't alphabetized. "Are you sure you're all right?" She reached up and placed her palm on his forehead.

"Couldn't be better." The broom clattered to the floor, his hands were on her waist, and he pulled her to him with a speed that left her breathless. Among other things.

"What are you doing?" she squealed.

"I haven't quite decided yet. There are so many possibilities." He bent his head and nuzzled her behind the ear, and her knees threatened to buckle. "Your ears." His mouth was warm, his breath hot, and she was getting dizzy. "Your neck, of course." He moved to the part he'd named, a quick glide of his tongue against the side of her neck that made her want to pull him down on the nearest table.

"Why are you doing this?" she gasped.

"Mostly because it feels good. Don't you think it feels good?"

She was going down for the last time. His palms were creeping up her ribs, his thumbs sweeping to within an inch of her breasts. Just barely, she managed to grab on to enough sanity to pull herself from his embrace and throw herself two quick steps backward.

"Just what do you think you're doing?"

"We've been taking things much too seriously around here, don't you think? I'm tired of it. Time to lighten up and have some fun." He reached for her.

"Now, see here." She threw her arm out in front to stop him and pressed the back of her other hand to her head. She had to think. How was she supposed to think when the thoughts were whirling in her head like drunken birds and she was so darn hot she felt like she should go jump right into the bay?

"I see just fine."

Oh, he was dangerous, with the turquoise blue of his eyes gleaming, and that brilliant smile that would make any woman want to fling herself at his feet, just in case he might look at her that way again. He advanced on her steadily.

"No!" She backed up, bumping into one of the tables.

"No what? No, don't come here? Or no, don't stop?"

"Yes! I mean, no! I mean . . . " Holy horse apples, she was confused. "I can't talk."

"Don't worry. You don't need to talk."

He planted his arms on the table on either side of her and leaned over her, his breath hot and sweet and utterly tempting. She bent backward, her back arching to get away, to keep from hurtling herself at him and pressing her mouth right to his.

"I don't know what's going on," she protested.

"Oh, now, Angel, you know better than that. I know you're innocent, but you're not naive. You'll figure it out."

"Now, just a minute—"

"Oh, it'll take more than a minute. A whole lot more than a minute."

She gaped at him, knowing that she must look like a fool with her jaw hanging half to the floor and a red flush staining her cheeks.

She ducked under his arm and slipped a few feet away. If she had any brains at all, she'd run right up the stairs right now and lock herself in her room. She couldn't seem to make herself move. Her blasted curiosity was getting the better of her again; she couldn't wait to hear what shocking thing was going to come out of his mouth next.

He pushed away from the table, turned to her, and grinned again, a smile that was full of anticipation and pleasure. Oh, Lord, surely that wasn't meant for her. No man had ever looked at her like that.

"J.J., you've been drinking, haven't you? You did too good of a job drowning your sorrows."

"Not a bit." He took one step toward her. "Why don't you come here and smell my breath and see?"

"Oh, no." She wasn't that stupid. No way was she leaning forward, that close to his mouth. Even if he wasn't up to something, she didn't trust herself that much. It would be far too easy to decide to taste for herself.

He gave a heavy sigh. "All my hopes, shattered. Cruel woman," he said forlornly.

She laughed; she couldn't help it. She knew that

was exactly what he wanted but, darn it, it was too much fun. All the while she'd been growing up, she'd watched her sisters flirt, seen them entrance every man in the neighborhood with nothing more than the tilt of their heads and a husky giggle.

She'd thought she was utterly inept at flirting. She hadn't known that she simply hadn't had the right partner before. And she hadn't known that it was so much fun.

"There, there. You'll survive." She reached out to pat his shoulder consolingly. It was all he needed. He took her hand, gave a quick tug, and pulled her snugly up against the hard length of his body before she even had time to blink.

"Lord, you're quick."

"No, I'm not. I promise you, Angel, I'm not quick."

But he was close. Close, and hot, and hard, and intoxicating, and his head was lowering over hers, down and down and—

She escaped just in time, skittering out of his grasp the instant before his lips met hers. It was a near thing; she knew if she'd felt the entrancing touch of his mouth, she would have been completely lost.

"Now, J.J." She wagged her finger at him. "Just give me a minute to think, okay?"

"You think too much."

"There's no such thing. You, of all people, should know that."

"I'm reformed. I'm not going to think so much anymore. From now on, I'm going to go with what I feel."

She had no idea what to make of this. Last night, when he'd leaped to her defense, she'd been flattered. It had been unexpectedly nice to have someone play knight in shining armor, even if it hadn't been necessary. She'd been warmed by the realization that he must have been watching her, that he had been ready to fight for her without a moment's hesitation.

It hadn't taken her long to get over it, to realize that it hadn't meant anything. He'd simply acted on instinct, on that reflex he had to protect the people in his world. It had nothing to do with his feelings for her; that had been clear from how quickly he'd dismissed her afterward, briskly brushing off her thanks.

Now this. She was thrown completely off balance, lost to something entirely beyond her realm of experience. And undeniably, overwhelmingly tempted simply to give in, to fall into his strong arms and his hot, blue gaze, to forget that she needed to worry about things like the future.

"Why would you even *want* to do this? I'm not your type, and you know it."

"How do you know that? If you saw what happens to my body every time I see you, you wouldn't say that."

He wasn't giving her any time to think. He was sneaky, insinuating one arm around her waist, letting his mouth descend dangerously close to hers.

She jumped back.

"Stop it. Don't touch me," she ordered. If he touched her, there wasn't any way she'd manage to make the right decision here, and the right decision was absolutely crucial.

"How am I supposed to seduce you if you won't let me touch you?"

"S-seduce me?" He'd said it so easily, as if he were merely asking her to lunch. He was so calm, and she was on the verge of hyperventilating. "Whoever said anything about seduction?"

"What did you think this was all about? I thought I was being perfectly obvious."

He was utterly gorgeous, elegant and sophisticated and golden. And far, far too dangerous to her future. Any woman in her right mind would turn him down, but Angie was quite certain she was no longer in her right mind.

"Now see here." She pressed her hand against her heaving chest, trying to calm her racing heart. "You can't seduce me."

"I can't?" His boyish frown was almost as appealing as his smile. "How disappointing. Are you quite certain?"

"I think so," she said, praying that she was right.

"Think?" He brightened visibly, light flashing in his pure eyes. "There's a chance then, isn't there?"

"No, there's not. I didn't mean that at all." He grabbed her hand and busied himself kissing her wrist. She was sure he could feel the pulse beating there, so heavily was her heart pounding the blood through her veins. "I told you not to touch me."

"Well, now, that's not very sporting of you, is it?"

His mouth opened as he spoke, and his tongue was warm and moist as it grazed the tender skin inside her wrist. "What do you mean?"

"I don't know how I am to seduce you if I'm not even allowed to touch you."

"I told you, you're not going to seduce me!" She pulled her hand away from his hot mouth and shoved her fist into the safety of her pocket.

His grin was utterly wicked. "I'm not sure you should count on that."

"I said you're not going to seduce me, and that's that! If I don't want to be seduced, I won't be. I'm not that weak."

"No, you're not weak. Thank God."

"Good. We're agreed."

"Yep." He folded his arms across the breadth of his chest, and she was vaguely disappointed that, with them in that position, he couldn't be planning to try and touch her again. "I'm going to try and seduce you, and you're going to try not to give in."

"I don't think that's what I agreed to."

"Isn't it?"

"Nooo," she said slowly, not entirely sure of anything anymore. She couldn't have agreed to let him try and seduce her, could she?

"Of course, just to make it fair, you're going to have to let me touch you sometimes."

"No!" If he touched her, she'd probably end up trying to seduce *him*.

"Wow. I must be even closer than I thought, if you're so close to surrendering that you can't even let me touch you."

"That's not it." She couldn't tell him how close he was to the truth. He'd waste no time in pressing his advantage.

"That's good. I'm so glad we agree that I can touch you after all."

"No!" she shouted, horrified. How had it come to this? She was quite certain she'd made herself clear. "How about . . . " She pondered her dilemma for a moment. "How about you can touch me only where I'm not covered by clothes?"

There, that should do it. It wouldn't give him much to work with.

Her relief lasted only until she saw his gleaming, satisfied grin. He looked like a man who fully expected to get what he wanted.

She was suddenly sure she'd just made the most dangerous bargain of her life.

28

She was ready.

Angie tugged at her restrictive collar and nodded at her reflection in satisfaction.

Every square inch of skin possible was covered. Her boots were laced up to her knees. Her split skirt was tightly buttoned, and she'd added a knotted sash for good measure. The sleeves of her blouse came halfway down her palms, and the neckline bunched up underneath her chin. She was swaddled from head to toe.

Now if only she didn't feel as if she was going to choke to death. She also needed to figure out how the heck she was supposed to ride like this.

This morning, she'd escaped just after making that ridiculous bargain with J.J. She still wasn't quite sure how he'd maneuvered her into that one. She'd fled up to her room, but not before he called after her that he'd meet her for his riding lesson just after lunch.

It was nearly one o'clock now. She would delay a bit longer, put it off as long as possible, if she wasn't absolutely sure he'd make note of the fact that she was late and assume it was because she wasn't up to the challenge of fending him off.

She wasn't entirely sure she was.

Sucking in a deep breath, she tightened the knot on her sash. There. Let his clever fingers get that untied, she thought in satisfaction. Though she'd probably have to cut it off herself when it came time to get undressed tonight.

She turned in front of the mirror, checking her attire one last time. She was going to sweat to death, but that was better than the alternative.

She'd have to be a nun to be more covered up than she was. Surely she would be safe like this. What could the man do with a few bare inches of her face and hands?

On further reflection, she snatched up an oversized, floppy hat and jammed it on her head. Now properly armored, she marched out the door to meet her fate.

J.J. took one look at her and burst out laughing.

He'd been waiting for her out in the yard. He'd been ready a good fifteen minutes early, so as to get a good jump on her. So to speak.

Angel was already saddled and tethered to a post. J.J. had every intention of keeping his hands free, and he didn't want his concentration divided, so he'd made certain his tasks were complete before Angie arrived. This way, he'd be free while she was busy. Too busy to fend him off, he hoped.

As soon as he saw her, wrapped in acres of fabric, striding out from the Rose with that grim, determined look on her face, he knew she was close to caving in. If she hadn't been right on the verge of it, she wouldn't have gone to so much trouble to try and protect herself. It was all he could do to keep from rubbing his hands together in anticipation.

"Decide to join an order, did you?"

She scowled at him fiercely. "No. I just thought it was a bit brisk today, that's all."

J.J. squinted up at the summer sun. Though there certainly wasn't the heat that there had been before the rain, it was far from cool. "I see."

"I'm going to saddle my horse." She rapidly disappeared into the stables.

He followed. It took a moment for his eyes to adjust to the dim light inside. By then, she was already leading Lancelot from his stall.

By damn, she was alluring. He'd spent the entire morning after she left, as he swept and lugged and washed, planning precisely what he was going to do to her.

None of those fantasies was one bit as arousing as simply watching her move. The energy, the life—she fairly threw off sparks as she dashed around the stables. He just knew she'd start to hum with heat the instant he touched her.

She buckled the halter and turned to fetch the saddle blanket. When she saw J.J. standing there, she stopped cold.

"Do you need something?" she asked crossly.

"Oh, yes."

"You know where everything is."

"I surely hope so. But I'll wait until you're done."

He watched the comprehension dawn on her clear, sharp features. "Oh, no." She shook her head wildly, almost dislodging that sorry hat, and had to clamp it back on her head. "If you don't have a reason for being in here, get out."

"I have a reason."

"I mean a legitimate reason. Something to do with horses."

"Well, okay, I've never tried it that way, but I've heard—"

"Stop!" She nearly strangled on the word.

"Stop what?

"Looking at me. Grinning at me. Talking to me."

"You're not leaving me a whole lot of other options, then." He swooped, catching her hands and pulling her off balance toward him. She stiffened, holding herself away.

He linked his fingers with hers, careful not to let any part of him touch anywhere she was bundled in all that absurd fabric.

"J.J., I—"

"Hush. I get to touch you, remember?"

"Only where . . . " Her voice trailed off. Only there, she thought, as he tasted the place where her ear met her jaw. Oh, dear. She felt her heart pick up speed, and knew he could feel the rapid thud of her pulse where he kissed her.

How could she have thought this was a reasonable bargain? How could she have let herself be talked into it?

The only logical explanation was that she'd rather liked the idea herself. Liked that he might woo her, that he would touch her, that his thumb would softly rub the back of her hand the way it was right now.

She'd thought this would be a safe way to experience just a bit of what all those other women got to, all the things her sisters whispered about when they thought she wasn't around to hear.

But it wasn't safe at all. How could it be, when his tongue was flirting along the edge of her high collar, and it was all she could do not to tilt her head back to give her more access?

She jumped back, away from him. "I—I've got to get this horse saddled," she stammered. She'd half expected him to be annoyed with her for not allowing him his part of the deal.

He didn't look annoyed. His eyes were very blue,

hot as a desert sky, and his even features were touched with a hint of color. He was smiling, but not one of his stock, practiced smiles she'd seen him use before. This smile was all searing, tempting, powerful anticipation.

"Holy horse apples," she muttered under her breath. Get ahold of yourself, Angie. This would never do. She'd rip off her clothes and fling herself at him long before the summer was up at this rate. Then what was she going to do? More interestingly, what would he do?

Trying to ignore him—an impossibility if ever there was one—she went ahead and readied the horse, knowing that J.J. was watching her. Knowing that he was plotting and planning her downfall, the rat, yet unable to shake being extraordinarily pleased that he was.

She rubbed the softness of Lancelot's nose, then checked the bit one more time, certain she could feel the warmth of J.J.'s gaze on her back. Darn it all, it seemed like he didn't even have to touch her to touch her.

J.J. didn't know when was the last time he'd had so much fun.

It had been years since he'd had to work for sex, to play these games of seduction and lure. He hadn't realized how alluring they could be, in and of themselves. The planning, the fantasies, the careful observation, the light conversation that had so many undercurrents. It was the best foreplay he'd ever had.

Half of him was tempted to draw it out, to savor the anticipation. The other half was damn certain he was going to burst before he ever got to lay one hand on the woman.

Her head was bent over the horse's nose. Her braid slipped over her shoulder, and it exposed a tiny, tempting section of her neck. So small, barely enough room to place a kiss, and he was utterly caught by its enticement.

He knew she felt his approach, for she went still as he slipped up behind her, the tension vibrating through her small body. But she didn't move away, didn't say a word of denial. God, was she waiting for his touch?

He blew gently on her neck, a warm current of air that stirred the fine hairs. Her scent came to him, warm and sweet and completely woman. His tongue stroked her there, a bare touch at the base of her hairline, and he felt her shiver. Closing his eyes, he let the world narrow to the touch of his mouth on her exquisite, soft skin.

Her shoulders squared, and she tried to swat him away as she would a fly. "Stop that."

"Why?" he murmured against her cheek.

"Because you're annoying me, and it's interrupting my work."

He stepped back and chuckled when she grabbed her horse and dashed out of the stables as if it had just caught on fire.

Yes, he thought in satisfaction, it wouldn't be long now.

29

He was going to die.

J.J. yanked his pillow out from under his head and hurled it across the room. It kept bunching up under his head, annoying him, and it was keeping him awake.

Except he'd be lying to himself if he really thought that was what was keeping him awake.

It had been going on for two weeks. Two weeks in which he'd woken up every morning certain that Angie would come to him sometime during that day, that she'd give in and tumble over into the sensuality that shimmered about her with every quick step she took. Two incredibly long weeks in which he'd retired to his bed every night, alone. And more frustrated than he could ever recall being.

His windows were wide open, letting in the damp, cold night. Haze sifted across his room, blurring his vision. It was far too cold to be sleeping with the window open, but it was the only way he could think of to bring his overheated body down to a reasonable temperature. He refused to resort to dumping a bucket of ice water on his head. He wasn't that far gone.

Yet.

He'd spent every second that he could manage with her. It wasn't always easy; he suspected Angie had taken to hiding herself away whenever she could, for she spent even less time in the saloon than ever before.

But she'd never come right out and told him to go away, or asked to go back on their bargain. He wouldn't have had the heart to keep trying if she'd truly seemed distressed, if she'd actually asked him outright to stop.

Instead, every time she laid eyes on him, her big brown eyes would darken. It was so easy to read, the longing and anticipation mixed with apprehension. She couldn't seem to pull herself away, but couldn't seem to bring herself to give in completely.

He'd spent all those sleepless nights thinking up new ways to touch her. He knew her body in a way he'd never known a woman's body before, a richness of tiny, intimate details that added up to *her*. The way she smelled in the morning, just after her wash, all soapy and floral and clean. And the way she smelled at night, spicy, warm, womanly.

He shifted restlessly, feeling as if he were ready to burst from his skin. How much more of this could he take?

He lay there, in that dark, hazy place between wakefulness and sleep, between fantasy and dreams filled with burning, naked skin and smoke.

He could almost smell the smoke, as if these unbearably heated visions had ignited his bed, and he chuckled hoarsely at the thought.

Blinking, he tried to clear the fog from his brain and his eyes, newly aware that he could scarcely see the foot of the bed through the darkness. Must be exceptionally foggy tonight.

He gulped in a deep breath, and it was harsh, tinged with smoke.

Smoke! No one who lived in San Francisco could ever take smoke lightly, not after living through the devastating fires in the early part of the decade, fires that had roared through the slap-dash wooden buildings and leveled everything they touched.

He grabbed for his pants and jumped into them, hastily buttoning them over his naked body. If there was a fire somewhere, he'd be ready to go. That was how they'd all survived, by pitching in to save whatever was sparked by the destructive flames, no matter whose place it was.

There was a loud clatter of hooves, thundering by, quickly fading into the distance. Someone was in a hurry.

Perhaps it was down at the docks, at the over-stuffed warehouses. He was heading for the door, ready to go out and check it out, when the sound stopped him dead.

A faint whoosh, and a distant crackle.

No! He leaped for the window and stuck his head out, looking down. Where? Not here. Please, not here.

The back of the Rose, the far distant corner. He squinted against the haze, swearing at the thick fog that cloaked his vision.

There, a faint, dreadful, orange-red glow, creeping up the side of the Rose.

J.J. dived for the door. It resounded against the wall with a huge crash even as he shouted.

"Fire! Fire!"

He dashed into the hallway, finding, to his relief, that the air was clearer. It couldn't have gone that far, then.

There were shrieks, the soft, rapid tattoo of bare feet, and people began to pop out all along the hallway.

"Get out!" he hollered. "There's a fire."

The girls were fast, gone down the stairs in a flash of loose fabric and bare skin.

Rose appeared from her room, a swish of pink silk and pale hair. "J.J.?"

He gave her a quick squeeze of gratitude for her calm. "Just get out. I'll be right behind you."

"Let me do something."

Stitch was still shrugging into a loose black shirt when he came out of his room. "What should I do?"

J.J. jerked his thumb at Rose. "Get her out of here first, okay? Then check and make sure everybody's outside. Then we'll have to get a bucket brigade going."

Stitch nodded and hustled Rose toward the stairs. J.J. turned and took off down the hall at a dead run.

He hadn't seen Angie.

Damn it, why had he put her in the last room? Right above the corner where he'd seen the fire.

Fear was hot and acid, churning in his gut, burning the back of his throat. Even as he knew that it couldn't be that bad—not yet—he couldn't prevent the stabbing, searing picture of her frightened face.

Please, God. Please.

The loud bang of the door shattered in his head. "Angie!" he shouted. Waves of gray fog and hazy smoke rolled to him, past him, out the door. It was uncomfortably warm in the room, and the soft hiss of the fire was just barely audible.

"Angie!"

"What?" The voice from the bed was cross. "Go away. I'm sleeping."

"There's a fire."

"Please, leave me alone. You can seduce me tomorrow," she said sleepily.

Huddled down into the bed, she looked absurdly small among the piles of pillows and blankets.

He didn't waste any more time arguing with her, simply yanked off the covers and scooped her in his arms.

"What?" she squawked in outrage.

They were already through the door and halfway down the stairs. "I told you, there's a fire."

He felt her sudden stiffness. "Where?"

"Here." His feet thundered down the stairs.

"Shit, J.J." She jerked up, finally awake. "Put me down. We'll run."

"Not a chance, Angie. You might fall asleep again."

He beat a path across the empty space of the main room.

"This is a ridiculous conversation."

"I know." He shouldn't be grinning at the way "shit" had popped out of her mouth. He knew he was going nuts, but he didn't realize he'd gone completely around the bend. But he was just so damn relieved that she was safe and sound.

They burst right out the open door and into the street. J.J. set her down and took a quick head count. Everyone was there but Stitch.

"Where is he?"

"He went next door to get us some help."

"Good. Let's get to work."

There was a large reservoir behind the stables, kept there and filled ever since J.J. and David had first built the Rose. Helped by a half-dozen men from the neighboring boardinghouse, there was soon a solid line of people from the water to the Rose, passing dripping buckets from hand to hand, Stitch at the tail of the line, J.J. at its head.

The fire had been started outside, at the back corner, where there was the telling, charred remains of kerosene soaked rags. It had licked up along the inside wall, almost crumbling it, though it still looked fairly solid from the outside. But dousing the flames hidden inside the wall was proving to be an exhausting task.

J.J. had tried to keep Angie out of it, tried to stick her safely away in the stables, wrapped in a warm blanket. He'd underestimated her toughness, and she, clad only in her nightgown, had taken her place in the line next to Tommy and passed on the heavy buckets without missing a beat.

The girls had clustered helplessly around until someone shooed them into the barn. Rose had devoted herself to serving glasses of water and a few sandwiches to the men fighting the blaze.

The fire was finally out. Dawn came, bringing gray, only marginally effective light. J.J. sent everyone off to bed with thanks for their help and a promise that drinks for them were on the house, permanently.

He shoved his hands in his pockets. Squinting through the thick, smoky fog, he stared at the blackened back corner of the Rose. The damage was minimal; it wouldn't take more than a few days to get the place back into shape.

He wondered if he should give up. He swallowed, and his throat was raw from the smoke he'd inhaled.

Was it really worth it? Had he endangered people's lives because he was too stupid to let go of something when it was long past its time, just because the place was his?

Angie's hands were cool as she slipped them around his waist, hugging him softly, and leaned against his side. He drew a deep, ragged breath. Never before had she touched him first.

"You should get some rest."

"I'm not tired."

He slipped his arm around her shoulder, warmed when she didn't move away. She fit against him so sweetly, and he realized that he couldn't remember the last time a woman's touch had been only that. Not a prelude to something more, but a comfort, a companionship, a sharing.

Her hair was loose, straggling down around her face, and a large streak of soot smudged the sharp lines of her face. He'd never seen anything quite so appealing.

"How about you? Shouldn't you be resting?"

"It's odd. I feel too jumpy. Like I've got all kinds of energy left." Her face was sober as she studied the dark splotch that marred the side of the Rose. "We were lucky. It could have been worse."

"No. No one was intended to get hurt. They wouldn't have started such a small fire otherwise."

"What do you mean?"

He studied the few threads that were left of the cloth that had been wedged up against the wall. "It started only here, not all along the side."

"Someone started it?" She sounded dazed.

"Hermanson."

"Are you sure?"

"Who else?" She shivered, and he rubbed his hand along her upper arm to warm her. "I told you what kind of man he was, Angel. He wants what he wants. This was just a warning. If he'd wanted it gone, it would be gone."

"What are you going to do?"

"I'm not sure. I can't prove it. We'll just wait him out, for the moment. It's not that much longer. I'll think of something."

She was shaking now, her body vibrating against him. He liked the feel, if not the cause.

"You're cold."

"Maybe a little."

"Come on." They walked toward the door. "I'll tuck you in."

Her room proved uninhabitable. The closest to the source of the fire, it reeked of smoke; on the outside wall, the silk wall covering was darkened and singed. J.J.'s throat threatened to close when he thought of just how dangerous it had been.

"Come on. You can sleep in David's old room until we get this repaired."

"Oh, I couldn't—" She flushed, stammered, and he was charmed.

"What are you thinking, Angel? All the other rooms are filled. There's a whole sitting room between us."

"Oh." Was that wishful thinking that had him catching a note of disappointment in her voice?

J.J. left her in the sitting room, tucked carefully on a burgundy-striped couch with a spare blanket in her lap, while he went to fetch some warm water. She tried to relax while she waited, tried to let sleep begin to creep up on her.

She should have been exhausted. Instead, she felt light, her heart tripping into a wildly rapid beat.

The soft, gray morning light was filtering into the room when J.J. returned and carefully shut the door behind him. He was still wearing only his pants, and the bare expanse of his chest was nearly too much for her. It was the one thing she knew she shouldn't look at, yet she couldn't seem to tear her eyes away.

His pants rode low on his hips, his skin was a dusky bronze, and even in all her dreams, she hadn't imagined he would look like this. Lean, nearly sleek, long muscles that shifted smoothly under tawny skin. Just a hint of golden hair sprinkled over his smooth chest, just enough for her to want to touch it and see if it would feel as soft and springy as it looked.

He'd washed before coming back in, thick hair darkened by water and dripping on his shoulders. His skin was still damp, gleaming softly when he moved, and she knew she was probably lost.

It wasn't fair, she thought. How was a woman expected to withstand this? No woman could possibly be that strong. Especially not her, who didn't have the will or the experience to resist.

God, she was lovely. He knew they both should have been completely sapped of strength, but all it took was one look at her and life began to pump through his veins.

She was so small, and it was so misleading. She had more strength and fire in her than anyone he'd ever known. She'd lugged those buckets with the best of them. The water had sloshed out, on her, and her nightgown was still wet, clinging to her, and the dark shadows of her nipples were clearly visible through the damp cotton.

He gulped and sat down on the small table in front of the couch, setting the pan of warmed water next to him. Water dripped back as he picked up a soft cloth and wrung it out with a strong twist.

"I'm sorry about your place," she said softly, in that low, husky drawl that never failed to surprise him. Never failed to arouse him.

"It doesn't matter." It was a shock how little it mattered. It could be fixed. "For a moment, I thought I might have lost you."

His hand was gentle under her jaw as he lifted her face, brushing the cloth softly over her cheek, wiping away the remnants of the night's work. An ache settled into her heart, into her soul. He couldn't possibly mean that the way it sounded.

"You called me Angie." She was mesmerized by the subtle stroke of his fingers against her skin, the slow glide of the warm, wet cloth. He was bent close to her, so close she would need only to lean forward a few inches and she could press her mouth to his. Even after all her dreaming, it surprised her just how much she wanted to.

"When?"

"When you were carrying me. It's the first time you've ever called me that."

"Yeah, well, don't get used to it. I say all kinds of things when a fire is raging, Angel." One was raging now, starting slow and creeping up inside him, threatening to take over the last rational thought in his head.

"I can do that," she said when he dipped the cloth in the water once again.

"You never let me have any fun." He deftly evaded

her attempt to take the cloth, and she gave up. Why bother? It felt too good, and it was far too tempting simply to let him do what he was so intent on doing. She was rapidly discovering she was shamefully vulnerable to temptation.

She'd nearly tumbled over the edge a thousand times in the last weeks, every time he brushed his finger along the edge of her jaw or his lips whispered over her brow.

Only a raging terror of what she might become if she allowed it had kept her back. It would be so easy, she thought, to allow him to cloud her mind, to let her dreams and plans get pushed away by pure, intoxicating physical sensation. She'd seen it happen to many women, and she'd always assumed she was immune.

Instead, she found she'd simply never before met the man who could tempt her.

"There." He smiled down at her. "Got rid of all that soot."

She snorted, trying to make it sound casual, when her heart was thumping in a way that was about as far from casual as she could get. "I'm not sure it matters. I'm used to running around with smudges on my face."

"You're right, it doesn't matter." He dropped the cloth into the pan with a plop. His hands came up to cradle her face, his palms warm and wet. "You're beautiful no matter what."

She tried to laugh, tried to toss off his words, the way she knew she should. They came so easily from him, flattery and compliments that made a woman's head spin. She'd heard him use his charm on women before. Yet, she'd never heard that note in his voice, that warm vibrancy that resounded in her soul.

He picked up her foot and set it in his lap.

"What are you doing?" she exclaimed.

He caught her foot when she tried to pull it away, ignoring her mortified gasp when he started to wash the sole.

"You were out there without any shoes. You shouldn't have been." He looked up at her, his eyes intent. "Let me."

Oh, Lord. She would let him do anything, as long as he'd look at her like that again.

Lean fingers rimmed her ankle, rubbing gently. She jerked when the cloth skimmed her arch.

"Hey!"

"Ticklish?" His grin was pure pleasure.

"A little."

"I don't suppose you'd care to tell me where else."

"No."

He sighed heavily. "I didn't think so."

It seemed to take hours for him to complete his task, his touch unbelievably gentle. His hair was drying into thick waves, the pure gold gleaming softly. She fought to keep her gaze from the bare, broad expanse of his chest. She was, as always, surprised that for a man so lean and elegantly built, he had an amazing amount of muscle.

Her foot rested in his lap, his warmth seeping through his pants and into her. She was overwhelmingly aware of exactly where her heel was.

Suddenly conscious of where her gaze was resting, she forced it up, and found herself looking straight into his eyes.

"Oh, no." Knowledge was there, and her cheeks heated with mortification. How could she have so blatantly stared at his lap?

God. He thought he was handling it, that he was managing to be here with her without rushing head-long into uncontrollable passion. It wouldn't be fair to her; she was too tired, and too vulnerable, stuck in here alone with him.

He'd managed to keep his touch light, and forced himself to keep his hands from wandering up her leg, even though the urge to find out just how firm the muscle of her calf was was almost too much for him.

But then he'd looked up to find her looking at her foot, where it rested just an inch from his groin. Her eyes glazed with passion, and he couldn't keep from hardening rapidly. He knew if she glanced down once again, the change would be all too obvious.

Slowly, slowly, he lifted her foot to his mouth, letting his tongue slide around her ankle, his fingers massaging her heel. She took a great gulp of air, her eyes widening. He pressed a soft kiss to her arch, and she trembled.

"J.J.," she said helplessly.

"Yes?" he said, waiting for her to remind him of their agreement, dreading that she would tell him to stop.

That's all it would have taken. He couldn't bring himself to push the issue now. For all his plans, he found he couldn't seduce her if there was a shred of doubt in her eyes, a hint of hesitation in her manner. He watched her carefully, looking for a bit of fear, certain she would withdraw from him now.

He gave her all the time he could. When all she did was, once more, whisper his name, the sound sighing out of her, he set her foot down and moved to join her on the couch, knowing even the words his mind had chosen were significant.

To join with her.

30

Where to begin? The possibilities seemed limitless, tempting.

Her hands, he decided. He loved the quick, sharp motions she made with them, the slender fingers. He linked one of his own with hers, pressing the palms together, twining the fingers. Then, as slowly as he could manage, he lifted the other to his mouth.

He'd learned her hands well the last few weeks, since they were one of the few things allowed him. He knew just where to start, at the satiny skin on the back. He kissed it, openmouthed, lightly touching his tongue to her, and heard her soft gasp.

Gently, he turned her hand over, fascinated by the contrast of the smooth skin on one side and the hard, textured calluses on her palm. It showed her work, showed that she wasn't a woman who waited for life to come to her. His mouth roamed her hand, rasping over the slight roughness, exploring the places where it changed from ridged to smooth. So much to learn.

Her hand began to shake. He wondered if he was trembling, too, even as he knew he was.

He found her wrist, where the skin was tender and beat with the rhythm of her heart. His tongue flirted with the lacy edge of her sleeve, tracing a circle around the fabric that barred him from a new expanse of skin.

"J.J." Her voice was husky, ragged. He loved the way it sounded, loved that he could make her sound like that.

He dropped her hands and hooked a palm around the back of her neck, drawing her closer. She came willingly.

"Only the skin that's bare. I promise."

Her lips were waiting for him, parted on a soft breath. God, she was sweet, as if she'd been sipping honey, all warm breath and eager tongue and yielding warmth. His fingers played with the hair at the back of her neck, and he deepened the gentle pressure.

Angie thought she understood passion, thought she'd been introduced thoroughly to all its temptations in the past few weeks. Yet nothing he'd done to her, no time he had kissed her before, had prepared her for this.

Her thoughts were clouded, her senses sharp. She smelled smoke and soap and strong, spicy male. There was sound, the slight, ragged edge to his breathing, the rasp of fabric as he shifted on the couch. And always, touch, the way his fingers slid along her neck, her jaw, and made her shiver. The way his lips and his tongue found every last sensitive spot in her own, made need shimmer through all the untouched corners of her body.

Heat swirled through her, as insidious and enveloping as the morning fog. Oh, God. Why this? Why now? Life had been so much simpler before she experienced this. And so much paler.

She'd never let him stay this long without pulling away, never given him the extravagance of time. Patience was hard to come by, restraint nearly impossible. He slipped his mouth down her jawline to her neck. Her scent was strongest here, sweetness and warmth, and her skin was finer even than he had dreamed.

He knew he was shaking, fighting the need to sweep the flimsy gown from her body and find all those places hidden from him for so long. To find out if the skin on the rest of her body could possibly taste as sweet.

It had to be her invitation. Even as the sharp edge of hunger nearly rent him in two, even as the power of desire nearly pushed him beyond all control, he had to wait for her to ask.

She wouldn't tell him no, wouldn't stop him even if he tried. The soft whimpers she made in the back of her throat told him that. But acceptance wasn't enough. He'd promised her it would be only at her invitation, and by God, he'd stick to it. Though if she didn't, he had no idea how he'd manage to make it through the next few minutes, much less the rest of his life.

The collar of her nightgown was high and frilly, stopping the foray of his mouth. He traced the cords in her neck, the gentle valley between them, the firm curves around the sides. His fingers winnowed through her hair, massaging her scalp, exploring the full length of the dark, rumpled silk.

If he had ever wanted anything so much as to have that cloth swept away, to be able to continue his explorations down, and down, he couldn't remember it. It would have required thinking, and thinking was something he was utterly incapable of at the moment.

"Only the parts you leave bare," he murmured again, his voice muffled against her neck. "Bare . . . skin."

His tongue dipped just beneath the edge of the gown, dampening her flesh, reaching only as far as he could.

He felt her small hands on his chest, clutching him close for a moment, then abruptly pushing him back.

He let her go. Oh, God, he thought. Now. Now she would stop him.

She said nothing, only looked at him, her eyes dark and shining, her mouth trembling. How could he not reach for her again? He didn't have the strength.

She wasn't this strong. He was far too beautiful, his chest heaving with each gulping breath, his hair tumbling over his forehead.

A long time ago, she was certain she'd come to terms with the things she would have to give up in this life, because having them would mean giving up too much of herself. She was sure she'd made the right decision. Must she give this up too?

She'd managed to hold him off this long, even though his determined seduction had made her head spin and her body shake, only because she didn't know if she could give in without involving her heart. That would have been certain disaster.

Now she knew it was too late. Her heart was already involved. And, if she must have the pain that was sure to follow, couldn't she at least have the pleasure? Couldn't she have one glorious night to remember on all those endless nights that she would sleep alone?

It was his stillness that decided her, the way he looked at her with so much longing in his eyes but didn't try to touch her again.

She reached up to her collar and yanked it open with such force that buttons popped off, raining down on the floor and rolling away.

Heat flashing in his eyes, he slowly reached out his hand, brushing it down the skin she'd just exposed, circling around the slight weight of her breast.

"So beautiful," he said.

She swallowed, embarrassment mingling with the luscious feel of his fingers sweeping over her skin. "Small," she said, half-apologizing.

"No." He shook his head. "Women never seem to

understand." His touch was gentle, the slight roughness of his palm making her shiver. "It has nothing to do with size. It has only to do with something that is so quintessentially *woman*."

He bent his head, and she gasped. His tongue, hot and wet, came out and flicked the tip of her breast, just once, and her nipple puckered up immediately.

His voice held a note of awe. "And everything to do with the way they respond when I touch you."

It hadn't been nearly enough. Raking her fingers through his hair, she pulled him back to her. He obliged, his tongue stroking one nipple while his thumb brushed her other in the same rhythm.

She leaned back, feeling the curved, hard arm of the sofa against her back. Why had no one ever told her, never warned her of the unbearable sweetness of a man's mouth at her breast, the wonderful tugging that pulled rivers of delight from somewhere deep inside?

As many times as he'd dreamed about this, J.J. realized that the fantasies didn't even come close to the reality. Her nipples were tight, small, unbelievably responsive. He nuzzled the hollow between her breasts, his cheek resting against the softness of her inner curves. He ran his hands down her ribs, reveling in the firmness of muscle at her waist, her supple strength. What fool was it who thought women should be soft and cushiony?

She vibrated under his hands, shimmering with heat. He moaned against her skin, shifting himself to rest over her, trying to find a place for his knees on the narrow couch. Carefully, he lowered himself to rest against her, the heat of her thighs cradling him, and he nearly burst when he felt the pressure against his erection.

Squeezing his hips tightly with her strong thighs, she jerked against him, seeking relief.

"Oh, no. Don't do that." He groaned. He'd embarrass himself right here if she kept that up.

"Please," she whispered, her head rolling back. "Please."

"I . . . can't. You're still covered. I promised you." Even as he spoke, his lips moved over her breast, cherishing every curve, every hollow.

"Get up," she ordered.

"Oh, Angel—"

"Get up!"

Reluctantly, he sat up, fighting himself every inch of the way. He deserved this, he supposed. Deserved every bit of agony he was going through right now.

Ah, hell. Nobody deserved this.

Angie scrambled up, yanked her nightgown over her head, and hurled it across the room. It drifted down, settling over a chair like a discarded white flag.

Shocked, he stared at her. It was the last thing he'd expected.

"Well? What are you waiting for?"

"I thought you . . . I . . . "

Her scowl was fierce. "Don't you dare back out on me now, Johnston."

Grinning like a fool, he stood up and scooped her into his arms.

"What are you doing?"

"I'm taking you to bed." His smile disappeared, and his eyes grew tender. "Please, Angel. Let me take you to bed."

Even now, he was giving her one last chance to be sure. And that alone would have decided her. She laid her palm against his jaw, feeling the light scrape of his beard when he turned his head to place a kiss in her palm. "Oh, yes. Just hurry."

Her head rested against his chest, the soft spill of her hair tickling his skin as he carried her. Never had the distance to his bed been so long. Never had he crossed it so quickly.

The room was filled with gray light, softening the

heavy lines of the furniture, the shiny gleam on the brass bed. A man's room. Angie registered it only for an instant, before all her attention focused squarely back on J.J.

The world tipped, and he laid her on the billowy softness of the bed. She smiled up at him, at this golden man who belonged to her for this time.

He stood over her, and all the masks he wore for the world were stripped away. No more polish, no more charm; just naked need. For her.

His hands moved to the waistband of his pants, and her gaze followed. Though her breath came hard, and heat flashed through her, she couldn't look away. She'd thrown off her clothes for him; now he removed his for her.

He released the buttons and shoved his pants down, letting them drop to the floor, and stepped out of them. He didn't move, didn't hide, just stood there and let her look her fill.

His erection fit the rest of him, elegant and bold and fascinating.

"I didn't know it would point up," she blurted out, then cursed herself for saying the first thing that popped into her head. She sounded like an idiot.

But all he did was grin, delighted, and everything was well. She lifted her arms, waiting for him, and he came to her.

His weight was delicious, settling heavily over her. There was the faint tickle of his chest hair against her breasts, the heat of his belly pressed against hers, the blinding, unbelievably wonderful pressure of his hardness against her. She raised her knees and tilted her hips to increase the contact.

"Oh, God, Angel," he rasped out.

She was greedy, her hands racing over his body, sweeping down the muscled expanse of his ribs, digging into the tight roundness of his hips as if she were trying to feel, to touch, to remember, as much as she could. She bit his shoulder and writhed beneath him, humming under his hands, crackling with energy and life.

He was no less crazed, no less desperate. He tried to be slow, tried to be gentle, but she wouldn't let him. If his mouth brushed hers, she cried in protest and pulled him closer. When his hands gently molded her breast, she whispered and arched into his palm. When he moved over her, sweat-slicked skin gliding over skin, she wrapped her arms around him and yanked him close.

"Slow," he mumbled, trying to remind himself of reality, trying to find some semblance of control. "Slow."

"No," she said, sinking her teeth into the hard curve of his shoulder. "I like fast."

"Gentle," he said, lightly brushing his hand down her belly, sliding his middle finger deeply into her. "Soft."

"No." She shuddered, strong muscles tightening around his finger. She searched, found, wrapping her hand around his erection. "Hard."

"Not yet," he insisted, stroking her gently, making her shudder and strain against his hand.

"Now!" She urged him on, stroking his length, palming the soft weight beneath in her hand.

This was impossible, she knew. No way a human body could survive such pleasure, such heat, and come back whole. No way she was still part of this earth. And she couldn't summon the will to give a damn.

He'd tried so hard, tried to take this easy, tried to make sure she had all the pleasure he could give her. Tried to focus on the small things, the sleek, misty taste of her skin, the way her breath caught every time he kissed her. But when she squeezed him, her small fingers tightening firmly around his hardness, he had no reserve left, no way to hold back.

Raising up on his arms, he probed carefully. He didn't want to hurt her. He only wanted her to be happy.

But her hips shifted restlessly beneath him, and her softness was so hot, so sleek, parting easily for him, that he slid right inside before he thought to hold back.

She stiffened abruptly in his arms.

"Oh, God." His muscles quivering with strain, he dropped his forehead to hers. "I'm sorry."

"I thought it was supposed to hurt," she said, bewildered.

"It didn't?"

Her forehead crinkled. "My sisters said it was supposed to hurt."

He started to smile.

"What is it?" she asked suspiciously. "Is there something wrong with me?"

"How long have you been riding horses?"

"All my life, of course."

"Astride?"

"Well, yes." Comprehension dawned. "Oh, I see."

He chuckled, a rumble coming from deep in his chest. He'd never laughed while making love, and so he'd never suspected that it was the most wonderfully erotic thing he'd ever felt, the laughter coming from deep inside while she trembled beneath him and the joy bubbled through him.

Suddenly she lifted her hips, sliding him in deeper, stroking his full length. Blood roared in his ears.

"Oh, God, Angel, don't do that."

"I can't help it." She moved again, struggling to get close enough, to find the source of this wonderful feeling that was far too much and not nearly enough.

"Don't!"

She paid him no mind. Why would she stop, when it felt so good?

And then he was shaking over her, his body pushing as deeply into her as he could go, his face buried against her neck. He was shuddering, groaning, and she felt a pulsing and liquid warmth spreading deep inside her.

He went still, his weight heavy and luscious. She wanted him to move.

"Is that it?"

"No." His face was pressed into the pillow, and she could barely make out his words. "That's not it. I promise."

He should have been embarrassed, he thought. He'd reacted like a schoolboy. Hell, he hadn't done it like that, that sudden, that sharp, even when he'd *been* a schoolboy.

It didn't matter what he should be. He felt too good, too incredibly, indelibly, unbelievably good. And as soon as he mustered the energy to move, he'd make it up to her.

Idly, Angie let her hand play up and down his spine, stroking slowly. Lord, he smelled good, all sweaty and male and some faint, warm fragrance she'd never encountered before but knew was sex. She'd expected it to feel good, but she never knew it smelled good, too.

He'd promised more. When would she get it? Not that this wasn't nice, him warm on her, in her, around her. But there was a sharp, sweet ache between her thighs, a low, heavy throb in her belly.

She wiggled a bit, just a bit, to get closer to him. There. A twinge of pleasure shot up her spine.

He lifted his head and smiled down at her, his eyes blue and sleepy. "Impatient?"

"Yes," she admitted.

"Good." His mouth was warm, gentle, his breath slipping into her as easily as his tongue. She sighed, wrapped her arms around his neck, and gave herself over to him. Whatever he wanted, whatever he needed. She'd go wherever he led.

His tongue was slick, slow, sliding wetly over the inside of her lower lip, gliding along the edges of her teeth, flirting with hers.

There was a humming in her head, a hazy cloud of

sensation that billowed and shifted. Ideas were vague, formless, too relentlessly physical to be thoughts.

He was moving slightly, his pelvis lazily rocking against hers. She felt him swelling again within her, filling her, stretching bigger, and an answering pleasure swelled within her again.

"Look at me." He rose over her, and she opened eyes that were blurred with passion to find him studying her. He was intense, the hot blue of his eyes never wavering from her.

His movements grew bigger, longer, deeper, stroking her fully, making the ache intensify, build, sharpen.

"Now," he said, his expression fierce, beautiful. "Now."

Nothing could be this good. No pleasure could be this strong. But she was wrong, and she broke beneath him, crying out, closing her eyes because any more sensation, even sight, was more than she could bear.

He watched her, the stunned agony sharpening her already sharp features, her head tossing from side to side, more beautiful than anything he'd ever seen. When she opened her eyes, they were dark, wild, dazed.

She blinked, then wrapped her arms around his shoulders and simply hugged him.

And then she watched him as he closed his eyes and surrendered to her.

31

J.J. felt as if he was ready to take on the world.

Energy was flowing through him, and he was just about to burst with exuberance. His heart thudded in his chest, tiny shivers of pleasure still ripped down his spine, and he was grinning like an idiot.

He should have been tired. Lord knew, he should have been exhausted, sapped of every single reserve. Instead, he felt as if he could go run that damn race by himself right now and beat the horses.

The air was cool on his sweat-slicked skin, and he inhaled deeply, filling his lungs with the scents of woman and sex and smoke. He would always remember exactly that smell.

He'd simply wrapped his arms around Angie and rolled over, bringing her with him, so now she rested softly on top of him, her warm cheek nestled against his neck, the soft spill of her hair flowing over her back and down his side.

Questions jumbled his brain. He wanted to know everything about her, every tiny, silly thing that had formed this unusual woman.

"Angel?" he ventured. "Tell me . . . " What? Everything? He could keep her here all day, talking, and never know even the start of all he wanted. "Tell me about your family. Or your childhood. Or the trip here. Whatever you want."

Silence.

"Angel?"

His only response was a soft, rumbling snore.

Darn it, how could she go to sleep right now? Didn't she know he would want to talk to her? He was wide awake, full of energy and well-being.

The least she could have done was talked to him a bit before she winked out.

Angie blinked awake slowly. Late afternoon light filtered through the window, casting a pale rectangle across the bed where she lay, stark naked, snuggled up against J.J.'s side.

She supposed she should have felt at least slightly embarrassed. He was as naked as she; they were both sprawled on top of the covers, in full light and bare to each others' sight.

Right now, though, curiosity was much more important than modesty.

His features were relaxed and open in sleep, one arm thrown loosely over his head, his face turned slightly toward her. She watched the steady rise and fall of his chest, and couldn't resist brushing her hand down the long slope of his ribs and the ridged expanse of his belly.

"Having fun?"

She looked up into smiling blue eyes. "You are . . . magnificent."

The corners of his eyes crinkled as he laughed. "Finally. Does that mean you like me as well as my horse now?"

"Hmm." Her hand slipped down farther, down to his hard-muscled thighs. "You're running neck and neck."

The texture of the skin under her palm changed, becoming smooth and hairless. "What's this?"

The light in his eyes dimmed. "Just an old scar."

"A scar? From what?"

He sighed and slipped an arm around her shoulders. "I don't suppose you'd be willing to just leave it at that, huh?"

"You know me better than that, don't you?"

"Yeah." His fingers drifted soothingly over her back, and she wondered if he was even aware of it. "How about I make you a deal?"

"Don't you think we've made enough of those?" she teased.

"God, I love your dimples." He planted a kiss on her cheek. "I'll answer your questions if you answer some for me."

"Of course. Why wouldn't I?"

"You weren't very interested in telling me anything about yourself before."

"Well, that was before . . . " She was a bit embarrassed after all.

"Yes." His head fell back on the pillow, and he closed his eyes. "It's not that much of a story, anyway. I was a rather, uh, enthusiastic child. Didn't like to listen to anyone, always wanted to try new things. Including my father's new gelding."

She winced. "Ouch. How old were you?"

"Four."

"Four?"

He nodded. "I couldn't even pull myself up on him, of course. But I could try. And when I slipped, the horse stepped on my thigh. Busted my leg but good."

"You don't limp or anything."

"Children's bones heal well, the doctor said. I was in bed for months, though."

And you've been afraid of horses ever since, she thought. She would have liked to comfort that little boy.

Instead, she massaged his thigh with her hand. "I'm sorry."

"It's no big deal," he said lightly. "Happens all the time."

"That doesn't necessarily make it any easier."

"No." He was quiet for a moment, as if making up his mind about something. Under her ear, she heard his heartbeat pick up speed.

"When they brought me in hurt, my mother went into labor."

His body went rigid, and she knew there was something much more here. "It wasn't your fault."

"I know that." He held a fistful of her hair, rubbing the strands between his fingers. "It was time, anyway. Had my sister six hours later."

She waited, knowing there must be something else. She rubbed his leg, trying to relax the tight knot of muscle. "They put my mother in the room next to mine, so the nurse could take care of both of us." His voice was low, strained. "That's the last time I ever saw her."

"Oh, J.J."

"She caught a fever, with the birth."

"It wasn't your fault."

"I know that!" She knew he didn't mean it, and so forgave the anger in his voice. "I'm an adult. We grow up, and we go on."

Except what you believe in your head and in your heart are two different things, aren't they? she thought.

"It's just—You should know this about me. Before it goes any further. I have this tendency not to be there when people need me. I wasn't there when my father died, either, or when my sister was stuck taking care of him all by herself. I'm always too busy taking care of my own life."

He really was oblivious to all the good he'd done for people, she realized. For Rose and Tommy and Josiah and her and all the others who'd crossed his path. She wanted to tell him that no one blamed him for a little bad timing. She wanted to comfort him, to hold him, but she knew that he wouldn't want comfort. He was too proud, too in control of himself and his life, to let her do anything but simply accept what he told her.

And she would do it, damn it. If that's what he wanted. So she did the only thing she could think of. She turned her face against him, searching out his nipple with her mouth, stroking it with the flat of her tongue.

Slowly, she moved her hand from his thigh, seeking, stroking.

"Oh, my."

"Don't worry about it," he mumbled, giving himself over to her touch. "Just the usual morning thickness."

It wasn't, though. If his intention had been to get her out of his system, to reduce this wild craving to some sort of manageable level so that he could get on with his life, he'd failed miserably. His dreams last night had been filled with her, made all the more vivid and colorful by knowing what he'd been missing.

He was terribly afraid that he was going to spend the rest of his life plotting ways to get her back into bed. There was only one solution he could see.

Slipping his hands behind her head, he pulled her up for a deep kiss, relishing the feel of her skin slipping over his, the soft push of her breasts against his chest. Shamelessly, he kissed her, sending his tongue deep until she was humming and dazed with passion.

"So," he said, turning his attention to the skin behind her ear. She was sensitive there, shivering with each slow stroke of his tongue. "When shall we have the wedding?"

"Oh, I . . . " His words penetrated. She snapped away from him, sitting up and shoving her hair out of her eyes to stare at him. "Married?"

"Of course."

"But—but why?" she stammered, eyes wide with shock.

"It's the right thing to do, of course."

"The right thing to do," she repeated.

Oops, wrong answer, he figured, watching her mouth thin and brows draw together. He braced himself.

She slugged him, her fist thunking squarely in the middle of his chest.

Damn it, that hurt. She pulled her hand back and shook it, trying to force some blood back into her tingling fingers. He looked unfazed, even having the nerve to grin at her.

"Cut that out."

"Okay." He obligingly wiped the grin off his face, but his eyes were lit with humor.

"So, you think we should get married."

"As I said, it seems like the right thing to do." He linked his arms behind his head, settling back comfortably, and she longed to punch him again. He looked so damn sure of himself.

"Why?"

"Because we already had the wedding night, Angel."

"Oh? And I suppose you always propose to every woman you sleep with? Don't all those turndowns get depressing after a while?"

"Well, no, actually. I never did this before."

"Really? I couldn't tell," she said coolly.

He actually blushed. "That's not what I meant, and you know it. I mean, suggesting marriage."

She wouldn't be charmed by that, wouldn't feel like she was special when she knew it wasn't the case.

"Oh? Why am I so lucky, then?"

"Well, you were a virgin, for one thing."

"Ohhhh." She gritted her teeth and nodded her head. "It's only the virgins you propose to, then."

"Well, actually, you're the first one of those, too."

"I see. So, did the woman who took your virginity propose to you?"

"Of course not." He looked puzzled. "A few of them since then, though."

He was such a man. This was exactly the reason she was never getting married.

"No."

"No?" He looked puzzled. "What do you mean, no?"

"No, we're not getting married."

"What?" That shook his complacency. He sat up, scattering pillows to the floor, and she tried to keep her gaze on his face. Too dangerous to look lower. It would make her weak. "Of course we are."

"No, we're not."

"Why won't you marry me? I thought we were pretty good at it."

They were mind-shatteringly wonderful at it, and he knew it. "That's not a reason to get married."

"Of course it is. Why else?" He grinned, trying to charm her, and reached to pull her into his arms. "Aw, come on, Angel. Marry me." He bent to kiss her neck. One way or the other, he'd convince her of this, though he couldn't have said why it seemed so vital.

She planted her hands on his chest to hold him off, stiffening her arms. "It's not just you, J.J. I'm not marrying anybody."

"Why not?" He wasn't worried. Not the way her fingers were already starting to twitch across his chest, lightly stroking, exploring, even though she clearly wasn't aware of what she was doing. "You never really have explained that."

"I know."

He wondered if she had any idea what she looked like, sitting there, bare to the world, in the misty soft light. Her dark hair, tangled from the night before, streamed over her round, honey-toned shoulders, and her assertive little breasts were just waiting for his touch. His mouth. He swallowed heavily and dragged his gaze up to her face, knowing that was the only way he'd hear what she had to say. He had to listen, so he could make the right argument and talk her into this marriage with the minimum of fuss. Otherwise, he might never get his life back to normal.

"It really has nothing to do with you. It's the world." Impatiently, she shoved her hair back, tucking it behind her ear. "Marriage isn't good for women."

What a ridiculous thing to say. She probably didn't want to hear that, though, so he probed for more answers. "What makes you think that?"

"I don't think. I know." She began to gesture with her hands, warming to her subject. "My mother was an opera singer, before she met my father. She never performed again after she married him."

"Did you ever think that that was her choice?"

"That's not the point." She stabbed the air. "One of my sisters has the most wonderful eye for clothes. She wanted to open a dress shop. You should have seen the gowns she made herself."

"That's nice," he said cautiously.

"They were so beautiful. Then she married our neighbor's son, and he decreed that no wife of his was going to make her own clothes. People would think he was poor. And the only thing she ever makes now is christening gowns."

"Is that so bad?"

"There's more." She jabbed him in the chest. "My other sister was a teacher."

He was beginning to see a pattern here. "And now she only teaches her own children, right?"

"Yes." She beamed at him, as if he were her own prize pupil. "See what I mean?"

"Well, not really. It doesn't have to be that way, does it?"

"Yes, it does! Everyone thinks a married woman should be busy taking care of her husband and family. What if that's not what she's good at?"

"Can't she do both?"

"No!" she said vehemently. "Even if she tried, no one would let her. They'd all say she should be home instead of neglecting her family for her silly hobbies."

"I swear to God, Angel. I'd let you have all the horses you want to, and I won't interfere at all." Not that it would be much of a sacrifice.

"You wouldn't even mean to." Her color was high, rose blushing across her sharp cheekbones, and he wanted, more than anything, to kiss her into submission. Only the suspicion that she might hit him again if he tried kept him back. "Even my brother, who is, I'm sure, a wonderful husband, told his wife she could keep painting when they got married. I'm sure Tony meant it, too, but with all the girls I doubt my sister-in-law has much time to work on her art, and—"

"Hold it right there!" J.J. shouted, snapping to attention. "Repeat that."

"Repeat what?" What was the matter with J.J.? He'd gone white, all the blood draining from his cheeks, and he looked like he might keel over in a dead faint at any minute. "J.J., are you all right? You want me to call someone?"

"No. The part about your brother, Tony, and his wife, the artist, and their daughters. That part."

"Oh, well, I guess I didn't tell you about him yet, did I? J.J., I'm going to go get you a cold cloth, okay? I just want you to lie back down and—"

"Don't you dare move!" he roared. He sagged back against the pillows. "Please, please, tell me your last name isn't Winchester."

"Well, of course it is. I know I probably should have told you before, but—"

"Damn it all to hell!" J.J. sprang off the bed and dived for his bureau. He yanked open the drawer, and started throwing out clothes, muttering under his breath, "No, no, that won't do." He held up a silk shirt, frowned at it, shook his head, and tossed it away, where it floated

down to join the rest in a rapidly growing pile. "A-ha!"
He pulled out a high-necked, simple cotton shirt. "Here.
Put this on for now." He hurled it at her and turned back
to his clothes.

She caught the shirt in midair. He wanted her to
wear his clothes? "J.J., what—"

"Don't talk. Get dressed." He pulled open the next
drawer so hard it came right out of its slot, dropping to
the floor and J.J.'s foot. "Ouch! Damn it all to hell!" He
tugged open another drawer and pawed through a pile of
trousers. The room was rapidly beginning to resemble a
badly run laundry.

"Now wait a minute," she began.

"Here." He threw a pair of faded denims at her.
"They're not going to fit, but they'll have to do for the
moment." He tugged out a pair of pants for himself and
stuck one leg in, nearly tripping himself. "Well? What
are you waiting for? Get dressed!"

He should know by now that she didn't respond
well to orders. "Not until you tell me what's so urgent."

"We have to get married."

"I thought we already had this discussion."

"That was before." He had his other leg through
now and was trying to shove the buttons through the
wrong holes.

"Before what?"

"Damn it all, Angel, would you just get dressed!" he
hollered.

"Why?" she shouted back.

"Because if we don't, your brother is going to kill us
both!"

32

•

"*What has my brother* got to do with this?"

He rounded on her, and she clutched his shirt to her chest.

"Oh, God." He flared at her. "Smile," he ordered.

Figuring this was probably not the time to argue with him about trivial matters, she bared her teeth.

"God. The dimples. I should have known."

"Known what?" They probably heard her yell all the way down on the waterfront. Probably sent the incoming ships back out to sea, away from the screeching monster that inhabited San Francisco, but holy horse apples, the man was making her mad.

"Why didn't you tell me that you had a brother here?"

"Oh, well. I thought if you knew that I had someplace to go, you'd kick me out."

"You damn well got that right." He'd thrown a shirt over his shoulders, and it hung, loose and unbuttoned, exposing a decent wedge of chest. If she was lucky, maybe he'd forget to button it up.

"Look, I'm sorry, all right!"

"Sorry's not going to help us now. The only thing that's going to save us is to get you dressed and get ourselves to a preacher before your brother gets here."

Uh-oh. "Tony's coming here?"

"My sister's coming to visit. My sister, the artist, and she's bringing her damned husband."

Life couldn't be this unfair. Her next word came out on a squeak. "Tony?"

"Tony."

An hour later, Angie sat at a table in the Rose and glumly picked at her dinner. She nibbled a slightly charred piece of toast while the yolks of the greasy fried eggs stared accusingly at her.

J.J. had hustled her back into her room and into some "decent" clothes before she even had a chance to assimilate what he'd told her. His sister. Her brother. Oh, dear. She'd landed herself right in the middle of it this time.

It was only when he'd nearly dragged her out the front door in search of the nearest preacher that she finally put her foot down.

She wasn't going to marry him, Tony or no Tony.

She pierced the yolk with her fork and dribbled trails of bright yellow all over her plate.

"Not hungry?" J.J. slid into the chair beside her.

He was neatly attired in his usual flawless white suit, his hair perfectly combed. He scarcely looked like a man who'd spent the entire night fighting a fire, and the whole morning afterward in bed.

If only she could forget about that "in bed" part. It was the one thing her mind kept getting stuck on, playing it over and over again.

"Holy horse apples," she muttered. For all her resolve about being strong and independent, all it had taken was a few kisses and she'd tumbled right over into wantonness. And what a blazingly lovely wantonness it was.

"What did you say? I didn't catch that."

"It doesn't matter. And, no, I'm not particularly hungry."

"Good." He plucked the fork from her fingers and scooped himself a large bite of egg. "Why aren't you hungry?"

"Does there have to be a reason?"

"Guilty conscience, huh?" He grinned and kept chewing.

"Why should I have a guilty conscience?" He could at least look worried, she thought, annoyed.

"Because you took advantage of my body and now you won't do the right thing and marry me." His turquoise and gold ring glittered as he cut another piece of egg.

"What! Why, you—"

"Here. Eat." He shoved the forkful into her mouth. "Having second thoughts? Worried about your brother after all?"

She swallowed hard before she could answer. "Of course not. Tony's a reasonable man. He'll understand."

That stopped J.J. cold, absolute incredulity written across his face. "Oh, sure."

"He certainly will." She made a face. "Maybe."

"Well, I can think of only one thing to do."

She hadn't seen him move that fast since the day she met him, when he'd disarmed the thief down on the waterfront. He set down the fork, captured her arm, and pulled her into his lap before she could let out so much as an outraged squawk.

"J.J., wait, I—"

"I've already been waiting all day." He settled her comfortably and busied himself nuzzling the back of her neck.

"All day?" she scoffed. "We've only been up . . . two hours." The last words were increasingly difficult to get out, as air was rapidly becoming in short supply. It was clear her body wasn't too crazy about her one-time-for-the-memories theory. She wanted him again, and as quickly as possible.

"An eternity," he murmured. His hands were around her waist, slowly edging up to her breasts. She felt her nipples harden in response, ready for him. Shameful things. Had they no decorum at all? "J.J., we can't."

"Sure we can. I doubt they'll be here for an hour or two."

With his thumbs, he began to rim the undercurves of her breasts, and his mouth found the hollow of her throat where her pulse thudded hard. What had she been trying to say? "No, I mean, we *can't*."

"Of course we can, Angel. We've already proven that."

The room was spinning around her, a dizzying whirl of color and light. She summoned all her strength, put her hands on his chest to stop him, and pushed him away. "No, I don't mean just now. I mean ever again."

"Angel," he said reproachfully. His eyes were so deep and blue a woman could fall right into them. His thumbs kept circling her breasts, never quite near enough for relief, never far enough away to forget about. "It'll only get better. I promise."

Better? Her mind boggled. "It's not that, J.J."

"What is it, then?" he asked, his voice soft and coaxing. She was quite certain there was no woman in the world who could resist him when he used that tone of voice.

"I could get pregnant."

"Well, yes, I suppose you could."

The idea didn't seem to faze him in the slightest. "What would I do then?"

Pregnant? he thought. She'd have to marry him then. "I believe I've already suggested something along those lines."

"No." Her arms were still holding him off, but her elbows were weakening. As was her resolve. "I can't take that chance, J.J."

"Hmm." Lord help him if he didn't rather like that idea.

Every moment since he awoke had only confirmed his suspicions. There was only one way he was ever going to get his life back on course. He had to stop thinking about her all the time, had to be able to put women and sex back into the nice, neat corner where he'd always kept them.

It seemed that the only way to do that was to have her be his, where he had the right to reach for her any time he wanted. Then he'd be able to string together more than two coherent thoughts about something besides her. "Would it really be so bad?"

"Y—yes."

He grinned. She'd hesitated, by heavens. He liked that.

All he would have had to do was steer her to Rose. She'd have been able to fix Angie up with that sponge thing that she used. But damned if he didn't find the smell of vinegar slightly unromantic.

It was an unheroic, unfair thought. He couldn't help it. There seemed to be no way to get the traitorous idea out of his mind:

If she got pregnant, then she'd *have* to marry him.

Her hands were still firmly placed on his chest, holding him away, but her rear was moving slightly on his lap.

"Angel," he said softly, and her eyes softened, too. He lifted one hand to her face, stroking lightly down the angle of her jaw. Suddenly, she twisted her hands in his shirt, yanking him closer, and her mouth started to descend toward his. He grinned and puckered up.

"Hey, J.J."

At the rude shout, his eyes flew open.

"What the hell you doin'? That's not Rose."

"Hell!" J.J. swore as Angie flew off his lap as fast as a cat on a hot skillet. But J.J. knew it was too late.

"Rose'll roast your hide but good if she catches you. You—oh, *Dio,* what the hell is going on?"

Shooting one quick glance toward Angie, J.J. stood up. Her hands tucked behind her back, she was looking down while one toe scraped a circle on the floor.

J.J. gave a deep sigh and turned to face his brother-in-law. "Hello, Tony."

Tony was standing stock-still, his face registering shock. He had his youngest daughter, eighteen-month-old Jenny, slung on his hip, and he looked as if he'd just been hit by lightning. Behind him, a perplexed Jessie, J.J.'s sister, was trailing along, a twin firmly attached to each hand.

"Oh, Angie," Tony said on a big sigh.

"Hello, Tony." Her voice was very small. "I'm so happy to see you."

Tony lowered his gaze on J.J. How could he not have seen it before? J.J. wondered. The same coloring. The same dimples. Only because he looked at Tony as little as possible had he not noticed. That, and the fact that he'd been too obsessed by Angie's femininity to start looking for anything that reminded him of a man.

"J.J., I really am going to have to hurt you, you know."

J.J.'s shoulders slumped. "Yeah, I kinda figured that."

Jessie stepped up in a swirl of blue-checked skirts and small, red-headed girls. "What the hell is going on here?"

"Jesus, Tony, haven't you broken her of that habit yet? She still swears too much," J.J. asked with a grimace.

"Don't start." He thrust Jenny at his wife. "Here, you take the baby and get them all out of the way."

"I most certainly will not! Not until you tell me exactly what is going on here."

Tony planted his fists on his hips. "Jess, meet my baby sister, Angelina."

Jessie's mouth fell open. "Oh, dear."

"Yeah." He still held Jenny, outstretched, and her chubby arms flailed the air. "Take her, Jess."

"I don't think so," she said slowly.

"Angie, meet your niece." He stuck Jenny in Angie's arms, who grabbed her reflexively.

There was the crack of bone on bone. One quick jab from Tony's fist and J.J. snapped back, bowing over the table.

"Wait!" Angie shrieked, setting off the little girl in her arms, who wailed with gusto.

"Quiet!" Tony bellowed, sparking a round of giggles between the twins.

J.J. tested his jaw. "Nice to see you have them all so cowed, Tony."

Interesting. Tony turned the most amazing shade of red when he was angry. He pulled back his fist, ready to let fly again, and paused. "You're not going tell me you've already married her, are you?"

"No. But wait!" He threw up a hand to block the blow. "I tried, Winchester. I swear it. She turned me down."

Tony rounded on his sister, who was frantically trying to calm the screaming Jenny. "Is this true?"

"Well, yes, but—"

"Aw, Angelina, how could you?" He bunched his fists and turned back to J.J. "You should have talked her into it, Johnston."

"Well, actually, that was what I was trying to do when you walked in."

Wrong thing to say, J.J. figured when Tony started to wind up again. He braced himself for the blow. After all, he supposed he deserved it.

"That's enough." Jessie had had all that she could take. She let go of her daughters and grabbed Tony's arm. "Not in front of the girls, at least, Tony."

"I suppose you're right." Tony lowered his arm and J.J. relaxed.

"Now then." Jessie bent to the four-year-old twins, nearly identical except that one had blue eyes and the other brown. "You take your little sister and go into the kitchen. I'll bet Josiah made some cookies just for you."

"But, Mommy," Laura protested, "is Daddy going to hurt Uncle J.J.?" Hannah nodded solemnly in agreement.

"No." Jessie shot a stern look at her husband. "I won't let him."

"Jess—" Tony started to protest, but was cut off by his wife's glare.

"Now, go." Angie reluctantly put down her niece. Each sister took one of Jenny's hands, and all three headed for the kitchen, Laura keeping up a constant chatter about cookies and horses and grown-ups who play too rough.

Tony waited only until the girls disappeared down the hallway. This punch caught J.J. in the stomach.

"Stop!" Angie couldn't take any more. She threw herself in front of J.J. "Why don't you hit him back?"

"Angie!" Tony was clearly shocked.

"I can't, Angel." Half in apology, he ran the back of his hand down the curve of her cheek. "Everything he's worried about is true. I seduced you, I slept with you, and that's that."

"Now you've done it. Why did you have to say it straight out like that?"

A small smile lifted the left corner of his mouth. "You did't really think he wouldn't know, did you, Angel?"

"Angel?" Tony's voice was heavy with disgust. "Isn't that cute?"

"Oh, shut up!" And here she'd thought Tony was the most understanding of brothers.

"That's it." He looped a hand around his sister's wrist and began to drag her toward the door. Leaning back on her heels, she skidded along behind him.

"Where are we going?"

"We're going to get you hitched. If you're lucky, Father will never find out about this. C'mon, J.J."

"Fine by me."

"Enough." She wrenched her arm free and stood her ground, determined not to go anywhere. "What is it with you men and this obsession with weddings?"

"He slept with you, and he's marrying you. End of discussion."

"Oh? And why is that?"

He threw up his hands. "Isn't it obvious? He deflowered you, Angie."

"And you're so certain of that?"

His hands twitched, as if he was tempted to throttle her. He tried to stare her down. She simply lifted her chin and met his gaze without giving an inch.

Clearly, he wasn't getting the answer from her. He turned to J.J. instead. "Well?"

J.J. simply grinned with male satisfaction.

"There, you see? It's your own fault, Angie. That's what you get for always being so reckless. You slept with the man, and you're just going to have to marry him."

"Oh, yes?" She poked him in the chest. "Then I'll ask you the same question I asked him. You went ahead and married the girl who took your virginity, hmm?"

"Well, of course not, but—"

"Aha!"

"Aha, what?" Tony frowned. "It's not the same."

"You all keep saying that. But nobody seems quite able to explain to me why not."

"Yes, honey," Jessie put in. "I would rather like to hear that, myself."

Tony groaned. They were ganging up on him.

Angie shot a grateful glance at her sister-in-law. They might never have met before, but she knew a kindred spirit when she saw one.

"There, Tony, you see? Your wife agrees with me," she said smugly.

"Jessie," Tony said warningly to his wife, who merely smiled innocently at him.

"What do you expect? It's their lives. Not yours, not mine. I think we should probably let them work it out between themselves."

"But, *cara,*" he protested.

"But nothing. Anything else is bound to be a mistake, Tony."

"I'm so glad we all agree." Angie gave a huge sigh of relief, ignoring J.J.'s snort. "Tony, I do believe I'm really going to like your wife. I'm glad to see your taste in women has improved so much."

33

The Winchester family stayed for three days.

The fire had left the saloon short of bedrooms, so J.J. had, to his disgust, been forced to give his room over to the Winchester clan. He'd grumbled long and colorfully about trying to fit his frame on the small, hard sofa in the sitting room while his brother-in-law got his bed and the girls, David's room. Angie knew he was less worried about his back than frustrated about having no place to get her alone, as soon as he talked her into it again. Which he tried to do every time her brother was out of earshot.

Her room was still uninhabitable, so she'd bunked with Rose. It wasn't nearly as bad as she'd expected, though Rose had drilled her far into the night on debits and credits and tables.

With Tony's help, they'd made a good deal of progress cleaning up the Rose. They'd be able to open again that weekend.

She should have been delighted to have them there.

Except Angie knew that if they had stayed any longer, she would have run screaming into the night.

It wasn't that she wasn't thrilled to see her brother. She loved him as much as ever, was rapidly growing fond of her new sister-in-law, and was head over heels about her nieces.

But she felt as if she were being pulled in several different directions at once.

J.J. and Tony were like two dogs who wanted the same bone, snarling and snapping at each other over the slightest thing. Even Jessie's interference couldn't smooth things out. She admitted to Angie that they'd never been exactly fond of each other—J.J. thought Tony couldn't possibly be good enough for her, and Tony was roundly insulted by it—but this had sent them over the edge.

The two men agreed wholeheartedly on one thing: she should marry J.J. Tony grumbled and complained about her abysmal taste in men, but clearly thought that, now that she'd made her bed, she'd damn well better lie in it, preferably before their father found out.

J.J. proposed at least once a day. Whenever he got that wicked gleam in his eye, whenever he managed to brush against her in passing, she knew what he was up to. It wouldn't have been nearly so bad if a tiny, treacherous, and utterly foolish corner of her heart wasn't quite entranced by the idea. Even though she knew it would be a complete and total disaster. Sooner or later, she'd resent what she'd been forced to give up.

She found refuge with Jessie, who talked mostly of children and horses and continually prodded for news of the Winchesters at home. Sometimes, though, she'd catch Jessie watching her with a speculative gleam in her eye and wonder what Jessie was plotting.

The Winchesters were to leave just after lunch. Tony was outside, checking the wagon and packing it up. Angie and Jessie were in J.J.'s sitting room, watching J.J. play with his nieces.

He was down on the floor, wearing holes through the knees of his white suit. Both twins, copper curls shining like new pennies, were perched on his back, and he was doing his darndest to buck them both off, while Jenny squealed and clapped in delight.

"Oof," he said, collapsing suddenly to the rug while Laura thumped his side with her heels. "Horsey's tired."

"No!" she squealed. "Want to ride more, Uncle. More."

"You should have known they'd ride well, J.J.," Jessie put in.

"Yeah," Laura agreed. "Not like you."

"What?" J.J. rolled over and gathered the girls close. "What do you mean?"

"Daddy said you ride like an old lady."

"Me?" He tried to frown at them but ended up grinning instead. "Not anymore. Your aunt Angie taught me how."

"Really?"

"Of course. He's my best student, you know. Also my only one, but who's counting?"

The girls squeaked when J.J. found a ticklish spot on their sides.

There was a tiny, painful catch in the corner of Angie's heart.

Never would she have guessed how good J.J. would be with the children. Laura chattered nonstop, words spilling out of her like water from a pitcher, and he answered every one of her questions with amazing patience. Hannah hardly spoke at all, letting her vocal twin do the work while her disconcertingly adult brown eyes calmly observed everything. J.J. always made sure that Hannah, so quiet, was never overlooked, and he often succeeded in drawing a word or two out of her in answer.

And Jenny—who could not love Jenny—all shiny and fresh and sticky fingered, with a grin as big as California and a hug for everyone who came within her reach? Even now, unwilling to be left out of the fun, she launched herself at J.J.'s lap. He caught her easily, pulled her into his arms, and simply held her for a quiet moment, resting his cheek against the top of her head, before he tossed her up in the air.

"He's very good with them, isn't he?" Jessie said, regarding Angie with an odd, soft smile on her face.

"Yes. I don't know why I'm so surprised."

"Because not that many people ever see this side of him. He's too careful most of the time."

"Careful. Tony says I'm never careful enough."

"And you've heard that an awful lot these few days, haven't you?" Jessie said, sympathy clear in her voice.

Angie shrugged, trying to look nonchalant. "It's nothing new."

"Perhaps not." Jessie looked over at her brother. "J.J., why don't you take the girls downstairs? They should probably have something to eat before we leave."

J.J. peered out from under a tangle of small, chubby arms and legs. "Now?"

"Yes, now."

"Why?"

"Because I asked you to."

He sat up and his gaze slid from Jessie to Angie and back. "Sis, I—"

"Please."

"Okay. C'mon, ladies. Perhaps you would be so kind as to join me for luncheon." He got to his feet and easily lifted Jenny to his hip, the movement seeming completely natural to him. He ushered the other two out in front of him, promising them sandwiches without the crust, and frowned warningly back over his shoulder at Jessie before he closed the door behind himself.

"Now then." Jessie smiled brilliantly. "What's this I hear about not wanting to get married?"

Angie barely suppressed a groan. "Not you, too. I thought you were on my side."

"Come now," Jessie said, her voice rich with laughter, "you can hardly blame me for wanting my brother to hang on to the best thing that's ever happened to him."

"Really?" Jessie thought that? "Why?"

"You make him laugh."

"Everybody makes him laugh."

"No." Jessie gestured to her face. "Only here. Everyone makes him laugh here." She pressed her midsection. "You make him laugh here. Where it matters."

"Maybe." Laughter. How could that possibly be enough? "For how long, though? We need such different things. I can't see a middle ground."

"If you love him enough, you'll find it."

"L-love," Angie sputtered. The word had never been mentioned, had never even popped up in her mind. Now that it was there, she was terribly afraid she'd never root it out. Even when it so clearly didn't apply. "No one's said anything about love."

"No, I suppose not." Jessie shook her head. "Tell me. J.J. said you have some sort of objection on principle to getting married."

"He talked to you about me?"

"I asked."

"Oh." She wasn't disappointed, she told herself.

"Would you mind explaining it to me?"

"I'll try." She rubbed the back of the couch, the hard curves of the wood smooth under her fingers. "Marriage just doesn't allow women a lot of . . . room. If your talents lie in something outside the home and the children, you either let them go, or they're taken from you."

"Not all husbands are like that."

"I know that." There was a nick in the wood, and her finger caught on the edge. "It's not just your husband. It's everyone out there." She waved her hand vaguely in the direction of the city. "They all think you should be home taking care of things like a good little girl."

"Angelina," Jessie said crisply. "That's something you're going to have to fight whether you're married or not. There'll always be a fair number of people who believe you should be tucked safely away at home."

"I suppose so." She leaned forward, intent on making herself understood. "But every woman I know has given up so much to get married. I know that it is their choice, but there's something about it that seems to sap their talent. My mother, my sisters . . ."

"Me?"

Angie cleared her throat awkwardly. "Well, yes."

Jessie studied her for a moment, her eyes a cloudy blue gray. "Wait here." She reached over and patted Angie's hand, then disappeared through the door to J.J.'s room.

Angie fidgeted and tapped her foot on the floor, trying to ignore her curiosity. What could it be? Obviously, it had to be something that was meant to convince her, but she hadn't a clue.

Jessie backed into the room, lugging a huge canvas. It was round, at least three feet in diameter.

"How did you get it circular?"

Jessie grinned. "I had it stretched over a barrel hoop. Clever, don't you think?"

"Um-hmm," Angie said noncommittally. There couldn't be anything in a painting that would convince her that she and J.J. could find a life that wouldn't require one of them to give up more than they were willing to.

"Look," Jessie said. "I'm not going to try and convince you about marrying J.J. That's up to the two of you. But this nonsense about a family blunting your gifts . . . well, I finished this a week ago. Brought it along for J.J. What do you think?"

Frowning anxiously, she turned the painting around.

At first glance, it was a simple landscape, a small

cabin in a hidden valley, surrounded on all sides by sheer, forested mountains. The cabin was right in the center of the painting, the mountains spreading out all around it. The painting changed the farther one looked from the center, the trees becoming oddly formed, the outlines more and more vague, the mountains hazy and twisted. The color faded, too, so gradually it was almost unnoticeable, until, near the edge, Angie realized it was only dense, flat shades of gray.

But the cabin, and the area immediately surrounding it—here the color was vibrant, so intense it nearly hurt the eyes. The edges were sharp, the images clean and clear, the brilliant red hair on the three little girls who played in the wildflowers in front of the cabin so detailed Angie thought she could see the individual strands.

"Jessie," Angie said softly, catching herself before she reached out to the center of the painting, certain it would be warm to the touch, so vivid and alive did it appear.

"You like it?"

"It's wonderful."

Jessie nodded in satisfaction. "J.J. wanted a portrait of the three girls. Not exactly what he had in mind, perhaps, but I think it works."

"I think I can hear them laughing."

"Yes." Jessie smiled at her expectantly. "And?"

"And what?"

She gave an exasperated sigh. "You are as bad as he is. Heaven help you both. Neither one of you would notice the obvious if you fell and landed right in the middle of it."

"Hey, I . . . " She couldn't possibly be as bad as J.J. Could she?

"Having a family doesn't take away from your talent at all. Your time, maybe, though it's certainly worth it. But the richness it adds can only be good." Jessie looked down at the painting, pride—for both the work and her daughters—clear in her expression. "I could always paint, Angie. But now . . . now I have something to paint about."

Right before they left, Tony came up with the idea that if Angie wasn't going to marry J.J., she should come home and live with them, where he could watch out for her. At least she wouldn't be living in sin.

Angie firmly turned him down, insisting that she had a job to do, though she'd be more than happy to see him if he came to visit her again. Especially if he brought her nieces along.

Then he pulled her close and said: "You do know, Angie, that Father will never let you take over, right?"

She shook her head violently, so that the ends of her braid whipped around. "He will. Once he sees what I can do."

"No." Tony's voice was soft and heavy with regret. "He should. He's a good man, Ang, but he thinks business needs a man's touch."

She didn't believe him, so he simply let her go and swung up onto the wagon to join his family.

He made it quite clear that he'd be back. Then he exchanged significant if not friendly glances with J.J., and the two shook hands. Odd, since they'd managed not to come within five feet of each other the entire three days. The whole thing made Angie a bit nervous.

The next two weeks rolled by at a crawl. Angie moved back into her room. It still smelled faintly of smoke, but it was better than sharing a room with Rose, who had taken to dropping unsubtle hints about how much they liked having her around and how long was she going to stay?

Angie and J.J. talked of nothing but horses. Anytime he tried to bring up something else, she would cut him off abruptly and walk away as quickly as she could manage. She was clearly too weak to listen to what he had to say. She might give in, and then where would they be?

She'd be stuck in this town, trying to learn to be a saloon hostess or a barmaid or some such nonsense, probably spilling drinks all over the best customers and longing to be out riding in the hills of Kentucky.

And he'd be saddled with a wife who was of no help to him at all. Sooner or later, when the novelty wore off, he'd tire of her and go looking for someone with a bit of sophistication and polish. Someone more like himself.

Except every now and then she'd turn from doing some routine task and find him watching her, such warmth and tenderness in his eyes that her heart squeezed.

They worked, long and hard, getting ready for the race. It was the only safe, reasonable excuse for being in each others' company. But their tempers were short, and they snapped at each other more than they meant to.

Angie knew he didn't mean it, any more than she did. But there had to be some release for the energy that crackled between them the instant they were in the same room, and hollering at him seemed like as good a solution as any.

But two weeks, it seemed, was all J.J. was willing to wait.

34

"Let's take the day off."

Angie stopped rechecking the bridle and looked over at J.J. "You're not serious."

"Of course I am. Why wouldn't I be?" He had his own horse saddled—he'd beaten her out this morning—and was waiting for her to finish before they took off on one more combination training run and riding lesson.

He couldn't have suggested just forgetting it. For one thing, the race was too close, barely a week away, and she knew precisely how much it meant to him. Enough for him to submit to spending four hours or more a day on the back of a horse for an entire month.

For another, she'd finally run into someone who worked harder than she did. He worked at a slower pace, steadier, but he simply never stopped. She wondered if he even slept. Come to think of it, she hadn't even seen him sleeping the night they'd—

Oh, bad thought. She'd been trying so hard to keep it out of her mind, but there it was, big and vivid and powerful in her memory as it had been in life. Her fingers fumbled with the buckles.

"Why would you want to take a day off, with the race so close?" Suspicious, she narrowed her eyes at him. He had to be up to something.

He just grinned at her, and it was all she could do to keep from sagging against Lancelot's side. Damn, shouldn't she be immune to that smile by now?

"We've been working too hard. Don't you think we deserve a little free time?"

"I don't know . . . "

"Aw, come on. We'll ride there, so you'll have plenty of time to tell me what I'm doing wrong."

"Ride where?"

"Come along and find out. I'll even feed you."

Ah, now he had her. He'd known that appealing to her curiosity was the one thing that would likely get her to agree.

He'd managed to behave himself the entire two weeks only by dint of more willpower than he ever suspected he had, and he only hoped to God he'd never have to call on that much again.

It had been a test of sorts. To see if he could put her out of his mind. Find out if the infatuation would fade, if he could force himself to forget that incredible night and get back to his life.

He'd failed. He would have been a bit more upset if he wasn't so certain what he was going to do next.

But he'd seen the look in her eyes every time he came close to her, the way her breathing changed and her cheeks bloomed with color. She hadn't been able to forget, either.

So today, he'd begin his campaign. And he would win, because he was certain that, deep inside, she wanted the same thing he did.

"Come along, Angel. You'll like it, I promise. Don't you want to get out of the city for a day?"

Out of the city. Ah, that sounded like heaven to Angie. It would be green, and she'd be able to breathe air that smelled the way it was supposed to, of grass and wildflowers and sunshine. Maybe even a little bit like animals, instead of too many people too close together.

"All right. I give in."

He fervently hoped so.

They rode for nearly an hour, following J.J.'s instructions, out of the city and on a twisting, up and down path through the hills. Angie thought they stayed near the sea, for above the clatter of hooves, she could sometimes hear the crash and sliding retreat of waves, though she couldn't see them.

The fog was thick, the air damp, cool, and tinged with salt. The gray was nearly impenetrable, lush and shadowy. Sometimes she was certain she could reach out and grab a handful of it, and it would feel like reaching into the sea, cold and briny and pouring through her fingers.

True to his word, he let her critique his riding on the way up. He'd never be a natural rider; he was still far too stiff on the horse, and once in a while he tried to force control on the animal, rather than coaxing Angel into it. However, if it wasn't pretty, his riding was serviceable. Angie felt she'd done her job. That part of it, at least.

There was still the race, of course. Angel was in top form, and she felt they had a good chance. She should have been excited. What she'd planned for was close, and soon she'd be able to go on and start her breeding farm.

Except that would mean leaving J.J., and, as much as she'd tried to cut him out of her mind in the last two weeks, she wasn't able to do it. She was beginning to accept that he would always be there. She'd simply have to learn to live with it. That didn't mean she wasn't greedy for these last days. She couldn't give in and let him touch her, but she relished the thought that, at least, he was never too far away.

"Whoa." J.J. pulled Angel to a stop. "We're here."

"Here? You promised me there'd be a view."

"There will be."

The bluff was thick with dark grass, splotched with brilliant orange-red poppies. She could still hear the sea, its rhythm a low, soothing counterpoint to her own heartbeat. Life always had a rhythm, she thought.

He wouldn't let her do a thing except dismount. Since there was nothing else to look at but fog and the horses, she watched him. He was far more interesting.

Out of his saddlebag came a large green-striped blanket, which he spread over the ground with a flourish. He pulled out a crusty chunk of bread, an orange half-round of cheese, and a tin box, which opened to reveal a few handfuls of precious, ruby raspberries. He unearthed a sack of puffy, pale steamed buns.

"What are those?"

"From the Chinese teahouse. They're filled with sweet beans. Try one, you'll like it."

He tossed one to her and she bit in. The thick, rich filling oozed out.

"What do you think?"

"Mmm."

"Madam," he said grandly. "Luncheon is served."

She dropped a curtsy. "I'd be honored."

Once she was settled on the blanket, he pulled out one last bundle and sat down next to her. A little closer than was probably smart, a little farther away than she wanted.

While she nibbled on a heel of bread, crumbs from the crisp crust drifting down, he unwrapped the cloth, revealing a bottle of wine and two thick, cut-crystal glasses.

"Wine?"

She was unable to find enough air for words. He took her silence as assent.

The wine was golden and light, sunshine concentrated in liquid form.

"It's good."

He nodded, refilling her glass. "Apples. Jessie has a friend who makes it."

The fog enveloped them, muffling sound, shifting and blurring outlines. Was there really a world out there? There was no sign of it, nothing that seemed to matter. Perhaps they were high, floating in the middle of a cloud, lost somewhere in heaven. She could almost pretend they never had to come back to earth.

They talked little while they ate the simple food, her appetite sharp after the morning ride. Now and then, he'd reach over and pop a raspberry in her mouth, smiling as the flavors, sweet and tangy, just enough of each, burst on her tongue.

Finally, he packed away everything but the wine and turned to her.

She'd known it was coming, had read it in every yearning look in his eyes. Yet pulling away was impossible.

Nothing that happened here mattered, anyway. Here, in the soft, misty gray, nothing she did was part of the world.

His face was almost severe as he lifted one hand to her collar, hovering close to the first button. Then he stopped, as if waiting for her answer.

He hadn't meant to give her a choice. He'd planned to overwhelm her, to give her no time to listen to anything but the way he made her feel.

But he wanted her to say yes, he found. Wanted her to take that step toward him, instead of merely not running away.

"Yes," she said, her voice as soft and lush as the fog.

Oh, that smile, she thought. Sunshine. Golden hair, golden man.

Golden wine.

He leaned forward to kiss her and he tasted of the wine, a faint spice underlying the sweetness. His knuckles rubbed against her as he worked her buttons free, but he touched her nowhere else, just the gentle pressure of his lips. She rested her arms on his shoulders, ready to pull him close.

"Oh, no," he murmured. "Not this time. This time, we take it slow." No matter if it killed him, he thought.

He drew back. Her blouse was open to the waist, exposing the thin white of her chemise and her skin, lightly sheened with mist. He dipped his thumb in the wine, then ran it across the firm curve of her lips, and they glistened wetly. His tongue traced the same path, savoring the taste of her.

He painted her collarbone with the golden liquid. Cool wine, warm touch, hot mouth. Her head fell back loosely and she twisted handfuls of the blanket, trying to keep her hands from urging him to move faster.

J.J. set the glass aside, nesting it in a tuft of grass rimmed by poppies, freeing both his hands. Her chemise pulled easily from her waistband, sweeping up to expose her breasts to the sea-heavy air.

He dipped his fingers again, trailing pale droplets of wine over the swells of her breasts, over her nipples. And she gave up trying to follow his instructions not to hurry him, wound her fingers in his hair, and pulled him down to her.

Her skin tasted of brine and salt and the sweetness that was hers alone. He'd been so sure he remembered it all vividly, every sigh and every soft place where her pulse beat close to the surface.

It couldn't possibly be better than he remembered. Yet it was, as the sea roared and her hips shifted restlessly, as his tongue formed around the hardened peak of her breast.

She tumbled back, taking him with her. The grass

beneath the blanket gave easily under their weight, sinking down, cushioning them.

Impatient, she opened his shirt, and the fine linen came loose, brushing her own bare sides as it hung down from him. His hands slipped down, tracing the edge of her waistband.

"These are a problem," he said. "Only time I ever wished you wore real skirts. I could just slip them up."

She made a soft sound of disappointment. "We're outside."

"So?"

"You can't mean . . . " The thought was shameful. Amazing how much she liked it.

"There's nothing out here but the hills and the poppies."

She was out of her skirts and drawers before he could take a shuddering breath. Billowing gray fog surrounded her as she lay, exposed, her blouse barely clinging to her shoulders and her chemise pushed up, rimming the upper curves of her breasts, drawing his eye to what lay beneath.

"Oh, my God."

"This is no time to pray, J.J."

It probably was a very good time to beg the Lord that he'd get out of this whole. He couldn't seem to form the thought, could only look at her, the slender, defined muscles of her legs and the compact curves of her hips.

He reached for the glass and poured a thin stream of wine on her breastbone. It slipped down, pooling in her navel and the concave curve of her belly.

She was no longer cool. Angie shut her eyes against the whirling world, unable to tell where sky and earth divided. Nothing seemed real except J.J., sipping the wine from her body and sending her into a warm, misty place where nothing was real but acute, sharp pleasure.

His mouth traced the angle of her hipbone, and his hands moved lower, gently parting her thighs.

Her moan blended with the sighing of the waves,

low, keening, ebbing and flowing with the sensations that seeped through her. He moved again, and there was the trickle of cool, young wine against her most intimate flesh.

She jerked once, in surprise.

"Shh," he said soothingly, thumbs tracing intricate designs on the skin of her inner thighs. "What does it feel like?"

It was hard to summon the strength to form the words, and they came out slowly. "It's . . . warm. Like holding spices in your mouth," she said, surprised.

"And this?"

If the wine had warmed, his tongue was hot, sending a searing stab of pleasure racing through her. She arched her back, giving over to the unbelievable heat of his mouth flat against her and his tongue licking the wine from her swollen flesh.

Her hands fisted, uncurled, bunched again, needing something to hold. *She* needed something to hold, an anchor in a world spun out of control and beyond the limits of her endurance.

She had to stay with him now, he thought. Now that her smell and feel and taste were so firmly burned in his brain that he knew it could never be obliterated, never even be blunted. This moment would always be razor sharp for him, the faint calls of the gulls blending with her broken cries, the rough scratch of the blanket and the first, slick resilience of her body under his hands.

She lifted against his mouth, then started to shudder, long, uneven convulsions that nearly sent him over the edge himself. She quieted slowly, faint aftertremors continuing for a long time, until she felt her hand come to rest on his head and urge him up to her.

He meant to hold her for a while, to let her calm before he started over again. Instead, she pushed at his shoulders, rolling him over on his back and climbing up to straddle him.

What few clothes she wore were rumpled and disarranged. The glossy, smooth length of her hair streamed down around her shoulders, and her eyes were luminous with exultation and sensuality.

"My Lord, Johnston, you managed all that and you still have your pants on!"

He laughed, joy and triumph so close together he couldn't distinguish one from the other. Her hands were deft, working on the buttons of his pants and his drawers before the last echoes of his amusement faded.

She didn't bother with removing his clothes, leaving them loose around his hips, his erection bare and proud. Bracing herself on his chest with her hands, she lifted up and positioned herself.

He raised his head to watch her sink down onto him. To see himself disappearing into her body, his dark gold hair contrasting with her deep brown curls.

The light was behind her, a background of blue-gray sky for elemental woman, all lithe, strong grace as she slid above him, full and rhythmic and powerful. When he reached his own pleasure, giving a hoarse shout, she sank down on him fully.

He stilled, then gave a sudden, last jerk.

"How did you do that?" he asked.

"What do you mean?"

"Whatever you just did."

"Oh, this?" Deep inside, she squeezed him tightly.

He gritted his teeth, jerking again with the ripple of pleasure. "Yeah, that."

"I don't know. I just sort of . . . tighten everything up inside."

"Oh, my God." It was an immense effort for a man who had not one drop of energy left in his entire body, but he ran his hand up the sleek length of her side. "You have the most incredible muscles."

She smiled at him, delighted, shoving the loose hair from her face, then looked around her in surprise.

"The fog's gone. The sun's out!"

"So it is." He lifted her off, turning on his side and bringing her down to tuck her securely against him, her back resting against his chest, so they could both look out at the view.

The fog had drifted out to sea, a low, lacy gray fringe between the sea and the sky. The sky was a warm, hazy blue, a marked contrast to the deep, gray-green ocean. The water was churning wildly, pulsing with waves edged with foam and spray.

"I told you there would be a view."

"You did. But there was one even before the sun came out."

He chuckled and nuzzled the back of her neck.

"What's that?" She pointed at a dark, wet rock out to sea that was covered in dark brown dots. Dots that moved.

"Sea lions. There are a lot of them out there." He looped his arm around her waist, and his hand swept up to tease her breasts, his fingers lightly circling her nipples.

This was too good. Angie couldn't even regret giving in and taking the chance she had promised herself she wasn't going to take. In a niggling corner of her mind, she wondered if that was exactly what she wanted. Then the choice would be taken out of her hands, and she wouldn't have to blame herself if it went wrong.

"I'm not going to marry you, you know," she said abruptly.

The last thing she expected from him was laughter, but that was exactly what she got.

"I didn't say a word."

"I know. But I can always tell when you're working yourself up to it."

"Oh, really?"

"Yes." She pondered the seething ocean. It looked so alive. "You should be grateful to me for turning you down, you know. Sooner or later you'd want someone else."

That annoyed him. He flipped her on her back, so he could look into her eyes.

"Good God, woman, is that what you're worried about? I was faithful to Rose all the time we were together, and I wasn't even in love with her."

For one second, all the air left her lungs. But then he went on.

"Not that I'm in love with you, of course. But it doesn't matter. It's been a long time since I've been interested in conquest, Angel."

"Oh." What else could she say? She wanted him to come back to Kentucky with her? Oh, he'd love that idea. No, he belonged here, with the gold and the sunshine and the sea. Or should she say she would stay here, as long as it felt right to both of them, and then she'd walk away? She'd never walk away. She'd crawl, clutching the bleeding remains of her heart and the tattered remnants of all her fine young dreams.

He reached out and plucked one of the flowers, pressing it into her hand. She twirled the hard, rough stem between her fingers, then turned back, facing the water. He pressed close behind her, comfortable and warm, fitting neatly curled around her.

They lay there on the hillside and watched the sea.

35

Rose stood in the darkened hallway, rubbing her damp palms on her skirts. It wasn't good for the fragile satin, but right now she didn't much care. That alone showed what a state she was in. Her heart was knocking against her ribs, her stomach was twisted, and she had to gulp just to get in enough air.

Her rap was timid.

No answer.

Damn it, why couldn't this be easy? If it was so hard just to knock on the blame door, what was the rest of it going to be like?

She raised her hand to knock louder, and hit only air. The door had been yanked open wide.

Stitch loomed over her, tall and thin, his hair silver in the dim light, his eyes a matching shade. Both his dark shirt and pants were unbuttoned, as if he'd thrown them on hastily to answer the door. Silver and black. Darkness and strength. All male.

This was all so crazy. Why did she feel as if it was

the only thing she could do? It had taken her all summer to work up to this point. She wasn't backing out now.

His hand still on the latch, he simply stood there, waiting, as if he had all the time and patience in the world. She thought maybe he did.

When it was clear he wasn't going to ask, she did. "Can I come in?"

Silently, he stepped aside and allowed her to enter. To her surprise, he didn't close the door behind her.

"Don't you want to shut the door?"

"No. I want you to know you still got a way out, 'cept you choose to stay."

"Oh." She started to pace, through the bar of light cast by the faint moonlight coming through the window, into the shadows, and back into the light, her skirts swishing around her ankles. She twisted her fingers together until the skin burned.

She'd rehearsed it in her head, over and over again. There was nothing left to do but just spill it.

"I got married when I was sixteen." A lifetime ago. "My Johnny was the best." Pausing a moment at the window, she stared out at the ghostly, silver-rimmed shadows in the yard. She couldn't remember his face clearly anymore. She hated that.

"He also had gold fever. Wanted to come out here. Of course, I came with him. What else was I going to do?"

Her heels clicked hollowly on the wooden floor. "We had everything. A claim, each other, a baby on the way."

She stopped in front of him, looking up at his bony, unsmiling face, finding strength in his silver eyes. Lord, if only she could breathe, could force away the tight constriction in her chest. "It only took one night to take it all away."

He found her hand in the dark, linking his fingers with hers, and she found comfort in the rough-skinned touch of his palm on hers. "All of it," she repeated. "Johnny. The baby. Even me."

"Not you."

"Yes." Squeezing his hand tightly, she looked up into his face, willing him to understand. "The Rose that was there before those claim jumpers hit us doesn't exist anymore. This Rose . . . I'm someone else entirely now."

"Aren't we all?"

"Yes."

His thumb rubbed the back of her hand, gently, slowly. "Have you ever told anyone this before?"

"Only one."

She saw a faint twitch in his jaw. "J.J.?"

"No. Only Jessie, once, a long time ago."

He brushed her cheekbone, wiping away the single tear, then rubbed his fingers together, as if testing the moisture. "Why now, Rose?"

"Tomorrow's the race. I wanted you to know, whatever happens tomorrow, that it makes no difference in this. In us."

She would have sworn he couldn't smile like that, all flashing teeth and male satisfaction. And when she saw it, she knew he understood what her telling him this now meant.

The heel of his boot caught the corner of the door, and he pushed it slowly shut behind him, just before he pulled her into his arms.

The racetrack was several miles inland and several hundred yards up from San Francisco. It was as straight and flat as it could be made, which meant not much. It ran along the flattest tops of the hills, between the peaks, for nearly a mile and a half.

Angie pulled the horse to a stop and appraised the place, reaching down to give Angel a pat.

Up here, it was far warmer than down by the bay, a

brisk wind sweeping across the high spots, bending the brown-green grass. They'd spent a fair amount of time up here in the last few weeks, running the course, trying to familiarize Angel with the slight changes in grade and the long, loping curves.

Usually it was empty of everything but the drying grass and a few scrub bushes. Today there was a large clump of men and horses clustered around the starting line, all milling and jostling with sharp, frenetic energy. Apparently, not all the gamblers had left San Francisco with the gold rush.

She looked over at J.J., who was sitting on Lancelot and studying the crowd through eyes that were sharply focused. His face was carefully blank, and she knew he only wiped it so clean of emotion when he felt the most and was determined that no one else would know.

So much rode on this day. She'd done what she could to stack the odds in their favor. There was no doubt that Angel was the best-trained, best-conditioned, and fastest horse. Her light weight would be an added advantage. But there were always holes and rocks in the paths, sudden lameness, and other things that could destroy even her careful plans.

She swallowed heavily, trying to keep her breakfast in her stomach. Angel danced beneath her, whacking her leg with his tail, and she knew her nervousness had transmitted to her mount.

How much she wanted to do this for J.J. No matter what happened, she would have to leave after this, and she wanted to be able to leave something behind.

Since that afternoon on the bluff above the sea, she'd barely seen him. Shaken by the power of their time together, and how easily she'd gone to him again, she'd said the hell with bargains and shut him completely away. She'd thought it was the only way to keep things under control, to find the strength to do what she had to do.

He was hatless, and the wind shearing off the high hills ruffled his thick golden curls and the loose white cotton of his shirt. He looked so beautiful that she felt a pang in her chest, and she suddenly wished she hadn't wasted the last week. If that was all she ever was to have, she should have taken full advantage of it.

It was too late. He'd drawn away completely, becoming remote and untouchable. This morning, when they met at the stables, she tried to make him smile and failed totally. His unresponsiveness was her own fault. She'd pulled away, and he'd gone on, and damn her for wanting to take it back.

"So what do you think of Lancelot?" she asked.

Lancelot's ears pricked when he heard his name. J.J. only continued to study the crowd. "He's fine. Just like you said."

This morning, she'd insisted on riding Angel, claiming that the horse needed to know who was riding him today. J.J. had looked at her then, an odd, hard set to his jaw, and agreed. She'd suggested he take Lance instead. Though J.J. didn't like the idea, she'd told him that Lance was better mannered than any horse he was ever likely to run across.

"We'd better get down there," J.J. said flatly. "Time to enter the race."

J.J. nudged Lancelot gently through the crowd. There'd been a couple of makeshift posts to tie their horses to, but he hadn't wanted to take the chance. Too easy for someone to get to them, slip them something that would make them sick or put a little notch in their fetlock. Angel was so clearly the class of the horseflesh here.

Damn it, he felt proud of the horse. Amazing.

And he was proud of the woman. He sneaked a quick peek at Angie. There were few women here, and none so young and small. It wasn't the place for her to be, but he hadn't had the heart to leave her behind completely. Anything they accomplished today was going to be her victory. Though not exactly in the way she was planning.

She wasn't going to like it. He knew that already. But she was going to be safe, and that was enough for him.

He knew she'd been a little hurt at his coldness this morning. Her sparkling energy had dimmed, just a bit, when he abruptly turned away from her.

He'd been hurt, too, when she pulled away so completely after they returned from their picnic. He hadn't thought she'd be able to deny him any longer. His initial instinct had been to hound her day and night, seduce her until she was either pregnant or gave in from sheer exhaustion.

He hadn't been able to do it. Damn it, he wanted her to come to him on her own. He needed her to have the choice. And the only way he could give her the freedom and time she needed was to stay as far away as possible.

A fellow who more closely resembled a bear than a man took note of her passing and reached up to grab her reins. With no signal J.J. could see, Angie had Angel swing his hindquarters abruptly to the left, as if making a quick side turn. The man had to jump out of the way to keep from being banged by the horse's huge rump, and got caught across the face with a whap of tail.

Angie never looked down, but there was a hint of dimple flirting with the corner of her mouth. Good thing he wasn't close enough to kiss her, or it would be all over.

This was no place to bring a woman. But Angie looked completely undisturbed and in control. She was relaxed and confident.

He leaned over. "You've got that Colt with you again, don't you?"

She looked faintly surprised that he was talking to her, then her dimples deepened. "I certainly do."

"Where?"

"The classic spot, of course. Strapped to the outside of my thigh. Wanta check?"

The image that bloomed in his mind nearly made him swallow his tongue. "How do you expect me to ride a horse, when you say things like that to me?"

The crowd was getting thicker as they neared the center, swarming around and buzzing like bees. Hermanson was holding court right in the middle, surrounded by tight, concentric circles of men. Not ten feet away, close enough so they could keep an eye on each other but far enough away that they didn't have to acknowledge each other's existence, L.J. Hooper stood in the middle of his own group of followers.

"Time to go to work." J.J. nudged Lance to a halt, debating. It would be immeasurably easier to give his entrance fee to Hooper. Hermanson wasn't going to like it.

It might have been easier, but it wouldn't have been as much fun.

Lancelot picked his way through the crowd, stopping a bare two feet from Hermanson, who looked disconcerted at the size of the horse in front of him for only a moment until his jovial mask clicked neatly into place.

"Johnston, isn't it? How delightful you could come watch our little games."

Hermanson's elegantly cut gray suit was too heavy for the warm summer air and probably cost as much as most people's yearly rent. A diamond stickpin winked from his chest.

Hard to believe the man was going to race a horse in that get-up. Which, J.J. supposed, was exactly the point. Hermanson was proving he could afford to.

"I'm not watching." J.J. pulled a hefty pouch from his waistband and tossed it at Hermanson, who caught it reflexively. "I'd like to enter my horse, Angel. There's the entry fee."

"Angel?" Hermanson's grin was beatific. "Going to bat his wings and fly to the end?"

"Oh, he flies all right. But with only his feet."

Ezekiel weighed the pouch in his right hand. "Sorry. I don't believe I can allow you to enter." He made a motion to toss the bag back.

"Really?" J.J.'s calm voice stopped him. "I wonder what L.J. would think of that, hmm? Should we ask him?"

The cold, hard light of Hermanson's eyes was nearly hidden by his beaming smile. "Oh, I don't think we need to do that. You're in." Dull gold gleamed from his waistline as he lifted his pocket watch and flipped open the lid. "Fifteen minutes to start!" he called. An enthusiastic cheer greeted his announcement.

J.J. backed his horse away, studying the crowd until he found whom he was looking for. He turned to Angie, who was making her own thorough inspection.

"Angel, let's move over there for a moment."

She followed him as he headed toward a slight thinning of the crowd, over in the shadow of one of the higher hills.

"J.J., I've been looking at the horses. I don't think there's much here. Hooper has a big black stallion that's more show than depth. Too big, for one thing. He looks ready to go, but controlling him will be tough. Nothing else comes close, except Hermanson's."

"We had to expect that. Which one?"

"The bay gelding over there, I think. He sent a handler over to it. He has beautiful conformation, J.J., but I don't think he's got the speed."

"We'll soon find out, won't we?" He halted Lance just at the edge of the crowd. "Well, well, look who's here."

"Tony! What are you doing here?" Angie asked, her slow drawl lit with delight. "Where are Jessie and the girls?"

"I left them back at our place. This is just a quick little trip."

"What are you doing here?"

"What do you mean, what am I doing here?" His grin was innocent, and J.J. wondered, once again, how he couldn't have noticed their kinship. Maybe because Angie seemed to run through the day at double Tony's relaxed pace.

Or maybe because he hadn't exactly been thinking with his head.

"I couldn't miss the chance to see my baby strut his stuff," Tony went on.

"He's just exceptional." She reached down to give Angel a companionable thunk. "You did well, brother."

"Almost as well as you could have?"

"Almost. Of course, I did get to him before there was too much damage."

"Stitch," J.J. said abruptly. "I didn't know you were here."

A whipcord lean strip of black, his battered hat pulled low over his eyes, Stitch stepped out of the crowd and joined Tony. "Mebbe I like racin'."

"Uh-huh."

"Or Rose asked me to come."

"Protecting your interests is more like it."

"That, too."

The low rumbling of the crowd was increasing in intensity, punctuated by an occasional, ringing hoot.

"Must be gettin' close to race time," Stitch said.

"Oh, I'd better get—"

"Wait a second, Angie," Tony said quickly. "Come on down and give me a hug."

"I don't think there's time."

"There's time," J.J. said quietly.

Angie sprang off the horse and dashed over to her brother. His arms closed around her, holding her tight.

"Hey, Tony, I'm going to need all the breath I can get."

He finally loosened her, and she turned toward her horse.

Except all she saw was the familiar deep chestnut rump, heading for the starting line with J.J. clamped on his back.

"Hey, wait a minute—" She started after them, but her arm was still held firmly. "Tony, you're still hanging on to me. I have to go." She jerked away, but he didn't release her. "Let go!"

"No, Angie," he said quietly.

"But I have to . . ." Her voice trailing off, she looked up at her brother, whose eyes were soft with sympathy but whose jaw was hard with determination.

"You two planned this, didn't you?"

"Yep."

"Damn it, we have a better chance if I ride!"

"Maybe." Her arm was going to fall out of its socket if he didn't let go soon. Frustration mixed with fear made her stomach churn.

"Tony, please, you have to help me! I'm begging you, he could get hurt."

"So could you. Which is exactly what we're trying to avoid."

She looked around frantically. If only there were a rock or a stick or something that she could hit him with. Not too hard, of course. Just enough to let her get away.

There was always her gun, though she didn't know how she could get it out from underneath her skirts without him catching on.

Oh, damn, it was hopeless. She couldn't hurt him, and she knew it.

"You know how I ride! I won't get hurt."

"Ang, this isn't the kind of thing you're used to. You know how to ride, but you don't know California. If someone pulls a knife on you, what are you going to do?"

"While I'm riding?"

"Yes, while you're riding."

They'd never get close enough to use it, she thought, stamping her foot, oddly satisfied by the quick stab of pain that shot up through her heel.

He wasn't going to let her go. Time to change tactics.

"Well, how about you at least let me go over to the finish line and see him off?" she said in her sweetest voice.

"Oh, come off it. You don't really think I'd fall for that? No telling what kind of a ruckus you'd cause if I let you go over there."

God, she wanted to slug him. Stubborn man. She needed help.

"Stitch, surely you want to see your investment protected, right? Can't you see that your best chance is to make sure I'm the one riding?"

Stitch didn't even bother to say no, just shook his head once and went back to scanning the crowd.

"Angie, I am sorry." Tony's other hand—the one that wasn't clamped around her arm—came up to awkwardly stroke her hair. "Can't you see he needs to do this?"

"No," she said stubbornly. "I don't even care if he wins, Tony. But I couldn't see him hurt."

"I know." He dropped a quick kiss on her forehead, then dragged her, still protesting, up to the side of a hill where they could watch the race.

36

J.J. selected an end spot at the starting line. It made his route a bit longer, but it kept him away from the crush of the rest of the horses. With any luck, Angel's initial burst of speed would be enough to put him ahead of the pack, and then he could veer in along the most direct path.

The leather reins bit into his fingers, he held them so tightly. He should loosen them up, but he couldn't make himself relax that much.

There were only seven horses racing. Most of the throng were apparently there only for the spectacle and the side betting. It seemed few men in San Francisco could afford to come up with the entrance stake. Or, perhaps, most were smart enough not to get between Hermanson and Hooper, whose vicious feud was legendary.

J.J. took a great gulp of air and let it out slowly, telling himself to relax. There was no way he'd be able to find the right rhythm, letting himself go with Angel's strides, if he was sitting there stiff as a poker.

Beneath him, he could feel Angel's muscles bunch in anticipation, as if he knew he was about to do something he was bred, born, and raised for. He wasn't dancing and nipping like the other horses; it seemed as if he were saving all his strength for the task ahead.

Good thing the horse knew what he was doing, because J.J. sure didn't. He decided he'd direct Angel as little as possible, trusting in the horse's training and instinct. It was a far sight better than trusting his own.

"To the line!"

Oh, God. J.J. said a quick prayer for deliverance. Oddly, he didn't think of saving the Rose.

Most of all, he wanted to make Angie proud of him.

He lifted his knees further against Angel's shoulders and hunched low, curling and uncurling his fingers around the reins. He wished to God he'd learned to ride a horse a long time ago. Most of these men had been riding their whole lives. Who did he think he was, competing with them?

His heart thudded loudly in his chest, and his breathing became rapid.

He had the best horse, he repeated to himself again and again. Angie said so, and she knew.

"Hey there, J.J. You looking a might peaked. Wouldn't do if you were to fall off even before we got started." Hermanson had maneuvered his big bay between J.J. and Hooper's black. His smile was firmly in place. He looked like a man who had no worries at all.

"Don't worry about me—"

Crack!

The abrupt pistol firing caught J.J. by surprise. Angel, however, knew what to do. He lurched forward, nearly toppling J.J., who tightened his grip, closed his eyes, and hung on, hearing the faint echo of Hermanson's triumphant shout over the loud thunder of pounding hooves.

The race was meant to take only a few minutes.

J.J. was certain a lifetime had gone by in the first quarter mile.

Angie was going to yell at him about his rhythm. His butt was getting pounded black and blue, and he could feel the jarring already setting up a stiffness in his back.

Damn it, he had to do better than this. She was depending on him.

He chanced cracking open one eye. So far, so good. They seemed to be about level with the rest.

They were approaching the first turn, an easy left one in his direction. He opened both eyes. Brown hills were a blur, flying by at a dizzying pace. His eyes stung from wind and dust, and he blinked to clear them of moisture and grit. All right then, he'd compromise. He'd squint.

Trying to take the shortest path, the horses were swinging in his direction, crowding him on the inside of the curve. Hermanson's mount brushed his leg, and Angel moved farther to the left, tightly hugging the edge of the crude track, trying to stay away from the pack.

J.J. tried simply to keep his hands light and hang on. The horse was the experienced one here.

First casualty. In the far corner of his vision, he saw the bearlike man bend over and shove a skinny, pale man, who went over the side of his horse and disappeared.

Damn, he'd known that might happen. There was simply too much at stake here.

He lowered his head, hunching over his horse's neck, out of the worst of the wind.

"Come on, Angel, *go!*"

The next half mile went by in a blur. Angel's powerful legs churned beneath him, eating up the hard-packed trail, slowly pulling ahead of the rest of the pack. J.J. simply hung on and prayed.

Jesus, they were winning. They were going to make it after all!

Not much farther. Keep low, hang on. Don't screw it up now, he told himself.

A flash of silver glinted in the corner of his vision. He turned his head, looking back.

Hermanson, looking amazingly unruffled on the back of his pounding bay, was pulling even with Angel's hindquarters.

And he was clutching a knife.

"Damn it!" J.J. bellowed. Clutching mane and reins in one hand, he frantically clawed for the pistol he'd shoved in the back of his waistband.

How the hell was he going to hang on with one hand, turn around in the saddle, and aim at the same time?

Prayer was probably his best shot.

J.J. aimed the pistol at Hermanson's belly. Behind Ezekiel, a full length back, the rest of the jostling horses kicked up a thick cloud of dust.

He felt himself beginning to slip sideways, a sickening lurch, and he tried to clamp his legs more firmly around Angel's laboring sides. Hermanson was leaning over, arm outstretched, ready to plunge the blade in Angel's flanks. He obviously hadn't seen the gun trained on him.

J.J. gave another loud shout. Hermanson's gaze flicked up for a second, and he stopped stretching. Then he grinned and leaned forward again, his shattering, cold gaze holding J.J.'s.

Damn it. He obviously didn't believe J.J. would really shoot.

J.J. narrowed his eyes, trying to look threatening. He'd always been good at putting on a face; he only hoped to God this one was good enough. His finger tightened around the trigger.

A loud roar penetrated J.J.'s consciousness. He blinked and looked around.

They were on the other side of the finish line.

He'd done it, by damn!

The crowd surged around them, separating him from Hermanson. Bastard. He knew better than to think that this was the end. Somehow, there had to be a way to protect them all from Ezekiel.

Angie got to him first, quickly twisting through the men. She was jubilant, laughing, her eyes shimmering, and J.J. tumbled off the horse and into her arms.

She kept him from falling to the ground.

Damn, he felt good. He probably wouldn't sit properly for a week, his back was stiff, and his heart was still thundering with the aftereffects of exertion, exhilaration, and fear.

But he'd won. And Angie was there, hugging him fiercely, her firm, small body wrapped around his. Her head was tucked against his neck, the fine silk of her hair tickling him slightly, and he could feel the warm ebb and flow of her breath.

"Hmm. You're all sweaty."

"Sorry."

She tightened her grip on him. "I like it."

Maybe he should kiss her. Yeah, that sounded like a good idea.

His hands shook as he cupped her jaw, lifting her face up. Her skin was flushed, rosy and fine, and her lips were gently parted.

A *great* idea.

"All right, that's enough." Tony clamped his hand on J.J.'s shoulder and dragged him away from Angie.

"Aw, come on. To the victor go the spoils, and all that."

Angie had pulled away reluctantly from J.J.'s embrace but had stayed close to his side. She playfully poked his stomach. "Spoils?"

He grinned down at her and draped his arm around her shoulders. She allowed it to stay. Damn, but life was good sometimes.

"Don't push it," Tony said. "I let you squash her as long as I could stand it. You're asking a lot."

"I know." J.J. regarded his brother-in-law and grew serious. "I owe you two, now."

"Two?"

"Once for giving me the horse in the first place. And now, for keeping her safe today."

"Forget it." Tony stuck his hand out. "What is family for?"

"Family." Their handshake was rapid but firm. "Yes."

"All right," J.J. continued, turning his attention back to Angie. "You're not too mad at me?"

"I should be, but . . . " Her dimples appeared and her teeth flashed, small and even and white. "How can I be mad? We *won*!"

"That's it exactly. *We.*" Her shoulder was firm and round beneath the light cotton, and he squeezed it. "No way in hell could I have done it without you."

"Just remember that, please."

He wanted to get her out of here. Get her alone, and preferably naked, while the heady rush of victory still surged through his veins and beat, wild and primitive, in his soul.

Except he'd promised himself he would push her no more. The next time, she'd have to come to him.

And he rather thought her brother would find a way to stop him, too.

He sighed regretfully. "What do you say we go collect our winnings, huh?"

"Sounds good to me."

Stitch stepped forward. "J.J., 'fore ya do, could I talk to you a minute?"

What could the man want? There was no clue in his angular, emotionless face. Still, he doubted Stitch would have asked unless he had something to say worth listening to.

"Fine." He let Angie go and stepped aside with Stitch, getting away from the crowd of well-wishers with a bit of difficulty until Stitch glared at them all and they quickly stepped back.

"What is it?" His side felt cool where Angie had been, and he missed her warmth. How was he ever going to let her go? How could he not?

"I'm guessin' old Ezekiel prob'ly ain't going to be too thrilled about you winnin'. And about me not sellin' my shares to him."

"I'd say that's a fair guess. Don't worry, though. I'll figure something out." Eventually, he thought. He just hoped it wouldn't be too late.

"Thought ya might be interested in this." He pulled a stiff, folded square of paper out from his shirt pocket.

What possible good could that be? J.J. plucked the paper from Stitch's hand, opened it, and quickly read it.

"Is this true?"

"Oh, yeah."

"I heard rumors, but . . . " J.J. frowned at the paper. It couldn't possibly be this easy. "Are you sure?"

"I still got a few friends from the old days. The information is reliable."

"I don't want to know." The paper crinkled slightly. J.J. folded it carefully and tucked it away in his pocket. "Why?"

Stitch clamped down on a chaw of tobacco. "Why not? I'm gettin' mine the same, either way."

J.J. stared at him, wanting the rest of the story, wondering at Stitch's motives.

"I'm retired from being the bad guy, ain't you heard?"

"Well, I did hear something to that effect. Still . . . "

"Rose."

"You take care of her right or I'll come kill you."

A hint of a smile lightened Stitch's austere features. "I wouldn't expect anything else."

"Good."

Ezekiel, surrounded by his hangers-on who were busily trying to get in good by consoling him on his obviously unfair loss, was on the far side of the crowd. J.J. took off toward him, grabbing Angie's hand as he went by, bringing her along with him.

"So." Ezekiel was still wearing that same, friendly, unthreatening smile. The threat was all in his eyes, cold and sharp as shattered ice. J.J. wondered if Hermanson had ever managed to kill someone, just with that look. "I suppose you're here to collect your winnings."

"That we are."

Hermanson snapped his fingers at one of his lackeys, who scurried forward with a large, bulging bag. He took it and handed it over with the casual air of one who was turning over something of no more importance than a spare chicken egg. "Don't spend it all in one place."

"Actually, I intend to."

"I wouldn't, if I were you. Things could happen. Fires, for instance. Floods, robberies. Who knows?" His voice was smooth, almost mesmerizing.

"Really? Well, we've already had the fire, so I'm not too concerned."

"One can never be too concerned."

"What would you recommend, then? Perhaps I'll get interested in land deals."

Ezekiel sniffed and turned away, dismissing J.J., making it clear he couldn't possibly be interested in J.J.'s plans.

"Maybe like the one you got hooked up with back in fifty-one."

Ezekiel didn't turn, but his body went still.

"Of course, I heard that there was some speculation that you really didn't own the land that you sold."

"Don't be ridiculous." Hermanson's voice went flat. "It was in the clerk's records. Everything was in order."

"Well, now, I heard that clerk isn't around here anymore. Pity, isn't it? No one to verify it."

"Nothing to verify. I had the deeds."

"Well, people can write new deeds, can't they?"

"I tire of this." A casual flick of his hand and three men scrambled for the privilege of bringing his carriage around.

"Oh, that's too bad. Perhaps I'll take a trip. New Orleans is nice, don't you think?"

"New Orleans." A vein pulsed slightly under the thin skin at Ezekiel's temple.

"Heard it's a nice place to retire to. If you have enough money, that is. Clerk couldn't do it on his salary."

"No."

"You know, if anything should happen to any of my friends, or to the Rose, I just might have to take a trip down to New Orleans."

"You wouldn't like it there. It's bad for your health."

"Maybe." J.J. passed the bag of money to Angie and went to stand in front of Ezekiel. "You're so dusty from the race." He brushed the brown grime off Ezekiel's gray suit. "You know," he said conversationally, "if something happened to me, I have friends who'd make that trip to New Orleans instead."

Hermanson, his eyes narrowed to chips of clear glass, stared up at J.J. Finally, he nodded curtly. "Yes, I suppose there would be." He was in his carriage and on his way immediately.

"What was that all about?" Angie sounded vaguely curious, but she was too busy poking her nose into the bulging sack of money to pay too much attention.

"Just a little fire prevention," J.J. murmured. "Oh, come on, Angel. Let's go home and count our winnings."

37

The gold pieces were spread in a loose, tumbling pile over the table. They gleamed dully in the flickering gaslight, cold and tarnished.

Angie counted out another stack, for once able to concentrate on numbers. It was easier than dealing with abstracts in a ledger book; these were real, solid, and cool when she picked them up and warmed them in her palm.

Tonight, J.J. had declared the saloon closed, much to the disappointment of the customers who wanted to celebrate J.J.'s win. He'd insisted he was tired, and wanted to celebrate one night in peace.

The large room was empty and hushed, save for the soft chink of coins. Wood glowed warmly in the low, golden light. J.J. sat at the table with her, patiently counting his own stacks, his head bent over the piles.

Just for a moment, she thought of bumping the tables, scattering all the carefully counted money, just so they would have to start over again. At least, for a little longer, he'd stay across from her, where she could look up and see the golden gleam of his hair and the intimate flash of his smile.

Damn it, she'd known it was going to be hard to leave. What she hadn't known until now was just how much it was going to hurt.

"So." J.J. picked up a coin, rubbing it between his thumb and forefinger. "Our bargain is complete."

"Yes." A hard, painful knot thickened in her throat.

"What are your plans?"

He said it so casually, as if he were asking a slight acquaintance. As if it meant nothing to him. She forced herself to sound as unconcerned.

"I suppose I'll go looking for some land to get started on. And some horses."

"What you wanted." Carefully, he set the coin down on top of a precisely stacked pile and started toying with his ring.

"Yes." She tried to smile. "Do you think you'd consider letting me use Angel? For stud?" Foolishness. It was nothing more than an excuse to believe she would see him again, now and then. Perhaps it would be bearable, if she could at least count on that small pleasure. Was it too much to ask?

"Of course."

The ring caught the light; the turquoise looked dark blue in the dimness, as deep and unreadable as his eyes.

"Will you give me a good deal?"

"Angel, you know I could never ask you to pay. I owe you too much." He lifted his finger and placed it across her lips, silencing her protests. "We're partners, remember? Partners don't try to make money off of each other."

The pressure of his finger was firm, his skin slightly roughened with calluses. It was only a flash, an instant of temptation, but she almost gave in, opening her mouth and taking his finger inside.

He moved his finger, gently tracing the curve of her lower lip, a slow, even, back and forth stroke that brought to mind too many other memories.

"Stay."

"What?" She tried to concentrate on something other than the distraction of his touch. "You want me to stay?"

"Why not?"

"J.J., we've talked about this . . . " God, it was too tempting. Too easy to forget all the good reasons why she couldn't.

"Hush and listen." His fingers slipped around her neck, his thumb stroking the tender skin under her ear. "I promise I won't bring up marriage anymore, all right? First off, you're not planning to go all that far away, correct?"

"Yes," she said, unable to disguise the husky note of her voice. Oh, what he could do to her, just with the lightest brush of his fingers and the wicked gleam of his smile. "All my best customers would more than likely be here in San Francisco."

"Well, then, why don't you stay? You could get some land close to town, go out during the day. You could bring some here to the stables during foaling season, so they'd be nearby. You have to live someplace, Angel. Why not here?"

His words were as seductive as the slow glide of his palm, rubbing down the curve between her neck and her shoulder.

"For how long?"

"As long as you want."

Forever. She almost said it but snatched the words back just in time.

Why shouldn't she stay? Tony was right. Her father might never let her have the Meadows. Hell, he might have already turned it over to one of her brothers-in-law. And, even if there was a chance, it would take years to build her business to the level it would take to convince him of her competence.

Years that she could spend alone.

Or years that she could spend here. At least until J.J. tired of her. Why shouldn't she be greedy? Why shouldn't she take whatever time she could have? It couldn't possibly hurt any worse to say good-bye then than it did now.

"What about . . . you know . . . babies?"

He laughed low, a seductive sound that shimmered in the air and settled into her heart. "I know why you're so determined to have a stud farm. Always thinking about breeding." His hand was on her shoulder now, lightly polishing. "There are ways around that, Angel."

It could work. Warmth bubbled in her, spreading, seeping into every corner. She opened her mouth to say yes.

"Angelina!" The door to the Rose crashed open and rebounded. "Where are you, my Angelina?"

"Oh my God." She froze, her hands going flat on the table. "Daddy?"

"Yes, my baby. Ah, the worry you've caused us!"

Her father was a big man, striding across the floor and seeming to take up more than his share of the room. He didn't look much like Angie, J.J. thought, for he had light brown hair and pale hazel eyes. When he reached the table, he hauled Angie out of her chair and into his arms, squeezing her tightly, his large body all but swallowing up her small frame.

"I don't know whether to kiss you, I'm so happy to see you, or beat you for what you did. We were so frantic!"

"I left a note telling you why I left. And that you shouldn't worry about me."

"How can a parent not worry about you! It's impossible." Now that her father was closer, J.J. could see the resemblance to Tony, the squared jaw and broad cheekbones.

Her father's brows drew together abruptly when he took in J.J.

"Angelina, what is this?" he demanded. "Who is this man?"

"Oh . . . uh . . . this is J.J. Tony's brother-in-law. J.J., my father, Edward Winchester."

"Ah!" His face cleared, and he smiled, delighted. "Jessie's brother! I am so pleased to meet you." His beefy hand grabbed J.J.'s in a firm shake. "But, Angelina," he went on, "what are you doing here? In a place like this?"

"I . . . well, I . . . " She gulped air, then squared her strong, narrow shoulders. "I didn't want to go to Tony. If he helped me, it wouldn't prove to you what I needed to be able to show you. I needed to do it on my own."

"You children. So foolish." Edward shook his head sadly. "Don't you know what could have happened to you?"

"Yes, well, I thought I'd be safe enough here. J.J.'s family, after all." She gave J.J. a warning glance.

Did she really think he would give her away? He was half-tempted, just to see the fireworks.

"Well, we won't tell your mama you've been in a saloon, will we? She wouldn't understand."

"Mama? Is she here?"

"No, of course not. I mean when we get home."

"I'm not going home."

"Of course you're going home!" Edward looked astonished. "You love the Meadows. Even more than I do, I think."

"Too much to watch someone else run it."

"No, you misunderstand. Come, sit down. We have to talk."

"Uh, maybe I'd better . . . " J.J. slid uneasily out of his seat. He had the sharp, irrational fear that if he left her now, he might never see her again. But he could think of no excuse for horning in on their private conversation.

"No." Her eyes were dark, pleading. No way in the world he could resist them. "Stay."

"Yes, stay." Edward clapped him so hard on the back he nearly flew into the table. "Later I must thank you properly for watching over my Angelina. Now, you can listen to what I have to tell her."

They all settled around the table. Angie looked anxious, J.J. thought. Her gaze was focused on the tabletop she was absently rubbing with her forefinger. One long strand of hair kept sliding down around her face, and she tucked it back behind her ear, where it promptly slid loose again.

God knew, *he* was anxious. For many reasons, not the least of which was the fact that her father had every right to break each bone in J.J.'s body. For another, Edward's presence threw another, unknown factor into the equation. Before his arrival, J.J. was certain he'd almost talked Angie into staying, at least for a time. As long as she was here, there was always a chance that, someday, she'd give in to the rest.

J.J. shifted in his chair, wishing that he was able to reach out for her hand. He thought it might make her feel better. For damn certain it would make him feel better. If only he hadn't closed the saloon tonight. Somehow, the idea of the light and noise and crowds seemed comforting.

Only Edward seemed completely unconcerned. He beamed at his daughter, then reached across and patted her hand.

"By God, Angelina, but you have guts!" His laughter bellowed up in the open room. "I always knew that. From the time you were so little and managed to ride your brother's horse. But this—even *I* didn't know you had this in you, to take yourself all the way across the country by yourself."

She shrugged carelessly, as if what she had done was nothing. "What else could I do?"

"I should have known it. Somehow, though, I keep expecting you to be like one of your sisters."

When her face went still like that, all the light and energy winking out, she was hurt. J.J. wondered if her father knew that.

"Don't expect it, Daddy. Ever."

"I know that now. All will be well. And you'll come back to Winchester Meadows with me, and your mother will stop yelling at me for how stupid I am."

"I told you, I—"

"No, no, you don't understand." He waved his arms in the air. "It's yours."

"Mine? What?"

"The Meadows. I was wrong. I know that now. Lord knows, I've heard it enough since you left, a million times every day. And, so, it will be yours."

"You can't mean that." She looked stunned, her eyes glittering in the soft light. The strand of hair fell over her shoulder again and lay against the upper curve of her breast. This time, she didn't notice and brush it back.

"Of course I mean it. Not all at once, certainly. I won't retire quite as quickly as I thought. We will work together, you and I, just as we did when you were young. I will teach you everything you need to know, and then the Meadows will be yours."

"I . . . " She turned to J.J., a silent plea in her eyes.

Oh, God. For so long, he thought he hadn't had a heart. Just vague, formless, and ultimately unimportant feelings were all he'd had. Now, by the empty aching hole where his heart should have been, he knew he'd had one all along.

He was going to have to let her go.

He couldn't ask her to sacrifice this. He couldn't take from her the one thing she'd always wanted above all else. She had a chance for it now, and he should be happy for her.

But God, how it hurt. He wanted to throw himself

at her feet and beg her not to leave him. Except he couldn't do that to her, couldn't hold her with *his* emotion. Could only hold her with her own.

He forced his lightest smile on his face, blessing all the years of practice he'd had. He'd need every bit of skill not to let her see through it.

"That's wonderful, Angie," he said, his voice sounding monotonously flat even to his own ears. "What you've always wanted."

"Yes." What she'd always wanted, she thought. Now, she was on the verge of having it, and she felt hollow. There was nothing of the heady anticipation she'd felt a half hour ago, when he'd asked her to stay.

Oh, God. All she'd ever wanted, and it wasn't what she wanted at all.

He was letting her go so easily, a perfect, smooth smile on his handsome face. She searched for just a trace of sadness, of regret. It only confirmed how shallow his feelings for her were. He liked her well enough when she was here, but not enough to fight for her to stay.

Ask me to stay, she thought. Please, ask me to stay.

Tell me you want to stay, he begged silently. Don't you know I can't ask this of you? Tell me you want stay.

"I wish you the best of luck." He would have extended his hand for her to shake, it seemed the appropriate gesture. But his hands were trembling, and he couldn't make them stop long enough to raise them above the level of the table.

If only, just once, he'd said the word *love*. She'd have thrown herself at his feet and begged him to let her stay. But it was perfectly obvious; he wanted her there because they were compatible in bed. They were convenient, and, oddly enough, friends.

It wasn't enough.

Say it. She closed her eyes, willing him to, just once, say "love." She only needed it once; just that would do for the rest of her life.

"Well." He was using his host voice, that warm, impersonal tone he always adopted with his best customers. "I think I'll go on to bed, leave you two to plan."

She heard the scrape of his chair as he stood up, heard the fading echo of his footsteps as he climbed the stairs. Her throat burned, and she squeezed her eyes shut until she was certain that the tears wouldn't spill down her cheeks.

When she opened them, he was already at his doorway. All she saw was the faint glow of his white-clad back until he disappeared into the darkness of his room.

38

The Rose was unnaturally, unsettlingly quiet. Angie stood in front of J.J.'s door, listening to the faint, rare squeaks and whisperings of the building, and breathing in the scents of wax and beer and the lingering, nearly imaginary hint of smoke.

She shivered, cool in the thin, slippery silk robe that Rose had loaned her. It was the only thing she wore.

She took a deep, shaky breath for courage and reached for the doorknob. She was going to do this.

Why was she even worrying about it? Since this was essentially what J.J. wanted from her, anyway, there was no reason for him to turn her away.

Her father was gone, back to his own hotel. It had taken all her powers of persuasion to get him out the door without her, but she'd finally prevailed, her resolve bolstered by the fact that he'd informed her they were leaving first thing in the morning.

If this was the only night left to her, she would damn well make the most of it.

The door, its hinges well oiled, well kept like everything else of J.J.'s, opened easily at her touch. She shut it behind her.

The floorboards were cold against her bare feet. The room was dark, too dark to see anything but the dull outlines of bulky shapes.

J.J. was in his bed, though. She could hear the deep, steady rhythm of his breathing, and her own slowed to match it. The air was heavy, pushing into her lungs, and she thought she could smell a hint of him: rich, spicy, male musk.

She untied the robe and let it slide to the floor, the fine silk whispering against her, making a slight hiss as it settled down.

"What do you want?" He sounded grumpy from sleep, his voice rough.

"To say good-bye."

"Well, you said it." He cursed himself for being so short. Even now, he didn't want to hurt her. But how much was he expected to take? How long was he supposed to pretend, to let her go freely along her way without worrying about the heartbroken man she left behind?

"I didn't mean with words."

The mattress gave as she sat down beside him, bringing with her a hint of warmth and the faint scent of wildflowers and hay.

"Do . . . do you want me to go?"

"No." No, he didn't want her to go. Not now, not ever. "When are you leaving?"

"Tomorrow. Early."

"I'll see you off." He could have bit his tongue for saying that. It was too much to ask of himself, to wave casually as she rode away.

"No." The low, smoky whisper of her voice floated through the darkness, seeming to drift around him, to entwine him more deeply under her spell. He'd always loved that about her, that slow seductive voice in that tight, quick body. "I'd rather our good-byes be now."

He rolled toward her, intending to take her into his arms, to push her down into the soft mattresses. He wanted to drown himself in her, to lose the reality of tomorrow completely in the dream of tonight.

"No." She stopped him, her hands gentle on his chest as she pushed him back against his pillows. "Let me."

This was to be her night, the one that was to keep her through the rest of her life. So she would take all she could, do everything she'd ever dreamed of, imprint every corner of her mind with taste and scent and motion, so that she could draw them out whenever she needed them and relive them all.

Not too soon. Soon would be too painful. Eventually, though, she would need the memories, and she would store them up against those gray, passionless days.

A moan escaped him as her hands gently explored the planes and swells of his chest and her mouth found the hollow of his throat. Already, the pleasure was too sharp, a sweet-sad ache that made his blood thicken and his head spin.

Always in his life, he had given pleasure, been the one who decided where and how and how much. It allowed him to stay in control, to separate his body and his mind and his heart. Never had he simply accepted pleasure, let it swell and break over him, permitted it to be so huge and powerful and overwhelming.

She moved her mouth up, along the tendons of his throat and the beard-shadowed slope of his jaw until she found his mouth. He opened for her, and her tongue moved in quick, stabbing little motions that urged his to join in the play.

She lay down on him, her breasts fitting against his chest, his erection pulsing against the curve of her belly. He spread his legs wide, so hers fell comfortably between them, and he stroked the length of her back, his slow caresses an exciting counterpoint to her swift, inciting ones.

Yes, she thought. This is what she wanted. Her golden man turned as dark and desperate as she, the hungry kisses and the hungry hands, their cries and sighs and ragged breathing swirling above them.

She felt as if she were a falcon, flying blind, finding her way through the darkness only by feel, searching, seeking, needing. Trying to find that one arc through the air that was so perfect and pure that she wouldn't care if she crashed to earth afterward, for it had been enough.

She rained kisses, openmouthed, wet, and hot, on his face, neck, and chest. The nubby points of his nipples were firm against her tongue, the flat planes of his chest warm and silky. His hands combed through her hair, again and again, swishing through the entire length.

He bowed up, his harsh cry splitting the darkness, when she moved lower yet and found him with her mouth. Silky, marble-hard, vibrating against her tongue. Alive and strong, like him.

Suddenly he lifted her, turned her, settling her against the bed, and rolled himself on her.

"But I wasn't finished—"

"Yes, you were." His hoarse growl rumbled low in her ear, and anything more she would have said was lost in her gasp of pleasure when he slid easily into her.

She wanted to make it last, to spend those endless, perfect moments when nothing had meaning but the growing edge of pleasure. But it was too near, sharp, sweet and clear, and she shuddered once more with each time he stroked into her.

"Oh, please," he whispered, over and over. "Angel, please."

When she finally quieted, fading into that easy, warm haze, he pulled out of her abruptly, making her cry out with the sudden loss.

He pressed himself against her leg, once, twice, and

she felt him shudder and his warmth spurt against her thigh.

He was calm now, still, sweet, and heavy over her. She was grateful for the darkness, so he couldn't see the dampness in her eyes.

It had been too much. And it wasn't nearly enough.

It would never, ever be enough.

"Why did you do that?" she asked.

"I couldn't let your dreams be taken away from you, Angel."

Sometimes, dreams had too high a price.

He rolled off her, drawing her leg up across his thighs and draping her arm over his chest. She nestled there, close and secure.

"Sleep now, Angel. My Angel."

She slept.

And in the morning, she stood by the bed while the early morning light washed the room to pale gray and watched him sleep, the blankets twisted down around his lean hips, his face relaxed and far too beautiful.

"Good-bye, J.J."

"You stupid idiot."

"Go away." J.J. didn't even glance Rose's way, merely went back to wiping down the bar after the noon crowd had left, readying for the evening to come.

"Do you really think you can fool me?"

"Fool you about what?" he said, his voice smooth and uninterested.

He looked as he always had, Rose thought. Golden and polished. Perfect, absolutely in control, dressed impeccably in white and standing behind a bar that didn't have the slightest hint of a smudge on its gleaming surface.

It had been so much better when Angie was here, when his hair was rumpled and he wore those faded denims, when there was some emotion in those turquoise eyes. Now, they looked just like the stone in his ring: smooth, beautiful, and lifeless.

"She only left this morning, J.J. You could catch up with her."

He simply kept rubbing the glossy oak of the bar. "Was there something you wanted?"

What else could she do? She'd tried. If he was insistent on letting her go, there wasn't anything she could do.

"I came to tell you I'm leaving."

His even strokes slowed. "With Stitch?"

"Yes."

He flipped the cloth over his shoulder and came around to her, then linked his hands with her. "Are you sure this is what you want?"

"Sure?" Her laugh was a little breathless, a little scared. "I'm not sure of anything, except that I can't seem to do anything else."

He leaned down. His mouth was warm, a gentle kiss between two good friends who somehow never quite managed to be more.

"If you ever need me, you know where to find me. I'll be right here, at the Rose."

"That's too bad, J.J."

His smile was a little sad.

"It's time to let this place go," Rose went on. "None of us need it anymore."

His fingers tightened around hers. "It's what I have."

"It wouldn't have to be."

She'd been wrong. She'd thought it would be better to see any emotion, rather than the impersonal blankness. But she hadn't wanted to see this, the bleak emptiness, the loneliness.

"It was her dream, Rose. I couldn't take it away from her."

"Oh, damn. Haven't you learned by now that what people want isn't necessarily what they need?"

"You're not making sense."

"I would slug you if I thought it would knock any sense into your stubborn head. I bet you didn't even tell her you loved her, did you?"

His silence was her answer.

"Shit!"

He gave the ghost of a smile, then hugged her. "You're hanging around with Stitch too much. Picking up his bad habits."

"You should have told her, J.J."

"It wouldn't have mattered."

"It *always* matters."

He squeezed her a little too tightly, forcing the air from her lungs, as if he needed something to hold on to.

"Shit, J.J., you really are an idiot."

Angie stared glumly at the rump of her father's gelding, just as she had for the last ten miles, plodding along behind the slow-moving stage.

She'd been so certain she was prepared for the pain of saying good-bye to J.J. That she was ready to be content with the life she'd planned and her special memories.

Unholy horse apples. She *hurt,* damn it. Her eyes, her throat. Her stomach, her chest.

She felt not one bit of anticipation at going home, at seeing the Meadows and finally fulfilling her life's dream. Shouldn't she be feeling just a little bit of satisfaction, a bit of happiness?

It wasn't going to be enough. She needed him in her life, no matter what else there was. Without him, without love, the rest was only trimmings; it sounded nice enough, but she had no heart for it.

So what if he didn't love her? He cared for her, he'd made her smile, he'd be faithful, and they were downright wonderful in bed.

And anyway, she loved him enough for both of them.

A quick signal, and Lance spun around in a tight circle. They headed back the way they'd come.

"Angelina!" her father shouted. "What are you doing?"

"I'm going home!"

39

The last stage station before entering San Francisco was nearly empty. Angie figured it probably didn't do a booming business; it was too close to the city to be a necessary stop.

She'd wanted to ride through the night, impatient to get back. She didn't want to waste another second.

Her father couldn't ride all night, though. He wasn't up for it anymore, even though he insisted he was. No matter how she tried, she hadn't managed to convince him he should go on ahead to Kentucky. He'd see her safely back to San Francisco as a father should. It was his duty—and it would give him a bit more time to try and change her mind.

Despite its apparent lack of business, the simple, wooden stage stop was well kept. Most importantly, the stables were in good shape, nicely swept and with decent fodder.

Now if she could only find some food for herself. It was past supper, and the two plank tables that sat squarely in the middle of the single room were cleared.

She was hungry, darn it. And she was going to need some fortification before she saw J.J. and explained to him that he was going to have to marry her after all. It was the only way her father was ever going to let her stay in San Francisco, and let them both live.

J.J. She'd been so busy thinking of him that now she was seeing things, a golden-haired man dressed in white bent over a bundle in the far corner of the room.

Then he straightened, and she knew it wasn't her imagination. No one else moved with such elegance and lean grace.

"J.J.?"

Frowning, he turned, searching the dim room. When he saw her, his face lit with that incredible, brilliant smile. He crossed the room in an instant.

"J.J., what are you doing here?"

"I'm coming after you, of course."

"After me? But that's what—"

"Now, see here, young man." Angie had forgotten there was anyone else in the place. She'd most especially forgotten that her father was there, until his voice boomed in her ear loudly enough to make her wince. "It appears to me that you and I are going to have a bit of a talk."

"Yes, sir." J.J. nodded, but his gaze never left Angie's face. "But I think perhaps I need to talk to your daughter a minute, first."

"Hell, you two had months to talk to each other and nothing came of It. Better you listen to me this time—"

"Daddy." Angie laid a calming hand on his arm. "Just for a moment. Please?"

He'd never been able to resist her. That smile, that pleading tone of voice, was why she'd been able to talk him into letting her tail after him at the Meadows, all the time she'd been growing up, even to the breakings and the breedings and all those other places little girls shouldn't have been.

He still wasn't immune. "Oh, all right," he agreed, then waved a warning finger at J.J. "You've got ten minutes, you hear? Then I'm coming out to get you. And you don't want me to do that."

"Yes, sir."

The night air was cool and dry, pure and still as crystal. They were in the foothills. The scent of pine was strong and pungent, and the moon poured silvery light over the dark earth.

Hand in hand, laughing, they ran into the woods, until the sounds from the inn faded. Their footsteps were muffled by pine needles, and when they stopped, there was only the faint creak of rubbing branches and the sound of their rapid breathing.

"Now, what are you doing here?" she asked.

"Hush. Wait." He cradled her face in his palms, lifting it up to the moonlight filtering through the trees. "Just let me look at you first."

"You just saw me yesterday."

"Exactly. That's far too long."

She waited as long as she could. "Please, J.J."

"All right." His eyes were intent; his voice, hushed. "Before anything else, there's something I should have told you ages ago." His thumbs rubbed softly, reverently, under her chin, along her neck. "I love you."

"Oh, God." She vaulted at him, the force of her jump sending them both to the earth. She landed on his chest and planted ecstatic kisses over his face and neck.

"Good thing the ground was soft." He laughed and threw his arms around her to hold her there. "I take it this means you rather like the idea."

"No, of course not. Why would I?" she mumbled between taking small nips of his neck.

"Angel, listen to me."

Propping herself up on her arms, she looked down at him. He was gilded in silver moonlight, his eyes gleaming with what could only be joy.

"I don't want to listen. I want you to kiss me."

"Soon enough." He tenderly brushed the hair off her face, his fingers whispering over her skin. "If I asked you to marry me again, would the answer be different?"

Damn it, she wasn't going to cry. "J.J., I love you."

He stared up at her, the muscles in his throat working. "Does . . . does that mean yes?"

"Of course it means yes!"

"Then why are you crying?"

"Oh, shut up and kiss me."

He did, lifting his mouth to hers, sending his tongue deep and slow, a dark, seductive rhythm that made her want to move on top of him. She smelled pine and cold, earth and him, and warmth bloomed through her chilled body.

He broke away, tucking her head against his neck, his hand slowly stroking down the length of her hair and back. She listened to the loud thump of his heart.

"I can't believe we're lying out here in the forest in the middle of the night. Daddy's going to come after us soon enough."

"That's my plan, Angel. If he catches us, you'll have to marry me for sure."

"Good. Then we can start looking for some land right away. Not too far from the Rose, for you, of course, but I will need several acres."

"Nope. Can't do that."

"J.J., you promised me we'd find space for the horses! You can't—"

"It's too late."

"How can it be too late?" She was warming up now, readying for a good, hearty fight. She'd marry him anyway, but he was going to learn right now that she wasn't going to be a quiet, decorative, citified wife.

"I already sold the Rose."

"You what?" She leaned back, looking down into his face. He looked serious. "You didn't."

He nodded, watching her closely. "I did."

"Oh, J.J., you can't let that obnoxious Hermanson get the Rose."

"I didn't. I sold it to L. J. Hooper."

"Hooper."

"Yeah. Let the two of them fight it out between them. It's not worth it."

"But you love the Rose."

"I don't need it anymore. I have everything I ever wanted, right here."

She gave a snort of disbelief. "More like I'm everything you *never* wanted."

"No." He drew back to look at her, and she knew his brilliant, tender smile was for her alone. "Everything I *thought* I didn't want. So I wasn't too smart before. I learned better. Besides, I was kind of figuring you needed a partner."

"A partner?" she repeated slowly. He couldn't mean it.

"Well, you never really did catch on to keeping books. And you're really not that great at charming customers, either, Angel."

"I know," she admitted ruefully.

"So I figure you need somebody to handle the business end of things. Someone who won't muddle with you when you're doing what you do best—dealing with the horses. In fact, someone who would just as soon stay as far away as possible from them."

"Have anyone in mind?" It was difficult, trying to keep the thread of the conversation, when his hips were slowly lifting and falling against hers, and there were too many frustrating layers of cloth between them.

"Maybe." With his tongue, he traced a line from just under her ear down to her jaw. "Someone who just happens to have a nice chunk of capital to work with, too, so could buy in evenly."

"Hmm." She shivered when his mouth found the spot where her pulse thrummed. "The thing I do best? Working with horses?"

"Well, okay, maybe the thing you do second best."

Author's Note

The rumor of a gold strike at the Fraser River, British Columbia, that emptied San Francisco nearly overnight actually happened in April 1858. But there was no way to get my heroine west that early in the year (snow in the mountain passes, you know), so I moved the date back to June. There was no gold; most of those who were able to return to San Francisco did so by the fall. Also, though the history books state that the gas streetlights in San Francisco were turned off in 1857 because the city refused to pay the bills, I could find no mention of when they were turned back on. I left them off, for atmosphere. I hope I'll be forgiven these small liberties with history, for I did it for love.

Winner Take All by **Terri Herrington**

Logan Brisco is the smoothest, slickest, handsomest man ever to grace the small town of Serenity, Texas. Carny Sullivan is the only one who sees the con man behind that winning smile, and she vows to save the town from his clutches. But saving herself from the man who steals her heart is going to be the greatest challenge of all.

The Honeymoon by **Elizabeth Bevarly**

Newlyweds Nick and Natalie Brannon are wildly in love, starry-eyed about the future...and in for a rude awakening. Suddenly relocated from their midwestern hometown to San Juan, Puerto Rico, where Nick is posted with the U.S. Coast Guard, Natalie hopes for the best. But can true love survive the trials and tribulations of a not-so-perfect paradise?

Ride the Night Wind by **Jo Ann Ferguson**

As the only surviving member of a powerful family, Lady Audra fought to hold on to her vast manor lands against ruthless warlords. But from the moonlit moment when she encountered the mysterious masked outlaw known as Lynx, she was plunged into an even more desperate battle for the fate of her heart.

To Dream Again by **Laura Lee Guhrke**

Beautiful widow Mara Elliot had little time for shining promises or impractical dreams. But when dashing inventor Nathaniel Chase became her unwanted business partner, Mara found his optimism and reckless determination igniting a passion in her that suddenly put everything she treasured at risk.

Reckless Angel by **Susan Kay Law**

Angelina Winchester's dream led her to a new city, a new life, and a reckless bargain with Jeremiah Johnston, owner of the most notorious saloon in San Francisco. Falling in love was never part of their deal. But soon they would discover that the last thing they ever wanted was exactly what they needed most.

A Slender Thread by **Lee Scofield**

Once the center of Philadelphia's worst scandal, Jennifer Hastings was determined to rebuild her life as a schoolteacher in Kansas. She was touched when handsome and aloof Gil Prescott entrusted her with the care of his newborn son while he went to fight in the Civil War. When Gil's return unleashed a passion they had ignored for too long, they thought they had found happiness—until a man from Jennifer's past threatened to destroy it.

Alone in a Crowd by Georgia Bockoven

After a terrible accident, country music sensation Cole Webster must undergo reconstructive surgery which gives him temporary anonymity. Before he can reveal his true identity, Cole loses his heart to Holly, a beautiful woman who values her privacy above all else. Cole must come to terms with who he is and what he's looking for in life before he can find love and true happiness.

Destiny Awaits by Suzanne Elizabeth

When wealthy and spoiled Tess Harper was transported back in time to Kansas, 1885, it didn't take her long to find trouble. Captivating farmer Joseph Maguire agreed to bail her out on one condition—that she live with him and care for his two orphaned nieces. Despite the hardships of prairie life, Tess soon realized that this love of a lifetime was to be her destiny.

Broken Vows by Donna Grove

To Rachel Girard, nothing was more important than her family's cattle ranch, which would one day be hers. But when her father declared she must take a husband or lose her birthright, Rachel offered footloose bounty hunter Caleb Delaney a fortune if he'd marry her—then leave her! Cal knew he'd be a fool to refuse, but he would soon wonder if a life without Rachel was worth anything at all.

Lady in Blue by Lynn Kerstan

A delightful, sexy romance set in the Regency period. Wealthy and powerful Brynmore Talgarth never wanted a wife, despite pressure to restore the family's reputation by marrying well. But once he met young, destitute, and beautiful Clare Easton, an indecent proposal led the way to a love neither knew could exist.

The Long Road Home by Mary Alice Monroe

Bankrupt and alone after her financier husband dies, Nora MacKenzie's life is shattered. After fleeing to a sheep farm in Vermont, she meets up with the mysterious C. W. Friendship soon blossoms into love, but C. W. is keeping some dangerous secrets that could destroy them both.

Winter Bride by Teresa Southwick

Wyoming rancher Matt Decker needed a wife. His mother sent him Eliza Jones, the young woman who had adored Matt when they were children. Eliza was anxious to start a new life out west, but the last thing Matt wanted was to marry someone to whom he might become emotionally attached.

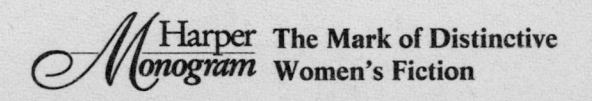